CLASSIC SCOTTISH
SHORT STORIES

CLASSIC
SCOTTISH
SHORT STORIES

Selected and Introduced by
J. M. REID

Oxford New York
OXFORD UNIVERSITY PRESS

Oxford University Press, Great Clarendon Street, Oxford OX2 6DP

Oxford New York
Athens Auckland Bangkok Bogota Buenos Aires Calcutta
Cape Town Chennai Dar es Salaam Delhi Florence Hong Kong Istanbul
Karachi Kuala Lumpur Madrid Melbourne Mexico City Mumbai
Nairobi Paris São Paolo Singapore Taipei Tokyo Toronto Warsaw
and associated companies in
Berlin Ibadan

Oxford is a registered trade mark of Oxford University Press

First published as Scottish Short Stories 1963
Reprinted three times
First issued as an Oxford University Press paperback with the title
Classic Scottish Short Stories 1989

British Library Cataloguing in Publication Data
Data available

Library of Congress Cataloging in Publication Data
Scottish short stories.
Classical Scottish short stories / selected and introduced by J. M. Reid.
p. cm.
Reprinted Originally published: Scottish Short stories. London:
New York: Oxford University Press, 1963. (The World's Classics)
1. Short stories, Scottish.   I. Reid, J. M. (James Macarthur), 1901-1970.   II. Title.
823'.01089411—dc20   PR8676.C5   1989   89-36495
ISBN 0-19-282686-7

10

Printed in Great Britain by
Cox & Wyman Ltd,
Reading, Berkshire

CONTENTS

INTRODUCTION

A SHORT story should be something between a poem and a reflection, a novel and an anecdote. The very best stories have a little of the character of all four.

This description may not be acceptable for all times and countries but it seems to come naturally from what has been written by Scotsmen in the last century and a half. Perhaps a book of Scottish short stories should really begin with a selection of folk tales from Gaelic and Scots, which could exhibit almost every sort of material used later by writers for the printing-press—legend, the supernatural, social comment, history, satire and plain fun.

Scottish story-telling has its roots in this tradition, which gives it a national character. Tales of the fireside were told to entertain: the heirs of this art have no need to be ashamed if they write for their readers' enjoyment. Almost the first (and almost the most nearly perfect) of Scottish literary short stories, 'Wandering Willie's Tale' from Sir Walter Scott's *Redgauntlet*, has the form of a folk legend, with a final, but carefully unobtrusive, twist to fit it for an age that read David Hume. It has a tightness, a concentrated action and symbolism, which are too rare in Scott's novels. It re-creates not the facts of history but the spirit of the Scottish past. Scott, who did not love the Presbyterian enthusiasts of the seventeenth century, makes his narrator and the chief character in his story, both of whom had good reason to disagree with the Covenanters, find the persecutors of these 'Hill folk' in Hell. This is absolutely true to popular tradition: very few Scots Lowlanders of Wandering Willie's day, whatever their politics, would have expected to find these men anywhere else. Steenie's meeting with the damned is wonderfully dramatic: it also fills the story with a special sort of irony which gives it its peculiar flavour.

The feeling for the eerie and supernatural has had a peculiar importance for Scottish writers. It reappears time and again in the short stories of R. L. Stevenson—grimly in 'Thrawn Janet', with the quality of a laughing South Seas fairy tale in 'The Isle of Voices'. It is as strong in the best of Eric Linklater's stories today as in the plays of his friend James Bridie. This is one folk tradition which Scotsmen have found valuable when they wanted both to heighten tension in a few pages and to suggest that the everyday world around them is not enough.

For it must be admitted that more than half the stories in this collection do not attempt to paint the world of their writers' days exactly. The book could not have represented Scottish fiction adequately if its balance had been weighted towards any sort of concentration on contemporary scenes. Certainly Fred Urquhart's G.I. bride belongs firmly to 1946, as Dorothy K. Haynes's housewife does to the 1950's. But most Scots writers of fiction have been inclined to set their subjects in the past, even if the period they write of is only twenty years away. We are a historically minded people with a strong sense of the changing flow of time, and any collection of this sort is bound to take its readers as far back as living traditions of the past could carry the writers whose work it contains.

In one other respect its balance may perhaps seem surprising. The Industrial Revolution came to Scotland early. For more than a century most Scotsmen have lived in towns or near mines, mills, and foundries. Yet Scots have preferred to write and read about countrysides and villages rather than about cities, about fields rather than factories. The Gaelic Highlands and Isles have a far greater place in Scottish literature (written in English) than in the daily life and experience of the mass of Scots people. Nearly a century and a half ago the novelist John Galt showed more interest in the beginnings of industrial life than most of his successors seemed to feel in its very active development.

In our own day writers have begun to be rather more

willing to look at urban things and people, but when one tries to find the best that has been written in Scotland through six or seven generations one soon discovers not only that a remarkably high proportion of authors have come from the Highlands, the villages, or very small towns, but that even those who (like R. L. Stevenson and John Buchan) were brought up in cities usually chose to write about less crowded places. Naturally, since the Scots have always been a wandering people, a good deal of their fiction is set in other parts of the world; but the picture of their own country that they present is overwhelmingly a rural one. Even when an editor deliberately seeks, as I have done, to find city stories which can rank with those from the country the rural scene breaks in. The late John Macnair Reid had to take the singing mother of his story from Glasgow to a village church. Ian Macpherson's clerk and Ian H. Finlay's painter must flee from the towns.

When their imaginations are roused Scotsmen seem to reject the industrial background they have made for themselves: they are unwilling to look closely at human nature except in the setting of fields or heather. The figures which recur most persistently in their fiction are those of husbands and wives, ministers and farming folk. Possibly they are better prepared than most other people (though, no doubt, unconsciously) to see the end of the industrial age which has been the framework of existence for the great majority of them.

The stories of this collection fall naturally into four groups. To begin with most writers (and almost all readers) in Scotland liked to keep close to the fireside pattern. Publications like *Wilson's Tales of the Borders*, from which Thomas Gillespie's 'The Fair Maid of Cellardykes' comes, had an enormous vogue among the early Victorians and their predecessors. This sort of narrative, often artless enough, was certainly the most popular in Scotland itself for at least a century.

With Robert Louis Stevenson the story became, much

more deliberately, an art-form, carefully shaped in words precisely and appropriately chosen. He remains the most impressive of Scots short-story writers. Perhaps the form suited him even better than the novel usually did: it gave him just room enough to say what he wanted to say well. Stevenson's successors, who used words with something of his exuberant precision, are R. B. Cunninghame Graham, John Buchan, and Neil Munro in his richly decorated treatment of a folk theme. 'The Lost Pibroch' is a poem: 'Hurricane Jack', on the other hand, is a high-spirited anecdote meant not for the literary-minded but for the readers of a Glasgow evening paper. This was the other side of Munro's work (it was published under a pseudonym) but its background is the same narrow fifty miles of firth, sea-loch, and hill which fed his imagination.

While Stevenson still lived the strain of simple rural story-telling won a new public among English as well as Scottish readers for the writers of the Kailyard. This school has had a very bad name for more than half a century. It did, indeed, sink quickly into shameless sentimentality or uncomfortably comfortable humour. Its writers created a false image of Scotland which has been much resented by their countrymen: in letters they were very much what the 'Scoatch comic' has been for the theatre.

But there were some skilful story-tellers among them, most notably J. M. Barrie. Before he had discovered the commercial value of sentimentality—or, perhaps, had learned to look back sentimentally on the land he had left for London—he produced, in *Auld Licht Idylls*, some of the most effective short stories in the traditional Scottish rural vein that have ever been written. 'The Courting of T'now-head's Bell' is one of these. S. R. Crockett's 'The Lammas Preaching' is a less accomplished, though still not contemptible, fruit of the Kailyard. Characteristically enough, both these men describe a rural society that belonged to their fathers' day rather than to their own.

For a time just before and after the 1914–18 war Scots

authors tended to give their readers the Kailyard in reverse
—country life quite deliberately unsentimentalized. Lewis
Grassic Gibbon is the great figure of this reaction: his
countryside lies within a few miles of Barrie's Thrums,
but the sharp light that beats on it is as different from the
Kailyard's as his almost metrical and alliterative prose,
Scots in idiom, though English in spelling, is from Barrie's
easy and economical flow.

Others, however, were now beginning to write without
sentimentality or reaction against false sentiment but with
genuine sympathy for the life they described. No one has
dealt with the world of Highland crofters and fishermen
more convincingly than Neil Gunn. He still tells a story
in the old sense, though with a modern awareness of
psychological complexities. He was one of the first recruits
of the Scottish Renaissance movement which has brought
a revived national feeling into the arts. It has influenced most
writers since—very notably Grassic Gibbon.

Though very few of the authors whose work is reprinted
here have written without thought of readers outside Scotland itself, almost all use words and phrases which are not
English. 'Wandering Willie's Tale' and 'Thrawn Janet' are
in a slightly anglicized Lowland Scots. Some others dis-
guised their native speech, but it is the basis of their style.
Neil Munro and Neil Gunn have each used a Gaelic–
English of his own. Their stories, like Naomi Mitchison's
'On an Island', need to be read with a Highland accent.

None of this should be particularly difficult for English-
men or Americans. But a glossary which, it is hoped, pro-
vides the necessary key to unfamiliar words and phrases,
Scots and Gaelic, should make the way still plainer for them.

J. M. REID

Wandering Willie's Tale

SIR WALTER SCOTT

(1771–1832)

YE maun have heard of Sir Robert Redgauntlet of that Ilk, who lived in these parts before the dear years. The country will lang mind him; and our fathers used to draw breath thick if ever they heard him named. He was out wi' the Hielandmen in Montrose's time; and again he was in the hills wi' Glencairn in the saxteen hundred and fifty-twa; and sae when King Charles the Second came in, wha was in sic favour as the Laird of Redgauntlet? He was knighted at Lonon court, wi' the King's ain sword; and being a red-hot prelatist, he came down here, rampauging like a lion, with commissions of lieutenancy (and of lunacy, for what I ken), to put down a' the Whigs and Covenanters in the country. Wild wark they made of it; for the Whigs were as dour as the Cavaliers were fierce, and it was which should first tire the other. Redgauntlet was aye for the strong hand; and his name is kenn'd as wide in the country as Claverhouse's or Tam Dalyell's. Glen, nor dargle, nor mountain, nor cave could hide the puir Hill-folk when Redgauntlet was out with bugle and bloodhound after them, as if they had been sae mony deer. And troth when they fand them, they didna mak muckle mair ceremony than a Hielandman wi' a roebuck. It was just, 'Will ye tak the test?' If not, 'Make ready—present—fire!' and there lay the recusant.

Far and wide was Sir Robert hated and feared. Men thought he had a direct compact with Satan; that he was proof against steel, and that bullets happed aff his buff-coat like hailstanes from a hearth; that he had a mear that would turn a hare on the side of Carrifra Gauns—and muckle to the same purpose, of whilk mair anon. The best blessing they

wared on him was, 'Deil scowp wi' Redgauntlet!' He wasna
a bad maister to his ain folk though, and was weel aneugh
liked by his tenants; and as for the lackies and troopers that
raid out wi' him to the persecutions, as the Whigs ca'd those
killing times, they wad hae drunken themsells blind to his
health at ony time.

Now you are to ken that my gudesire lived on Redgauntlet's
grund; they ca' the place Primrose Knowe. We had lived on
the grund, and under the Redgauntlets, since the riding days,
and lang before. It was a pleasant bit; and I think the air is
callerer and fresher there than onywhere else in the country.
It's a' deserted now; and I sat on the broken door-cheek
three days since, and was glad I couldna see the plight the
place was in; but that's a' wide o' the mark. There dwelt my
gudesire, Steenie Steenson, a rambling, rattling chiel he had
been in his young days, and could play weel on the pipes; he
was famous at 'Hoopers and Girders', a' Cumberland
couldna touch him at 'Jockie Lattin', and he had the finest
finger for the back-lilt between Berwick and Carlisle. The
like o' Steenie wasna the sort that they made Whigs o'. And
so he became a Tory, as they ca' it, which we now ca'
Jacobites, just out of a kind of needcessity, that he might
belang to some side or other. He had nae ill-will to the Whig
bodies, and liked little to see the blude rin, though, being
obliged to follow Sir Robert in hunting and hosting, watching and warding, he saw muckle mischief, and maybe did
some, that he couldna avoid.

Now Steenie was a kind of favourite with his master, and
kenn'd a' the folks about the castle, and was often sent for to
play the pipes when they were at their merriment. Auld
Dougal MacCallum, the butler, that had followed Sir Robert
through gude and ill, thick and thin, pool and stream, was
specially fond of the pipes, and aye gae my gudesire his gude
word wi' the laird; for Dougal could turn his master round
his finger.

Weel, round came the Revolution, and it had like to have
broken the hearts baith of Dougal and his master. But the

change was not a'thegither sae great as they feared, and other folk thought for. The Whigs made an unco crawing what they wad do with their auld enemies, and in special wi' Sir Robert Redgauntlet. But there were ower mony great folks dipped in the same doings to mak a spick and span new warld. So Parliament passed it a' ower easy; and Sir Robert, bating that he was held to hunting foxes instead of Covenanters, remained just the man he was. His revel was as loud, and his hall as weel lighted, as ever it had been, though maybe he lacked the fines of the Nonconformists, that used to come to stock his larder and cellar; for it is certain he began to be keener about the rents than his tenants used to find him before, and they behoved to be prompt to the rent-day, or else the laird wasna pleased. And he was sic an awsome body that naebody cared to anger him; for the oaths he swore, and the rage that he used to get into, and the looks that he put on, made men sometimes think him a devil incarnate.

Weel, my gudesire was nae manager—no that he was a very great misguider—but he hadna the saving gift, and he got twa terms' rent in arrear. He got the first brash at Whitsunday put ower wi' fair word and piping; but when Martinmas came, there was a summons from the grund-officer to come wi' the rent on a day preceese, or else Steenie behoved to flit. Sair wark he had to get the siller; but he was weel-freended, and at last he got the haill scraped thegither—a thousand merks; the maist of it was from a neighbour they ca'd Laurie Lapraik—a sly tod. Laurie had walth o' gear—could hunt wi' the hound and rin wi' the hare—and be Whig or Tory, saunt or sinner, as the wind stood. He was a professor in this Revolution warld; but he liked an orra sough of this warld, and a tune on the pipes weel aneugh at a bye-time; and abune a', he thought he had gude security for the siller he lent my gudesire ower the stocking at Primrose Knowe.

Away trots my gudesire to Redgauntlet Castle, wi' a heavy purse and a light heart, glad to be out of the laird's danger.

Weel, the first thing he learned at the castle was that Sir Robert had fretted himsell into a fit of the gout, because he did not appear before twelve o'clock. It wasna a'thegither for sake of the money, Dougal thought; but because he didna like to part wi' my gudesire aff the grund. Dougal was glad to see Steenie, and brought him into the great oak parlour, and there sat the laird his leesome lane, excepting that he had beside him a great ill-favoured jackanape, that was a special pet of his—a cankered beast it was, and mony an ill-natured trick it played; ill to please it was, and easily angered—ran about the haill castle, chattering and yowling, and pinching and biting folk, especially before ill weather, or disturbances in the state. Sir Robert ca'd it Major Weir, after the warlock that was burnt;[1] and few folk liked either the name or the conditions of the creature—they thought there was something in it by ordinar—and my gudesire was not just easy in his mind when the door shut on him, and he saw himself in the room wi' naebody but the laird, Dougal MacCallum, and the major, a thing that hadna chanced to him before.

Sir Robert sat, or, I should say, lay, in a great armed chair, wi' his grand velvet gown, and his feet on a cradle; for he had baith gout and gravel, and his face looked as gash and ghastly as Satan's. Major Weir sat opposite to him, in a red laced coat, and the laird's wig on his head; and aye as Sir Robert girned wi' pain, the jackanape girned too, like a sheep's-head between a pair of tangs—an ill-faured, fearsome couple they were. The laird's buff-coat was hung on a pin behind him, and his broadsword and his pistols within reach; for he keepit up the auld fashion of having the weapons ready, and a horse saddled day and night, just as he used to do when he was able to loup on horseback, and away after ony of the Hill-folk he could get speerings of. Some said it was for fear of the Whigs taking vengeance, but I judge it was just his auld custom—he wasna gien to fear onything. The rental-book, wi' its black cover and brass clasps, was lying beside

---

[1] A celebrated wizard, executed [1670] at Edinburgh for sorcery and other crimes.

him; and a book of sculduddry sangs was put betwixt the leaves, to keep it open at the place where it bore evidence against the goodman of Primrose Knowe, as behind the hand with his mails and duties. Sir Robert gave my gudesire a look as if he would have withered his heart in his bosom. Ye maun ken he had a way of bending his brows that men saw the visible mark of a horse-shoe in his forehead, deep-dinted, as if it had been stamped there.

'Are ye come light-handed, ye son of a toom whistle?' said Sir Robert. 'Zounds! if you are——'

My gudesire, with as gude a countenance as he could put on, made a leg, and placed the bag of money on the table wi' a dash, like a man that does something clever. The laird drew it to him hastily. 'Is it all here, Steenie, man?'

'Your honour will find it right,' said my gudesire.

'Here, Dougal,' said the laird, 'gie Steenie a tass of brandy downstairs, till I count the siller and write the receipt.'

But they werena weel out of the room when Sir Robert gied a yelloch that garr'd the castle rock. Back ran Dougal—in flew the livery-men—yell on yell gied the laird, ilk ane mair awfu' than the ither. My gudesire knew not whether to stand or flee, but he ventured back into the parlour, where a' was gaun hirdie-girdie—naebody to say 'come in' or 'gae out'. Terribly the laird roared for cauld water to his feet, and wine to cool his throat; and 'Hell, hell, hell, and its flames', was aye the word in his mouth. They brought him water, and when they plunged his swoln feet into the tub, he cried out it was burning; and folk say that it *did* bubble and sparkle like a seething cauldron. He flung the cup at Dougal's head, and said he had given him blood instead of burgundy; and, sure aneugh, the lass washed clotted blood aff the carpet the neist day. The jackanape they ca'd Major Weir, it jibbered and cried as if it was mocking its master. My gudesire's head was like to turn: he forgot baith siller and receipt, and downstairs he banged; but as he ran, the shrieks came faint and fainter; there was a deep-drawn shivering groan, and word gaed through the castle that the laird was dead.

Weel, away came my gudesire wi' his finger in his mouth, and his best hope was that Dougal had seen the money-bag, and heard the laird speak of writing the receipt. The young laird, now Sir John, came from Edinburgh to see things put to rights. Sir John and his father never gree'd weel. Sir John had been bred an advocate, and afterwards sat in the last Scots Parliament and voted for the Union, having gotten, it was thought, a rug of the compensations; if his father could have come out of his grave he would have brained him for it on his awn hearthstane. Some thought it was easier counting with the auld rough knight than the fair-spoken young ane— but mair of that anon.

Dougal MacCallum, poor body, neither grat nor graned, but gaed about the house looking like a corpse, but directing, as was his duty, a' the order of the grand funeral. Now, Dougal looked aye waur and waur when night was coming, and was aye the last to gang to his bed, whilk was in a little round just opposite the chamber of dais, whilk his master occupied while he was living, and where he now lay in state, as they ca'd it, weel-a-day! The night before the funeral, Dougal could keep his awn counsel nae langer: he came doun with his proud spirit, and fairly asked auld Hutcheon to sit in his room with him for an hour. When they were in the round, Dougal took ae tass of brandy to himsell and gave another to Hutcheon, and wished him all health and lang life, and said that, for himsell, he wasna lang for this world; for that, every night since Sir Robert's death, his silver call had sounded from the state chamber, just as it used to do at nights in his lifetime, to call Dougal to help to turn him in his bed. Dougal said that, being alone with the dead on that floor of the tower (for naebody cared to wake Sir Robert Redgauntlet like another corpse), he had never daured to answer the call, but that now his conscience checked him for neglecting his duty; for, 'though death breaks service,' said MacCallum, 'it shall never break my service to Sir Robert; and I will answer his next whistle, so be you will stand by me, Hutcheon.'

Hutcheon had nae will to the wark, but he had stood by Dougal in battle and broil, and he wad not fail him at this pinch; so down the carles sat ower a stoup of brandy, and Hutcheon, who was something of a clerk, would have read a chapter of the Bible; but Dougal would hear naething but a blaud of Davie Lindsay, whilk was the waur preparation.

When midnight came, and the house was quiet as the grave, sure aneugh the silver whistle sounded as sharp and shrill as if Sir Robert was blowing it, and up gat the twa auld serving-men and tottered into the room where the dead man lay. Hutcheon saw aneugh at the first glance; for there were torches in the room, which showed him the foul fiend in his ain shape, sitting on the laird's coffin! Ower he couped as if he had been dead. He could not tell how lang he lay in a trance at the door, but when he gathered himself he cried on his neighbour, and getting nae answer, raised the house, when Dougal was found lying dead within twa steps of the bed where his master's coffin was placed. As for the whistle, it was gaen anes and aye; but mony a time was it heard at the top of the house on the bartizan, and amang the auld chimneys and turrets, where the howlets have their nests. Sir John hushed the matter up, and the funeral passed over without mair bogle-wark.

But when a' was ower, and the laird was beginning to settle his affairs, every tenant was called up for his arrears, and my gudesire for the full sum that stood against him in the rental-book. Weel, away he trots to the castle, to tell his story, and there he is introduced to Sir John, sitting in his father's chair, in deep mourning, with weepers and hanging cravat, and a small walking rapier by his side, instead of the auld broadsword that had a hundredweight of steel about it, what with blade, chape, and basket-hilt. I have heard their communing so often tauld ower, that I almost think I was there mysell, though I couldna be born at the time.

'I wuss ye joy, sir, of the head seat, and the white loaf, and the braid lairdship. Your father was a kind man to friends and followers; muckle grace to you, Sir John, to fill his shoon

—his boots, I suld say, for he seldom wore shoon, unless it were muils when he had the gout.'

'Ay, Steenie,' quoth the laird, sighing deeply, and putting his napkin to his een, 'his was a sudden call, and he will be missed in the country; no time to set his house in order: weel prepared Godward, no doubt, which is the root of the matter, but left us behind a tangled hesp to wind, Steenie. Hem! hem! We maun go to business, Steenie; much to do, and little time to do it in.'

Here he opened the fatal volume. I have heard of a thing they call Doomsday Book—I am clear it has been a rental of back-ganging tenants.

'Stephen,' said Sir John, still in the same soft, sleekit tone of voice—'Stephen Stevenson, or Steenson, ye are down here for a year's rent behind the hand, due at last term.'

Stephen. 'Please your honour, Sir John, I paid it to your father.'

Sir John. 'Ye took a receipt then, doubtless, Stephen, and can produce it?'

Stephen. 'Indeed I hadna time, an it like your honour; for nae sooner had I set doun the siller, and just as his honour Sir Robert, that's gaen, drew it till him to count it, and write out the receipt, he was ta'en wi' the pains that removed him.'

'That was unlucky,' said Sir John, after a pause. 'But ye maybe paid it in the presence of somebody. I want but a *talis qualis* evidence, Stephen. I would go ower strictly to work with no poor man.'

Stephen. 'Troth, Sir John, there was naebody in the room but Douglas MacCallum, the butler. But, as your honour kens, he has e'en followed his auld master.'

'Very unlucky again, Stephen,' said Sir John, without altering his voice a single note. 'The man to whom ye paid the money is dead; and the man who witnessed the payment is dead too; and the siller, which should have been to the fore, is neither seen nor heard tell of in the repositories. How am I to believe a' this?'

Stephen. 'I dinna ken, your honour; but there is a bit

memorandum note of the very coins—for, God help me! I had to borrow out of twenty purses—and I am sure that ilka man there set down will take his grit oath for what purpose I borrowed the money.'

Sir John. 'I have little doubt ye *borrowed* the money, Steenie. It is the *payment* to my father that I want to have some proof of.'

Stephen. 'The siller maun be about the house, Sir John. And since your honour never got it, and his honour that was canna have ta'en it wi' him, maybe some of the family may have seen it.'

Sir John. 'We will examine the servants, Stephen; that is but reasonable.'

But lackey and lass, and page and groom, all denied stoutly that they had ever seen such a bag of money as my gudesire described. What was waur, he had unluckily not mentioned to any living soul of them his purpose of paying his rent. Ae quean had noticed something under his arm, but she took it for the pipes.

Sir John Redgauntlet ordered the servants out of the room, and then said to my gudesire, 'Now, Steenie, ye see you have fair play; and, as I have little doubt ye ken better where to find the siller than ony other body, I beg, in fair terms, and for your own sake, that you will end this fasherie; for, Stephen, ye maun pay or flit.'

'The Lord forgie your opinion,' said Stephen, driven almost to his wit's end—'I am an honest man.'

'So am I, Stephen,' said his honour; 'and so are all the folks in the house, I hope. But if there be a knave amongst us, it must be he that tells the story he cannot prove.' He paused, and then added, mair sternly, 'If I understand your trick, sir, you want to take advantage of some malicious reports concerning things in this family, and particularly respecting my father's sudden death, thereby to cheat me out of the money, and perhaps take away my character, by insinuating that I have received the rent I am demanding. Where do you suppose this money to be? I insist upon knowing.'

My gudesire saw everything look sae muckle against him that he grew nearly desperate; however, he shifted from one foot to another, looked to every corner of the room, and made no answer.

'Speak out, sirrah,' said the laird, assuming a look of his father's—a very particular ane, which he had when he was angry: it seemed as if the wrinkles of his frown made that selfsame fearful shape of a horse's shoe in the middle of his brow—'speak out, sir! I *will* know your thoughts. Do you suppose that I have this money?'

'Far be it frae me to say so,' said Stephen.

'Do you charge any of my people with having taken it?'

'I wad be laith to charge them that may be innocent,' said my gudesire; 'and if there be any one that is guilty, I have nae proof.'

'Somewhere the money must be, if there is a word of truth in your story,' said Sir John; 'I ask where you think it is, and demand a correct answer?'

'In hell, if you *will* have my thoughts of it,' said my gudesire, driven to extremity—'in hell! with your father, his jackanape, and his silver whistle.'

Down the stairs he ran, for the parlour was nae place for him after such a word, and he heard the laird swearing blood and wounds behind him, as fast as ever did Sir Robert, and roaring for the bailie and the baron-officer.

Away rode my gudesire to his chief creditor, him they ca'd Laurie Lapraik, to try if he could make onything out of him; but when he tauld his story, he got but the warst word in his wame—thief, beggar, and dyvour were the saftest terms; and to the boot of these hard terms, Laurie brought up the auld story of his dipping his hand in the blood of God's saunts, just as if a tenant could have helped riding with the laird, and that a laird like Sir Robert Redgauntlet. My gudesire was by this time far beyond the bounds of patience, and while he and Laurie were at deil speed the liars, he was wanchancie aneugh to abuse Lapraik's doctrine as weel as the man, and said things that garr'd folks' flesh grue that heard them; he wasna just himsell, and he had lived wi' a wild set in his day.

At last they parted, and my gudesire was to ride hame through the wood of Pitmurkie, that is a' fou of black firs, as they say. I ken the wood, but the firs may be black or white for what I can tell. At the entry of the wood there is a wild common, and on the edge of the common a little lonely change-house, that was keepit then by a hostler-wife—they suld hae ca'd her Tibbie Faw—and there puir Steenie cried for a mutchkin of brandy, for he had had no refreshment the haill day. Tibbie was earnest wi' him to take a bite o' meat, but he couldna think o't, nor would he take his foot out of the stirrup, and took off the brandy wholely at two draughts, and named a toast at each—the first was, the memory of Sir Robert Redgauntlet, and might he never lie quiet in his grave till he had righted his poor bond-tenant; and the second was, a health to Man's Enemy, if he would but get him back the pock of siller, or tell him what came o't, for he saw the haill world was like to regard him as a thief and a cheat, and he took that waur than even the ruin of his house and hauld.

On he rode, little caring where. It was a dark night turned, and the trees made it yet darker, and he let the beast take its ain road through the wood; when, all of a sudden, from tired and wearied that it was before, the nag began to spring, and flee, and stend, that my gudesire could hardly keep the saddle; upon the whilk, a horseman, suddenly riding up beside him, said, 'That's a mettle beast of yours, freend; will you sell him?' So saying, he touched the horse's neck with his riding-wand, and it fell into its auld heigh-ho of a stumbling trot. 'But his spunk's soon out of him, I think,' continued the stranger, 'and that is like mony a man's courage, that thinks he wad do great things till he come to the proof.'

My gudesire scarce listened to this, but spurred his horse, with 'Gude e'en to you, freend.'

But it's like the stranger was ane that doesna lightly yield his point; for, ride as Steenie liked, he was aye beside him at the selfsame pace. At last my gudesire, Steenie Steenson, grew half angry, and, to say the truth, half feared.

'What is it that ye want with me, freend?' he said. 'If ye be a robber, I have nae money; if ye be a leal man, wanting company, I have nae heart to mirth or speaking; and if ye want to ken the road, I scarce ken it mysell.'

'If you will tell me your grief,' said the stranger, 'I am one that, though I have been sair misca'd in the world, am the only hand for helping my freends.'

So my gudesire, to ease his ain heart, mair than from any hope of help, told him the story from beginning to end.

'It's a hard pinch,' said the stranger; 'but I think I can help you.'

'If you could lend the money, sir, and take a lang day—I ken nae other help on earth,' said my gudesire.

'But there may be some under the earth,' said the stranger. 'Come, I'll be frank wi' you; I could lend you the money on bond, but you would maybe scruple my terms. Now, I can tell you that your auld laird is disturbed in his grave by your curses, and the wailing of your family, and if ye daur venture to go to see him, he will give you the receipt.'

My gudesire's hair stood on end at this proposal, but he thought his companion might be some humorsome chield that was trying to frighten him, and might end with lending him the money. Besides, he was bauld wi' brandy, and desperate wi' distress; and he said he had courage to go to the gate of hell, and a step farther, for that receipt.

The stranger laughed.

Weel, they rode on through the thickest of the wood, when, all of a sudden, the horse stopped at the door of a great house; and, but that he knew the place was ten miles off, my father would have thought he was at Redgauntlet Castle. They rode into the outer courtyard, through the muckle faulding yetts, and aneath the auld portcullis; and the whole front of the house was lighted, and there were pipes and fiddles, and as much dancing and deray within as used to be in Sir Robert's house at Pace and Yule, and such high seasons. They lap off, and my gudesire, as seemed to him, fastened his horse to the very ring he had tied him to that morning, when he gaed to wait on the young Sir John.

'God!' said my gudesire, 'if Sir Robert's death be but a dream!'

He knocked at the ha' door just as he was wont, and his auld acquaintance, Dougal MacCallum, just after his wont, too, came to open the door, and said, 'Piper Steenie, are ye there, lad? Sir Robert has been crying for you.'

My gudesire was like a man in a dream; he looked for the stranger, but he was gane for the time. At last he just tried to say, 'Ha! Dougal Driveower, are ye living? I thought ye had been dead.'

'Never fash yoursell wi' me,' said Dougal, 'but look to yoursell; and see ye tak naething frae onybody here, neither meat, drink, or siller, except just the receipt that is your ain.'

So saying, he led the way out through halls and trances that were weel kenn'd to my gudesire, and into the auld oak parlour; and there was as much singing of profane sangs, and birling of red wine, and speaking blasphemy and sculduddry, as had ever been in Redgauntlet Castle when it was at the blythest.

But, Lord take us in keeping! what a set of ghastly revellers they were that sat round that table! My gudesire kenn'd mony that had long before gane to their place, for often had he piped to the most part in the hall of Redgauntlet. There was the fierce Middleton, and the dissolute Rothes, and the crafty Lauderdale; and Dalyell, with his bald head and a beard to his girdle; and Earlshall, with Cameron's blude on his hand; and wild Bonshaw, that tied blessed Mr. Cargill's limbs till the blude sprung; and Dumbarton Douglas, the twice-turned traitor baith to country and king. There was the Bluidy Advocate MacKenyie, who, for his worldly wit and wisdom, had been to the rest as a god. And there was Claverhouse, as beautiful as when he lived, with his long, dark, curled locks, streaming down over his laced buff-coat, and his left-hand always on his right spule-blade, to hide the wound that the silver bullet had made.[1] He sat apart from them all, and looked at them with a melancholy, haughty countenance; while the rest hallooed, and sung, and laughed, that the room rang. But their smiles were fearfully contorted from time to time; and their laughter passed into such wild sounds as made my gudesire's very nails grow blue, and chilled the marrow in his banes.

They that waited at the table were just the wicked serving-men and troopers that had done their work and cruel bidding on earth. There was the Lang Lad of the Nethertown, that helped to take Argyle; and the bishop's summoner, that they called the Deil's Rattle-bag; and the wicked guardsmen, in their laced coats; and the savage Highland Amorites, that shed blood like water; and mony a proud serving-man, haughty of heart and bloody of hand, cringing to the rich, and making them wickeder than they would be; grinding the poor to powder, when the rich had broken them to fragments. And mony, mony mair were coming and ganging, a' as busy in their vocation as if they had been alive.

Sir Robert Redgauntlet, in the midst of a' this fearful riot, cried, wi' a voice like thunder, on Steenie Piper to come to the board-head where he was sitting, his legs stretched out before him, and swathed up with flannel, with his holster pistols aside him, while the great broadsword rested against his chair, just as my gudesire had seen him the last time upon earth—the very cushion for the jackanape was close to him, but the creature itsell was not there; it wasna its hour, it's likely; for he heard them say as he came forward, 'Is not the major come yet?' And another answered, 'The jackanape will be here betimes the morn.' And when my gudesire came forward, Sir Robert, or his ghaist, or the deevil in his likeness, said, 'Weel, piper, hae ye settled wi' my son for the year's rent?'

[1] These men were regarded by the Covenanters as their principal persecutors under Charles II and James VII.

With much ado my father gat breath to say that Sir John would not settle without his honour's receipt.

'Ye shall hae that for a tune of the pipes, Steenie,' said the appearance of Sir Robert. 'Play us up, "Weel hoddled, Luckie".'

Now this was a tune my gudesire learned frae a warlock, that heard it when they were worshipping Satan at their meetings, and my gudesire had sometimes played it at the ranting suppers in Redgauntlet Castle, but never very willingly; and now he grew cauld at the very name of it, and said, for excuse, he hadna his pipes wi' him.

'MacCallum, ye limb of Beelzebub,' said the fearfu' Sir Robert, 'bring Steenie the pipes that I am keeping for him!'

MacCallum brought a pair of pipes might have served the piper of Donald of the Isles. But he gave my gudesire a nudge as he offered them; and looking secretly and closely, Steenie saw that the chanter was of steel, and heated to a white heat; so he had fair warning not to trust his fingers with it. So he excused himself again, and said he was faint and frightened, and had not wind aneugh to fill the bag.

'Then ye maun eat and drink, Steenie,' said the figure; 'for we do little else here; and it's ill speaking between a fou man and a fasting.'

Now these were the very words that the bloody Earl of Douglas said to keep the king's messenger in hand, while he cut the head off MacLellan of Bombie, at the Threave Castle, and that put Steenie mair and mair on his guard. So he spoke up like a man, and said he came neither to eat, or drink, or make minstrelsy, but simply for his ain—to ken what was come o' the money he had paid, and to get a discharge for it; and he was so stout-hearted by this time, that he charged Sir Robert for conscience' sake (he had no power to say the holy name), and as he hoped for peace and rest, to spread no snares for him, but just to give him his ain.

The appearance gnashed its teeth and laughed, but it took from a large pocket-book the receipt, and handed it to Steenie. 'There is your receipt, ye pitiful cur; and for the money, my dog-whelp of a son may go look for it in the Cat's Cradle.'

My gudesire uttered mony thanks, and was about to retire when Sir Robert roared aloud, 'Stop though, thou sack-doudling son of a whore! I am not done with thee. HERE we do nothing for nothing; and you must return on this very day twelvemonth to pay your master the homage that you owe me for my protection.'

My father's tongue was loosed of a suddenty, and he said aloud, 'I refer mysell to God's pleasure, and not to yours.'

He had no sooner uttered the word than all was dark around him, and he sunk on the earth with such a sudden shock, that he lost both breath and sense.

How lang Steenie lay there, he could not tell; but when he came to himsell, he was lying in the auld kirkyard of Red-gauntlet parochine, just at the door of the family aisle, and the scutcheon of the auld knight, Sir Robert, hanging over his head. There was a deep morning fog on grass and grave-stane around him, and his horse was feeding quietly beside the minister's twa cows. Steenie would have thought the whole was a dream, but he had the receipt in his hand, fairly written and signed by the auld laird; only the last letters of his name were a little disorderly, written like one seized with sudden pain.

Sorely troubled in his mind, he left that dreary place, rode through the mist to Redgauntlet Castle, and with much ado he got speech of the laird.

'Well, you dyvour bankrupt,' was the first word, 'have you brought me my rent?'

'No,' answered my gudesire, 'I have not; but I have brought your honour Sir Robert's receipt for it.'

'How, sirrah? Sir Robert's receipt! You told me he had not given you one.'

'Will your honour please to see if that bit line is right?'

Sir John looked at every line, and at every letter, with much attention, and at last at the date, which my gudesire had not observed—' "From my appointed place," he read, "this twenty-fifth of November." What! That is yesterday! Villain, thou must have gone to Hell for this!'

'I got it from your honour's father; whether he be in Heaven or Hell, I know not,' said Steenie.

'I will delate you for a warlock to the privy council!' said Sir John. 'I will send you to your master, the devil, with the help of a tar-barrel and a torch!'

'I intend to delate mysell to the presbytery,' said Steenie, 'and tell them all I have seen last night, whilk are things fitter for them to judge of than a borrel man like me.'

Sir John paused, composed himsell, and desired to hear the full history; and my gudesire told it him from point to point, as I have told it you—word for word, neither more nor less.

Sir John was silent again for a long time, and at last he said, very composedly, 'Steenie, this story of yours concerns the honour of many a noble family besides mine; and if it be a leasing-making, to keep yourself out of my danger, the least you can expect is to have a red-hot iron driven through your tongue, and that will be as bad as scauding your fingers with a red-hot chanter. But yet it may be true, Steenie; and if the money cast up, I shall not know what to think of it. But where shall we find the Cat's Cradle? There are cats enough about the old house, but I think they kitten without the ceremony of bed or cradle.'

'We were best ask Hutcheon,' said my gudesire; 'he kens a' the odd corners about as weel as—another serving-man that is now gane, and that I wad not like to name.'

Aweel, Hutcheon, when he was asked, told them that a ruinous turret, lang disused, next to the clock-house, only accessible by a ladder, for the opening was on the outside, and far above the battlements, was called of old the Cat's Cradle.

'There will I go immediately,' said Sir John; and he took (with what purpose, Heaven kens) one of his father's pistols from the hall-table, where they had lain since the night he died, and hastened to the battlements.

It was a dangerous place to climb, for the ladder was auld and frail, and wanted ane or twa rounds. However, up got Sir John, and entered at the turret door, where his body stopped the only little light that was in the bit turret. Something flees at him wi' a vengeance, maist dang him back ower; bang gaed the knight's pistol, and Hutcheon, that held the ladder, and my gudesire that stood beside him, hears a loud skelloch. A minute after, Sir John flings the body of the jackanape down to them, and cries that the siller is fund, and that they should come up and help him. And there was the bag of siller sure aneugh, and mony orra things besides that had been missing for mony a day. And Sir John, when he had riped the turret weel, led my gudesire into the dining-parlour, and took him by the hand, and spoke kindly to him, and said he was sorry he should have doubted his word, and that he would hereafter be a good master to him, to make amends.

'And now, Steenie,' said Sir John, 'although this vision of yours tends, on the whole, to my father's credit, as an honest man, that he should, even after his death, desire to see justice done to a poor man like you, yet you are sensible that ill-dispositioned men might make bad constructions upon it, concerning his soul's health. So, I think, we had better lay the haill dirdum on that ill-deedie creature, Major Weir, and say naething about your dream in the wood of Pitmurkie. You had taken ower muckle brandy to be very certain about ony thing; and, Steenie, this receipt (his hand shook while he held it out), it's but a queer kind of document, and we will do best, I think, to put it quietly in the fire.'

'Od, but for as queer as it is, it's a' the voucher I have for my rent,' said my gudesire, who was afraid, it may be, of losing the benefit of Sir Robert's discharge.

'I will bear the contents to your credit in the rental-book, and give you a discharge under my own hand,' said Sir John, 'and that on the spot. And, Steenie, if you can hold your tongue about this matter, you shall sit, from this term downward, at an easier rent.'

'Mony thanks to your honour,' said Steenie, who saw easily in what corner the wind was; 'doubtless I will be conformable to all your honour's commands; only I would willingly speak wi' some powerful minister on the subject, for I do not like the sort of soumons of appointment whilk your honour's father——'

'Do not call the phantom my father!' said Sir John, interrupting him.

'Weel, then, the thing that was so like him,' said my gudesire; 'he spoke of my coming back to him this time twelvemonth, and it's a weight on my conscience.'

'Aweel, then,' said Sir John, 'if you be so much distressed in mind, you may speak to our minister of the parish; he is a douce man, regards the honour of our family, and the mair that he may look for some patronage from me.'

Wi' that my gudesire readily agreed that the receipt should be burnt, and the laird threw it into the chimney with his ain hand. Burn it would not for them, though; but away it flew up the lum, wi' a lang train of sparks at its tail, and a hissing noise like a squib.

My gudesire gaed down to the manse, and the minister, when he had heard the story, said it was his real opinion that, though my gudesire had gaen very far in tampering with dangerous matters, yet, as he had refused the devil's arles (for such was the offer of meat and drink), and had refused to do homage by piping at his bidding, he hoped, that if he held a circumspect walk hereafter, Satan could take little advantage by what was come and gane. And, indeed, my gudesire, of his ain accord, lang forswore baith the pipes and the brandy; it was not even till the year was out, and the fatal day passed, that he would so much as take the fiddle, or drink usquebaugh or tippenny.

Sir John made up his story about the jackanape as he liked himsell; and some believe till this day there was no more in the matter than the filching nature of the brute. Indeed, ye'll no hinder some to threap that it was nane o' the Auld Enemy that Dougal and Hutcheon saw in the laird's room, but only that wanchancie creature, the major, capering on the coffin; and that, as to the blawing on the laird's whistle that was heard after he was dead, the filthy brute could do that as weel as the laird himsell, if no better. But Heaven kens the truth, whilk first came out by the minister's wife, after Sir John and her ain gudeman were baith in the moulds. And then, my gudesire, wha was failed in his limbs, but not in his judgment or memory—at least nothing to speak of—was obliged to tell the real narrative to his freends for the credit of his good name. He might else have been charged for a warlock.

The Fair Maid of Cellardykes

THOMAS GILLESPIE

(1777–1844)

I DID not like the idea of having all the specimens of the fine arts in Europe collected into one *bonne bouche* at the Louvre. It was like collecting, while a boy, a handful of strawberries, and devouring them at one indiscriminating gulp. I do not like floral exhibitions, for the same reason. I had rather a thousand times meet my old and my new friends in my solitary walks, or in my country rambles. All museums in this way confound and bewilder me; and had the Turk not been master of Greece, I should have preferred a view of the Elgin marbles in the land of their nativity. And it is for a similar reason that my mind still reverts, with a kind of dreamy delight, to the time when I viewed mankind in detail, and in all their individual and natural peculiarities, rather than *en masse*, and in one regimental uniform.

Educate up! Educate up! Invent machinery—discover agencies—saddle nature with the panniers of labour—and, at last, stand alongside of her, clothed, from the peasant to the prince, in the wonders of her manufacture, and merrily whistling, in idle unconcern, to the tune of her unerring dispatch! But what have we gained? One mass of similarities: the housemaid, the housekeeper, the lady, and the princess, speaking the same language, clothed in the same habiliments, and enjoying the same immunities from corporeal labour—the colours of the rainbow whirled and blended into one glare of white! Towards this *ultimatum* we are now fast hastening.

Where is the shepherd stocking-weaver, with his wires and his fingers moving invisibly? Where the 'wee and the muckle wheel', with the aged dames, in pletted toys, singing 'Tarry woo'? Where the hodden-grey clad patriarch, sitting in the midst of his family, and mixing familiarly, and in perfect equality with all the household—servant and child? My heart constantly warms to these recollections; and I feel as if wandering over a landscape variegated by pleasant and contrasting colouring, and overshadowed with associations which have long been a part of myself.

One exception to the general progression and assimilation still happily remains to gratify, I must confess, my liking for things as they were. The fisher population of Newhaven, Buckhaven, and Cellardykes[1]—(my observation extends no farther, and I limit my remarks accordingly)—are, in fact, the Scottish highlanders, the Irish, the Welsh, and the Manx of Fisherdom. Differing each somewhat from the other, they are united by one common bond of character—they are varieties of the same animal—the different species under one genus. I like this. I am always in high spirits when I pass through a fishing village or a fisher street.

No accumulation of filth in every hue—of shell, and gill, and fish-tail—can disgust me. I even smell a sweet savour from their empty baskets, as they exhale themselves dry in the sunbeam. And then there is a hue of robust health over all. No mincing of matters. Female arms and legs of the true

---

[1] Newhaven, fishing suburb of Edinburgh; Buckhaven, now united with the port of Methil, Fife; Cellardyke (today without a final 's'), now part of Anstruther, Fife. [Editor.]

Tuscan order—cheeks and chins where neither the rose nor the bone has been stinted. Children of the dub and the mire—all agog in demi-nudity, and following nature most vociferously. Snug, comfortable cabins, where garish day makes no unhandsome inquiries, and where rousing fires and plentiful meals abide from June to January. They have a language, too, of their own—the true Mucklebacket[1] dialect; and freely and firmly do they throw from them censure, praise, or ribaldry. The men are here but men; mere human machines—useful, but not ornamental—necessary incumbrances rather than valuable protectors.

'Poor creature!' says Meg of the Mucklebacket, 'she canna maintain a man.'

Sir Walter saw through the character I am labouring to describe; and, in one sentence, put life and identity into it. I know he was exceedingly fond of conversing with fisherwomen in particular. But, whilst such are the general features, each locality I have mentioned has its distinctive lineaments.

The Newhaven fisherwoman (for the man is unknown) is a bundle of snug comfort. Her body, her dress, her countenance, her basket, her voice, all partake of the same character of *enbonpointness*. Yet there is nothing at all untidy about her. She may ensconce her large limbs in more plaiden coverings than the gravedigger in *Hamlet* had waistcoats, but still she moves without constraint; and under a burden which would press my lady's waiting-maid to the carpet, she moves free, firm, elastic. Her tongue is not labour-logged, her feet are not creel-retarded; but, altogether unconscious of the presence of hundreds, she holds on her way and her discourse as if she were a caravan in the desert. She is to be found in every street and alley of Auld Reekie, till her work is accomplished. Her voice of call is exceedingly musical, and sounds sweetly in the ears of the infirm and bedrid. All night long she holds her stand close by the theatre, with her

[1] The name of a family of fisher folk in Sir Walter Scott's *The Antiquary*. [Editor.]

broad knife and her opened oyster. In vain does the young spark endeavour to engage her in licentious talk. He soon discovers that, wherever her feelings or affections tend, they do not point in his favour. Thus, loaded with pence, and primed with gin, she returns by midnight to her home—there to share a supper-pint with her man and her neighbours, and to prepare, by deep repose, for the duties of a new day. Far happier and far more useful she, in her day and generation, than that thing of fashion which men call a beau or a belle—in whose labours no one rejoices, and in whose bosom no sentiment but self finds a place.

In Buckhaven, again, the Salique law prevails. There men are men, and women mere appendages. The sea department is here all in all. The women, indeed, crawl a little way, and through a few deserted fields, into the surrounding country; but the man drives the cart, and the cart carries the fish; and the fish are found in all the larger inland towns eastward.

Cellardykes is a mixture of the two—a kind of William and Mary government, where, side by side, at the same cart, and not unfrequently in the same boat, are to be found man and woman, lad and lass. Oh, it is a pretty sight to see the Cellardyke fishers leaving the coast for the herring-fishing in the north! I witnessed it some years ago, as I passed to Edinburgh; and this year I witnessed it again.

Meeting and conversing with my old friend the minister of the parish of Kilrenny, we laid us down on the sunny slope of the brae facing the east and the Isle of May, whilst he gave me the following narrative:

Thomas Laing and Sarah Black were born and brought up under the same roof—namely, that double-storied tenement which stands somewhat by itself, overlooking the harbour. They entered by the same outer door, but occupied each a separate story. Thomas Laing was always a stout, hardy, fearless boy, better acquainted with every boat on the station than with his single questions, and far fonder of little Sarah's company than of the schoolmaster's. Sarah was likewise a healthy, stirring child, extremely sensitive and easily offended, but capable, at the same time, of the deepest feelings of gratitude and attachment. Thomas Laing was, in fact, her champion, her Don Quixote, from the time when he could square his arms and manage his fists; and much mischief and obloquy did he suffer among his companions on account of his chivalrous defence of little Sally.

One day whilst the fisher boys and girls were playing on the pier, whilst the tide was at the full, a mischievous boy, wishing to annoy Thomas, pushed little Sall into the harbour, where, but for Thomas's timely and skilful aid (for he was an excellent swimmer), she would probably have been drowned. Having placed his favourite in a condition and place of safety, Tom felled the offender, with a terrible fister, to the earth.

The blow had taken place on the pit of the stomach, and was mortal. Tom was taken up, imprisoned, and tried for manslaughter; but, on account of his youth—being then only thirteen—he was merely imprisoned for a certain number of months. Poor Sally, on whose account Tom had incurred the punishment of the law, visited him, as did many good-natured fishermen, whilst in prison, where he always expressed extreme contrition for his rashness. After the expiry of his imprisonment, Tom returned to Cellardykes, only to take farewell of his parents, and his now more than ever dear Sally. He could not bear, he said, to face the parents of the boy whose death he had occasioned.

He promised to spend one night at home; but he had no such intention—and, for several years, nobody knew what had become of Thomas Laing. The subject was at first a speculation, then a wonder, next an occasional recollection; and, in a few months, the place which once knew bold Tom Laing, knew him no more. Even his parents, engaged as they were in the active pursuits of fishing, and surrounded as they were by a large and dependent family, soon learned to forget him.

One bosom alone retained the image of Tom, more faithfully and indelibly than ever did coin the impression of royalty. Meanwhile, Sarah grew—for she was a year older than Tom—into womanhood, and fairly took her share in all the more laborious parts of a fisher's life. She could row a boat, carry a creel, or drive a cart with the best of them; and, whilst her frame was thus hardened, her limbs acquired a consistency and proportion which bespoke the buxom woman rather than the bonny lass. Her eye, however, was large and brown, and her lips had that variety of expression which lips only can exhibit. Many a jolly fisher wished and attempted to press these lips to his; but was always repulsed. She neither spoke of her Thomas, nor did she grieve for him much in secret; but her heart revolted from a union with any other person whilst Thomas might still be alive.

Upon a person differently situated, the passion (for passion assuredly it was) which she entertained for her absent lover, might and would have produced very different effects. Had Sarah been a young boarding-school miss, she would assuredly either have eloped with another, or have died in a madhouse; had she been a sentimental sprig of gentility, consumption must have followed: but Sarah was neither of these. She had a heart to feel, and deeply too; but she knew that labour was her destiny, and that when 'want came in at the door, love escapes by the window'. So she just laboured, laughed, ate, drank, and slept, very much like other people. Yet few sailors came to the place whom she did not question about Thomas; and many a time and oft did she retire to the rocks of a Sabbath eve, to think of and pray for Thomas Laing.

People imagine, from the free and open manner, and talk of the fisherwomen, that they are all or generally people of doubtful morality. Never was there a greater mistake. To the public in general they are inaccessible; they almost universally intermarry with one another; and there are fewer cases (said my reverend informant) of public or sessional reproof in Cellardykes, than in any other district of my parish. But, from the precarious and somewhat solitary nature of their employment, they are exceedingly superstitious; and I had access to know, that many a sly sixpence passed from Sally's pocket into old Effie the wise woman's, with the view of having the cards cut and cups read for poor Thomas.

Time, however, passed on—with time came, but did not pass misfortune. Sally's father, who had long been addicted, at intervals, to hard drinking, was found one morning dead at the bottom of a cliff, over which, in returning home inebriated, he had tumbled. There were now three sisters, all below twelve, to provide for, and Sally's mother had long been almost bedrid with severe and chronic rheumatism; consequently, the burden of supporting this helpless family devolved upon Sarah, who was now in the bloom and in the strength of her womanhood. Instead of sitting down, however, to lament what could not be helped, Sarah immediately redoubled her diligence. She even learned to row a boat as well as a man, and contrived, by the help of the men her father used to employ, to keep his boat still going.

Things prospered with her for a while; but, in a sudden storm, wherein five boats perished with all on board, she lost her whole resources. They are a high-minded people those Cellardyke fishers. The Blacks scorned to come upon the session. The young girls salted herrings, and cried haddocks in small baskets through the village and the adjoining burghs, and Sarah contrived still to keep up a cart for country service.

Meanwhile, Sarah became the object of attention through the whole neighbourhood. Though somewhat larger in feature and limb than the Venus de Medicis, she was, notwithstanding, tight, clean, and sunny—her skin white as snow, and her frame a well-proportioned Doric—just such a helpmate as a husband who has to rough it through life might be disposed to select.

Captain William M'Guffock, or, as he was commonly called, Big Bill, was the commander of a coasting craft, and a man of considerable substance. True, he was considerably older than Sally, and a widower, but he had no family, and a 'bien house to bide in'. You see that manse-looking tenement there, on the broad head towards the east—that was Captain M'Guffock's residence when his seafaring avocations did not demand his presence elsewhere. Well, Bill came acourting to Sally; but Sally 'looked asclent and unco skeich'. Someway or other, whenever she thought of matrimony—which she did occasionally—she at the same time thought of Thomas Laing, and, as she expressed it, her heart *scunnered* at the thought. Consequently, Bill made little progress in his courtship; which was likewise liable to be interrupted, for weeks at a time, by his professional voyages.

At last a letter arrived from on board a king's vessel, then lying in Leith Roads, apprising Thomas Laing's relatives that he had died of fever on the West India station. This news affected Sally more than anything which had hitherto happened to her. She shut herself up for two hours in her mother's bedroom, weeping aloud and bitterly, exclaiming, from time to time—

'Oh! my Thomas!—my own dearest Thomas! I shall never love man again. I am thine in life and in death—in time and in eternity!'

In vain did the poor bedrid woman try to comfort her daughter. Nature had her way; and, in less than three hours, Sarah Black was again in the streets, following, with a confused but a cheerful look, her ordinary occupation. This grief of Sarah's, had it been well nursed, might well have lasted a twelvemonth; but, luckily for Sarah, and for the labouring classes in general, she had not time to nurse her grief to keep it warm. 'Give us this day our daily bread', said a poor helpless mother and three somewhat dependent sisters—and Sarah's exertions were redoubled.

'Oh, what a feelingless woman!' said Mrs. Paterson to me, as Sarah passed her door one day in my presence, absolutely singing—'Oh, what a feelingless woman!—and her father dead, and her mother bedrid, and poor Thomas Laing, whom she made such a fuss about, gone too—and there is she, absolutely singing after all!'

Mrs. Paterson is now Mrs. Robson, having married her

second husband just six weeks after the death of the first,
whom her improper conduct and unhappy temper contri-
buted first to render miserable here, and at last to convey to
the churchyard! Verily (added the worthy clergyman), the
heart is deceitful above all things. But what, after all, could
poor Sarah do, but marry Will M'Guffock, and thus amply
provide, not only for herself, but for her mother and sister?
Had Thomas (and her heart heaved at the thought) still been
alive, she thought, she never would have brought herself to
think of it in earnest; but now that Thomas had long ceased
to think of her or of anything earthly, why should she not
make a man happy who seemed distractedly in love with her,
and at the same time honourably provide for her poor and
dependent relatives?

In the meantime, the sacramental occasion came round,
and I had a private meeting previous to the first communion
with Sarah Black. To me, in secret, she laid open her whole
heart as if in the presence of her God; and I found her,
though not a well-informed Christian by any means on
doctrinal points, yet well disposed and exceedingly humble;
in short, I had great pleasure in putting a token into her
hand, at which she continued to look for an instant, and
then returned it to me. I expressed surprise, at least by my
looks.

'I fear,' said she, 'that I am *unworthy*; for I have not told
you that I am thinking of marrying a man whom I cannot
love, merely to provide for our family. Is not this a sin?—
and can I, with an intention of doing what I know to be
wrong, safely communicate?'

I assured her that, instead of thinking it a sin, I thought
her resolution commendable, particularly as the object of
her real affection was beyond its reach; and I mention the
circumstance to show that there is often much honour, and
even delicacy of feeling, natural as well as religious, under
very uncongenial circumstances and appearances. Having
satisfied her mind on this subject, I had the pleasure to see
her at the communion table, conducting herself with much

seeming seriousness of spirit. I could see her shed tears, and formed the very best opinion of her from her conduct throughout.

In a few days or weeks after this, the proclamation lines were put into my hands, and I had the pleasure of uniting her to Captain M'Guffock in due course. They had, however, only been married a few weeks, when an occurrence of a very awkward character threw her and her husband, who was, in fact, an ill-tempered, passionate man, into much perplexity.

The captain was absent on a coasting voyage, as usual; and his wife was superintending the washing of some clothes, whilst the sun was setting. It was a lovely evening in the month of July, and the fishing boats were spread out all over the mouth of the Firth, from the East Neuk to the Isle of May, in the same manner in which you see them at present. Mrs. M'Guffock's mind assumed, notwithstanding the glorious scenery around her, a serious cast, for she could not help recalling many such evenings in which she had rejoiced in company and in unison with her beloved Thomas. She felt and knew that it was wrong to indulge such emotions; but she could not help it.

At last, altogether overcome, she threw herself forward on the green turf, and prayed audibly—'O my God, give me strength and grace to forget my own truly beloved Thomas! Alas! he knows not the struggles which I have to exclude him from my sinful meditations. Even suppose he were again to arise from the dead, and appear in all the reality of his youthful being, I must, and would fly from him as from my most dangerous foe.'

She lifted up her eyes in the twilight, and in the next instant felt herself in the arms of a powerful person, who pressed her in silence to his breast. Amazed and bewildered, she neither screamed nor fainted, but, putting his eager kisses aside, calmly inquired who he was who dared thus to insult her. She had no sooner pronounced the inquiry, than she heard the words, 'Thomas—your own Thomas!' pronounced in tones which could not be mistaken. This, indeed, over-powered her; and, with a scream of agony, she sank down dead on the earth.

This brought immediate assistance; but she was found lying by herself, and talking wildly about her Thomas Laing. Everybody who heard her concluded that she had either actually seen her lover's ghost, or that her mind had given way under the pressure of regret for her marriage, and that she was now actually a lunatic. For twelve hours she continued to evince the most manifest marks of insanity; but sleep at last soothed and restored her, and she immediately sent for me. I endeavoured to persuade her that it must be all a delusion, and that the imagination oftentimes created such fancies. I gave instances from books which I had read, as well as from a particular friend of my own who had long been subject to such delusive impressions, and at last she became actually persuaded that there had been no reality in what she had so vividly perceived, and still most distinctly and fearfully recollected. I took occasion then to urge upon her the exceeding sinfulness of allowing any image to come betwixt her and her lawful married husband; and left her restored, if not to her usual serenity, at least to a conviction that she had only been disturbed by a vision.

When her husband returned, I took him aside, and explained my views of the case, and stated my most decided apprehension that some similar impression might return upon her nerves, and that her sisters (her mother being now removed by death) should dwell in the same house with her. To this, however, the captain objected, on the score that, though he was willing to pay a person to take care of them in their own house, he did not deem them proper company, in short, for a *captain's wife*. I disliked the reasoning, and told him so; but he became passionate, and I saw it was useless to contend further.

From that day, however, Bill M'Guffock seemed to have become an altered man. Jealousy, or something nearly resembling it, took possession of his heart; and he even ventured to affirm that his wife had a paramour somewhere concealed, with whom, in his long and necessary absences, she associated. He alleged, too, that in her sleep she would repeat the name of her favourite, and in terms of present love and fondness. I now saw that I had not known the depth of 'a first love', otherwise I should not have advised this unhappy marriage, all advantageous as it was in a worldly point of view.

A sailor's life, however, is one of manifest risk, and in less than a twelvemonth Sarah M'Guffock was a young widow, without incumbrance, and with her rights to her just share of the captain's effects. Her sorrow for the death of her husband was, I believe, sincere; but I observed that she took an early opportunity of joining her sisters in her old habitation, immediately beneath that still tenanted by the friends of Laing.

Matters were in this situation, when I was surprised one evening, whilst sitting meditating in the manse of Kilrenny, about dusk, with a visit from a tall and well-dressed stranger. He asked me at once if I could give him a private interview for a few minutes, as he had something of importance to communicate. Having taken him into my study, and shut the door, I reached him a chair, and desired him to proceed.

'I had left the parish,' said the stranger, 'before you were minister of Kilrenny, in the time of worthy Mr. Brown, and therefore you will probably not know even my name. I am Thomas Laing!'

'I did not indeed,' said I, 'know you, but I have heard much about you; and I know one who has taken but too deep an interest in your fate. But how comes it,' added I, beginning to think that I was conversing either with a vision or an impostor—'how comes it that you are here, seemingly alive and well, whilst we have all been assured of your death some years ago?'

The stranger started, and immediately exclaimed— 'Dead!—dead!—who said I was dead?'

'Why,' said I, 'there was a letter came, I think, to your

own father, mentioning your death by fever in the West Indies.'

'Do I look like a dead man?' said the stranger; but, immediately becoming absent and embarrassed, he sat for a while silent, and then resumed: 'Some one,' said he, 'has imposed upon my dear Sarah, and for the basest of purposes. I now see it all. My dear girl has been sadly used.'

'This is, indeed, strange,' said I; 'but let me hear how it is that I have the honour of a visit from you at this time and in this place?'

'Oh,' replied Thomas Laing (for it was he in verity), 'I will soon give you the whole story:

'When I left this, fourteen years ago come the time, I embarked at Greenock, working my way out to New York. As I was an excellent hand at a rope and an oar, I early attracted the captain's notice, who made some inquiries respecting my place of birth and my views in life. I told him that I was literally "at sea", having nothing particularly in view—that I had been bred a fisher, and understood sailing and rowing as well as any one on board. The captain seemed to have something in his head, for he nodded to me, saying, "Very well, we will see what can be done for you when we arrive at New York." When we were off Newfoundland, we were overtaken by a terrible storm, which drove us completely out of our latitude, till, at last, we struck on a sandbank—the sea making for several hours a complete breach over the deck. Many were swept away into the devouring flood; whilst some of us—amongst several others the captain and myself—clung to what remained of the ship's masts till the storm somewhat abated. We then got the boat launched, and made for land, which we could see looming at some distance ahead. We got, however, entangled amongst currents and breakers; and, within sight of a boat which was making towards us from the shore, we fairly upset—and I remember nothing more till I awoke, in dreadful torment, in some fishermen's boat. Beside me lay the captain, the rest had perished.

'When we arrived at the land, we were placed in one of the fishermen's huts, where we were most kindly treated—assisting, as we did occasionally, in the daily labours of the cod fishery. I displayed so much alertness and skill in this employment, that the factor on the station made me an advantageous offer, if I would remain with them and assist in their labours. With this offer, having no other object distinctly in view, I complied. But my kind and good-hearted captain, possessing less dexterity in this employment, was early shipped at his own request for England.

'The most of the hands, about two hundred in all, on the station where I remained, were Scotch and Irish, and a merry, jovial set we were. The men had wives and families; and the governor or factor lived in a large slated house, very like your manse, upon a gentle eminence, a little inland. Towards the coast the land is sandy and flat; but in the interior there is much wood, a very rich soil, and excellent fresh water. Where we remained the water was brackish, and constituted the chief inconvenience of our station. The factor or agent, commonly called by the men the governor, used to visit us almost every day, and remained much on board when ships were loading for Europe. One fine summer's day we were all enjoying the luxury of bathing, when, all on a sudden, the shout was raised—"A shark! a shark!" I had just taken my place in the boat, and was still undressed, when I observed one man disappear, being dragged under the water by the sea monster. The factor, who was swimming about in the neighbourhood, seemed to be paralysed by terror, for he made for the boat, plashing like a dog, with his hands and arms frequently stretched out of the water. I saw his danger, and immediately plunged in to his rescue, which, with some difficulty, I at last effected.

'Poor Pat Moonie was seen no more; nor did the devouring monster reappear. The factor immediately acknowledged his obligations to me, by carrying me home with him, and introducing me to his lady and an only daughter—I think I never beheld a more beautiful creature; but I looked upon her as a being of a different order from myself, and I still thought of my own dear Sally and sweet home at Cellardykes.

'Through the factor's kindness, I got the management of a boat's crew, with considerable emolument which belonged to the situation. I then behoved to dress better, at least while on land, than I used to do, and I was an almost daily visitor at Codfield House, the name of the captain's residence. My affairs prospered; I made, and had no way of spending money. The factor was my banker, and his fair daughter wrote out the acknowledgements for her father to sign.

'One beautiful Sabbath-day, after the factor—who officiated at our small station as clergyman—had read us prayers and a sermon, I took a walk into the interior of the country, where, with a book in her hand, and an accompaniment of Newfoundland dogs, I chanced to meet with Miss Woodburn, the factor's beautiful child. She was only fourteen, but quite grown, and as blooming a piece of womanhood as ever wore kid gloves or black leather. She seemed somewhat embarrassed at my presence, and blushed scarlet, entreating me to prevent one of her dogs from running away with her glove, which he was playfully tossing about in his mouth. The dog would not surrender his charge to any one but to his mistress; and, in the struggle, he bit my hand somewhat severely. You may see the marks of his teeth there still' (holding out his hand while he spoke).

'Poor Miss Woodburn knew not what to do first; she immediately dropped the book which she was reading— scolded the offending dog to a distance—took up the glove, which the dog at her bidding had dropped, and wrapped it close and firmly around my bleeding hand; a band of long grass served for thread to make all secure, and in a few days my hand was in a fair way of recovery—but not so my heart; I felt as if I had been all at once transformed into a gentleman—the soft touch of Miss Eliza's fair fingers seemed to have transformed me, skin, flesh, and bones, into another species of being. I shook like an aspen leaf whenever I thought of our interesting interview; and I could observe that Eliza changed colour, and looked out of the window whenever I entered the room. But, sir, I am too particular, and I will now hasten to a close.'

I entreated him (said the parson) to go on in his own way, and without any reference to my leisure. He then proceeded: 'Well, sir, from year to year I prospered, and from year to year got more deeply in love with the angel which moved about in my presence. At last our attachment became manifest to the young lady's parent; and, to my great surprise, it was proposed that we should make a voyage to New York, and there be united in matrimony.

All this while, sir, I thought of my own dear Sally, and the thought not unfrequently made me miserable; but what was Sally to me now?—perhaps she was dead—perhaps she was married—perhaps—but I could scarcely think it— she had forgot me; and then the blooming rosebud was ever in my presence, and hallowed me, by its superior purity and beauty, into a complete gentleman. Well, married we were at New York, and for several months I was the happiest of men, and my dear wife (I know it) the happiest of women; but the time of her labour approached—and child and mother lie buried in the cemetery at New York, where we had now fixed our residence.' (Here poor Thomas wept plentifully, and, after a pause, proceeded.)—'I could not reside longer in a place which was so dismally associated in my mind; so, having wound up my worldly affairs, and placed my little fortune—about one thousand pounds—in the bank, I embarked for Europe, along with my father and mother-in-law, who were going home to end their days in the place of their nativity, Belfast, in Ireland.

'I determined upon landing at the Cove of Cork, to visit once more my native village, and to have at least one interview with Sally. I learned, on my arrival at Largo, that Sally was married to the old captain. I resolved, however, ere I went finally to settle in Belfast, to have one stolen peep at my first love—my own dear Sally. I came upon her whilst

repeating my name in her prayers—I embraced her con-
vulsively—repeated her name twice in her hearing—heard
her scream—saw her faint—kissed her fondly again and
again—and, strangers appearing, I immediately absconded.'

'This,' said the minister, 'explains all;—but go on—I am
anxious to hear the conclusion of your somewhat eventful
history.'

'Why, I was off immediately for Belfast, where I at present
reside with my father-in-law, whose temper, since the loss
of his child, has been much altered for the worse. But I am
here on a particular errand, in which your kind offices, sir—
for I have heard of your goodness of heart—may be of
service to me. I observed the death of the old captain in the
newspaper, and I am here once more to enjoy an interview
with his widow. I wish you, sir, to break the business to her;
meanwhile, I will lodge at the Old Inn, Mrs. Laing's, at
Anstruther, and await your return.'

I agreed (continued the parson of Kilrenny) to wait upon
the widow; and to see, in fact, how the wind set, in regard to
'first love'. I found her, as I expected, neatly clad in her
habiliments of widowhood, and employed in making some
dresses for a sister's marriage. I asked and obtained a private
interview, when I detailed, as cautiously as I could, the par-
ticulars of Thomas Laing's history. I could observe that her
whole frame shook occasionally, and that tears came, again
and again, into her eyes. I was present, but a fortnight ago,
at their first interview at the inn; and I never saw two human
beings evince more real attachment for each other. On their
bended knees, and with faces turned towards heaven, did
they unite in thanking God that he had permitted them to
have another interview with each other in this world of un-
certainty and death.

It has been since discovered that the letter announcing
Laing's death was a forgery of the old captain, which has
reconciled his widow very much to the idea of shortening
her days of mourning. In a word, this evening, and in a few
hours, I am going to unite the widower and the widowed,

together with a younger sister and a fine young sailor, in the
holy bonds of matrimony; and, as a punishment for your
giving me all this trouble in narrating this story, I shall
insist upon your eating fresh herring, with the fresh-herring
Presbytery of St. Andrew's, which meets here at Mrs.
Laing's today, and afterwards witnessing the double ceremony.

To this I assented, and certainly never spent an evening
more agreeably than that which I divided betwixt the merry
lads of St. Andrew's Presbytery, and the fair dames and
maidens of Cellardykes, who graced the marriage ceremony.
Such dancing as there was, and such screaming, and such
music, and such laughing; yet, amidst it all, Mr. and Mrs.
Laing preserved that decent decorum, which plainly said,
'We will not mar the happiness of the young; but we feel
the goodness and providence of our God too deeply, to
permit us to join in the noisy part of the festivity.'

'The fair maid of Cellardykes', with her kind-hearted
husband—I may mention, for the satisfaction of my fair
readers in particular—may now be seen daily at their own
door, and in their own garden, on the face of the steep which
overlooks the village. They have already lived three years
in complete happiness, and have been blessed with two as
fine healthy children as a Cellardykes sun ever rose upon.
Mr. Laing has become an elder in the church, and both husband and wife are most exemplary in the discharge of their
religious, as well as relative duties. God has blessed them
with an ample competence; and sure is the writer of this
narrative, that no poor fisherman or woman ever applied to
this worthy couple without obtaining relief.

One circumstance more, and my narrative closes. As Mr.
Laing was one evening taking a walk along the seashore,
viewing the boats as they mustered for the herring fishing,
he was shot at from behind one of the rocks, and severely
wounded in the shoulder—the ball or slug-shot having
lodged in the clavicle, and refusing, for some days, to be
extracted. The hue-and-cry was immediately raised, but the

guilty person was nowhere to be seen. He had escaped in a boat, or had hid himself in a crevice of the rock, or in some private and friendly house in the village. Poor Thomas Laing was carried home to his distracted wife more dead than alive; and Dr. Goodsir being called, disclosed that, in his present state, the lead could not be extracted. Poor Sarah was never a moment from her husband's side, who fevered, and became occasionally delirious—talking incoherently of murder and shipwreck, and Woodburn, and love, and marriage, and Sarah Black. All within his brain was one mad wheel of mixed and confused colours, such as children make when they wheel a stick, dyed white, black, and red, rapidly around.

Suspicion, from the first, fell upon the brother of the boy Rob Paterson, whom Laing had killed many years before. Revenge is the most enduring, perhaps, of all the passions, and rather feeds upon itself than decays. Like fame, 'it acquires strength by time', and it was suspected that Dan Paterson, a reckless and a dissipated man, had done the deed. In confirmation of this supposition, Dan was nowhere to be found, and it was strongly suspected that his wife and his son, who returned at midnight with the boat, had set Dan on shore somewhere on the coast, and that he had effected his escape. Death, for some time, seemed every day and hour nearer at hand; but at last the symptoms softened, the fever mitigated, the swelling subsided, and, after much careful and skilful surgery, most admirably conducted by Dr. Goodsir's son, the ball was extracted. The wound closed without mortification; and, in a week or two, Mr. Laing was not only out of danger, but out of bed, and walking about, as he does to this hour, with his arm in a sling.

It was about the period of his recovery, that Dan Paterson was taken as he was skulking about in the west country, apparently looking out for a ship in which to sail to America. He was immediately brought back to Cellardykes, and lodged in Anstruther prison. Mr. Laing would willingly have forborne the prosecution; but the law behoved to have its course. Dan was tried for 'maiming with the intention of murder', and was condemned to fourteen years' transportation. This happened in the year 1822, the year of the King's visit to Scotland. Mr. and Mrs. Laing actually waited upon his Majesty King George the Fourth, at the palace of Dalkeith, and, backed by the learned judge and counsel, obtained a commutation of the punishment, from banishment to imprisonment for a limited period. The great argument in his favour was the provocation he had received.

Dan Paterson now inhabits a neat cottage in the village, and Mr. Laing has quite set him up with a boat of his own, ready rigged and fitted for use. He has entirely reformed, has become a member of a temperance society, and his wife and family are as happy as the day is long. Mr. and Mrs. Laing are supplied with the very best of fish, and stockings and mittens are manufactured by the Patersons for the little Laings, particularly during boisterous weather, when fishing is out of the question. Thus has a wise Providence made even the wrath of man to praise him. The truth of the above narrative may be tested any day, by waiting upon the Rev. Mr. Dickson, or upon the parties themselves at Braehead of Cellardykes.

The Gray Wolf

GEORGE MACDONALD

(1824–1905)

ONE evening-twilight in spring, a young English student, who had wandered northwards as far as the outlying fragments of Scotland called the Orkney and Shetland Islands, found himself on a small island of the latter group, caught in a storm of wind and hail, which had come on suddenly. It was in vain to look about for any shelter; for not only did

the storm entirely obscure the landscape, but there was
nothing around him save a desert moss.

At length, however, as he walked on for mere walking's
sake, he found himself on the verge of a cliff, and saw, over
the brow of it, a few feet below him, a ledge of rock, where
he might find some shelter from the blast, which blew from
behind. Letting himself down by his hands, he alighted
upon something that crunched beneath his tread, and found
the bones of many small animals scattered about in front of
a little cave in the rock, offering the refuge he sought. He
went in, and sat upon a stone. The storm increased in
violence, and as the darkness grew he became uneasy, for he
did not relish the thought of spending the night in the cave.
He had parted from his companions on the opposite side of
the island, and it added to his uneasiness that they must be
full of apprehension about him. At last there came a lull in
the storm, and the same instant he heard a footfall, stealthy
and light as that of a wild beast, upon the bones at the mouth
of the cave. He started up in some fear, though the least
thought might have satisfied him that there could be no very
dangerous animals upon the island. Before he had time to
think, however, the face of a woman appeared in the opening. Eagerly the wanderer spoke. She started at the sound
of his voice. He could not see her well, because she was
turned towards the darkness of the cave.

'Will you tell me how to find my way across the moor to
Shielness?' he asked.

'You cannot find it tonight,' she answered, in a sweet tone,
and with a smile that bewitched him, revealing the whitest
of teeth.

'What am I to do, then?'

'My mother will give you shelter, but that is all she has to
offer.'

'And that is far more than I expected a minute ago,' he
replied. 'I shall be most grateful.'

She turned in silence and left the cave. The youth followed.

She was barefooted, and her pretty brown feet went cat-like over the sharp stones, as she led the way down a rocky path to the shore. Her garments were scanty and torn, and her hair blew tangled in the wind. She seemed about five and twenty, lithe and small. Her long fingers kept clutching and pulling nervously at her skirts as she went. Her face was very gray in complexion, and very worn, but delicately formed, and smooth-skinned. Her thin nostrils were tremulous as eyelids, and her lips, whose curves were faultless, had no colour to give sign of indwelling blood. What her eyes were like he could not see, for she had never lifted the delicate films of her eyelids.

At the foot of the cliff they came upon a little hut leaning against it, and having for its inner apartment a natural hollow within. Smoke was spreading over the face of the rock, and the grateful odour of food gave hope to the hungry student. His guide opened the door of the cottage; he followed her in, and saw a woman bending over a fire in the middle of the floor. On the fire lay a large fish broiling. The daughter spoke a few words, and the mother turned and welcomed the stranger. She had an old and very wrinkled, but honest face, and looked troubled. She dusted the only chair in the cottage, and placed it for him by the side of the fire, opposite the one window, whence he saw a little patch of yellow sand over which the spent waves spread themselves out listlessly. Under this window there was a bench, upon which the daughter threw herself in an unusual posture, resting her chin upon her hand. A moment after, the youth caught the first glimpse of her blue eyes. They were fixed upon him with a strange look of greed, amounting to craving, but, as if aware that they belied or betrayed her, she dropped them instantly. The moment she veiled them, her face, notwithstanding its colourless complexion, was almost beautiful.

When the fish was ready, the old woman wiped the deal table, steadied it upon the uneven floor, and covered it with a piece of fine table-linen. She then laid the fish on a wooden

platter, and invited the guest to help himself. Seeing no
other provision, he pulled from his pocket a hunting knife,
and divided a portion from the fish, offering it to the mother
first.

'Come, my lamb,' said the old woman; and the daughter
approached the table. But her nostrils and mouth quivered
with disgust.

The next moment she turned and hurried from the hut.

'She doesn't like fish,' said the old woman, 'and I haven't
anything else to give her.'

'She does not seem in good health,' he rejoined.

The woman answered only with a sigh, and they ate their
fish with the help of a little rye bread. As they finished their
supper, the youth heard the sound as of the pattering of
a dog's feet upon the sand close to the door; but ere he had
time to look out of the window, the door opened, and the
young woman entered. She looked better, perhaps from
having just washed her face. She drew a stool to the corner
of the fire opposite him. But as she sat down, to his bewilder-
ment, and even horror, the student spied a single drop of
blood on her white skin within her torn dress. The woman
brought out a jar of whisky, put a rusty old kettle on the
fire, and took her place in front of it. As soon as the water
boiled, she proceeded to make some toddy in a wooden
bowl.

Meantime the youth could not take his eyes off the young
woman, so that at length he found himself fascinated, or
rather bewitched. She kept her eyes for the most part veiled
with the loveliest eyelids fringed with darkest lashes, and he
gazed entranced; for the red glow of the little oil-lamp
covered all the strangeness of her complexion. But as soon
as he met a stolen glance out of those eyes unveiled, his soul
shuddered within him. Lovely face and craving eyes alternated fascination and repulsion.

The mother placed the bowl in his hands. He drank
sparingly, and passed it to the girl. She lifted it to her lips,
and as she tasted—only tasted it—looked at him. He thought

the drink must have been drugged and have affected his brain. Her hair smoothed itself back, and drew her forehead backwards with it; while the lower part of her face projected towards the bowl, revealing, ere she sipped, her dazzling teeth in strange prominence. But the same moment the vision vanished; she returned the vessel to her mother, and rising, hurried out of the cottage.

Then the old woman pointed to a bed of heather in one corner with a murmured apology; and the student, wearied both with the fatigues of the day and the strangeness of the night, threw himself upon it, wrapped in his cloak. The moment he lay down, the storm began afresh, and the wind blew so keenly through the crannies of the hut, that it was only by drawing his cloak over his head that he could protect himself from its currents. Unable to sleep, he lay listening to the uproar which grew in violence, till the spray was dashing against the window. At length the door opened, and the young woman came in, made up the fire, drew the bench before it, and lay down in the same strange posture, with her chin propped on her hand and elbow, and her face turned towards the youth. He moved a little; she dropped her head, and lay on her face, with her arms crossed beneath her forehead. The mother had disappeared.

Drowsiness crept over him. A movement of the bench roused him, and he fancied he saw some four-footed creature as tall as a large dog trot quietly out of the door. He was sure he felt a rush of cold wind. Gazing fixedly through the darkness, he thought he saw the eyes of the damsel encountering his, but a glow from the falling together of the remnants of the fire revealed clearly enough that the bench was vacant. Wondering what could have made her go out in such a storm, he fell fast asleep.

In the middle of the night he felt a pain in his shoulder, came broad awake, and saw the gleaming eyes and grinning teeth of some animal close to his face. Its claws were in his shoulder, and its mouth in the act of seeking his throat. Before it had fixed its fangs, however, he had its throat in one hand, and sought his knife with the other. A terrible struggle followed; but regardless of the tearing claws, he found and opened his knife. He had made one futile stab, and was drawing it for a surer, when, with a spring of the whole body, and one wildly contorted effort, the creature twisted its neck from his hold, and with something betwixt a scream and a howl, darted from him. Again he heard the door open; again the wind blew in upon him, and it continued blowing; a sheet of spray dashed across the floor, and over his face. He sprung from his couch and bounded to the door.

It was a wild night—dark, but for the flash of whiteness from the waves as they broke within a few yards of the cottage; the wind was raving, and the rain pouring down the air. A gruesome sound as of mingled weeping and howling came from somewhere in the dark. He turned again into the hut and closed the door, but could find no way of securing it.

The lamp was nearly out, and he could not be certain whether the form of the young woman was upon the bench or not. Overcoming a strong repugnance, he approached it, and put out his hands—there was nothing there. He sat down and waited for the daylight: he dared not sleep any more.

When the day dawned at length, he went out yet again, and looked around. The morning was dim and gusty and gray. The wind had fallen, but the waves were tossing wildly. He wandered up and down the little strand, longing for more light.

At length he heard a movement in the cottage. By and by the voice of the old woman called to him from the door.

'You're up early, sir. I doubt you didn't sleep well.'

'Not very well,' he answered. 'But where is your daughter?'

'She's not awake yet,' said the mother. 'I'm afraid I have but a poor breakfast for you. But you'll take a dram and a bit of fish. It's all I've got.'

Unwilling to hurt her, though hardly in good appetite, he sat down at the table. While they were eating, the daughter came in, but turned her face away and went to the farther end of the hut. When she came forward after a minute or two, the youth saw that her hair was drenched, and her face whiter than before. She looked ill and faint, and when she raised her eyes, all their fierceness had vanished, and sadness had taken its place. Her neck was now covered with a cotton handkerchief. She was modestly attentive to him, and no longer shunned his gaze. He was gradually yielding to the temptation of braving another night in the hut, and seeing what would follow, when the old woman spoke.

'The weather will be broken all day, sir,' she said. 'You had better be going, or your friends will leave without you.'

Ere he could answer, he saw such a beseeching glance on the face of the girl, that he hesitated, confused. Glancing at the mother, he saw the flash of wrath in her face. She rose and approached her daughter, with her hand lifted to strike her. The young woman stooped her head with a cry. He darted round the table to interpose between them. But the mother had caught hold of her; the handkerchief had fallen from her neck; and the youth saw five blue bruises on her lovely throat—the marks of the four fingers and the thumb of a left hand. With a cry of horror he darted from the house, but as he reached the door he turned. His hostess was lying motionless on the floor, and a huge gray wolf came bounding after him.

There was no weapon at hand. Instinctively, he set himself firm, leaning a little forward, with half outstretched arms, and hands curved ready to clutch again at the throat upon which he had left those pitiful marks. But the creature as she sprung eluded his grasp, and just as he expected to feel her fangs, he found a woman weeping on his bosom, with her arms around his neck. The next instant, the gray wolf broke from him, and bounded howling up the cliff. Recovering himself as he best might, the youth followed, for it was the only way to the moor above, across which he must now make his way to find his companions.

All at once he heard the sound of a crunching of bones—

not as if a creature was eating them, but as if they were ground by the teeth of rage and disappointment; looking up, he saw close above him the mouth of the little cavern in which he had taken refuge the day before. Summoning all his resolution, he passed it slowly and softly. From within came the sounds of a mingled moaning and growling.

Having reached the top, he ran at full speed for some distance across the moor before venturing to look behind him. When at length he did so, he saw, against the sky, the girl standing on the edge of the cliff, wringing her hands. One solitary wail crossed the space between. She made no attempt to follow him, and he reached the opposite shore in safety.

Thrawn Janet

R. L. STEVENSON

(1850–94)

THE Reverend Murdoch Soulis was long minister of the moorland parish of Balweary, in the vale of Dule. A severe, bleak-faced old man, dreadful to his hearers, he dwelt in the last years of his life, without relative or servant or any human company, in the small and lonely manse under the Hanging Shaw. In spite of the iron composure of his features, his eye was wild, scared, and uncertain; and when he dwelt, in private admonitions, on the future of the impenitent, it seemed as if his eye pierced through the storms of time to the terrors of eternity. Many young persons, coming to prepare themselves against the season of the Holy Communion, were dreadfully affected by his talk. He had a sermon on 1st Peter, v. and 8th, 'The devil as a roaring lion', on the Sunday after every seventeenth of August, and he was accustomed to surpass himself upon that text both by the appalling nature of the matter and the terror of his bearing in the pulpit. The children were frightened into fits, and the old looked more than usually oracular, and were, all that day, full of those hints that Hamlet deprecated. The manse itself, where it stood by the water of Dule among some thick trees, with the Shaw overhanging it on the one side, and on the other many cold, moorish hill-tops rising towards the sky, had begun, at a very early period of Mr. Soulis's ministry, to be avoided in the dusk hours by all who valued themselves upon their prudence; and guidmen sitting at the clachan alehouse shook their heads together at the thought of passing late by that uncanny neighbourhood. There was one spot, to be more particular, which was regarded with especial awe. The manse stood between the high-road and the water of Dule, with a gable to each; its back was towards the kirk-town of Balweary, nearly half a mile away; in front of it, a bare garden, hedged with thorn, occupied the land between the river and the road. The house was two storeys high, with two large rooms on each. It opened not directly on the garden, but on a causewayed path, or passage, giving on the road on the one hand, and closed on the other by the tall willows and elders that bordered on the stream. And it was this strip of causeway that enjoyed among the young parishioners of Balweary so infamous a reputation. The minister walked there often after dark, sometimes groaning aloud in the instancy of his unspoken prayers; and when he was from home, and the manse door was locked, the more daring schoolboys ventured, with beating hearts, to 'follow my leader' across that legendary spot.

This atmosphere of terror, surrounding, as it did, a man of God of spotless character and orthodoxy, was a common cause of wonder and subject of inquiry among the few strangers who were led by chance or business into that unknown, outlying country. But many even of the people of the parish were ignorant of the strange events which had marked the first year of Mr. Soulis's ministrations; and among those who were better informed, some were naturally reticent, and others shy of that particular topic. Now and again, only, one of the older folk would warm into courage over his third tumbler, and recount the cause of the minister's strange looks and solitary life.

Fifty years syne, when Mr. Soulis cam' first into Ba'weary, he was still a young man—a callant, the folk said—fu' o' book learnin' and grand at the exposition, but, as was natural in sae young a man, wi' nae leevin' experience in religion. The younger sort were greatly taken wi' his gifts and his gab; but auld, concerned, serious men and women were moved even to prayer for the young man, whom they took to be a self-deceiver, and the parish that was like to be sae ill-supplied. It was before the days o' the Moderates—weary fa' them; but ill things are like guid—they baith come bit by bit, a pickle at a time; and there were folk even then that said the Lord had left the college professors to their ain devices, an' the lads that went to study wi' them wad hae done mair and better sittin' in a peat-bog, like their forebears of the persecution, wi' a Bible under their oxter and a speerit o' prayer in their heart. There was nae doubt, ony-way, but that Mr. Soulis had been ower lang at the college. He was careful and troubled for mony things besides the ae thing needful. He had a feck o' books wi' him—mair than had ever been seen before in a' that presbytery; and a sair wark the carrier had wi' them, for they were a' like to have smoored in the Deil's Hag between this and Kilmackerlie. They were books o' divinity, to be sure, or so they ca'd them; but the serious were o' opinion there was little service for sae mony, when the hail o' God's Word would gang in the neuk of a plaid. Then he wad sit half the day and half the nicht forbye, which was scant decent—writin', nae less; and first, they were feared he wad read his ser-mons; and syne it proved he was writin' a book himsel', which was surely no fittin' for ane of his years an' sma' experience.

Onyway it behoved him to get an auld, decent wife to keep

the manse for him an' see to his bit denners; and he was recommended to an auld limmer—Janet M'Clour, they ca'd her—and sae far left to himsel' as to be ower persuaded. There was mony advised him to the contrar, for Janet was mair than suspeckit by the best folk in Ba'weary. Lang or that, she had had a wean to a dragoon; she hadnae come forrit[1] for maybe thretty year; and bairns had seen her mumblin' to hersel' up on Key's Loan in the gloamin', whilk was an unco time an' place for a God-fearin' woman. Howsoever, it was the laird himsel' that had first tauld the minister o' Janet; and in thae days he wad have gane a far gate to pleesure the laird. When folk tauld him that Janet was sib to the deil, it was a' superstition by his way of it; an' when they cast up the Bible to him an' the witch of Endor, he wad threep it doun their thrapples that thir days were a' gane by, and the deil was mercifully restrained.

Weel, when it got about the clachan that Janet M'Clour was to be servant at the manse, the folk were fair mad wi' her an' him thegether; and some o' the guidwives had nae better to dae than get round her door-cheeks and chairge her wi' a' that was ken't again her, frae the sodger's bairn to John Tamson's twa kye. She was nae great speaker; folk usually let her gang her ain gate, an' she let them gang theirs, wi' neither Fair-guid-een nor Fair-guid-day; but when she buckled to, she had a tongue to deave the miller. Up she got, an' there wasnae an auld story in Ba'weary but she gart somebody lowp for it that day; they couldnae say ae thing but she could say twa to it; till, at the hinder end, the guidwives up and claught haud of her, and clawed the coats aff her back, and pu'd her doun the clachan to the water o' Dule, to see if she were a witch or no, soum or droun. The carline skirled till ye could hear her at the Hangin' Shaw, and she focht like ten; there was mony a guidwife bure the mark of her neist day an' mony a lang day after; and just in the hettest o' the collie-shangie, wha suld come up (for his sins) but the new minister.

[1] To come forrit—to offer oneself as a communicant.

'Women,' said he (and he had a grand voice), 'I charge you in the Lord's name to let her go.'

Janet ran to him—she was fair wud wi' terror—an' clang to him, an' prayed him, for Christ's sake, save her frae the cummers; an' they, for their pairt, tauld him a' that was ken't, and maybe mair.

'Woman,' says he to Janet, 'is this true?'

'As the Lord sees me,' says she, 'as the Lord made me, no a word o't. Forbye the bairn,' says she, 'I've been a decent woman a' my days.'

'Will you,' says Mr. Soulis, 'in the name of God, and before me, His unworthy minister, renounce the devil and his works?'

Weel, it wad appear that when he askit that, she gave a girn that fairly frichtit them that saw her, an' they could hear her teeth play dirl thegether in her chafts; but there was naething for it but the ae way or the ither; an' Janet lifted up her hand and renounced the deil before them a'.

'And now,' says Mr. Soulis to the guidwives, 'home with ye, one and all, and pray to God for His forgiveness.'

And he gied Janet his arm, though she had little on her but a sark, and took her up the clachan to her ain door like a leddy of the land; an' her scrieghin' and laughin' as was a scandal to be heard.

There were mony grave folk lang ower their prayers that nicht; but when the morn cam' there was sic a fear fell upon a' Ba'weary that the bairns hid theirsels, and even the menfolk stood and keekit frae their doors. For there was Janet comin' doun the clachan—her or her likeness, nane could tell—wi' her neck thrawn, and her heid on ae side, like a body that has been hangit, and a girn on her face like an unstreakit corp. By-an'-by they got used wi' it, and even speered at her to ken what was wrang; but frae that day forth she couldnae speak like a Christian woman, but slavered and played click wi' her teeth like a pair o' shears; and frae that day forth the name o' God cam' never on her lips. Whiles she would try to say it, but it michtnae be. Them that kenned best said

least; but they never gied that Thing the name o' Janet
M'Clour; for the auld Janet, by their way o't, was in muckle
hell that day. But the minister was neither to haud nor to
bind; he preached about naething but the folk's cruelty that
had gi'en her a stroke of the palsy; he skelpt the bairns that
meddled her; and he had her up to the manse that same
nicht, and dwalled there a' his lane wi' her under the
Hangin' Shaw.

Weel, time gaed by: and the idler sort commenced to
think mair lichtly o' that black business. The minister was
weel thocht o'; he was aye late at the writing, folk wad see
his can'le doon by the Dule water after twal' at e'en; and he
seemed pleased wi' himsel' and upsitten as at first, though
a'body could see that he was dwining. As for Janet she cam'
an' she gaed; if she didnae speak muckle afore, it was reason
she should speak less then; she meddled naebody; but she
was an eldritch thing to see, an' nane wad hae mistrysted wi'
her for Ba'weary glebe.

About the end o' July there cam' a spell o' weather, the
like o't never was in that country-side; it was lown an' het
an' heartless; the herds couldnae win up the Black Hill, the
bairns were ower weariet to play; an' yet it was gousty too,
wi' claps o' het wund that rumm'led in the glens, and bits o'
shouers that slockened naething. We aye thocht it but to
thun'er on the morn; but the morn cam', an' the morn's
morning, and it was aye the same uncanny weather, sair on
folks and bestial. Of a' that were the waur, nane suffered
like Mr. Soulis; he could neither sleep nor eat, he tauld his
elders; an' when he wasnae writin' at his weary book, he
wad be stravaguin' ower a' the country-side like a man
possessed, when a'body else was blythe to keep caller ben
the house.

Abune Hangin' Shaw, in the bield o' the Black Hill,
there's a bit enclosed grund wi' an iron yett; and it seems,
in the auld days, that was the kirkyaird o' Ba'weary, and
consecrated by the Papists before the blessed licht shone
upon the kingdom. It was a great howff o' Mr. Soulis's,

onyway; there he would sit an' consider his sermons; and indeed it's a bieldy bit. Weel, as he cam' ower the wast end o' the Black Hill ae day, he saw first twa, an' syne fower, an' syne seeven corbie craws fleein' round an' round abune the auld kirkyaird. They flew laigh and heavy, an' squawked to ither as they gaed; and it was clear to Mr. Soulis that something had put them frae their ordinar. He wasnae easy fleyed, an' gaed straucht up to the wa's; an' what suld he find there but a man, or the appearance of a man, sittin' in the inside upon a grave. He was of a great stature, an' black as hell, and his e'en were singular to see.[1] Mr. Soulis had heard tell o' black men, mony's the time; but there was something unco about this black man that daunted him. Het as he was, he took a kind o' cauld grue in the marrow o' his banes; but up he spak for a' that; an' says he: 'My friend, are you a stranger in this place?' The black man answered never a word; he got upon his feet, an' begude to hirsle to the wa' on the far side; but he aye lookit at the minister; an' the minister stood an' lookit back; till a' in a meenute the black man was ower the wa' an' rinnin' for the bield o' the trees. Mr. Soulis, he hardly kenned why, ran after him; but he was sair forjaskit wi' his walk an' the het, unhalesome weather; and rin as he likit, he got nae mair than a glisk o' the black man amang the birks, till he won doun to the foot o' the hill-side, an' there he saw him aince mair, gaun hap, step, an' lowp, ower Dule water to the manse.

Mr. Soulis wasnae weel pleased that this fearsome gangrel suld mak' sae free wi' Ba'weary manse; an' he ran the harder, an', wet shoon, ower the burn, an' up the walk; but the deil a black man was there to see. He stepped out upon the road, but there was naebody there; he gaed a' ower the gairden, but na, nae black man. At the hinder end, and a bit feared, as was but natural, he lifted the hasp and into the manse; and there was Janet M'Clour before his een, wi'

---

[1] It was a common belief in Scotland that the devil appeared as a black man. This appears in several witch trials, and I think in Law's *Memorials*, that delightful storehouse of the quaint and grisly.

her thrawn craig, and nane sae pleased to see him. And he aye minded sinsyne, when first he set his een upon her, he had the same cauld and deidly grue.

'Janet,' says he, 'have you seen a black man?'

'A black man?' quo' she. 'Save us a'! Ye're no wise, minister. There's nae black man in a' Ba'weary.'

But she didnae speak plain, ye maun understand; but yam-yammered, like a powney wi' the bit in its moo.

'Weel,' says he, 'Janet, if there was nae black man, I have spoken with the Accuser of the Brethren.'

And he sat down like ane wi' a fever, an' his teeth chittered in his heid.

'Hoots,' says she, 'think shame to yoursel', minister'; an' gied him a drap brandy that she keept aye by her.

Syne Mr. Soulis gaed into his study amang a' his books. It's a lang, laigh, mirk chalmer, perishin' cauld in winter, an' no very dry even in the tap o' the simmer, for the manse stands near the burn. Sae doun he sat, and thocht of a' that had come an' gane since he was in Ba'weary, an' his hame, an' the days when he was a bairn an' ran daffin' on the braes; and that black man aye ran in his heid like the ower-come of a sang. Aye the mair he thocht, the mair he thocht o' the black man. He tried the prayer, an' the words wouldnae come to him; an' he tried, they say, to write at his book, but he couldnae mak' nae mair o' that. There was whiles he thocht the black man was at his oxter, an' the swat stood upon him cauld as well-water; and there was other whiles, when he cam' to himsel' like a christened bairn and minded naething.

The upshot was that he gaed to the window an' stood glowrin' at Dule water. The trees are unco thick, an' the water lies deep an' black under the manse; an' there was Janet washin' the cla'es wi' her coats kilted. She had her back to the minister, an' he, for his pairt, hardly kenned what he was lookin' at. Syne she turned round, an' shawed her face; Mr. Soulis had the same cauld grue as twice that day afore, an' it was borne in upon him what folk said, that

Janet was deid lang syne, an' this was a bogle in her clay-
cauld flesh. He drew back a pickle and he scanned her
narrowly. She was tramp-trampin' in the cla'es, croonin' to
hersel'; and eh! Gude guide us, but it was a fearsome face.
Whiles she sang louder, but there was nae man born o'
woman that could tell the words o' her sang; an' whiles she
lookit side-lang doun, but there was naething there for her
to look at. There gaed a scunner through the flesh upon his
banes; and that was Heeven's advertisement. But Mr.
Soulis just blamed himsel', he said, to think sae ill of a puir,
auld afflicted wife that hadnae a freend forbye himsel'; an'
he put up a bit prayer for him and her, an' drank a little
caller water—for his heart rose again the meat—an' gaed
up to his naked bed in the gloaming.

That was a nicht that has never been forgotten in Ba'weary,
the nicht o' the seventeenth of August, seventeen hun'er an'
twal'. It had been het afore, as I hae said, but that nicht it
was hetter than ever. The sun gaed doun amang unco-
lookin' clouds; it fell as mirk as the pit; no a star, no a
breath o' wund; ye couldnae see your han' afore your face,
and even the auld folk cuist the covers frae their beds and
lay pechin' for their breath. Wi' a' that he had upon his
mind, it was gey and unlikely Mr. Soulis wad get muckle
sleep. He lay an' he tummled; the gude, caller bed that he
got into brunt his very banes; whiles he slept, and whiles he
waukened; whiles he heard the time o' nicht, and whiles
a tyke yowlin' up the muir, as if somebody was deid; whiles
he thocht he heard bogles claverin' in his lug, an' whiles he
saw spunkies in the room. He behoved, he judged, to be
sick; an' sick he was— little he jaloosed the sickness.

At the hinder end, he got a clearness in his mind, sat up
in his sark on the bedside, and fell thinkin' aince mair o' the
black man an' Janet. He couldnae weel tell how—maybe it
was the cauld to his feet—but it cam' in upon him wi' a
spate that there was some connexion between thir twa, an'
that either or baith o' them were bogles. And just at that
moment, in Janet's room, which was neist to his, there cam'

a stramp o' feet as if men were wars'lin', an' then a loud bang; an' then a wund gaed reishling round the fower quarters of the house; an' then a' was aince mair as seelent as the grave.

Mr. Soulis was feared for neither man nor deevil. He got his tinder-box, an' lit a can'le, an' made three steps o't ower to Janet's door. It was on the hasp, an' he pushed it open, an' keeked bauldly in. It was a big room, as big as the minister's ain, an' plenished wi' grand, auld, solid gear, for he had naething else. There was a fower-posted bed wi' auld tapestry; and a braw cabinet of aik, that was fu' o' the minister's divinity books, an' put there to be out o' the gate; an' a wheen duds o' Janet's lying here and there about the floor. But nae Janet could Mr. Soulis see; nor ony sign of a contention. In he gaed (an' there's few that wad hae followed him) an' lookit a' round, an' listened. But there was naethin' to be heard, neither inside the manse nor in a' Ba'weary parish, an' naethin' to be seen but the muckle shadows turnin' round the can'le. An' then a' at aince, the minister's heart played dunt an' stood stock-still; an' a cauld wund blew amang the hairs o' his heid. Whaten a weary sicht was that for the puir man's een! For there was Janet hangin' frae a nail beside the auld aik cabinet: her heid aye lay on her shoother, her een were steeked, the tongue projekit frae her mouth, and her heels were twa feet clear abune the floor.

'God forgive us all!' thocht Mr. Soulis; 'poor Janet's dead.'

He cam' a step nearer to the corp; an' then his heart fair whammled in his inside. For by what cantrip it wad ill-beseem a man to judge, she was hingin' frae a single nail an' by a single wursted thread for darnin' hose.

It's an awfu' thing to be your lane at nicht wi' siccan prodigies o' darkness; but Mr. Soulis was strong in the Lord. He turned an' gaed his ways oot o' that room, and lockit the door ahint him; and step by step, doon the stairs, as heavy as leed; and set doon the can'le on the table at the stairfoot. He couldnae pray, he couldnae think, he was dreepin' wi' caul' swat, an' naething could he hear but the dunt-dunt-duntin' o' his ain heart. He micht maybe have stood there an·hour, or maybe twa, he minded sae little; when a' o' a sudden, he heard a laigh, uncanny steer upstairs; a foot gaed to an' fro in the cha'mer whaur the corp was hingin'; syne the door was opened, though he minded weel that he had lockit it; an' syne there was a step upon the landin', an' it seemed to him as if the corp was lookin' ower the rail and doun upon him whaur he stood.

He took up the can'le again (for he couldnae want the licht), and as saftly as ever he could, gaed straucht out o' the manse an' to the far end o' the causeway. It was aye pit-mirk; the flame o' the can'le, when he set it on the grund, brunt steedy and clear as in a room; naething moved, but the Dule water seepin' and sabbin' doon the glen, an' yon unhaly footstep that cam' ploddin' doun the stairs inside the manse. He kenned the foot ower weel, for it was Janet's; and at ilka step that cam' a wee thing nearer, the cauld got deeper in his vitals. He commended his soul to Him that made an' keepit him; 'and, O Lord,' said he, 'give me strength this night to war against the powers of evil.'

By this time the foot was comin' through the passage for the door; he could hear a hand skirt alang the wa', as if the fearsome thing was feelin' for its way. The saughs tossed an' maned thegether, a lang sigh cam' ower the hills, the flame o' the can'le was blawn aboot; an' there stood the corp of Thrawn Janet, wi' her grogram goun an' her black mutch, wi' the heid aye upon the shoother, an' the girn still upon the face o't—leevin', ye wad hae said—deid, as Mr. Soulis weel kenned—upon the threshold o' the manse.

It's a strange thing that the saul of man should be that thirled into his perishable body; but the minister saw that, an' his heart didnae break.

She didnae stand there lang; she began to move again an' cam' slowly towards Mr. Soulis whaur he stood under the saughs. A' the life o' his body, a' the strength o' his speerit, were glowerin' frae his een. It seemed she was gaun to speak, but wanted words, an' made a sign wi' the left hand.

There cam' a clap o' wund, like a cat's fuff; oot gaed the can'le, the saughs skrieghed like folk; an' Mr. Soulis kenned that, live or die, this was the end o't.

'Witch, beldame, devil!' he cried, 'I charge you, by the power of God, begone—if you be dead, to the grave—if you be damned, to hell.'

An' at that moment the Lord's ain hand out o' the Heevens struck the Horror whaur it stood; the auld, deid, desecrated corp o' the witch-wife, sae lang keepit frae the grave and hirsled round by deils, lowed up like a brunstane spunk and fell in ashes to the grund; the thunder followed, peal on dirling peal, the rairing rain upon the back o' that; and Mr. Soulis lowped through the garden hedge, and ran, wi' skelloch upon skelloch, for the clachan.

That same mornin' John Christie saw the Black Man pass the Muckle Cairn as it was chappin' six; before eicht, he gaed by the change-house at Knockdow; an' no lang after, Sandy M'Lellan saw him gaun linkin' doun the braes frae Kilmackerlie. There's little doubt but it was him that dwalled sae lang in Janet's body; but he was awa' at last; and sinsyne the deil has never fashed us in Ba'weary.

But it was a sair dispensation for the minister; lang, lang he lay ravin' in his bed; and frae that hour to this, he was the man ye ken the day.

The Isle of Voices

R. L. STEVENSON

(1850–94)

KEOLA was married with Lehua, daughter of Kalamake, the wise man of Molokai, and he kept his dwelling with the father of his wife. There was no man more cunning than that prophet; he read the stars, he could divine by the bodies of the dead, and by the means of evil creatures: he could go alone into the highest parts of the mountain, into the region of the hobgoblins, and there he would lay snares to entrap the spirits of the ancient.

For this reason no man was more consulted in all the Kingdom of Hawaii. Prudent people bought, and sold, and married, and laid out their lives by his counsels; and the King had him twice to Kona to seek the treasures of Kamehameha. Neither was any man more feared: of his enemies, some had dwindled in sickness by the virtue of his incantations, and some had been spirited away, the life and the clay both, so that folk looked in vain for so much as a bone of their bodies. It was rumoured that he had the art or the gift of the old heroes. Men had seen him at night upon the mountains, stepping from one cliff to the next; they had seen him walking in the high forest, and his head and shoulders were above the trees.

This Kalamake was a strange man to see. He was come of the best blood in Molokai and Maui, of a pure descent; and yet he was more white to look upon than any foreigner: his hair the colour of dry grass, and his eyes red and very blind, so that 'Blind as Kalamake, that can see across tomorrow', was a byword in the islands.

Of all these doings of his father-in-law, Keola knew a little by the common repute, a little more he suspected, and the rest he ignored. But there was one thing troubled him. Kalamake was a man that spared for nothing, whether to eat or to drink, or to wear; and for all he paid in bright new dollars. 'Bright as Kalamake's dollars', was another saying in the Eight Isles. Yet he neither sold, nor planted, nor took hire—only now and then from his sorceries—and there was no source conceivable for so much silver coin.

It chanced one day Keola's wife was gone upon a visit to Kaunakakai, on the lee side of the island, and the men were forth at the sea-fishing. But Keola was an idle dog, and he lay in the veranda and watched the surf beat on the shore and the birds fly about the cliff. It was a chief thought with him always—the thought of the bright dollars. When he lay down to bed he would be wondering why they were so many, and when he woke at morn he would be wondering why they were all new; and the thing was never absent from his mind. But this day of all days he made sure in his heart of some discovery. For it seems he had observed the place where Kalamake kept his treasure, which was a lock-fast desk against the parlour wall, under the print of Kamehameha the Fifth, and a photograph of Queen Victoria with her crown; and it seems again that, no later than the night before, he found occasion to look in, and behold! the bag lay there empty. And this was the day of the steamer; he could see her smoke off Kalaupapa; and she must soon arrive with a month's goods, tinned salmon and gin, and all manner of rare luxuries for Kalamake.

'Now if he can pay for his goods today,' Keola thought, 'I shall know for certain that the man is a warlock, and the dollars come out of the Devil's pocket.'

While he was so thinking, there was his father-in-law behind him, looking vexed.

'Is that the steamer?' he asked.

'Yes,' said Keola. 'She has but to call at Pelekunu, and then she will be here.'

'There is no help for it then,' returned Kalamake, 'and I must take you in my confidence, Keola, for the lack of anyone better. Come here within the house.'

So they stepped together into the parlour, which was a very fine room, papered and hung with prints, and furnished with a rocking-chair, and a table and a sofa in the European style. There was a shelf of books besides, and a family Bible in the midst of the table, and the lock-fast writing desk against the wall; so that anyone could see it was the house of a man of substance.

Kalamake made Keola close the shutters of the windows, while he himself locked all the doors and set open the lid of the desk. From this he brought forth a pair of necklaces hung with charms and shells, a bundle of dried herbs, and the dried leaves of trees, and a green branch of palm.

'What I am about,' said he, 'is a thing beyond wonder.
The men of old were wise; they wrought marvels, and this
among the rest; but that was at night, in the dark, under the
fit stars and in the desert. The same will I do here in my own
house and under the plain eye of day.'

So saying, he put the Bible under the cushion of the sofa
so that it was all covered, brought out from the same place
a mat of a wonderfully fine texture, and heaped the herbs
and leaves on sand in a tin pan. And then he and Keola put
on the necklaces and took their stand upon the opposite
corners of the mat.

'The time comes,' said the warlock; 'be not afraid.'

With that he set flame to the herbs, and began to mutter
and wave the branch of palm. At first the light was dim
because of the closed shutters; but the herbs caught strongly
afire, and the flames beat upon Keola, and the room glowed
with the burning; and next the smoke rose and made his
head swim and his eyes darken, and the sound of Kalamake
muttering ran in his ears. And suddenly, to the mat on
which they were standing came a snatch or twitch, that
seemed to be more swift than lightning. In the same wink
the room was gone and the house, the breath all beaten from
Keola's body. Volumes of light rolled upon his eyes and
head, and he found himself transported to a beach of the
sea, under a strong sun, with a great surf roaring: he and
the warlock standing there on the same mat, speechless,
gasping and grasping at one another, and passing their
hands before their eyes.

'What was this?' cried Keola, who came to himself the
first, because he was the younger. 'The pang of it was like
death.'

'It matters not,' panted Kalamake. 'It is now done.'

'And, in the name of God, where are we?' cried Keola.

'That is not the question,' replied the sorcerer. 'Being
here, we have matter in our hands, and that we must attend
to. Go, while I recover my breath, into the borders of the
wood, and bring me the leaves of such and such a herb,

and such and such a tree, which you will find to grow there plentifully—three handfuls of each. And be speedy. We must be home again before the steamer comes; it would seem strange if we had disappeared.' And he sat on the sand and panted.

Keola went up the beach, which was of shining sand and coral, strewn with singular shells; and he thought in his heart—

'How do I not know this beach? I will come here again and gather shells.'

In front of him was a line of palms against the sky; not like the palms of the Eight Islands, but tall and fresh and beautiful, and hanging out withered fans like gold among the green, and he thought in his heart—

'It is strange I should not have found this grove. I will come here again, when it is warm, to sleep.' And he thought, 'How warm it has grown suddenly!' For it was winter in Hawaii, and the day had been chill. And he thought also, 'Where are the grey mountains? And where is the high cliff with the hanging forest and the wheeling birds?' And the more he considered, the less he might conceive in what quarter of the islands he was fallen.

In the border of the grove, where it met the beach, the herb was growing, but the tree further back. Now, as Keola went toward the tree, he was aware of a young woman who had nothing on her body but a belt of leaves.

'Well!' thought Keola, 'they are not very particular about their dress in this part of the country.' And he paused, supposing she would observe him and escape; and seeing that she still looked before her, stood and hummed aloud. Up she leaped at the sound. Her face was ashen; she looked this way and that, and her mouth gaped with the terror of her soul. But it was a strange thing that her eyes did not rest upon Keola.

'Good day,' said he. 'You need not be so frightened; I will not eat you.' And he had scarce opened his mouth before the young woman fled into the bush.

'These are strange manners,' thought Keola. And, not thinking what he did, ran after her.

As she ran, the girl kept crying in some speech that was not practised in Hawaii, yet some of the words were the same, and he knew she kept calling and warning others. And presently he saw more people running—men, women and children, one with another, all running and crying like people at a fire. And with that he began to grow afraid himself, and returned to Kalamake bringing the leaves. Him he told what he had seen.

'You must pay no heed,' said Kalamake. 'All this is like a dream and shadows. All will disappear and be forgotten.'

'It seemed none saw me,' said Keola.

'And none did,' replied the sorcerer. 'We walk here in the broad sun invisible by reason of these charms. Yet they hear us; and therefore it is well to speak softly, as I do.'

With that he made a circle round the mat with stones, and in the midst he set the leaves.

'It will be your part,' said he, 'to keep the leaves alight, and feed the fire slowly. While they blaze (which is but for a little moment) I must do my errand; and before the ashes blacken, the same power that brought us carries us away. Be ready now with the match; and do you call me in good time lest the flames burn out and I be left.'

As soon as the leaves caught, the sorcerer leaped like a deer out of the circle, and began to race along the beach like a hound that has been bathing. As he ran, he kept stooping to snatch shells; and it seemed to Keola that they glittered as he took them. The leaves blazed with a clear flame that consumed them swiftly; and presently Keola had but a handful left, and the sorcerer was far off, running and stopping.

'Back!' cried Keola. 'Back! The leaves are near done.'

At that Kalamake turned, and if he had run before, now he flew. But fast as he ran, the leaves burned faster. The flame was ready to expire when, with a great leap, he bounded on the mat. The wind of his leaping blew it out;

and with that the beach was gone, and the sun and the sea, and they stood once more in the dimness of the shuttered parlour, and were once more shaken and blinded; and on the mat betwixt them lay a pile of shining dollars. Keola ran to the shutters; and there was the steamer tossing in the swell close in.

The same night Kalamake took his son-in-law apart, and gave him five dollars in his hand.

'Keola,' said he, 'if you are a wise man (which I am doubtful of) you will think you slept this afternoon on the veranda, and dreamed as you were sleeping. I am a man of few words, and I have for my helpers people of short memories.'

Never a word more said Kalamake, nor referred again to that affair. But it ran all the while in Keola's head—if he were lazy before, he would now do nothing.

'Why should I work,' thought he, 'when I have a father-in-law who makes dollars of sea-shells?'

Presently his share was spent. He spent it all upon fine clothes. And then he was sorry:

'For,' thought he, 'I had done better to have bought a concertina, with which I might have entertained myself all day long.' And then he began to grow vexed with Kalamake.

'This man has the soul of a dog,' thought he. 'He can gather dollars when he pleases on the beach, and he leaves me to pine for a concertina! Let him beware: I am no child, I am as cunning as he, and hold his secret.' With that he spoke to his wife Lehua, and complained of her father's manners.

'I would let my father be,' said Lehua. 'He is a dangerous man to cross.'

'I care that for him!' cried Keola; and snapped his fingers. 'I have him by the nose. I can make him do what I please.' And he told Lehua the story.

But she shook her head.

'You may do what you like,' said she; 'but as sure as you thwart my father, you will be no more heard of. Think of this person, and that person; think of Hua, who was a noble of the House of Representatives, and went to Honolulu every year; and not a bone or a hair of him was found. Remember Kamau, and how he wasted to a thread, so that his wife lifted him with one hand. Keola, you are a baby in my father's hands; he will take you with his thumb and finger and eat you like a shrimp.'

Now Keola was truly afraid of Kalamake, but he was vain too; and these words of his wife's incensed him.

'Very well,' said he, 'if that is what you think of me, I will show how much you are deceived.' And he went straight to where his father-in-law was sitting in the parlour.

'Kalamake,' said he, 'I want a concertina.'

'Do you, indeed?' said Kalamake.

'Yes,' said he, 'and I may as well tell you plainly, I mean to have it. A man who picks up dollars on the beach can certainly afford a concertina.'

'I had no idea you had so much spirit,' replied the sorcerer. 'I thought you were a timid, useless lad, and I cannot describe how much pleased I am to find I was mistaken. Now I begin to think I may have found an assistant and successor in my difficult business. A concertina? You shall have the best in Honolulu. And tonight, as soon as it is dark, you and I will go and find the money.'

'Shall we return to the beach?' asked Keola.

'No, no!' replied Kalamake; 'you must begin to learn more of my secrets. Last time I taught you to pick shells; this time I shall teach you to catch fish. Are you strong enough to launch Pili's boat?'

'I think I am,' returned Keola. 'But why should we not take your own, which is afloat already?'

'I have a reason which you will understand thoroughly before tomorrow,' said Kalamake. 'Pili's boat is the better suited for my purpose. So, if you please, let us meet there as soon as it is dark; and in the meanwhile, let us keep our own counsel, for there is no cause to let the family into our business.'

Honey is not more sweet than was the voice of Kalamake, and Keola could scarce contain his satisfaction.

'I might have had my concertina weeks ago,' thought he, 'and there is nothing needed in this world but a little courage.'

Presently after he spied Lehua weeping, and was half in a mind to tell her all was well.

'But no,' thinks he; 'I shall wait till I can show her the concertina; we shall see what the chit will do then. Perhaps she will understand in the future that her husband is a man of some intelligence.'

As soon as it was dark father and son-in-law launched Pili's boat and set the sail. There was a great sea, and it blew strong from the leeward; but the boat was swift and light and dry, and skimmed the waves. The wizard had a lantern, which he lit and held with his finger through the ring; and the two sat in the stern and smoked cigars, of which Kalamake had always a provision, and spoke like friends of magic and the great sums of money which they could make by its exercise, and what they should buy first, and what second; and Kalamake talked like a father.

Presently he looked all about, and above him at the stars, and back at the island, which was already three parts sunk under the sea, and he seemed to consider ripely his position.

'Look!' says he, 'there is Molokai already far behind us, and Maui like a cloud; and by the bearing of these three stars I know I am come where I desire. This part of the sea is called the Sea of the Dead. It is in this place extraordinarily deep, and the floor is all covered with the bones of men, and in the holes of this part gods and goblins keep their habitation. The flow of the sea is to the north, stronger than a shark can swim, and any man who shall here be thrown out of a ship it bears away like a wild horse into the uttermost ocean. Presently he is spent and goes down, and his bones are scattered with the rest, and the gods devour his spirit.'

Fear came on Keola at the words, and he looked, and by

the light of the stars and the lantern, the warlock seemed to change.

'What ails you?' cried Keola, quick and sharp.

'It is not I who am ailing,' said the wizard; 'but there is one here very sick.'

With that he changed his grasp upon the lantern, and, behold! as he drew his finger from the ring, the finger stuck and the ring was burst, and his hand was grown to be of the bigness of three.

At that sight Keola screamed and covered his face.

But Kalamake held up the lantern. 'Look rather at my face!' said he—and his head was huge as a barrel; and still he grew and grew as a cloud grows on a mountain, and Keola sat before him screaming, and the boat raced on the great seas.

'And now,' said the wizard, 'what do you think about that concertina? and are you sure you would not rather have a flute? No?' says he; 'that is well, for I do not like my family to be changeable of purpose. But I begin to think I had better get out of this paltry boat, for my bulk swells to a very unusual degree, and if we are not the more careful, she will presently be swamped.'

With that he threw his legs over the side. Even as he did so, the greatness of the man grew thirty-fold and forty-fold as swift as sight or thinking, so that he stood in the deep seas to the armpits, and his head and shoulders rose like a high isle, and the swell beat and burst upon his bosom, as it beats and breaks against a cliff. The boat ran still to the north, but he reached out his hand, and took the gunwale by the finger and thumb, and broke the side like a biscuit, and Keola was spilled into the sea. And the pieces of the boat the sorcerer crushed in the hollow of his hand and flung miles away into the night.

'Excuse me taking the lantern,' said he; 'for I have a long wade before me, and the land is far, and the bottom of the sea uneven, and I feel the bones under my toes.'

And he turned and went off walking with great strides;

and as often as Keola sank in the trough he could see him no longer; but as often as he was heaved upon the crest, there he was striding and dwindling, and he held the lamp high over his head, and the waves broke white about him as he went.

Since first the islands were fished out of the sea, there was never a man so terrified as this Keola. He swam indeed, but he swam as puppies swim when they are cast in to drown, and knew not wherefore. He could but think of the hugeness of the swelling of the warlock, of that face which was great as a mountain, of those shoulders that were broad as an isle, and of the seas that beat on them in vain. He thought, too, of the concertina, and shame took hold upon him; and of the dead men's bones, and fear shook him.

Of a sudden he was aware of something dark against the stars that tossed, and a light below, and a brightness of the cloven sea; and he heard speech of men. He cried out aloud and a voice answered; and in a twinkling the bows of a ship hung above him on a wave like a thing balanced, and swooped down. He caught with his two hands in the chains of her, and the next moment was buried in the rushing seas, and the next hauled on board by seamen.

They gave him gin and biscuit and dry clothes, and asked him how he came where they found him, and whether the light which they had seen was the lighthouse, Lae o Ka Laau. But Keola knew white men are like children and only believe their own stories; so about himself he told them what he pleased, and as for the light (which was Kalamake's lantern) he vowed he had seen none.

This ship was a schooner bound for Honolulu, and then to trade in the low islands; and by a very good chance for Keola she had lost a man off the bowsprit in a squall. It was no use talking. Keola durst not stay in the Eight Islands. Word goes so quickly, and all men are so fond to talk and carry news, that if he hid in the north end of Kauai or in the south end of Kaü, the wizard would have wind of it before a month, and he must perish. So he did what seemed the most prudent, and shipped sailor in the place of the man who had been drowned.

In some ways the ship was a good place. The food was extraordinarily rich and plenty, with biscuits and salt beef every day, and pea-soup and puddings made of flour and suet twice a week, so that Keola grew fat. The captain also was a good man, and the crew no worse than other whites. The trouble was the mate, who was the most difficult man to please Keola had ever met with, and beat and cursed him daily, both for what he did and what he did not. The blows that he dealt were very sore, for he was strong; and the words he used were very unpalatable, for Keola was come of a good family and accustomed to respect. And what was the worst of all, whenever Keola found a chance to sleep, there was the mate awake and stirring him up with a rope's end. Keola saw it would never do; and he made up his mind to run away.

They were about a month out from Honolulu when they made the land. It was a fine starry night, the sea was smooth as well as the sky fair; it blew a steady trade; and there was the island on their weather bow, a ribbon of palm trees lying flat along the sea. The captain and the mate looked at it with the night glass, and named the name of it, and talked of it, beside the wheel where Keola was steering. It seemed it was an isle where no traders came. By the captain's way, it was an isle besides where no man dwelt; but the mate thought otherwise.

'I don't give a cent for the directory,' said he. 'I've been past here one night in the schooner *Eugenie*; it was just such a night as this; they were fishing with torches, and the beach was thick with lights like a town.'

'Well, well,' says the captain, 'its steep-to, that's the great point; and there ain't any outlying dangers by the chart, so we'll just hug the lee side of it. Keep her romping full, don't I tell you!' he cried to Keola, who was listening so hard that he forgot to steer.

And the mate cursed him, and swore that Kanaka was

for no use in the world, and if he got started after him with a belaying pin, it would be a cold day for Keola.

And so the captain and mate lay down on the house together, and Keola was left to himself.

'This island will do very well for me,' he thought; 'if no traders deal there, the mate will never come. And as for Kalamake, it is not possible he can ever get as far as this.'

With that he kept edging the schooner nearer in. He had to do this quietly, for it was the trouble with these white men, and above all with the mate, that you could never be sure of them; they would all be sleeping sound, or else pretending, and if a sail shook, they would jump to their feet and fall on you with a rope's end. So Keola edged her up little by little, and kept all drawing. And presently the land was close on board, and the sound of the sea on the sides of it grew loud.

With that, the mate sat up suddenly upon the house.

'What are you doing?' he roars. 'You'll have the ship ashore!'

And he made one bound for Keola, and Keola made another clean over the rail and plump into the starry sea. When he came up again, the schooner had payed off on her true course, and the mate stood by the wheel himself, and Keola heard him cursing. The sea was smooth under the lee of the island; it was warm besides, and Keola had his sailor's knife, so he had no fear of sharks. A little way before him the trees stopped; there was a break in the line of the land like the mouth of a harbour; and the tide, which was then flowing, took him up and carried him through. One minute he was without, and the next within: had floated there in a wide shallow water, bright with ten thousand stars, and all about him was the ring of the land, with its string of palm trees. And he was amazed, because this was a kind of island he had never heard of.

The time of Keola in that place was in two periods—the period when he was alone, and the period when he was there with the tribe. At first he sought everywhere and found no man; only some houses standing in a hamlet, and the marks of fires. But the ashes of the fires were cold and the rains had washed them away; and the winds had blown, and some of the huts were overthrown. It was here he took his dwelling; and he made a fire drill, and a shell hook, and fished and cooked his fish, and climbed after green cocoanuts, the juice of which he drank, for in all the isle there was no water. The days were long to him, and the nights terrifying. He made a lamp of cocoa-shell, and drew the oil of the ripe nuts, and made a wick of fibre; and when evening came he closed up his hut, and lit his lamp, and lay and trembled till morning. Many a time he thought in his heart he would have been better in the bottom of the sea, his bones rolling there with the others.

All this while he kept by the inside of the island, for the huts were on the shore of the lagoon, and it was there the palms grew best, and the lagoon itself abounded with good fish. And to the outer side he went once only, and he looked but the once at the beach of the ocean, and came away shaking. For the look of it, with its bright sand, and strewn shells, and strong sun and surf, went sore against his inclination.

'It cannot be,' he thought, 'and yet it is very like. And how do I know? These white men, although they pretend to know where they are sailing, must take their chance like other people. So that after all we may have sailed in a circle, and I may be quite near to Molokai, and this may be the very beach where my father-in-law gathers his dollars.'

So after that he was prudent, and kept to the land side.

It was perhaps a month later, when the people of the place arrived—the fill of six great boats. They were a fine race of men, and spoke a tongue that sounded very different from the tongue of Hawaii, but so many of the words were the same that it was not difficult to understand. The men besides were very courteous, and the women very towardly; and they made Keola welcome, and built him a house, and gave him a wife; and what surprised him the most, he was never sent to work with the young men.

And now Keola had three periods. First he had a period of being very sad, and then he had a period when he was pretty merry. Last of all came the third, when he was the most terrified man in the four oceans.

The cause of the first period was the girl he had to wife. He was in doubt about the island, and he might have been in doubt about the speech, of which he had heard so little when he came there with the wizard on the mat. But about his wife there was no mistake conceivable, for she was the same girl that ran from him crying in the wood. So he had sailed all this way, and might as well have stayed in Molokai; and had left home and wife and all his friends for no other cause but to escape his enemy, and the place he had come to was that wizard's hunting ground, and the shore where he walked invisible. It was at this period when he kept the most close to the lagoon side, and as far as he dared, abode in the cover of his hut.

The cause of the second period was talk he heard from his wife and the chief islanders. Keola himself said little. He was never so sure of his new friends, for he judged they were too civil to be wholesome, and since he had grown better acquainted with his father-in-law the man had grown more cautious. So he told them nothing of himself, but only his name and descent, and that he came from the Eight Islands, and what fine islands they were; and about the king's palace in Honolulu, and how he was a chief friend of the king and the missionaries. But he put many questions and learned much. The island where he was was called the Isle of Voices; it belonged to the tribe, but they made their home upon another, three hours' sail to the southward. There they lived and had their permanent houses, and it was a rich island, where were eggs and chickens and pigs, and ships came trading with rum and tobacco. It was there the schooner had gone after Keola deserted; there, too, the mate had died, like the fool of a white man that he was. It seems, when the ship came, it was the beginning of the sickly season in that isle, when the fish of the lagoon are poisonous, and all who eat of them swell up and die. The mate was told of it; he saw the boats preparing, because in that season the people leave that island and sail to the Isle of Voices; but he was a fool of a white man, who would believe no stories but his own, and he caught one of these fish, cooked it and ate it, and swelled up and died, which was good news to Keola. As for the Isle of Voices, it lay solitary the most part of the year; only now and then a boat's crew came for copra, and in the bad season, when the fish at the main isle were poisonous, the tribe dwelt there in a body. It had its name from a marvel, for it seemed the sea-side of it was all beset with invisible devils; day and night you heard them talking one with another in strange tongues; day and night little fires blazed up and were extinguished on the beach; and what was the cause of these doings no man might conceive. Keola asked them if it were the same in their own island where they stayed, and they told him no, not there; nor yet in any other of some hundred isles that lay all about them in that sea; but it was a thing peculiar to the Isle of Voices. They told him also that these fires and voices were ever on the sea-side and in the seaward fringes of the wood, and a man might dwell by the lagoon two thousand years (if he could live so long) and never be any way troubled; and even on the sea-side the devils did no harm if let alone. Only once a chief had cast a spear at one of the voices, and the same night he fell out of a cocoanut palm and was killed.

Keola thought a good bit with himself. He saw he would be all right when the tribe returned to the main island, and right enough where he was, if he kept by the lagoon, yet he had a mind to make things righter if he could. So he told the high chief he had once been in an isle that was pestered the same way, and the folk had found a means to cure that trouble.

'There was a tree growing in the bush there,' says he, 'and it seems these devils came to get the leaves of it. So the people of the isle cut down the tree wherever it was found, and the devils came no more.'

They asked what kind of tree this was, and he showed them the tree of which Kalamake burned the leaves. They found it hard to believe, yet the idea tickled them. Night after night the old men debated it in their councils, but the high chief (though he was a brave man) was afraid of the matter, and reminded them daily of the chief who cast a spear against the voices and was killed, and the thought of that brought all to a stand again.

Though he could not yet bring about the destruction of the trees, Keola was well enough pleased, and began to look about him and take pleasure in his days; and, among other things, he was the kinder to his wife, so that the girl began to love him greatly. One day he came to the hut, and she lay on the ground lamenting.

'Why,' said Keola, 'what is wrong with you now?'

She declared it was nothing.

The same night she woke him. The lamp burned very low, but he saw by her face she was in sorrow.

'Keola,' she said, 'put your ear to my mouth that I may whisper, for no one must hear us. Two days before the boats begin to be got ready, go you to the sea-side of the isle and lie in a thicket. We shall choose that place beforehand, you and I; and hide food; and every night I shall come near by there singing. So when a night comes and you do not hear me, you shall know we are clean gone out of the island, and you may come forth again in safety.'

The soul of Keola died within him.

'What is this?' he cried. 'I cannot live among devils. I will not be left behind upon this isle. I am dying to leave it.'

'You will never leave it alive, my poor Keola,' said the girl; 'for to tell you the truth, my people are eaters of men; but this they keep secret. And the reason they will kill you before we leave is because in our island ships come, and Donat-Kimaran comes and talks for the French, and there is a white trader there in a house with a veranda, and a catechist. Oh, that is a fine place indeed! The trader has barrels filled with flour; and a French warship once came in the lagoon and gave everybody wine and biscuit. Ah, my poor Keola, I wish I could take you there, for great is my love to you, and it is the finest place in the seas except Papeete.'

So now Keola was the most terrified man in the four oceans. He had heard tell of eaters of men in the south islands, and the thing had always been a fear to him; and here it was knocking at his door. He had heard besides, by travellers, of their practices, and how when they are in a mind to eat a man, they cherish and fondle him like a mother with a favourite baby. And he saw this must be his own case; and that was why he had been housed, and fed, and wived, and liberated from all work; and why the old men and the chiefs discoursed with him like a person of weight. So he lay on his bed and railed upon his destiny; and the flesh curdled on his bones.

The next day the people of the tribe were very civil, as their way was. They were elegant speakers, and they made beautiful poetry, and jested at meals, so that a missionary must have died laughing. It was little enough Keola cared for their fine ways; all he saw was the white teeth shining in their mouths, and his gorge rose at the sight; and when they were done eating, he went and lay in the bush like a dead man.

The next day it was the same, and then his wife followed him.

'Keola,' she said, 'if you do not eat, I tell you plainly you will be killed and cooked tomorrow. Some of the old chiefs are murmuring already. They think you are fallen sick and must lose flesh.'

With that Keola got to his feet, and anger burned in him.

'It is little I care one way or the other,' said he. 'I am between the devil and the deep sea. Since die I must, let me die the quickest way; and since I must be eaten at the best of it, let me rather be eaten by hobgoblins than by men. Farewell,' said he, and he left her standing, and walked to the sea-side of that island.

It was all bare in the strong sun; there was no sign of man, only the beach was trodden, and all about him as he went, the voices talked and whispered, and the little fires sprang up and burned down. All tongues of the earth were spoken there; the French, the Dutch, the Russian, the Tamil, the Chinese. Whatever land knew sorcery, there were some of its people whispering in Keola's ear. That beach was thick as a cried fair, yet no man seen; and as he walked he saw the shells vanish before him, and no man to pick them up. I think the devil would have been afraid to be alone in such a company; but Keola was past fear and courted death. When the fires sprang up, he charged for them like a bull. Bodiless voices called to and fro; unseen hands poured sand upon the flames; and they were gone from the beach before he reached them.

'It is plain Kalamake is not here,' he thought, 'or I must have been killed long since.'

With that he sat him down in the margin of the wood, for he was tired, and put his chin upon his hands. The business before his eyes continued: the beach babbled with voices, and the fires sprang up and sank, and the shells vanished and were renewed again even while he looked.

'It was a by-day when I was here before,' he thought, 'for it was nothing to this.'

And his head was dizzy with the thought of these millions and millions of dollars, and all these hundreds and hundreds of persons culling them upon the beach and flying in the air higher and swifter than eagles.

'And to think how they have fooled me with their talk of mints,' says he, 'and that money was made there, when it is clear that all the new coin in all the world is gathered on these sands! But I will know better the next time!' said he.

And at last, he knew not very well how or when, sleep fell on Keola, and he forgot the island and all his sorrows.

Early the next day, before the sun was yet up, a bustle woke him. He awoke in fear, for he thought the tribe had caught him napping; but it was no such matter. Only, on the beach in front of him, the bodiless voices called and shouted one upon another, and it seemed they all passed and swept beside him up the coast of the island.

'What is afoot now?' thinks Keola. And it was plain to him it was something beyond ordinary, for the fires were not lighted nor the shells taken, but the bodiless voices kept posting up the beach, and hailing and dying away; and others following, and by the sound of them these wizards should be angry.

'It is not me they are angry at,' thought Keola, 'for they pass me close.'

As when hounds go by, or horses in a race, or city folk coursing to a fire, and all men join and follow after, so it was now with Keola; and he knew not what he did, nor why he did it, but there, lo and behold! he was running with the voices.

So he turned one point of the island, and this brought him in view of a second; and there he remembered the wizard trees to have been growing by the score together in a wood. From this point there went up a hubbub of men crying not to be described; and by the sound of them, those that he ran with shaped their course for the same quarter. A little nearer, and there began to mingle with the outcry the crash of many axes. And at this a thought came at last into his mind that the high chief had consented; that the men of the tribe had set-to cutting down these trees; that word had gone about the isle from sorcerer to sorcerer, and these were all now assembling to defend their trees. Desire of strange things swept him on. He posted with the voices, crossed the beach, and came into the borders of the wood, and stood astonished. One tree had fallen, others were part hewed away. There was the tribe clustered. They were back to back, and bodies lay, and blood flowed among their feet. The hue of fear was on all their faces; their voices went up to heaven shrill as a weasel's cry.

Have you seen a child when he is all alone and has a

wooden sword, and fights, leaping and hewing with the empty air? Even so the man-eaters huddled back to back, and heaved up their axes, and laid on, and screamed as they laid on, and behold! no man to contend with them! only here and there Keola saw an axe swinging over against them without hands; and time and again a man of the tribe would fall before it, clove in twain or burst asunder, and his soul sped howling.

For awhile Keola looked upon this prodigy like one that dreams, and then fear took him by the midst as sharp as death, that he should behold such doings. Even in that same flash the high chief of the clan espied him standing, and pointed and called out his name. Thereat the whole tribe saw him also, and their eyes flashed, and their teeth clashed.

'I am too long here,' thought Keola, and ran further out of the wood and down the beach, not caring whither.

'Keola!' said a voice close by upon the empty sand.

'Lehua! is that you?' he cried, and gasped, and looked in vain for her; but by the eyesight he was stark alone.

'I saw you pass before,' the voice answered; 'but you would not hear me. Quick! get the leaves and the herbs, and let us flee.'

'You are there with the mat?' he asked.

'Here, at your side,' said she. And he felt her arms about him. 'Quick! the leaves and the herbs, before my father can get back!'

So Keola ran for his life, and fetched the wizard fuel; and Lehua guided him back, and set his feet upon the mat, and made the fire. All the time of its burning, the sound of the battle towered out of the wood; the wizards and the man-eaters hard at fight; the wizards, the viewless ones, roaring out aloud like bulls upon a mountain, and the men of the tribe replying shrill and savage out of the terror of their souls. And all the time of the burning, Keola stood there and listened, and shook, and watched how the unseen hands of Lehua poured the leaves. She poured them fast, and the flame burned high, and scorched Keola's hands; and she speeded and blew the burning with her breath. The last leaf was eaten, the flame fell, and the shock followed, and there were Keola and Lehua in the room at home.

Now, when Keola could see his wife at last he was mighty pleased, and he was mighty pleased to be home again in Molokai and sit down beside a bowl of poi—for they make no poi on board ships, and there was none in the Isle of Voices—and he was out of the body with pleasure to be clean escaped out of the hands of the eaters of men. But there was another matter not so clear, and Lehua and Keola talked of it all night and were troubled. There was Kalamake left upon the isle. If, by the blessing of God, he could but stick there, all were well; but should he escape and return to Molokai, it would be an ill day for his daughter and her husband. They spoke of his gift of swelling, and whether he could wade that distance in the seas. But Keola knew by this time where that island was—and that is to say, in the Low or Dangerous Archipelago. So they fetched the atlas and looked upon the distance in the map, and by what they could make of it, it seemed a far way for an old gentleman to walk. Still, it would not do to make too sure of a warlock like Kalamake, and they determined at last to take counsel of a white missionary.

So the first one that came by Keola told him everything. And the missionary was very sharp on him for taking the second wife in the low island; but for all the rest, he vowed he could make neither head nor tail of it.

'However,' says he, 'if you think this money of your father's ill gotten, my advice to you would be, give some of it to the lepers and some to the missionary fund. And as for this extraordinary rigmarole, you cannot do better than keep it to yourselves.'

But he warned the police at Honolulu that, by all he could make out, Kalamake and Keola had been coining false money, and it would not be amiss to watch them.

Keola and Lehua took his advice, and gave many dollars

to the lepers and the fund. And no doubt the advice must have been good, for from that day to this, Kalamake has never more been heard of. But whether he was slain in the battle by the trees, or whether he is still kicking his heels upon the Isle of Voices, who shall say?

Miss Christian Jean

R. B. CUNNINGHAME GRAHAM

(1852–1936)

Two pictures hang upon my study wall, faded and woolly, but well stippled up, the outlines of the hills just indicated with a fine reed pen, showing the water, coloured saffron, deepening to pink in the deep shadows of the lake. Although one picture is a sunset and the other done as it would seem at sunrise, they show a country which even yet is undefiled by any human step.

So accurately is the dark brown tree set in position on the border of the fleecy lake, one feels an artist, superior to mere Nature, has been about the task. The castle, on the mountain top in one of the two masterpieces, is at the bottom of the hill in its compeer, and in the two a clear blue sky throws a deep shadow over the unruffled water, on which float boats with tall white sails, progressing without wind.

Still, with their frames, which are but fricassees of gingerbread well gilt, to me they say a something all the art of all the masters leaves unsaid.

A masterpiece speaks of imagination in its maker; but those pale blue-grey hills and salmon-coloured pinkish lakes, castles which never could have been inhabited, boats sailing in a calm, and trees that seem to rustle without breeze, set me reflecting upon things gone by, and upon places of which I was once part, places which still ungratefully live on, whilst that of me which lived in them is dead.

A long low Georgian room, in which the pictures hung, with its high mantelpiece, its smell of damp and Indian curiosities, and window looking out on the sunk garden underneath the terraces, the sides of which were honey-combed by rabbits, rises in my view, making me wonder in what substance of the body or the mind they have been stamped.

How few such rooms remain, and how few houses such as that, to which the dark and dampish chamber, with its three outside walls, and deep-cut mouldings on the windows and the doors, was library. We called it 'book-room', in the Scottish way, although the books were few and mostly had belonged to a dead uncle who had bought them all in India, and on their yellowing leaves were stains of insects from the East, and now and then a grass or flower from Hyderabad or Kolapur (as pencilled notes upon the margin said), transported children to a land so gorgeous that the like of it was never seen on earth. These books were all well chosen, and such as men read fifty years ago—Macaulay's *Essays*, with the *Penny Cyclopaedia*, Hume, Smollett, Captain Cook, the *Life of Dost Mohammed*, Elphinstone's *Cabul Mission*, with Burckhardt's *Travels*, enthralling Mungo Park, and others of the kind that at hill stations in the rains, or in the plains during the summer, must have passed many an hour of boredom and of heat away for their dead purchaser. The rest were books of heraldry and matters of the kind together with a set of Lever and of Dickens, with plates by Cruikshank or by Hablot Brown. One in particular set forth a man upon a horse, with a red fluttering cloak streaming out in the wind, galloping in the midst of buffaloes with a long knife between his teeth. But books and furniture and Indian curiosities, with the high Adam chimney-piece and portraits of the favourite hounds and horses of three generations, were, as it were, keyed up to the two water-colours, one of which hung up above a cabinet sunk far into the wall and glazed, the other over a low double door, deep as an embrasure.

All through the house the smell of damp, of kingwood furniture, and roses dried in bowls, blended and formed a scent which I shall smell as long as life endures. This may, of course, have been mere fancy; but often in old houses some picture or some piece of furniture appears to give the keynote to the rest. But it seemed evident to me that, in some strange mysterious way, the pictures, outstanding in their badness, had stamped themselves upon the house more than the Reynoldses and Raeburns on the walls, though they were pictures of my ancestors, and the two water-colours represented no known landscape upon earth. They entered into my ideas so strongly (though they were unobtrusive in themselves) that, looking from the window-seat in the deep bay of the sunk window in the dining-room, across the terraces, over the sea of laurels, beyond the rushy 'park', and out upon the moss and the low lumpy hills that ran down to the distant lake, almost divided into two by a peninsula set with dark pine trees and with planes, the landscape seemed unfinished and lacking interest without the castles and the chrome-laden skies of the twin masterpieces.

It may be, too, that the unnatural landscape caused me to form unnatural views of life, finding things interesting and people worthy of remark whom others found quite commonplace, merely upon their own account, and not from the surroundings of their lives. So everyone connected with the house of the two works of art became mixed up somehow with them in a mysterious way, as well as things inanimate and trees, the vegetation and the white mist which half the year hung over moss and woods, shrouding the hills and everything in its unearthly folds, making them strange and half unreal, as is a landscape in a dream.

Perhaps the fact that the house stood just at the point where Lowlands end and the great jumble of the Highland hills begins, and that the people were compounded of both simples, Saxon and Celtic mixed in equal parts, gave them and all the place an interest such as clings to borderlands the whole world over, for even forty years ago one talked of 'up above the pass' as of a land distinct from where we lived. Down from those regions wandered men speaking a strange tongue, shaggy, and smelling of a mixture of raw wool and peat smoke, whose dogs obeyed them in a way in which no dog of any man quite civilized, broken to railways and refreshment-rooms, obeys his master's call. The bond of union may have been that both slept out in the wet dew, huddling together in the morning round the fire for warmth, or something else, the half-possession of some sense that we have lost, by means of which, all unknown to themselves, the drover and his dog communicated. Communion, very likely, is the word, the old communion of all living things, the lost connexion between man and all the other animals, which modern life destroys.

But, be that as it may, the men and dogs seemed natives, and we who lived amongst the mosses and the hills seemed strangers, by lack of something or by excess of something else, according to your view.

The herds of ponies that the men drove before them on the road fell naturally into the scheme of Nature; sorrels and yellow chestnuts, creams and duns, they blended with the scrubbing woods and made no blot upon the shaggy hills. Instinctively they took the long-forgotten fords, crossing below the bridges, and standing knee-deep in the stream, the water dripping from the ropy tails and burdock-knotted manes. The herds of kyloes too have gone, which looked like animals of some race older than our own. The men who drove them, with their rough clothes of coarse grey wool, their hazel crooks, and plaids about their shoulders, whether the wind blew keenly or midges teased in August, all have disappeared. Their little camps upon the selvedge of the roads are all forgotten, although I know them still, by the bright grass that grows upon the ashes of the fires. Or have they gone, and are the hills brown, lumpy, heather-clad, and jewelled after rain by myriad streams, merely illusions; and is it really that I myself have gone, and they live on, deep down in the recesses of some fairy hill of which I am not free?

Men, too, like my friend Wallace of Gartchorrachan, have disappeared, and I am not quite sure if we should bless the Lord on that account. All through Menteith, and right 'across the hill' as far as Callander and Doune, he was well known, and always styled Laird Wallace, for though our custom is to call men by the title of their lands, thus making them *adscripti glebae* to the very soul, the word Gartchorrachan stuck in our throats, although we readily twist and distort the Gaelic place-names in our talk just as the Spaniards mutilate the Arab words, smoothing their corners and their angles out in the strong current of their speech.

Dressed in grey tweed with bits of buckskin let into the shoulders of his coat, for no one ever saw him leave his house without a gun, he was about the age that farmers in the north seem to be born at—that is, for years he had been grey, but yet was vigorous, wore spectacles, and his thick curly hair was matted like the wool upon a ram, whilst from his ears and nostrils grew thick tufts of bristles, just as a growth of twigs springs from the trunk of an old oak tree, where it has got a wound.

His house was like himself, old, grey, and rambling and smelt of gun oil, beeswax, and of camphor, for he was versed in entomology, and always had a case of specimens, at which he laboured with a glass stuck in his eye reminding me of Cyclops or of Polyphèmus, or of an ogre in a story-book. Botany and conchology, and generally those sciences which when pursued without a method soon became trifling and a pastime, were his joys, and he had cabinets in which the specimens reposed under a heavy coat of dust, but duly ticketed each with its Latin name.

He spoke good English as a general rule, and when un-moved, as was the custom with the people of his class and upbringing, but often used broad Scotch, which he employed after the fashion of a shield against the world, half in a joking way and half against the sin of self-revealment which we shun as the plague, passing our lives like pebbles in a brook, which rub against each other for an age, and yet remain apart.

In early life, he had contracted what he called a 'local liassong', the fruit of which had been a daughter whom he had educated, and who lived with him, half as his daughter, half as housekeeper. Her father loved her critically, and when she not infrequently swept china on the floor as she passed through the drawing-room (just as a tapir walks about a wood, breaking down all the saplings in its path), he would screw up one eye, and looking at her say, 'That's what you get from breeding from a cart-mare, the filly's sure to throw back to the dam.'

Withal he was a gentleman, having been in the army and travelled in his youth, but had not got much more by his experience than the raw youth of whom his father said, 'Aye, Willie's been to Rome and back again, and a' he's learnt is but to cast his sark aince every day.' But still he was a kindly man, the prey of anyone who had a specious story, the providence of all lame horses and of dogs quite useless for any kind of sport, all which he bought at prices far above the value of the most favoured members of their race.

His inner nature always seemed to be just struggling forth almost against his will, mastering his rough exterior, just as in pibrochs, after the skirling of the pipes has died away, a tender melody breaks out, fitful and plaintive, speaking of islands lost in misty seas, of things forgotten and mis- understood, of the faint, swishing noise of heather in the rain moved by the breeze at night, and which through minor modulations and fantastic trills ends in a wild lament for some Fingalian hero, like the wind sighing through the pines.

Nothing was more congenial to his humour than to unpack his recollections of the past, seated before the fire, an oily black cigar which he chewed almost like a quid between his teeth, and with a glass of whisky by his side.

After expatiating upon the excellences of his lame, jibbing chestnut mare, that he had bought at Falkirk Tryst from a quite honest dealer, but which had gone mysteriously so lame that even whisky for his groom had no effect in curing her, he usually used to lament upon the changes which the course of time had brought about. All was a grief to him, as it is really to all of us, if we all knew it, that some particular landmark of his life had disappeared. No one spoke Gaelic nowadays, although he never in his life had known a word of it. The use of 'weepers' and crape hat-bands by the country-folk on Sunday was quite discontinued, and no one took their collie dogs to church. Coffins were now no longer carried shoulder-high across the hills from lonely upland straths, as he remembered to have seen them in his youth. Did not some funeral party in his childhood, taking a short cut on a frozen loch, fall through and perish to a man?—a circumstance he naturally deplored, but still regretted, as men of older generations may have regretted highwaymen, as they sat safely by their fire. Although he never fished, he was quite certain no one now alive could busk a fly as well as a departed worthy of his youth, one Dan-a-Haltie, or make a withy basket or those osier loops which formerly were stuck between the 'divots' in a dry stone dike, projecting outwards like a torpedo netting, to stop sheep jumping from a field. Words such as *flauchtered feal* and *laroch* were hardly understood; shepherds read newspapers as they lay out upon the hill, the Shorter Catechism had been miserably abridged, and the old fir-tree by the Shannochill was blasted at the top.

All these complaints he uttered philosophically, not in a plaintive way, but as a man who, at his birth, had entered as it were into a covenant with life just as it was, which he for his part had faithfully observed, but was deceived by fate.

Then when he had relieved his mind he used to laugh and, puffing out the smoke of his thick black cigar, which hung about the tufts which sprung out of his nostrils, just as the

mist hangs dank about a bog, he would remark, 'I'm
haverin',' as if he was afraid of having to explain himself to
something in his mind. On these occasions, I used to let him
sit a little, and usually, he would begin again, after a look to
see if I had noticed the gag he suddenly had put upon himself, and then start off again. 'Ye mind my aunt, Miss
Christian Jean?' I did, eating her sweetmeats in my youth,
and trembling at her frown.

'Ye never heard me tell how it was I kisted her,' he said,
and then again fell into contemplation, and once again began.
'My aunt, Miss Christian Jean, was a survival of the fittest—
aye, ye know I am in some things quite opposed to Darwin,
the survival of the potter's wheel in the Fijis and several
other things . . . aye, haverin' again . . . or the most unfitted
to survive.

'She was a gentlewoman . . . yes, yes, the very word is
now half ludicrous, ye need not smile . . . lady is a poor sub-
stitute. Tall, dark, and masculine, and with a down upon
her upper lip that many a cornet of dragoons, for there
were cornets in those days, might well have envied, she was
a sort of providence, jealous and swift in chastisement, but
yet a providence to all the younger members of her race
who came across her path.

'I see her now, her and her maid, old Katherine Sinclair,
a tall, gaunt Highland woman, who might easily have walked
straight from the pages of *Rob Roy*, and her old butler,
Robert Cameron, grey and red-faced, and dressed eternally
in a black suit, all stained with snuff, a pawky sort of chiel,
religious and still with the spirit of revolt against all dog-
matism which modern life and cheap and stereotyped
instruction has quite stamped out today. My aunt kept order
in her house, that is as far as others were concerned. Each
day she read her chapter, in what she styled the Book, not
taking over heed how she selected it, so that the chapter
once was duly read. It happened sometimes that when she
came into the room where, as my cousin Andrew used to
say—ye mind that he was drowned in one of those Green's

ships, fell from aloft whilst they were reefing topsails in a dark night somewhere about the Cape.

'I've heard him say he could come down the weather-leach of a topsail, just like a monkey, by the bolt ropes. . . . Where was I, eh? Aye, I mind, he used to say that my aunt's prayers reminded him of service in a ship, with all hands mustered; so as I said, my aunt would sometimes open up the Book and come upon a chapter full of names, and how some one begat another body, and sometimes upon things perfectly awesome for a maiden lady to read aloud, for 'twas all one to her.

'Then the old butler would put his hand up to his mouth and whisper, "Mem, Miss Christian, Mem, ye're wandered," and she would close the book, or start again upon another chapter and maybe twice as long.

'My aunt and her two satellites kept such good order, that a visitor from England, seeing her neat and white-capped maids file in and take their seats facing the men-servants, expressed her pleasure at the well-ordered, comely worship, and received the answer, "Yes, my dear, ye see at family prayers we have the separation of the sexes, but I understand when they meet afterwards at the stair foot, the kissing beats the cracking of a whip."

'Poor Aunt Christian, I used to shiver at her nod, and well remember when a youth how she would flyte me when I pinched the maids, and say, "Laddie, I canna' have you making the girls squeal like Highland ponies; it is not decent, and decency comes after morality, sometimes, I think, before it, for it can be attained, whereas the other is a counsel of perfection set up on high, but well out of our reach."

'A pretty moralizer was my poor aunt, almost a heathen in her theory, guided by what she said were natural laws, and yet a Puritan in practice, whereas I always was a theoretic Puritan, but shaped my life exclusively by natural laws, as they appear to me.

'Let ministers just haver as they will, one line of conduct is not possible for nephews and for aunts. Take David, now, the man after the Lord's own heart, and ask yourself what would have happened if his aunt . . . aye, aye, I'm wandered from my tale . . . I ken I'm wandering.

'Well, well, it seemed as if my aunt might have gone on for ever, getting a little dryer and her face more peakit, as the years went by and her old friends dropped off and left her all alone. That's what it is, ye see; it's got to come, although it seems impossible whilst we sit talking here and drinking— that is, I drinking and you listening to me talk. One wintry day I was just sitting wiping the cee-spring of a gun, and looking out upon the avenue, when through the wreaths, I saw a boy on a bit yellow pony beast come trotting through the snow.

'It was before the days of telegrams, and I jaloused that there was something special, or no one would have sent the laddie out on such a day, with the snow drifted half a yard upon the ground, the trees all white with cranreuch like the sugar on a cake, and the first frost keen enough to split a pudding stone and grind it into sand.

'I sent the laddie to the kitchen fire, and ripped the envelope, whilst the bit pony rooted round for grass and walked upon the reins. The letter told me that my aunt had had a fit, was signed by "Robert Cameron, butler", and was all daubed with snuff, and in a postcript I was asked to hurry, for the time was short, and to come straight across the hill as the low road was blocked by the snow drifting and nobody could pass. I harnessed up my mare—not the bit blooded chestnut I drive now'—this was the way in which he spoke of the lame cripple which had conveyed him to my house—'but a stout sort of Highland mouse-coloured beastie that I had, rather short backit, a little hammer-headed, and with the hair upon the fetlocks like a Clydesdale. . . . Maun, I think ye dinna' often see such sort of beasts the now.' I mentally thanked God for it, and he again launched out in his tale.

'An awful drive, I'm tellin' ye! I hadna' got above Auchyle —ye mind, at the old bridge just where yon English tourist

coupit his creels, and gaed to heaven, maybe last summer—
when I saw I had a job. The snow balled in the mare's feet
as big as cabbages, and made her stotter in her gait, just like
a drunken curler ettlin' to walk upon a rink. I had to take
her by the head till we got on the flat ground, up about
Rusky. Man, it was arctic and the little loch lay like a sheet
of glass that had been breathed upon, with dead bulrushes
and reeds all sticking through the ice! The island in the
loch seemed like a blob of white, and the old tower (I dinna'
richtly mind, if, at one time, it belonged to some of your own
folk) loomed up like Stirling Castle or like Doune in the
keen frosty air. The little firwood on the east side of the old
change-house—that one they called Wright, or some such
name, once keepit—was full of roe, all sheltering like cows,
so cold and starved they scarcely steered when I passed by
and gave a shout to warm my lungs and hearten up the
mare; and a cock capercailzie, moping and miserable, sat on
a fir-tree like a barn-door fowl. I ploutered on just to where
there used to be a gate across the road, where ye see Uamh
Var and the great shoulder of Ben Ledi stretching up out
by the pass of Leny and the old chapel of St. Bryde. It was
fair awesome; I did not rightly know the landscape with the
familiar features blotted out. I very nearly got myself
wandered just in the straight about the Gart, for all the
dikes were sunk beneath the snow, and the hedge-tops
peeped up like box in an old cabbage-garden. At last I
reached the avenue, the mare fair taigled, and the ice hanging from her fetlocks and her mane and wagging to and fro.
The evergreens were, so to speak, a-wash, and looked like
beds of parsley or of greens, and underneath the trees the
squirrels' footsteps in the snow seemed those of some
strange birds, where they had melted and then frozen on
the ground. Across the sky a crow or two flew slowly,
flapping their wings as if the joint oil had been frozen in
their bones and cawing sullenly.

'On the high steps which led up to the door the butler met
me, and as he took my coat, said, "Laird, ye are welcome;

your poor dear auntie's going. Hech, sirs, 'twill be an awfu' nicht for the poor leddy to be fleein' naked through the air towards the judgement seat. Will ye tak' speerits or a dish o' tea after your coldsome drive, or will I tak' ye straight in to your aunt? I'm feared she willna' know you. But His will be done, though I could wish He micht hae held His hand a little longer; but we must not repine. I've just been readin' out to her from the old Book, ye ken, passin' the time awa' and waitin' for the end."

'All day my aunt lay dozing, half-conscious and half-stupefied, and all the day the butler, sitting by the bed, read psalms and chapters, to which she sometimes seemed to pay attention, and at others lay so still we thought that she was dead. Now and again he stopped his reading, and peering at his mistress with his spectacles pushed up, wiped off the tears that trickled down his face with his red handkerchief, and, as if doubting he were reading to the living or the dead, said, "Nod yer heid, Miss Christian," which she did feebly, and he, satisfied she understood, mumbled on piously in a thick undertone.

'Just about morning she passed away quite quietly, the maids and her butler standing round the bed, they crying silently, and he snorting in his red pocket-handkerchief, with the tears running down his face. The gaunt old Highland waiting-woman raised a high wail which echoed through the cold and silent house, causing the dogs to bark and the old parrot scream, and the butler stottered from the room, muttering that he would go and see if tea was ready, closing the door behind him with his foot, as if he feared the figure on the bed would scold him, as she had often done during her life, if it slammed to and made a noise.

'All the week through it snowed, and my aunt's house was dismal, smelling of cheese and honey, yellow soap, of jam, of grease burnt in the fire, and with the dogs and cats uncared for rambling about and sleeping on the chairs. The cold was penetrating, and I wandered up and down the stairs quite aimlessly, feeling like Alexander Selkirk in the melancholy house, which seemed an island cut off from the world by a white sea of snow. None of Aunt Christian's friends or relatives could come, as all the roads were blocked; even her coffin was not sent till a few hours before the funeral, the cart that brought it stalling in the snow, and the black-coated undertaker's men carrying it shoulder-high through the thick wreaths upon the avenue.

'The servants would not have a stranger touch the corpse, and the old butler and myself kisted my aunt, lifting her body from the bed between the two of us. A week had passed and she looked black and shrunken, and as I lifted her, the chill from the cold flesh struck me with horror, and welled into the bones. I could not kiss her as she lay like a mummy in the kist, for the shrunk face with the white clothes about the chin was not the same Aunt Christian's whom I had loved and before whom I trembled for so many years, but changed somehow and horrible to see.

'The butler did, looking at me, as I thought, half-reproachfully as I stood silently, not once crying but half stupefied, and then as she lay shrunken and brown on the white satin lining of the kist, we stood and looked at one another, just as we had been partners in a crime, till they began to hammer down the lid. A drearsome sound it makes. One feels the nails are sticking in the flesh, and every time ye hear it, it affects ye more than the last time, the same as an earthquake, as I mind I heard a traveller say one day in Edinburgh. What the old butler did, I do not mind; but I just dandered out into the garden, and washed my hands in snow, not that I felt a skunner at my poor Aunt Christian's flesh, but somehow I had to do it, for ye ken 'twas the first time.'

Laird Wallace stopped just as a horse props suddenly when he is fresh and changes feet, then breaking into Scotch, said: 'I have talked enough. That's how I kisted my Aunt Christian Jean, puir leddy, a sair job it was, and dreich. . . . Thank ye, nae soddy, I'll tak' a drop of Lagavoulin.' Then lighting a cigar, he said, 'Ring for my dog-cart, please,' and

when it came he clambered to the seat, and pointing to his
spavined mare, said, 'Man, a gran' beast clean thorough-
bred, fit to run for her life' (and this to me who knew her);
then bidding me good-night, drew his whip smartly on her
scraggy flank, and vanished through the trees.

The Lammas Preaching

S. R. CROCKETT

(1860–1914)

'AND I further intimate,' said the minister, 'that I will
preach this evening at Cauldshaws, and my text will be
from the ninth chapter of the book of Ecclesiastes and the
tenth verse, "Whatsoever thy hand findeth to do, do it with
thy might." '

'Save us,' said Janet MacTaggart, 'he's clean forgotten
"if it be the Lord's wull." Maybe he'll be for gaun whether
it's His wull or no'—he's a sair masterfu' man, the minister;
but he comes frae the Machars,[1] an' kens little aboot the
jealous God we hae amang the hills o' Gallowa'!'

The minister continued, in the same high, level tone in
which he did his preaching, 'There are a number of slug-
gards who lay the weight of their own laziness on the
Almighty, saying, "I am a worm and no man—how should
I strive with my Maker?" whenever they are at strife with
their own sluggishness. There will be a word for all such
this evening at the farmtown of Cauldshaws, presently
occupied by Gilbert M'Kissock—public worship to begin at
seven o'clock.'

The congregation of Barnessock kirk tumbled amicably
over its own heels with eagerness to get into the kirkyaird
in order to settle the momentous question, 'Wha's back
was he on the day?'

[1] The Eastern Lowlands of Wigtownshire.

Robert Kirk, Carsethorn, had a packet of peppermint lozenges in the crown of his 'lum' hat—deponed to by Elizabeth Douglas or Barr, in Barnbogrie, whose husband, Weelum Barr, put on the hat of the aforesaid Robert Kirk by mistake for his own, whereupon the peppermints fell to the floor and rolled under the pews in most unseemly fashion. Elizabeth Kirk is of opinion that this should be brought to the notice of Session, she herself always taking her peppermint while genteelly wiping her mouth with the corner of her handkerchief. Robert Kirk, on being put to the question, admits the fact, but says that it was his wife put them there to be near her hand.

The minister, however, ready with his word, brought him to shame by saying, 'O Robert, Robert, that was just what Adam said, "The woman Thou gavest me, she gave me to eat!" ' The aforesaid Robert Kirk thinks that it is meddling with the original Hebrew to apply this to peppermints, and also says that Elizabeth Kirk is an impident besom, and furthermore that, as all the country well knows—(Here the chronicler omits much matter actionable in the civil courts of the realm).

'Janet,' said the minister to his housekeeper, 'I am to preach tonight at Cauldshaws on the text, "Whatsoever thy hand findeth to do, do it with thy might." '

'I ken,' said Janet, 'I saw it on yer desk. I pat it ablow the clock for fear the wun's o' heeven micht blaw it awa' like chaff, an' you couldna do wantin' it!'

'Janet MacTaggart,' said the minister, tartly, 'bring in the denner, and do not meddle with what does not concern you.'

Janet could not abide read sermons; her natural woman rose against them. She knew, as she had said, that God was a jealous God, and, with regard to the minister, she looked upon herself as His vicegerent.

'He's young an' terrable ram-stam an' opeenionated—fu' o' buik-lear, but wi' little gracious experience. For a' that, the root o' the maitter 's in 'im,' said Janet, not unhopefully.

'I'm gaun to preach at Cauldshaws, and my text's "Whatsoever thy hand findeth to do, do it with thy might," ' said the minister to the precentor that afternoon, on the manse doorstep.

'The Lord's no' in a' his thochts. I'll gang wi' the lad mysel',' said the precentor.

Now, Galloway is so much out of the world that the Almighty has not there lifted His hand from reward and punishment, from guiding and restraining, as He has done in big towns where everything goes by machinery. Man may say that there is no God when he only sees a handbreadth of smoky heaven between the chimney-pots; but out on the fields of oats and bear, and up on the screes of the hillsides, where the mother granite sticks her bleaching ribs through the heather, men have reached great assurance on this and other matters.

The burns were running red with the mighty July rain when Douglas Maclellan started over the meadows and moors to preach his sermon at the farmtown of Cauldshaws. He had thanked the Lord that morning in his opening prayer for 'the bounteous rain wherewith He had seen meet to refresh His weary heritage.'

His congregation silently acquiesced, 'for what', said they, 'could a man from the Machars be expected to ken about meadow hay?'

When the minister and the precentor got to the foot of the manse loaning, they came upon the parish ne'er-do-weel, Ebie Kirgan, who kept himself in employment by constantly scratching his head, trying to think of something to do, and whose clothes were constructed on the latest sanitary principles of ventilation. The ruins of Ebie's hat were usually tipped over one eye for enlarged facilities of scratching in the rear.

'If it's yer wull, minister, I'll come to hear ye the nicht. It's drawing to mair rain, I'm thinkin'!' said the Scarecrow.

'I hope the discourse may be profitable to you, Ebenezer,

for, as I intimated this morning, I am to preach from the text, "Whatsoever thy hand findeth to do, do it with thy might." '

'Ay, minister,' said Ebie, relieving his right hand, and tipping his hat over the other eye to give his left free play. So the three struck over the fields, making for the thorn tree at the corner, where Robert Kirk's dyke dipped into the standing water of the meadow.

'Do you think ye can manage it, Maister Maclellan?' said the precentor. 'Ye're wat half-way up the leg already.'

'An' there's sax feet o' black moss water in the Laneburn as sure as I'm a leevin' sowl,' added Ebie Kirgan.

'I'm to preach at Cauldshaws, and my text is, "Whatsoever thy hand findeth to do, do it with thy might!" ' said the minister, stubbornly glooming from under the eaves of his eyebrows as the swarthy men from the Machars are wont to do. His companions said no more. They came to Camelon Lane, where usually Robert Kirk had a leaping pole on either bank to assist the traveller across, but both poles had gone down the water in the morning to look for Robert's meadow hay.

'Tak' care, Maister Maclellan, ye'll be in deep water afore ye ken. O man, ye had far better turn!'

The precentor stood up to his knees in water on what had once been the bank, and wrung his hands. But the minister pushed steadily ahead into the turbid and sluggish water.

'I canna come, oh, I canna come, for I'm a man that has a family.'

'It's no' your work; stay where ye are,' cried the minister, without looking over his shoulder; 'but as for me, I'm intimated to preach this night at Cauldshaws, and my text——'

Here he stepped into a deep hole, and his text was suddenly shut within him by the gurgle of moss water in his throat. His arms rose above the surface like the black spars of a windmill. But Ebie Kirgan sculled himself swiftly out, swimming with his shoeless feet, and pushed the minister before him to the further bank—the water gushing out of rents in his clothes as easily as out of the gills of a fish.

The minister stood with unshaken confidence on the bank. He ran peat water like a spout in a thunder plump, and black rivulets of dye were trickling from under his hat down his brow and dripping from the end of his nose.

'Then you'll not come any farther?' he called across to the precentor.

'I canna, oh, I canna; though I'm most awfu' wullin'. Kirsty wad never forgie me gin I was to droon.'

'Then I'll e'en have to raise the tune myself—though three times "Kilmarnock" is a pity,' said the minister, turning on his heel and striding away through the shallow sea, splashing the water as high as his head with a kind of headstrong glee which seemed to the precentor a direct defiance of Providence. Ebie Kirgan followed half a dozen steps behind. The support of the precentor's lay semi-equality taken from him, he began to regret that he had come, and silently and ruefully plunged along after the minister through the waterlogged meadows. They came in time to the foot of Robert Kirk's march dyke, and skirted it a hundred yards upward to avoid the deep pool in which the Laneburn waters were swirling. The minister climbed silently up the seven-foot dyke, pausing a second on the top to balance himself for his leap to the other side. As he did so Ebie Kirgan saw that the dyke was swaying to the fall, having been weakened by the rush of water on the farther side. He ran instantly at the minister, and gave him a push with both hands which caused Mr. Maclellan to alight on his feet clear of the falling stones. The dyke did not so much fall outward as settle down on its own ruins. Ebie fell on his face among the stones with the impetus of his own eagerness. He arose, however, quickly—only limping slightly from what he called a 'bit chack' on the leg between two stones.

'That was a merciful Providence, Ebenezer,' said the minister, solemnly; 'I hope you are duly thankful!'

'Dod, I am that!' replied Ebie, scratching his head vigorously with his right hand and rubbing his leg with his left. 'Gin I hadna gi'en ye that dunch, ye micht hae preachen nane at Cauldshaws this nicht.'

They now crossed a fairly level clover field, dank and laid with wet. The scent of the clover rose to their nostrils with almost overpowering force. There was not a breath of air. The sky was blue and the sun shining. Only a sullen roar came over the hill, sounding in the silence like the rush of a train over a far-away viaduct.

'What is that?' queried the minister, stopping to listen.

Ebie took a brisk sidelong look at him.

'I'm some dootsome that'll be the Skyreburn coming doon aff o' Cairnsmuir!'

The minister tramped unconcernedly on. Ebie Kirgan stared at him.

'He canna ken what a "Skyreburn warnin'" is—he'll be thinkin' it's some bit Machars burn that the laddies set their whurlie mills in. But he'll turn richt eneuch when he sees Skyreburn roarin' reed in a Lammas flood, I'm thinkin'!'

They took their way over the shoulder of the hill in the beautiful evening, leaning eagerly forward to get the first glimpse of the cause of that deep and resonant roar. In a moment they saw below them a narrow rock-walled gully, ten or fifteen yards across, filled to the brim with rushing water. It was not black peat water like the Camelon Lane, but it ran red as keel, flecked now and then with a revolving white blur as one of the Cauldshaws sheep spun downward to the sea, with four black feet turned pitifully up to the blue sky.

Ebie looked at the minister. 'He'll turn noo if he's mortal,' he said. But the minister held on. He looked at the water up and down the roaring stream. On a hill above, the farmer of Cauldshaws, having driven all his remaining sheep together, sat down to watch. Seeing the minister, he stood up and excitedly waved him back. But Douglas Maclellan from the Machars never gave him a look, and his shouting was of less effect than if he had been crying to an untrained collie.

The minister looked long up the stream, and at a point where the rocks came very close together, and many stunted pines were growing, he saw one which, having stood on the immediate brink, had been so much undercut that it leaned over the gully like a fishing-rod. With a keen glance along its length, the minister, jamming his dripping soft felt hat on the back of his head, was setting foot on the perilous slope of the uneven red-brown trunk, when Ebie Kirgan caught him sharply by the arm.

'It's no' for me to speak to a minister at ordinar' times,' he stammered, gathering courage in his desperation; 'but, oh, man, it's fair murder to try to gang ower that water!'

The minister wrenched himself free, and sprang along the trunk with wonderful agility.

'I'm intimated to preach at Cauldshaws this night, and my text is, "Whatsoever thy hand findeth to do, do it with thy might!" ' he shouted.

He made his way up and up the slope of the fir-tree, which, having little grip of the rock, dipped and swayed under his tread. Ebie Kirgan fell on his knees and prayed aloud. He had not prayed since his stepmother boxed his ears for getting into bed without saying his prayers twenty years ago. This had set him against it. But he prayed now, and to infinitely more purpose than his minister had recently done. But when the climber had reached the branchy top, and was striving to get a few feet farther, in order to clear the surging linn before he made his spring, Ebie rose to his feet, leaving his prayer unfinished. He sent forth an almost animal shriek of terror. The tree roots cracked like breaking cables and slowly gave way, an avalanche of stones plumped into the whirl, and the top of the fir crashed downwards on the rocks of the opposite bank.

'Oh, man, call on the name of the Lord!' cried Ebie Kirgan, the ragged preacher, at the top of his voice.

Then he saw something detach itself from the tree as it rebounded, and for a moment rise and fall black against the sunset. Then Ebie the Outcast fell on his face like a dead man.

.   .   .   .

In the white coverleted 'room' of the farmtown of Cauldshaws, a white-faced lad lay with his eyes closed, and a wet cloth on his brow. A large-boned, red-cheeked, motherly woman stole to and fro with a foot as light as a fairy. The sleeper stirred and tried to lift an unavailing hand to his head. The mistress of Cauldshaws stole to his bedside as he opened his eyes. She laid a restraining hand on him as he strove to rise.

'Let me up,' said the minister, 'I must away, for I'm intimated to preach at Cauldshaws, and my text is, "Whatsoever thy hand findeth to do, do it with thy might." '

'My bonny man,' said the goodwife, tenderly, 'you'll preach best on the broad o' yer back this mony a day, an' when ye rise your best text will be, "He sent from above, He took me, and drew me out of many waters!" '

The Courting of T'nowhead's Bell

J. M. BARRIE

(1860–1937)

FOR years it had been notorious in the square that Sam'l Dickie was thinking of courting T'nowhead's Bell, and that if little Sanders Elshioner (which is the Thrums pronunciation of Alexander Alexander) went in for her he might prove a formidable rival. Sam'l was a weaver in the Tenements, and Sanders a coal-carter whose trade mark was a bell on his horse's neck that told when coals were coming. Being something of a public man, Sanders had not perhaps so high a social position as Sam'l, but he had suceeeded his father on the coal cart, while the weaver had already tried several trades. It had always been against Sam'l, too, that once when the kirk was vacant he had advised the selection of the third minister who preached for it on the ground that it came expensive to pay a large number of candidates. The scandal of the thing was hushed up, out of respect for his father, who was a God-fearing man, but Sam'l was known by it in Lang Tammas's circle. The coal carter was called Little Sanders to distinguish him from his father, who was not much more than half his size. He had grown up with the name, and its inapplicability now came home to nobody. Sam'l's mother had been more far-seeing than Sanders's. Her man had been called Sammy all his life because it was the name he got as a boy, so when their eldest son was born she spoke of him as Sam'l while still in his cradle. The neighbours imitated her, and thus the young man had a better start in life than had been granted to Sammy, his father.

It was Saturday evening—the night in the week when Auld Licht young men fell in love. Sam'l Dickie, wearing a blue glengarry bonnet with a red ball on the top, came to the door of a one-story house in the Tenements and stood there wriggling for he was in a suit of tweeds for the first time that week, and did not feel at one with them. When his feeling of being a stranger to himself wore off he looked up and down the road, which straggles between houses and gardens, and then, picking his way over the puddles, crossed to his father's hen-house and sat down on it. He was now on his way to the square.

Eppie Fargus was sitting on an adjoining dyke knitting stockings, and Sam'l looked at her for a time.

'Is't yersel, Eppie?' he said at last.

'It's a' that,' said Eppie.

'Hoo's a' wi' ye?' asked Sam'l.

'We're juist aff an' on,' replied Eppie, cautiously.

There was not much more to say, but as Sam'l sidled off

the hen-house he murmured politely, 'Ay, ay.' In another minute he would have been fairly started, but Eppie resumed the conversation.

'Sam'l,' she said, with a twinkle in her eye, 'ye can tell Lisbeth Fargus I'll likely be drappin' in on her aboot Mununday or Teisday.'

Lisbeth was sister to Eppie, and wife of Tammas McQuhatty, better known as T'nowhead, which was the name of his farm. She was thus Bell's mistress.

Sam'l leant against the hen-house as if all his desire to depart had gone.

'Hoo d'ye kin I'll be at the T'nowhead the nicht?' he asked, grinning in anticipation.

'Ou, I'se warrant ye'll be after Bell,' said Eppie.

'A'm no sae sure o' that,' said Sam'l, trying to leer. He was enjoying himself now.

'A'm no sure o' that,' he repeated, for Eppie seemed lost in stitches.

'Sam'l?'

'Ay.'

'Ye'll be speirin' her sune noo, I dinna doot?'

This took Sam'l, who had only been courting Bell for a year or two, a little aback.

'Hoo d'ye mean, Eppie?' he asked.

'Maybe ye'll do't the nicht.'

'Na, there's nae hurry,' said Sam'l.

'Weel, we're a' coontin' on't, Sam'l.'

'Gae 'wa' wi' ye,' said Sam'l again.

'Bell's gei an' fond o' ye, Sam'l.'

'Ay,' said Sam'l.

'But am dootin' ye're a fell billy wi' the lasses.'

'Ay, oh, I d'na kin, moderate, moderate,' said Sam'l, in high delight.

'I saw ye,' said Eppie, speaking with a wire in her mouth, 'gae'in on terr'ble wi' Mysy Haggart at the pump last Saturday.'

'We was juist amoosin' oorsels,' said Sam'l.

'It'll be nae amoosement to Mysy,' said Eppie, 'gin ye brak her heart.'

'Losh, Eppie,' said Sam'l, 'I didna think o' that.'

'Ye maun kin weel, Sam'l, 'at there's mony a lass wid jump at ye.'

'Ou, weel,' said Sam'l, implying that a man must take these things as they come.

'For ye're a dainty chield to look at, Sam'l.'

'Do ye think so, Eppie? Ay, ay; oh, I d'na kin am onything by the ordinar.'

'Ye mayna be,' said Eppie, 'but lasses doesna do to be ower partikler.'

Sam'l resented this, and prepared to depart again.

'Ye'll no tell Bell that?' he asked, anxiously.

'Tell her what?'

'Aboot me an' Mysy.'

'We'll see hoo ye behave yersel, Sam'l.'

'No 'at I care, Eppie; ye can tell her gin ye like. I widna think twice o' tellin her mysel.'

'The Lord forgie ye for leein', Sam'l,' said Eppie, as he disappeared down Tammy Tosh's close. Here he came upon Henders Webster.

'Ye're late, Sam'l,' said Henders.

'What for?'

'Ou, I was thinkin' ye wid be gaen the length o' T'nowhead the nicht, an' I saw Sanders Elshioner makkin's wy there an oor syne.'

'Did ye?' cried Sam'l, adding craftily, 'but it's naething to me.'

'Tod, lad,' said Henders, 'gin ye dinna buckle to, Sanders'll be carryin' her off.'

Sam'l flung back his head and passed on.

'Sam'l!' cried Henders after him.

'Ay,' said Sam'l, wheeling round.

'Gie Bell a kiss frae me.'

The full force of this joke struck neither all at once. Sam'l began to smile at it as he turned down the school-wynd, and it came upon Henders while he was in his garden feeding his ferret. Then he slapped his legs gleefully, and explained the conceit to Will'um Byars, who went into the house and thought it over.

There were twelve or twenty little groups of men in the square, which was lit by a flare of oil suspended over a cadger's cart. Now and again a staid young woman passed through the square with a basket on her arm, and if she had lingered long enough to give them time, some of the idlers would have addressed her. As it was, they gazed after her, and then grinned to each other.

'Ay, Sam'l,' said two or three young men, as Sam'l joined them beneath the town clock.

'Ay, Davit,' replied Sam'l.

This group was composed of some of the sharpest wits in Thrums, and it was not to be expected that they would let this opportunity pass. Perhaps when Sam'l joined them he knew what was in store for him.

'Was ye lookin' for T'nowhead's Bell, Sam'l?' asked one.

'Or mebbe ye was wantin' the minister?' suggested another, the same who had walked out twice with Chirsty Duff and not married her after all.

Sam'l could not think of a good reply at the moment, so he laughed good-naturedly.

'Ondoobtedly she's a snod bit crittur,' said Davit, archly.

'An' michty clever wi' her fingers,' added Jamie Deuchars.

'Man, I've thocht o' makkin' up to Bell mysel,' said Pete Ogle. 'Wid there be ony chance, think ye, Sam'l?'

'I'm thinkin' she widna hae ye for her first, Pete,' replied Sam'l, in one of those happy flashes that come to some men, 'but there's nae sayin' but what she micht tak ye to finish up wi'.'

The unexpectedness of this sally startled every one. Though Sam'l did not set up for a wit, however, like Davit, it was notorious that he could say a cutting thing once in a way.

'Did ye ever see Bell reddin up?' asked Pete, recovering from his overthrow. He was a man who bore no malice.

104 **J. M. BARRIE**

'It's a sicht,' said Sam'l, solemnly.

'Hoo will that be?' asked Jamie Deuchars.

'It's weel worth yer while,' said Peter, 'to ging atower to the T'nowhead an' see. Ye'll mind the closed-in beds i' in the kitchen? Ay, weel, they're a fell spoilt crew, T'nowhead's litlins, an' no that aisy to manage. Th' ither lasses Lisbeth's hae'n had a michty trouble wi' them. When they war i' the middle o' their reddin up the bairns wid come tumlin' about the floor, but, sal, I assure ye, Bell didna fash lang wi' them. Did she, Sam'l?'

'She did not,' said Sam'l, dropping into a fine mode of speech to add emphasis to his remark.

'I'll tell ye what she did,' said Pete to the others. 'She juist lifted up the litlins, twa at a time, an' flung them into the coffin-beds. Syne she snibbit the doors on them, an' keepit them there till the floor was dry.'

'Ay, man, did she so?' said Davit, admiringly.

'I've seen her do't myself,' said Sam'l.

'There's no a lassie maks better bannocks this side o' Fetter Lums,' continued Pete.

'Her mither tocht her that,' said Sam'l; 'she was a gran' han' at the bakin', Kitty Ogilvy.'

'I've heard say,' remarked Jamie, putting it this way so as not to tie himself down to anything, ' 'at Bell's scones is equal to Mag Lunan's.'

'So they are,' said Sam'l, almost fiercely.

'I ken she's a neat han' at singein' a hen,' said Pete.

'An' wi't a',' said Davit, 'she's a snod, canty bit stocky in her Sabbath claes.'

'If onything, thick in the waist,' suggested Jamie.

'I dinna see that,' said Sam'l.

'I d'na care for her hair either,' continued Jamie, who was very nice in his tastes; 'something mair yallowchy wid be an improvement.'

'A'body kins,' growled Sam'l, ' 'at black hair's the bonniest.'

The others chuckled.

'Puir Sam'l!' Pete said.

Sam'l not being certain whether this should be received with a smile or a frown opened his mouth wide as a kind of compromise. This was position one with him for thinking things over.

Few Auld Lichts, as I have said, went the length of choosing a helpmate for themselves. One day a young man's friends would see him mending the washing tub of a maiden's mother. They kept the joke until Saturday night, and then he learned from them what he had been after. It dazed him for a time, but in a year or so he grew accustomed to the idea, and they were then married. With a little help he fell in love just like other people.

Sam'l was going the way of the others, but he found it difficult to come to the point. He only went courting once a week, and he could never take up the running at the place where he left off the Saturday before. Thus he had not, so far, made great headway. His method of making up to Bell had been to drop in at T'nowhead on Saturday nights and talk with the farmer about the rinderpest.

The farm kitchen was Bell's testimonial. Its chairs, tables, and stools were scoured by her to the whiteness of Rob Angus's saw-mill boards, and the muslin blind on the window was starched like a child's pinafore. Bell was brave, too, as well as energetic. Once Thrums had been overrun with thieves. It is now thought that there may have been only one, but he had the wicked cleverness of a gang. Such was his repute that there were weavers who spoke of locking their doors when they went from home. He was not very skilful, however, being generally caught, and when they said they knew he was a robber he gave them their things back and went away. If they had given him time there is no doubt that he would have gone off with his plunder. One night he went to T'nowhead, and Bell, who slept in the kitchen, was wakened by the noise. She knew who it would be, so she rose and dressed herself, and went to look for him with a candle. The thief had not known what to do when he

got in, and as it was very lonely he was glad to see Bell. She
told him he ought to be ashamed of himself and would not
let him out by the door until he had taken off his boots so
as not to soil the carpet.

On this Saturday evening Sam'l stood his ground in the
square, until by and by he found himself alone. There were
other groups there still, but his circle had melted away. They
went separately, and no one said good-night. Each took himself off slowly, backing out of the group until he was fairly
started.

Sam'l looked about him, and then, seeing that the others
had gone, walked round the townhouse into the darkness of
the brae that leads down and then up to the farm of T'nowhead.

To get into the good graces of Lisbeth Fargus you had to
know her ways and humour them. Sam'l, who was a student
of women, knew this, and so, instead of pushing the door
open and walking in, he went through the rather ridiculous
ceremony of knocking. Sanders Elshioner was also aware of
this weakness of Lisbeth's, but, though he often made up
his mind to knock, the absurdity of the thing prevented his
doing so when he reached the door. T'nowhead himself
had never got used to his wife's refined notions, and when
anyone knocked he always started to his feet, thinking there
must be something wrong.

Lisbeth came to the door, her expansive figure blocking
the way in.

'Sam'l,' she said.

'Lisbeth,' said Sam'l.

He shook hands with the farmer's wife, knowing that she
liked it, but only said, 'Ay, Bell,' to his sweetheart, 'Ay,
T'nowhead,' to McQuhatty, and 'It's yersel, Sanders,' to
his rival.

They were all sitting round the fire, T'nowhead with his
feet on the ribs, wondering why he felt so warm, and Bell
darned a stocking, while Lisbeth kept an eye on a goblet full
of potatoes.

'Sit into the fire, Sam'l,' said the farmer, not, however, making way for him.

'Na, na,' said Sam'l, 'I'm to bide nae time.' Then he sat into the fire. His face was turned away from Bell, and when she spoke he answered her without looking round. Sam'l felt a little anxious. Sanders Elshioner, who had one leg shorter than the other, but looked well when sitting, seemed suspiciously at home. He asked Bell questions out of his own head, which was beyond Sam'l, and once he said something to her in such a low voice that the others could not catch it. T'nowhead asked curiously what it was, and Sanders explained that he had only said, 'Ay, Bell, the morn's the Sabbath.' There was nothing startling in this, but Sam'l did not like it. He began to wonder if he was too late, and had he seen his opportunity would have told Bell of a nasty rumour that Sanders intended to go over to the Free Church if they would make him kirk-officer.

Sam'l had the goodwill of T'nowhead's wife, who liked a polite man. Sanders did his best, but from want of practice he constantly made mistakes. Tonight, for instance, he wore his hat in the house because he did not like to put up his hand and take it off. T'nowhead had not taken his off either, but that was because he meant to go out by and by and lock the byre door. It was impossible to say which of her lovers Bell preferred. The proper course with an Auld Licht lassie was to prefer the man who proposed to her.

'Ye'll bide a wee, an' hae something to eat?' Lisbeth asked Sam'l, with her eyes on the goblet.

'No, I thank ye,' said Sam'l, with true genteelity.

'Ye'll better?'

'I dinna think it.'

'Hoots aye; what's to hender ye?'

'Weel, since ye're sae pressin', I'll bide.'

No one asked Sanders to stay. Bell could not, for she was but the servant, and T'nowhead knew that the kick his wife had given him meant that he was not to do so either. Sanders whistled to show that he was not uncomfortable.

'Ay, then, I'll be stappin' ower the brae,' he said at last.

He did not go, however. There was sufficient pride in him to get him off his chair, but only slowly, for he had to get accustomed to the notion of going. At intervals of two or three minutes he remarked that he must now be going. In the same circumstances Sam'l would have acted similarly. For a Thrums man it is one of the hardest things in life to get away from anywhere.

At last Lisbeth saw that something must be done. The potatoes were burning, and T'nowhead had an invitation on his tongue.

'Yes, I'll hae to be movin,' said Sanders, hopelessly, for the fifth time.

'Guid nicht to ye, then, Sanders,' said Lisbeth. 'Gie the door a fling-to, ahent ye.'

Sanders, with a mighty effort, pulled himself together. He looked boldly at Bell, and then took off his hat carefully. Sam'l saw with misgivings that there was something in it which was not a handkerchief. It was a paper bag glittering with gold braid, and contained such an assortment of sweets as lads bought for their lasses on the Muckle Friday.

'Hae, Bell,' said Sanders, handing the bag to Bell in an offhand way as if it were but a trifle. Nevertheless he was a little excited, for he went off without saying good-night.

No one spoke. Bell's face was crimson, T'nowhead fidgeted on his chair, and Lisbeth looked at Sam'l. The weaver was strangely calm and collected, though he would have liked to know whether this was a proposal.

'Sit in by to the table, Sam'l,' said Lisbeth, trying to look as if things were as they had been before.

She put a saucerful of butter, salt, and pepper near the fire to melt, for melted butter is the shoeing-horn that helps over a meal of potatoes. Sam'l, however, saw what the hour required, and jumping up, he seized his bonnet.

'Hing the tatties higher up the joist, Lisbeth,' he said with dignity; 'I'se be back in ten meenits.'

He hurried out of the house, leaving the others looking at each other.

'What do ye think?' asked Lisbeth.

'I d'na kin,' faltered Bell.

'Thae tatties is lang o' comin' to the boil,' said T'nowhead.

In some circles a lover who behaved like Sam'l would have been suspected of intent upon his rival's life, but neither Bell nor Lisbeth did the weaver that injustice. In a case of this kind it does not much matter what T'nowhead thought.

The ten minutes had barely passed when Sam'l was back in the farm kitchen. He was too flurried to knock this time, and, indeed, Lisbeth did not expect it of him.

'Bell, hae!' he cried, handing his sweetheart a tinsel bag twice the size of Sanders's gift.

'Losh preserve's!' exclaimed Lisbeth; 'I'se warrant there's a shillin's worth.'

'There's a' that, Lisbeth—an' mair,' said Sam'l, firmly.

'I thank ye Sam'l,' said Bell, feeling an unwonted elation as she gazed at the two paper bags in her lap.

'Ye're ower extravegint, Sam'l,' Lisbeth said.

'Not at all,' said Sam'l; 'not at all. But I widna advise ye to eat thae ither anes, Bell—they're second quality.'

Bell drew back a step from Sam'l.

'How do ye ken?' asked the farmer shortly, for he liked Sanders.

'I spiered i' the shop,' said Sam'l.

The goblet was placed on a broken plate on the table with the saucer beside it, and Sam'l, like the others, helped himself. What he did was to take potatoes from the pot with his fingers, peel off their coats, and then dip them into the butter. Lisbeth would have liked to provide knives and forks, but she knew that beyond a certain point T'nowhead was master in his own house. As for Sam'l, he felt victory in his hands, and began to think that he had gone too far.

In the meantime Sanders, little witting that Sam'l had trumped his trick, was sauntering along the kirk-wynd with

his hat on the side of his head. Fortunately he did not meet
the minister.

The courting of T'nowhead's Bell reached its crisis one
Sabbath about a month after the events above recorded. The
minister was in great force that day, but it is no part of mine
to tell how he bore himself. I was there, and am not likely
to forget the scene. It was a fateful Sabbath for T'nowhead's
Bell and her swains, and destined to be remembered for the
painful scandal which they perpetrated in their passion.

Bell was not in the kirk. There being an infant of six
months in the house it was a question of either Lisbeth or
the lassie's staying at home with him, and though Lisbeth
was unselfish in a general way, she could not resist the
delight of going to church. She had nine children besides
the baby, and being but a woman, it was the pride of her
life to march them into the T'nowhead pew, so well watched
that they dared not misbehave, and so tightly packed that
they could not fall. The congregation looked at that pew,
the mothers enviously, when they sang the lines—

> 'Jerusalem like a city is
> Compactly built together.'

The first half of the service had been gone through on this
particular Sunday without anything remarkable happening.
It was at the end of the psalm which preceded the sermon
that Sanders Elshioner, who sat near the door, lowered his
head until it was no higher than the pews, and in that
attitude, looking almost like a four-footed animal, slipped
out of the church. In their eagerness to be at the sermon
many of the congregation did not notice him, and those who
did put the matter by in their minds for future investigation.
Sam'l, however, could not take it so coolly. From his seat in
the gallery he saw Sanders disappear, and his mind misgave
him. With the true lover's instinct he understood it all.
Sanders had been struck by the fine turn-out in the T'nowhead pew. Bell was alone at the farm. What an opportunity
to work one's way up to a proposal. T'nowhead was so

overrun with children that such a chance seldom occurred, except on a Sabbath. Sanders, doubtless, was off to propose, and he, Sam'l, was left behind.

The suspense was terrible. Sam'l and Sanders had both known all along that Bell would take the first of the two who asked her. Even those who thought her proud admitted that she was modest. Bitterly the weaver repented having waited so long. Now it was too late. In ten minutes Sanders would be at T'nowhead; in an hour all would be over. Sam'l rose to his feet in a daze. His mother pulled him down by the coat-tail, and his father shook him, thinking he was walking in his sleep. He tottered past them, however, hurried up the aisle, which was so narrow that Dan'l Ross could only reach his seat by walking sideways, and was gone before the minister could do more than stop in the middle of a whirl and gape in horror after him.

A number of the congregation felt that day the advantage of sitting in the loft. What was a mystery to those downstairs was revealed to them. From the gallery windows they had a fine open view to the south; and as Sam'l took the common, which was a short cut though a steep ascent, to T'nowhead, he was never out of their line of vision. Sanders was not to be seen, but they guessed rightly the reason why. Thinking he had ample time, he had gone round by the main road to save his boots—perhaps a little scared by what was coming. Sam'l's design was to forestall him by taking the shorter path over the burn and up the commonty.

It was a race for a wife, and several onlookers in the gallery braved the minister's displeasure to see who won. Those who favoured Sam'l's suit exultingly saw him leap the stream, while the friends of Sanders fixed their eyes on the top of the common where it ran into the road. Sanders must come into sight there, and the one who reached this point first would get Bell.

As Auld Lichts do not walk abroad on the Sabbath, Sanders would probably not be delayed. The chances were in his favour. Had it been any other day in the week Sam'l might have run. So some of the congregation in the gallery were thinking, when suddenly they saw him bend low and then take to his heels. He had caught sight of Sanders's head bobbing over the hedge that separated the road from the common, and feared that Sanders might see him. The congregation who could crane their necks sufficiently saw a black object, which they guessed to be the carter's hat, crawling along the hedge-top. For a moment it was motionless, and then it shot ahead. The rivals had seen each other. It was now a hot race. Sam'l, dissembling no longer, clattered up the common, becoming smaller and smaller to the onlookers as he neared the top. More than one person in the gallery almost rose to their feet in their excitement. Sam'l had it. No, Sanders was in front. Then the two figures disappeared from view. They seemed to run into each other at the top of the brae, and no one could say who was first. The congregation looked at one another. Some of them perspired. But the minister held on his course.

Sam'l had just been in time to cut Sanders out. It was the weaver's saving that Sanders saw this when his rival turned the corner; for Sam'l was sadly blown. Sanders took in the situation and gave in at once. The last hundred yards of the distance he covered at his leisure, and when he arrived at his destination he did not go in. It was a fine afternoon for the time of year, and he went round to have a look at the pig, about which T'nowhead was a little sinfully puffed up.

'Ay,' said Sanders, digging his fingers critically into the grunting animal; 'quite so.'

'Grumph,' said the pig, getting reluctantly to his feet.

'Ou ay; yes,' said Sanders thoughtfully.

Then he sat down on the edge of the sty, and looked long and silently at an empty bucket. But whether his thoughts were of T'nowhead's Bell, whom he had lost forever, or of the food the farmer fed his pig on, is not known.

'Lord preserve 's! Are ye no' at the kirk?' cried Bell, nearly dropping the baby as Sam'l broke into the room.

'Bell!' cried Sam'l.

Then T'nowhead's Bell knew that her hour had come.

'Sam'l,' she faltered.

'Will ye hae's Bell?' demanded Sam'l, glaring at her sheepishly.

'Ay,' answered Bell.

Sam'l fell into a chair.

'Bring's a drink o' water Bell,' he said.

But Bell thought the occasion required milk, and there was none in the kitchen. She went out to the byre, still with the baby in her arms, and saw Sanders Elshioner sitting gloomily on the pigsty.

'Weel, Bell,' said Sanders.

'I thocht ye'd been at the kirk, Sanders,' said Bell.

Then there was a silence between them.

'Has Sam'l spiered ye, Bell?' asked Sanders, solidly.

'Ay,' said Bell, again, and this time there was a tear in her eye. Sanders was little better than an 'orra man', and Sam'l was a weaver, and yet——. But it was too late now. Sanders gave the pig a vicious poke with a stick, and when it had ceased to grunt, Bell was back in the kitchen. She had forgotten about the milk, however, and Sam'l only got water after all.

In after days, when the story of Bell's wooing was told, there were some who held that the circumstances would have almost justified the lassie in giving Sam'l the go-by. But these perhaps forgot that her other lover was in the same predicament as the accepted one—that of the two, indeed, he was the more to blame, for he set off to T'nowhead on the Sabbath of his own accord, while Sam'l only ran after him. And then there is no one to say for certain whether Bell heard of her suitors' delinquencies until Lisbeth's return from the kirk. Sam'l could never remember whether he told her, and Bell was not sure whether, if he did, she took it in. Sanders was greatly in demand for weeks after to tell what he knew of the affair, but though he was twice asked to tea to the manse among the trees, and subjected thereafter to ministerial cross-examinations, this is all he

told. He remained at the pigsty until Sam'l left the farm,
when he joined him at the top of the brae, and they went
home together.

'It's yersel, Sanders,' said Sam'l.

'It is so, Sam'l,' said Sanders.

'Very cauld,' said Sam'l.

'Blawy,' assented Sanders.

After a pause—

'Sam'l,' said Sanders.

'Ay.'

'I'm hearin' yer to be mairit.'

'Ay.'

'Weel, Sam'l, she's a snod bit lassie.'

'Thank ye,' said Sam'l.

'I had aince a kin' o' notion o' Bell myself,' continued
Sanders.

'Ye had?'

'Yes, Sam'l; but I thocht better o't.'

'Hoo d'ye mean?' asked Sam'l, a little anxiously.

'Weel, Sam'l, mairitch is a terrible responsibeelity.'

'It is so,' said Sam'l, wincing.

'An' no the thing to tak up withoot conseedersation.'

'But it's a blessed and honourable state, Sanders; ye've
heard the minister on't.'

'They say,' continued the relentless Sanders, ' 'at the
minister doesna get on sair wi' the wife himsel.'

'So they do,' cried Sam'l, with a sinking at the heart.

'I've been telt,' Sanders went on, ' 'at gin ye can get the
upper han' o' the wife for a while at first, there's the mair
chance o' a harmonious exeestence.'

'Bell's no' the lassie,' said Sam'l appealingly, 'to thwart
her man.'

Sanders smiled.

'D'y ye think she is, Sanders?'

'Weel Sam'l, I d'na want to fluster ye, but she's been
ower lang wi' Lisbeth Fargus no' to hae learnt her ways. An
a'body kins what a life T'nowhead has wi' her.'

'Guid sake, Sanders, hoo did ye no speak o' this afore?'

'I thocht ye kent o't, Sam'l.'

They had now reached the square, and the U.P. kirk was coming out. The Auld Licht kirk would be half an hour yet.

'But, Sanders,' said Sam'l, brightening up, 'ye was on yer way to spier her yersel.'

'I was, Sam'l,' said Sanders, 'an I canna but be thankfu ye was ower quick for 's.'

'Gin't hadna been you,' said Sam'l, 'I wid never hae thocht o't.'

'I'm sayin' naething agin Bell,' pursued the other, 'but man Sam'l, a body should be mair deleeberate in a thing o' the kind.'

'It was michty hurried,' said Sam'l, woefully.

'It's a serious thing to spier a lassie,' said Sanders.

'It's an awfu thing,' said Sam'l.

'But we'll hope for the best,' added Sanders, in a hopeless voice.

They were close to the Tenements now, and Sam'l looked as if he were on his way to be hanged.

'Sam'l?'

'Ay, Sanders.'

'Did ye—did ye kiss her, Sam'l?'

'Na.'

'Hoo?'

'There's was varra little time, Sanders.'

'Half an 'oor,' said Sanders.

'Was there? Man Sanders, to tell ye the truth, I never thocht o't.'

Then the soul of Sanders Elshioner was filled with contempt for Sam'l Dickie.

The scandal blew over. At first it was expected that the minister would interfere to prevent the union, but beyond intimating from the pulpit that the souls of Sabbath-breakers were beyond praying for, and then praying for Sam'l and Sanders at great length, with a word thrown in for Bell, he let things take their course. Some said it was because

he was always frightened lest his young men should intermarry with other denominations, but Sanders explained it
differently to Sam'l.

'I hav'na a word to say agin the minister,' he said;
'they're gran' prayers, but Sam'l, he's a mairit man himsel.'

'He's a' the better for that, Sanders, isna he?'

'Do ye no see,' asked Sanders, compassionately, ' 'at he's
tryin' to mak the best o't?'

'Oh, Sanders, man!' said Sam'l.

'Cheer up, Sam'l,' said Sanders, 'it'll sune be ower.'

Their having been rival suitors had not interfered with
the friendship. On the contrary, while they had hitherto
been mere acquaintances, they became inseparables as the
wedding drew near. It was noticed that they had much to say
to each other, and that when they could not get a room to
themselves they wandered about together in the churchyard.
When Sam'l had anything to tell Bell he sent Sanders to tell
it, and Sanders did as he was bid. There was nothing that
he would not have done for Sam'l.

The more obliging Sanders was, however, the sadder
Sam'l grew. He never laughed now on Saturdays, and some-
times his loom was silent half the day. Sam'l felt that
Sanders's was the kindness of a friend for a dying man.

It was to be a penny wedding, and Lisbeth Fargus said it
was delicacy that made Sam'l superintend the fitting-up of
the barn by deputy. Once he came to see it in person, but he
looked so ill that Sanders had to see him home. This was on
the Thursday afternoon, and the wedding was fixed for
Friday.

'Sanders, Sanders,' said Sam'l, in a voice strangely unlike
his own, 'it'll a' be ower by this time the morn.'

'It will,' said Sanders.

'If I had only kent her langer,' continued Sam'l.

'It wid hae been safer,' said Sanders.

'Did ye see the yellow floor in Bell's bonnet?' asked the
accepted swain.

'Ay,' said Sanders, reluctantly.

'I'm dootin'—I'm sair dootin' she's but a flichty, licht-hearted crittur after a'.'

'I had ay my suspeecions o't,' said Sanders.

'Ye hae kent her langer than me,' said Sam'l.

'Yes,' said Sanders, 'but there's nae gettin' at the heart o' women. Man, Sam'l, they're desperate cunnin'.'

'I'm dootin't; I'm sair dootin't.'

'It'll be a warnin' to ye, Sam'l, no to be in sic a hurry i' the futur,' said Sanders.

Sam'l groaned.

'Ye'll be gaein up to the manse to arrange wi' the minister the morn's mornin',' continued Sanders, in a subdued voice.

Sam'l looked wistfully at his friend.

'I canna do't, Sanders,' he said, 'I canna do't.'

'Ye maun,' said Sanders.

'It's aisy to speak,' retorted Sam'l, bitterly.

'We have a' oor troubles, Sam'l,' said Sanders, soothingly, 'an' every man maun bear his ain burdens. Johnny Davie's wife's dead, an' he's no repinin'.'

'Ay,' said Sam'l, 'but a death's no a mairitch. We hae haen deaths in our family too.'

'It may a' be for the best,' added Sanders, 'an' there wid be a michty talk i' the hale country-side gin ye didna ging to the minister like a man.'

'I maun hae langer to think o't,' said Sam'l.

'Bell's mairitch is the morn,' said Sanders decisively.

Sam'l glanced up with a wild look in his eyes.

'Sanders,' he cried.

'Sam'l?'

'Ye hae been a guid friend to me, Sanders, in this sair affliction.'

'Nothing ava,' said Sanders; 'doun't mention'd.'

'But, Sanders, ye canna deny but what your rinnin oot o' the kirk that awfu' day was at the bottom o'd a'.'

'It was so,' said Sanders, bravely.

'An' ye used to be fond o' Bell, Sanders.'

'I dinna deny't.'

'Sanders, laddie,' said Sam'l, bending forward and speaking in a wheedling voice, 'I aye thocht it was you she likeit.'

'I had some sic idea mysel,' said Sanders.

'Sanders, I canna think to pairt twa fowk sae weel suited to ane anither as you an' Bell.'

'Canna ye, Sam'l?'

'She wid mak ye a guid wife, Sanders. I hae studied her weel and she's a thrifty, douce, clever lassie. Sanders, there's no the like o' her. Mony a time, Sanders, I hae said to mysel, "There's a lass ony man micht be prood to tak." A'body says the same, Sanders. There's nae risk ava, man, nane to speak o'. Tak her, laddie, tak her, Sanders; it's a grand chance, Sanders. She's yours for the spierin. I'll gie her up, Sanders.'

'Will ye, though?' said Sanders.

'What d'ye think?' asked Sam'l.

'If ye wid rayther,' said Sanders, politely.

'There's my han' on't,' said Sam'l. 'Bless ye, Sanders; ye've been a true frien' to me.'

Then they shook hands for the first time in their lives; and soon afterwards Sanders struck up the brae to T'nowhead.

Next morning Sanders Elshioner, who had been very busy the night before, put on his Sabbath clothes and strolled up to the manse.

'But—but where is Sam'l?' asked the minister; 'I must see himself.'

'It's a new arrangement,' said Sanders.

'What do you mean, Sanders?'

'Bell's to marry me,' explained Sanders.

'But—but what does Sam'l say?'

'He's willin',' said Sanders.

'And Bell?'

'She's willin', too. She perfers't.'

'It is unusual,' said the minister.

'It's a' richt,' said Sanders.

'Well, you know best,' said the minister.

'You see the hoose was taen, at ony rate,' continued Sanders. 'An I'll juist ging in til't instead o' Sam'l.'

'Quite so.'

'An' I cudna think to disappoint the lassie.'

'Your sentiments do you credit, Sanders,' said the minister; 'but I hope you do not enter upon the blessed state of matrimony without full consideration of its responsibilities. It is a serious business marriage.'

'It's a' that,' said Sanders, 'but I'm willin' to stan' the risk.'

So, as soon as it could be done, Sanders Elshioner took to wife T'nowhead's Bell, and I remember seeing Sam'l Dickie trying to dance at the penny wedding.

Years afterwards it was said in Thrums that Sam'l had treated Bell badly, but he was never sure about it himself.

'It was a near thing—a michty near thing,' he admitted in the square.

'They say,' some other weaver would remark, ' 'at it was you Bell liked best.'

'I d'na kin,' Sam'l would reply, 'but there's nae doot the lassie was fell fond o' me. Ou, a mere passin' fancy's ye micht say.'

The Lost Pibroch

NEIL MUNRO

(1864–1930)

To the make of a piper go seven years of his own learning and seven generations before. If it is in, it will out, as the Gaelic old-word says; if not, let him take to the net or sword. At the end of his seven years one born to it will stand at the start of knowledge, and leaning a fond ear to the drone, he may have parley with old folks of old affairs. Playing the tune of the 'Fairy Harp', he can hear his forefolks, plaided in skins, towsy-headed and terrible, grunting at the oars and snoring in the caves; he has his whittle and club in the 'Desperate Battle' (my own tune, my darling!), where the white-haired sea-rovers are on the shore, and a stain's on the edge of the tide; or, trying his art on Laments, he can stand by the cairn of kings, ken the colour of Fingal's hair, and see the moon-glint on the hook of the Druids!

Today there are but three pipers in the wide world, from the Sound of Sleat to the Wall of France. Who they are, and what their tartan, it is not for one to tell who has no heed for a thousand dirks in his doublet, but they may be known by the lucky ones who hear them. Namely players tickle the chanter and take out but the sound; the three give a tune the charm that I mention—a long thought and a bard's thought, and they bring the notes from the deeps of time, and the tale from the heart of the man who made it.

But not of the three best in Albainn today is my story, for they have not the Lost Pibroch. It is of the three best, who were not bad, in a place I ken—Half Town that stands in the wood.

You may rove for a thousand years on league-long brogues, or hurry on fairy wings from isle to isle and deep to deep, and find no equal to that same Half Town. It is not the splendour of it, nor the riches of its folk; it is not any great routh of field or sheep-fank, but the scented winds of it, and the comfort of the pine-trees round and about it on every hand. My mother used to be saying (when I had the notion of fairy tales), that once on a time, when the woods were young and thin, there was a road through them, and the pick of children of a country-side wandered among them into this place to play at sheilings. Up grew the trees, fast and tall, and shut the little folks in so that the way out they could not get if they had the mind for it. But never an out they wished for. They grew with the firs and alders, a quiet clan in the heart of the big wood, clear of the world out-by.

But now and then wanderers would come to Half Town,

through the gloomy coves, under the tall trees. There were packmen with tales of the out-world. There were broken men flying from rope or hatchet. And once on a day of days came two pipers—Gilian, of Clan Lachlan of Strathlachlan, and Rory Ban, of the Macnaghtons of Dundarave. They had seen Half Town from the sea—smoking to the clear air on the hill-side; and through the weary woods they came, and the dead quiet of them, and they stood on the edge of the fir-belt.

Before them was what might be a township in a dream, and to be seen at the one look, for it stood on the rising hill that goes back on Lochow.

The dogs barked, and out from the houses and in from the fields came the quiet clan to see who could be here. Biggest of all the men, one they named Coll, cried on the strangers to come forward; so out they went from the wood-edge, neither coy nor crouse, but the equal of friend or foe, and they passed the word of day.

'Hunting,' they said, 'in Easachosain, we found the roe come this way.'

'If this way she came, she's at Duglas Water by now, so you may bide and eat. Few, indeed, come calling on us in Half Town; but whoever they are, here's the open door, and the horn spoon, and the stool by the fire.'

He took them in and he fed them, nor asked their names nor calling, but when they had eaten well he said to Rory, 'You have skill of the pipes; I know by the drum of your fingers on the horn spoon.'

'I have tried them,' said Rory, with a laugh, 'a bit—a bit. My friend here is a player.'

'You have the art?' asked Coll.

'Well, not what you might call the whole art,' said Gilian, 'but I can play—oh yes! I can play two or three ports.'

'You can that!' said Rory.

'No better than yourself, Rory.'

'Well, maybe not, but—anyway, not all tunes; I allow you do "Mackay's Banner" in a pretty style.'

'Pipers,' said Coll, with a quick eye to a coming quarrel, 'I will take you to one of your own trade in this place— Paruig Dall, who is namely for music.'

'It's a name that's new to me,' said Rory, short and sharp, but up they rose and followed Big Coll.

He took them to a bothy behind the Half Town, a place with turf walls and never a window, where a blind man sat winding pirns for the weaver-folks.

'This,' said Coll, showing the strangers in at the door, 'is a piper of parts, or I'm no judge, and he has as rare a stand of great pipes as ever my eyes sat on.'

'I have that same,' said the blind man, with his face to the door. 'Your friends, Coll?'

'Two pipers of the neighbourhood,' Rory made answer. 'It was for no piping we came here, but by the accident of the chase. Still and on, if pipes are here, piping there might be.'

'So be it,' cried Coll; 'but I must go back to my cattle till night comes. Get you to the playing with Paruig Dall, and I'll find you here when I come back.' And with that he turned about and went off.

Paruig put down the ale and cake before the two men, and 'Welcome you are,' said he.

They ate the stranger's bite, and lipped the stranger's cup, and then, 'Whistle "The Macraes' March", my fair fellow,' said the blind man.

'How ken you I'm fair?' asked Rory.

'Your tongue tells that. A fair man has aye a soft bit in his speech, like the lapping of milk in a cogie; and a black one, like your friend there, has the sharp ring of a thin burn in frost running into an iron pot. "The Macraes' March", *laochain*.'

Rory put a pucker on his mouth and played a little of the fine tune.

'So!' said the blind man, with his head to a side, 'you had your lesson. And you, my Strathlachlan boy without beard, do you ken *Muinntir a' Ghlinne so?*'[1]

---

[1] Lament for the Massacre of Glencoe (1692). See below. [Editor.]

'How ken ye I'm Strathlachlan and beardless?' asked Gilian.

'Strathlachlan by the smell of herring-scale from your side of the house (for they told me yesterday the gannets were flying down Strathlachlan way, and that means fishing), and you have no beard I know, but in what way I know I do not know.'

Gilian had the *siubhal* of the pibroch but begun when the blind man stopped him.

'You have it,' he said, 'you have it in a way, the Macarthur's way, and that's not my way. But, no matter, let us to our piping.'

The three men sat them down on three stools on the clay floor, and the blind man's pipes passed round between them.

'First,' said Paruig (being the man of the house, and to get the vein of his own pipes)—'first I'll put on them "The Vaunting".' He stood to his shanks, a lean old man and straight, and the big drone came nigh on the black rafters. He filled the bag at a breath and swung a lover's arm round about it. To those who know not the pipes, the feel of the bag in the oxter is a gaiety lost. The sweet round curve is like a girl's waist; it is friendly and warm in the crook of the elbow and against a man's side, and to press it is to bring laughing or tears.

The bothy roared with the tuning, and then the air came melting and sweet from the chanter. Eight steps up, four to the turn, and eight down went Paruig, and the *piobaireachd* rolled to his fingers like a man's rhyming. The two men sat on the stools, with their elbows on their knees, and listened.

He played but the *urlar*, and the *crunluadh* to save time, and he played them well.

'Good indeed! Splendid, my old fellow!' cried the two; and said Gilian, 'You have a way of it in the *crunluadh* not my way, but as good as ever I heard.'

'It is the way of Padruig Og,' said Rory. 'Well I know it! There are tunes and tunes, and "The Vaunting" is not bad in its way, but give me "The Macraes' March".'

He jumped to his feet and took the pipes from the old man's hands, and over his shoulder with the drones.

'Stand back, lad!' he cried to Gilian, and Gilian went nearer the door.

The march came fast to the chanter—the old tune, the fine tune that Kintail has heard before, when the wild men in their red tartan came over hill and moor; the tune with the river in it, the fast river and the courageous that kens not stop nor tarry, that runs round rock and over fall with a good humour, yet no mood for anything but the way before it. The tune of the heroes, the tune of the pinelands and the broad straths, the tune that the eagles of Loch Duich crack their beaks together when they hear, and the crows of that country-side would as soon listen to as the squeal of their babies.

'Well! mighty well!' said Paruig Dall. 'You have the tartan of the clan in it.'

'Not bad, I'll allow,' said Gilian. 'Let me try.'

He put his fingers on the holes, and his heart took a leap back over two generations, and yonder was Glencoe! The grey day crawled on the white hills and the black roofs smoked below. Snow choked the pass, *eas* and corri filled with drift and flatted to the brae-face; the wind tossed quirky and cruel in the little bushes and among the smooring lintels and joists; the blood of old and young lappered on the hearthstone, and the bairn, with a knifed throat, had an icy lip on a frozen teat. Out of the place went the tramped path of the Campbell butchers—far on their way to Glenlyon and the towns of paper and ink and liars—*Muinntir a' ghlinne so, muinntir a' ghlinne so!*—'People, people, people of this glen, this glen, this glen!'

'Dogs! dogs! O God of grace—dogs and cowards!' cried Rory. 'I could be dirking a Diarmaid or two if by luck they were near me.'

'It is piping that is to be here,' said Paruig, 'and it is not piping for an hour nor piping for an evening, but the piping of Dunvegan that stops for sleep nor supper.'

So the three stayed in the bothy and played tune about while time went by the door. The birds flew home to the branches, the long-necked beasts flapped off to the shore to spear their flat fish; the rutting deers bellowed with loud throats in the deeps of the wood that stands round Half Town, and the scents of the moist night came gusty round the door. Over the back of Auchnabreac the sun trailed his plaid of red and yellow, and the loch stretched salt and dark from Cairn Dubh to Creaggans.

In from the hill the men and the women came, weary-legged, and the bairns nodded at their heels. Sleepiness was on the land, but the pipers, piping in the bothy, kept the world awake.

'We will go to bed in good time,' said the folks, eating their suppers at their doors; 'in good time when this tune is ended.' But tune came on tune, and every tune better than its neighbour, and they waited.

A cruisie-light was set alowe in the blind man's bothy, and the three men played old tunes and new tunes—salute and lament and brisk dances and marches that coax tired brogues on the long roads.

'Here's "Tulloch Ard" for you, and tell me who made it,' said Rory.

'Who kens that? Here's "Raasay's Lament", the best port Padruig Mor ever put together.'

'Tunes and tunes. I'm for "A Kiss o' the King's Hand".'

> 'Thug mi pòg 'us pòg 'us pòg,
> Thug mi pòg do làmh an righ,
> Cha do chuir gaoth an craicionn caorach,
> Fear a fhuair an fhaoilt ach mi!'[1]

Then a quietness came on Half Town, for the piping stopped, and the people at their doors heard but their blood thumping and the night-hags in the dark of the firwood.

[1] I got a kiss, a kiss, a kiss,
I got a kiss on the king's hand.
It was I alone who put the wind in the sheepskin,
The man who got the salute was me. [Editor.]

'A little longer and maybe there will be more,' they said to each other, and they waited; but no more music came from the drones, so they went in to bed.

There was quiet over Half Town, for the three pipers talked about the Lost Tune.

'A man my father knew,' said Gilian, 'heard a bit of it once in Moideart. A terrible fine tune he said it was, but sore on the mind.'

'It would be the tripling,' said the Macnaghton, stroking a reed with a fond hand.

'Maybe. Tripling is ill enough, but what is tripling? There is more in piping than brisk fingers. Am I not right, Paruig?'

'Right, oh! right. The Lost *Piobaireachd* asks for skilly tripling, but Macruimen himself could not get at the core of it for all his art.'

'You have heard it then!' cried Gilian.

The blind man stood up and filled out his breast.

'Heard it!' he said; 'I heard it, and I play it—on the *feadan*, but not on the full set. To play the tune I mention on the full set is what I have not done since I came to Half Town.'

'I have ten round pieces in my sporran, and a bonnet-brooch it would take much to part me from; but they're there for the man who'll play me the Lost *Piobaireachd*,' said Gilian, with the words tripping each other to the tip of his tongue.

'And here's a Macnaghton's fortune on the top of the round pieces,' cried Rory, emptying his purse on the table.

The old man's face got hot and angry. 'I am not,' he said, 'a tinker's minstrel, to give my tuning for bawbees and a quaich of ale. The king himself could not buy the tune I ken if he had but a whim for it. But when pipers ask it they can have it, and it's yours without a fee. Still if you think to learn the tune by my piping once, poor's the delusion. It is not a port to be picked up like a cockle on the sand, for it takes the schooling of years and blindness forbye.'

'Blindness?'

'Blindness indeed. The thought of it is only for the dark eye.'

'If we could hear it on the full set!'

'Come out, then, on the grass, and you'll hear it, if Half Town should sleep no sleep this night.'

They went out of the bothy to the wet short grass. Ragged mists shook o'er Cowal, and on Ben Ime sat a horned moon like a galley of Lorn.

'I heard this tune from the Moideart man—the last in Albainn who knew it then, and he's in the clods,' said the blind fellow.

He had the mouthpiece at his lip, and his hand was coaxing the bag, when a bairn's cry came from a house in the Half Town—a suckling's whimper, that, heard in the night, sets a man's mind busy on the sorrows that folks are born to. The drones clattered together on the piper's elbow and he stayed.

'I have a notion,' he said to the two men. 'I did not tell you that the Lost *Piobaireachd* is the *piobaireachd* of good-byes. It is the tune of broken clans, that sets the men on the foray and makes cold hearth-stones. It was played in Glenshira when Gilleasbuig Gruamach could stretch stout swordsmen from Boshang to Ben Bhuidhe, and where are the folks of Glenshira this day? I saw a cheery night in Carnus that's over Lochow, and song and story busy about the fire, and the Moideart man played it for a wager. In the morning the weans were without fathers, and Carnus men were scattered about the wide world.'

'It must be the magic tune, sure enough,' said Gilian.

'Magic indeed, *laochain*! It is the tune that puts men on the open road, that makes restless lads and seeking women. Here's a Half Town of dreamers and men fattening for want of men's work. They forget the world is wide and round about their fir-trees, and I can make them crave for something they cannot name.'

'Good or bad, out with it,' said Rory, 'if you know it at all.'

'Maybe no', maybe no'. I am old and done. Perhaps I have lost the right skill of the tune, for it's long since I put it on the great pipe. There's in me the strong notion to try it whatever may come of it, and here's for it.'

He put his pipe up again, filled the bag at a breath, brought the booming to the drones, and then the chanter-reed cried sharp and high.

'He's on it,' said Rory in Gilian's ear.

The groundwork of the tune was a drumming on the deep notes where the sorrows lie—'Come, come, come, my children, rain on the brae and the wind blowing.'

'It is a salute,' said Rory.

'It's the strange tune anyway,' said Gilian; 'listen to the time of yon!'

The tune searched through Half Town and into the gloomy pine-wood; it put an end to the whoop of the night-hag and rang to Ben Bhreac. Boatmen deep and far on the loch could hear it, and Half Town folks sat up to listen.

Its story was the story that's ill to tell—something of the heart's longing and the curious chances of life. It bound up all the tales of all the clans, and made one tale of the Gaels' past. Dirk nor sword against the tartan, but the tartan against all else, and the Gaels' target fending the hill-land and the juicy straths from the pock-pitted little black men. The winters and the summers passing fast and furious, day and night roaring in the ears, and then again the clans at variance, and warders on every pass and on every parish.

Then the tune changed.

'Folks,' said the reeds, coaxing. 'Wide's the world and merry the road. Here's but the old story and the women we kissed before. Come, come to the flat-lands rich and full, where the wonderful new things happen and the women's lips are still to try!'

'Tomorrow,' said Gilian in his friend's ear—'tomorrow I will go jaunting to the North. It has been in my mind since Beltane.'

'One might be doing worse,' said Rory, 'and I have the notion to try a trip with my cousin to the foreign wars.'

The blind piper put up his shoulder higher and rolled the air into the *crunluadh breabach* that comes prancing with variations. Pride stiffened him from heel to hip, and hip to head, and set his sinews like steel.

He was telling of the gold to get for the searching and the bucks that may be had for the hunting. 'What,' said the reeds, 'are your poor crops, slashed by the constant rain and rotting, all for a scart in the bottom of a pot? What are your stots and heifers—black, dun, and yellow—to milch-cows and horses? Here's but the same for ever—toil and sleep, sleep and toil even on, no feud nor foray nor castles to harry—only the starved field and the sleeping moss. Let us to a brisker place! Over yonder are the long straths and the deep rivers and townships strewn thick as your corn-rigs; over yonder's the place of the packmen's tales and the packmen's wares: steep we the withies and go!'

The two men stood with heads full of bravery and dreaming—men in a carouse. 'This,' said they, 'is the notion we had, but had no words for. It's a poor trade piping and eating and making amusement when one might be wandering up and down the world. We must be packing the haversacks.'

Then the *crunluadh mach* came fast and furious on the chanter, and Half Town shook with it. It buzzed in the ear like the flowers in the Honey Croft, and made commotion among the birds rocking on their eggs in the wood.

'*So! so!*' barked the *iolair* on Craig-an-eas. 'I have heard before it was an ill thing to be satisfied; in the morning I'll try the kids on Maam-side, for the hares here are wersh and tough.' 'Hearken, dear,' said the *londubh*. 'I know now why my beak is gold; it is because I once ate richer berries than the whortle, and in season I'll look for them on the braes of Glenfinne.' 'Honk-unk,' said the fox, the cunning red fellow, 'am not I the fool to be staying on this little brae when I know so many roads elsewhere?'

And the people sitting up in their beds in Half Town moaned for something new. 'Paruig Dall is putting the strange tune on her there,' said they. 'What the meaning of it is we must ask in the morning, but, *ochanoch*! it leaves one hungry at the heart.' And then gusty winds came snell from the north, and where the dark crept first, the day made his first showing, so that Ben Ime rose black against a grey sky.

'That's the Lost *Piobaireachd*,' said Paruig Dall when the bag sunk on his arm.

And the two men looked at him in a daze.

Sometimes in the spring of the year the winds from Lorn have it their own way with the Highlands. They will come tearing furious over the hundred hills, spurred the faster by the prongs of Cruachan and Dunchuach, and the large woods of home toss before them like corn before the hook. Up come the poor roots and over on their broken arms go the tall trees, and in the morning the deer will trot through new lanes cut in the forest.

A wind of that sort came on the full of the day when the two pipers were leaving Half Town.

'Stay till the storm is over,' said the kind folks; and 'Your bed and board are here for the pipers forty days,' said Paruig Dall. But 'No' said the two; 'we have business that your *piobaireachd* put us in mind of.'

'I'm hoping that I did not play yon with too much skill,' said the old man.

'Skill or no skill,' said Gilian, 'the like of yon I never heard. You played a port that makes poor enough all ports ever one listened to, and piping's no more for us wanderers.'

'Blessings with thee!' said the folks all, and the two men went down into the black wood among the cracking trees.

Six lads looked after them, and one said, 'It is an ill day for a body to take the world for his pillow, but what say you to following the pipers?'

'It might,' said one, 'be the beginning of fortune. I am weary enough of this poor place, with nothing about it but wood and water and tufty grass. If we went now, there might be gold and girls at the other end.'

They took crooks and bonnets and went after the two pipers. And when they were gone half a day, six women said to their men, 'Where can the lads be?'

'We do not know that,' said the men, with hot faces, 'but we might be looking.' They kissed their children and went, with *cromags* in their hands, and the road they took was the road the King of Errin rides, and that is the road to the end of days.

A weary season fell on Half Town, and the very bairns dwined at the breast for a change of fortune. The women lost their strength, and said, 'Today my back is weak, tomorrow I will put things to right,' and they looked slack-mouthed and heedless-eyed at the sun wheeling round the trees. Every week a man or two would go to seek something —a lost heifer or a wounded roe that was never brought back—and a new trade came to the place, the selling of herds. Far away in the low country, where the winds are warm and the poorest have money, black-cattle were wanted, so the men of Half Town made up long droves and took them round Glen Beag and the Rest.

Wherever they went they stayed, or the clans on the road-side put them to steel, for Half Town saw them no more. And a day came when all that was left in that fine place were but women and children and a blind piper.

'Am I the only man here?' asked Paruig Dall when it came to the bit, and they told him he was.

'Then here's another for fortune!' said he, and he went down through the woods with his pipes in his oxter.

Hurricane Jack

NEIL MUNRO

(1864–1930)

I VERY often hear my friend the Captain speak of Hurri-cane Jack in terms of admiration and devotion, which would suggest that Jack is a sort of demigod. The Captain always refers to Hurricane Jack as the most experienced seaman of modern times, as the most fearless soul that ever wore oilskins, the handsomest man in Britain, so free with his money he would fling it at the birds, so generally accomplished that it would be a treat to be left a month on a desert island alone with him.

'Why is he called Hurricane Jack?' I asked the Captain once.

'What the duvvle else would you caal him?' asked Para Handy. 'Nobody ever caals him anything else than Hurricane Jeck.'

'Quite so, but why?' I persisted.

Para Handy scratched the back of his neck, made the usual gesture as if he were going to scratch his ear, and then checked himself in the usual way to survey his hand as if it were a beautiful example of Greek sculpture. His hand, I may say, is almost as large as a Belfast ham.

'What way wass he called Hurricane Jeck?' said he. 'Well, I'll soon tell you that. He wass not always known by that name; that wass a name he got for the time he stole the sheep.'

'Stole the sheep!' I said, a little bewildered, for I failed to see how an incident of that kind would give rise to such a name.

'Yes; what you might call stole,' said Para Handy hastily; 'but, och! it wass only wan smaal wee sheep he lifted on a man that never went to the church, and chust let him take it! Hurricane Jeck would not steal a fly—no, nor two flies, from a Chrustian; he's the perfect chentleman in that.'

'Tell me all about it,' I said.

'I'll soon do that,' said he, putting out his hand to admire it again, and in doing so upsetting his glass. 'Tut, tut!' he said. 'Look what I have done—knocked doon my gless; it wass a good thing there wass nothing in it.

'Hurricane Jeck,' said the Captain, when I had taken the hint and put something in it, 'iss a man that can sail anything and go anywhere, and aalways be the perfect chentleman. A millionaire's yat or a washing-boyne—it's aal the same to Jeck; he would sail the wan chust as smert as the

other, and land on the quay as spruce ass if he wass newly
come from a baal. Oh, man! the cut of his jeckets! And
never anything else but 'lastic-sided boots, even in the
coorsest weather! If you would see him, you would see a
man that's chust sublime, and that careful about his 'lastic-
sided boots he would never stand at the wheel unless there
wass a bass below his feet. He'll aye be oiling at his hair,
and buying hard hats for going ashore with: I never saw a
man wi' a finer heid for the hat, and in some of the vessels
he wass in he would have the full of a bunker of hats. Hurricane Jeck wass brought up in the China clupper tred, only
he wassna called Hurricane Jeck then, for he hadna stole the
sheep till efter that. He wass captain of the *Dora Young*,
wan of them cluppers; he's a hand on a gaabert the now, but
aalways the perfect chentleman.'

'It seems a sad downcome for a man to be a gabbart hand
after having commanded a China clipper,' I ventured to
remark. 'What was the reason of his change?'

'Bad luck,' said Para Handy. 'Chust bad luck. The fellow
never got fair-play. He would aye be somewhere takin' a
gless of something wi' somebody, for he's a fine big cheery
chap. I mind splendid when he wass captain on the clupper,
he had a fine hoose of three rooms and a big decanter, wi'
hot and cold watter, oot at Pollokshaws. When you went
oot to the hoose to see Hurricane Jeck in them days, time
slupped bye. But he wassna known as Hurricane Jeck then,
for it wass before he stole the sheep.'

'You were just going to tell me something about that,'
I said.

'Jeck iss wan man in a hundred, and ass good ass two if
there wass anything in the way of trouble, for, man! he's
strong, strong! He has a back on him like a shipping-box,
and when he will come down Tarbert quay on a Friday
night after a good fishing, and the trawlers are arguing, it's
two yerds to the step with him and a bash in the side of his
hat for fair defiance. But he never hit a man twice, for he's
aye the perfect chentleman iss Hurricane Jeck. Of course,

you must understand, he wass not known as Hurricane Jeck till the time I'm going to tell you of, when he stole the sheep.

'I have not trevelled far mysel' yet, except Ullapool and the time I wass at Ireland; but Hurricane Jeck in his time has been at every place on the map, and some that's no'. Chust wan of Brutain's hardy sons—that's what he iss. As weel kent in Calcutta as if he wass in the Coocaddens, and he could taalk a dozen of their foreign kinds of languages if he cared to take the bother. When he would be leaving a port, there wassna a leddy in the place but what would be doon on the quay wi' her Sunday clothes on and a bunch o' floo'ers for his cabin. And when he would be sayin' good-bye to them from the brudge, he would chust take off his hat and give it a shoogle, and put it on again; his manners wass complete. The first thing he would do when he reached any place wass to go ashore and get his boots brushed, and then sing "Rule Britannia" roond aboot the docks. It wass a sure way to get freend or foe aboot you, he said, and he wass aye as ready for the wan as for the other. Brutain's hardy son!

'He made the fastest passages in his time that wass ever made in the tea trade, and still and on he would meet you like a common working-man. There wass no pride or non-sense of that sort aboot Hurricane Jeck; but, mind you, though I'm callin' him Hurricane Jeck, he wasna Hurricane Jeck till the time he stole the sheep.'

'I don't like to press you, Captain, but I'm anxious to hear about that sheep,' I said patiently.

'I'm comin' to't,' said Para Handy. 'Jeck had the duvvle's own bad luck; he couldna take a gless by-ordinar' but the ship went wrong on him, and he lost wan job efter the other, but he wass never anything else but the perfect chentleman. When he had not a penny in his pocket, he would borrow a shilling from you, and buy you a stick pipe for yourself chust for good nature——'

'A stick pipe?' I repeated interrogatively.

'Chust a stick pipe—or a wudden pipe, or whatever you like to call it. He had three medals and a clock that wouldna go for saving life at sea, but that wass before he wass Hurricane Jeck, mind you; for at that time he hadna stole the sheep.'

'I'm dying to hear about that sheep,' I said.

'I'll soon tell you about the sheep,' said Para Handy. 'It wass a thing that happened when him and me wass sailing on the *Elizabeth Ann*, a boat that belonged to Girvan, and a smert wan too, if she wass in any kind of trum at aal. We would be going here and there aboot the West Coast with wan thing and another, and not costing the owners mich for coals if coals wass our cargo. It wass wan Sunday we were passing Caticol in Arran, and in a place yonder where there wass not a hoose in sight we saw a herd of sheep eating gress near the shore. As luck would have it, there wass not a bit of butcher-meat on board the *Elizabeth Ann* for the Sunday dinner, and Jeck cocked his eye at the sheep and says to me, "Yonder's some sheep lost, poor things; what do you say to taking the punt and going ashore to see if there's anybody's address on them?"

' "Whatever you say yoursel'," I said to Jeck, and we stopped the vessel and went ashore, the two of us, and looked the sheep high and low, but there wass no address on them. "They're lost, sure enough," said Jeck, pulling some heather and putting it in his pocket—he wassna Hurricane Jeck then—"they're lost, sure enough, Peter. Here's a nice wee wan nobody would ever miss, that chust the very thing for a coal vessel," and before you could say "knife" he had it killed and carried to the punt. Oh, he iss a smert, smert fellow with his hands; he could do anything.

'We rowed ass caalm ass we could oot to the vessel, and we had chust got the deid sheep on board when we heard a roarin' and whustling.

' "Taalk about Arran being releegious!" said Jeck. "Who's that whustling on the Lord's day?"

'The man that wass whustling wass away up on the hill,

and we could see him coming running doon the hill the same ass if he would break every leg he had on him.

' "I'll bate you he'll say it's his sheep," said Jeck. "Weel, we'll chust anchor the vessel here till we hear what he hass to say, for if we go away and never mind the cratur he'll find oot somewhere else it's the *Elizabeth Ann*."

'When the fermer and two shepherds came oot to the *Elizabeth Ann* in a boat, she wass lying at anchor, and we were all on deck, every man wi' a piece o' heather in his jecket.

' "I saw you stealing my sheep," said the fermer, coming on deck, furious. "I'll have every man of you jiled for this."

' "Iss the man oot of his wuts?" said Jeck. "Drink—chust drink! Nothing else but drink! If you were a sober Christian man, you would be in the church at this 'oor in Arran, and not oot on the hill recovering from last night's carry-on in Loch Ranza, and imagining you are seeing things that's not there at aal, at aal."

' "I saw you with my own eyes steal the sheep and take it on board," said the fermer, nearly choking with rage.

' "What you saw was my freend and me gathering a puckle heather for oor jeckets," said Jeck, "and if ye don't believe me you can search the ship from stem to stern."

' "I'll soon do that," said the fermer, and him and his shepherds went over every bit of the *Elizabeth Ann*. They never missed a corner you could hide a moose in, but there wass no sheep nor sign of sheep anywhere.

' "Look at that, Macalpine," said Jeck. "I have a good mind to have you up for inflammation of character. But what could you expect from a man that would be whustling on the hill like a peesweep on a Sabbath when he should be in the church. It iss a good thing for you, Macalpine, it iss a Sabbath, and I can keep my temper."

' "I could swear I saw you lift the sheep," said the fermer, quite vexed.

' "Saw your auntie! Drink; nothing but the cursed

drink!" said Jeck, and the fermer and his shepherds went away with their tails behind their legs.

'We lay at anchor till it was getting dark, and then we lifted the anchor and took off the sheep that wass tied to it when we put it oot. "It's a good thing salt mutton," said Hurricane Jeck as we sailed away from Caticol, and efter that the name he always got wass Hurricane Jeck.'

'But why "Hurricane Jeck"?' I asked, more bewildered than ever.

'Holy smoke! am I no' tellin' ye?' said Para Handy. 'It wass because he stole the sheep.'

But I don't understand it yet.

The Company of the Marjolaine[1]

JOHN BUCHAN

(1875–1940)

'Qu'est-c' qui passe ici si tard,
Compagnons de la Marjolaine?'
CHANSONS DE FRANCE

I

. . . I CAME down from the mountains and into the pleasing valley of the Adige in as pelting a heat as ever mortal suffered under. The way underfoot was parched and white; I had newly come out of a wilderness of white limestone crags, and a sun of Italy blazed blindingly in an azure Italian sky. You are to suppose, my dear aunt, that I had had enough

---

[1] This extract from the unpublished papers of the Manorwater family has seemed to the Editor worth printing for its historical interest. The famous Lady Molly Carteron became Countess of Manorwater by her second marriage. She was a wit and a friend of wits, and her nephew, the Honourable Charles Hervey-Townshend (afterwards our Ambassador at The Hague), addressed to her a series of amusing letters while making, after the fashion of his contemporaries, the Grand Tour of Europe. Three letters, written at various places in the Eastern Alps and dispatched from Venice, contain the following short narrative. [Author's note.]

and something more of my craze for foot-marching. A fortnight ago I had gone to Belluno in a post-chaise, dismissed
my fellow to carry my baggage by way of Verona, and with
no more than a valise on my back plunged into the fastnesses
of those mountains. I had a fancy to see the little sculptured
hills which made backgrounds for Gianbellin, and there
were rumours of great mountains built wholly of marble
which shone like the battlements of the Celestial City. So at
any rate reported young Mr. Wyndham, who had travelled
with me from Milan to Venice. I lay the first night at Piave,
where Titian had the fortune to be born, and the landlord
at the inn displayed a set of villainous daubs which he swore
were the early works of that master. Thence up a toilsome
valley I journeyed to the Ampezzan country, where indeed
I saw my white mountains, but, alas! no longer Celestial.
For it rained like Westmoreland for five endless days, while
I kicked my heels in an inn and turned a canto of Ariosto
into halting English couplets. By and by it cleared, and I
headed westward towards Bozen, among the tangle of wild
rocks where the Dwarf King had once his rose garden. The
first night I had no inn, but slept in the vile cabin of a
forester, who spoke a tongue half Latin, half Dutch, which
I could not master. The next day was a blaze of heat, the
mountain paths lay thick with dust, and I had no wine from
sunrise to sunset. Can you wonder that, when the following
noon I saw Santa Chiara sleeping in its green circlet of
meadows, my thought was only of a deep draught and a cool
chamber? I protest that I am a great lover of natural beauty,
of rock and cascade, and all the properties of the poet; but
the enthusiasm of M. Rousseau himself would sink from
the stars to earth if he had marched since breakfast in a cloud
of dust with a throat like the nether millstone.

Yet I had not entered the place before Romance revived.
The little town—a mere wayside halting-place on the great
mountain road to the North—had the air of mystery which
foretells adventure. Why is it that a dwelling or a countenance catches the fancy with the promise of some strange

destiny? I have houses in my mind which I know will some
day and somehow be intertwined oddly with my life; and
I have faces in memory of which I know nothing save that I
shall undoubtedly cast eyes again upon them. My first
glimpses of Santa Chiara gave me this earnest of romance.
It was walled and fortified, the streets were narrow pits of
shade, old tenements with bent fronts swayed to meet each
other. Melons lay drying on flat roofs, and yet now and then
would come a high-pitched northern gable. Latin and
Teuton met and mingled in the place, and, as Mr. Gibbon
has taught us, the offspring of this admixture is something
fantastic and unpredictable. I forgot my grievous thirst and
my tired feet in admiration and a certain vague expectation
of wonders. Here, ran my thought, it is fated, maybe, that
Romance and I shall at last compass a meeting. Perchance
some princess is in need of my arm, or some affair of high
policy is afoot in this jumble of old masonry. You will laugh
at my folly, but I had an excuse for it. A fortnight in strange
mountains disposes a man to look for something at his next
encounter with his kind, and the sight of Santa Chiara would
have fired the imagination of a judge in Chancery.

I strode happily into the courtyard of the Tre Croci, and
presently had my expectation confirmed. For I found my
fellow, Gianbattista—a faithful rogue I got in Rome on a
Cardinal's recommendation—hot in dispute with a lady's-
maid. The woman was old, harsh-featured—no Italian
clearly, though she spoke fluently in the tongue. She rated
my man like a pickpocket, and the dispute was over a room.

'The signor will bear me out,' said Gianbattista. 'Was not
I sent to Verona with his baggage, and thence to this place
of ill manners? Was I not bidden engage for him a suite of
apartments? Did I not duly choose these fronting on the
gallery, and dispose therein the signor's baggage? And lo!
an hour ago I found it all turned into the yard and this
woman installed in its place. It is monstrous, unbearable! Is
this an inn for travellers, or haply the private mansion of
these Magnificences?'

'My servant speaks truly,' I said, firmly yet with courtesy, having no mind to spoil adventure by urging rights. 'He had orders to take these rooms for me, and I know not what higher power can countermand me.'

The woman had been staring at me scornfully, for no doubt in my dusty habit I was a figure of small count; but at the sound of my voice she started, and cried out, 'You are English, signor?'

I bowed an admission.

'Then my mistress shall speak with you,' she said, and dived into the inn like an elderly rabbit.

Gianbattista was for sending for the landlord and making a riot in that hostelry; but I stayed him, and bidding him fetch me a flask of white wine, three lemons, and a glass of *eau de vie*, I sat down peaceably at one of the little tables in the courtyard and prepared for the quenching of my thirst. Presently, as I sat drinking that excellent compound which was my own invention, my shoulder was touched, and I turned to find the maid and her mistress. Alas for my hopes of a glorious being, young and lissom and bright with the warm riches of the south! I saw a short, stout little lady, well on the wrong side of thirty. She had plump red cheeks, and fair hair dressed indifferently in the Roman fashion. Two candid blue eyes redeemed her plainness, and a certain grave and gentle dignity. She was notably a gentlewoman, so I got up, doffed my hat, and awaited her commands.

She spoke in Italian. 'Your pardon, signor, but I fear my good Cristine has done you unwittingly a wrong.'

Cristine snorted at this premature plea of guilty, while I hastened to assure the fair apologist that any rooms I might have taken were freely at her service.

I spoke unconsciously in English, and she replied in a halting parody of that tongue. 'I understand him,' she said, 'but I do not speak him happily. I will discourse, if the signor pleases, in our first speech.'

She and her father, it appeared, had come over the Brenner, and arrived that morning at the Tre Croci, where they purposed to lie for some days. He was an old man, very feeble, and much depending upon her constant care. Wherefore it was necessary that the rooms of all the party should adjoin, and there was no suite of the size in the inn save that which I had taken. Would I therefore consent to forgo my right, and place her under an eternal debt?

I agreed most readily, being at all times careless where I sleep, so the bed be clean, or where I eat, so the meal be good. I bade my servant see the landlord and have my belongings carried to other rooms. Madame thanked me sweetly, and would have gone, when a thought detained her.

'It is but courteous,' she said, 'that you should know the names of those whom you have befriended. My father is called the Count d'Albani, and I am his only daughter. We travel to Florence, where we have a villa in the environs.'

'My name,' said I, 'is Hervey-Townshend, an Englishman travelling abroad for his entertainment.'

'Hervey?' she repeated. 'Are you one of the family of Miladi Hervey?'

'My worthy aunt,' I replied, with a tender recollection of that preposterous woman.

Madame turned to Cristine, and spoke rapidly in a whisper.

'My father, sir,' she said, addressing me, 'is an old frail man, little used to the company of strangers; but in former days he has had kindness from members of your house, and it would be a satisfaction to him, I think, to have the privilege of your acquaintance.'

She spoke with the air of a vizier who promises a traveller a sight of the Grand Turk. I murmured my gratitude, and hastened after Gianbattista. In an hour I had bathed, rid myself of my beard, and arrayed myself in decent clothing. Then I strolled out to inspect the little city, admired an altar-piece, chaffered with a Jew for a cameo, purchased some small necessaries, and returned early in the afternoon with a noble appetite for dinner.

The Tre Croci had been in happier days a bishop's

lodging, and possessed a dining-hall ceiled with black oak and adorned with frescoes. It was used as a general *salle à manger* for all dwellers in the inn, and there accordingly I sat down to my long-deferred meal. At first there were no other diners, and I had two maids, as well as Gianbattista, to attend on my wants. Presently Madame d'Albani entered, escorted by Cristine and by a tall gaunt serving-man, who seemed no part of the hostelry. The landlord followed, bowing civilly, and the two women seated themselves at the little table at the farther end. 'Il Signor Conte dines in his room,' said Madame to the host, who withdrew to see to that gentleman's needs.

I found my eyes straying often to the little party in the cool twilight of that refectory. The man-servant was so old and battered, and yet of such a dignity, that he lent a touch of intrigue to the thing. He stood stiffly behind Madame's chair, handing dishes with an air of silent reverence—the lackey of a great noble, if ever I had seen the type. Madame never glanced towards me, but conversed sparingly with Cristine, while she pecked delicately at her food. Her name ran in my head with a tantalizing flavour of the familiar. Albani! D'Albani! It was a name not uncommon in the Roman States, but I had never heard it linked to a noble family. And yet I had,—somehow, somewhere; and in the vain effort at recollection I had almost forgotten my hunger. There was nothing bourgeois in the little lady. The austere servants, the high manner of condescension, spake of a stock used to deference, though, maybe, pitifully decayed in its fortunes. There was a mystery in these quiet folk which tickled my curiosity. Romance after all was not destined to fail me at Santa Chiara.

My doings of the afternoon were of interest to myself alone. Suffice it to say that when I returned at nightfall I found Gianbattista the trustee of a letter. It was from Madame, written in a fine thin hand on a delicate paper, and it invited me to wait upon the signor, her father, that evening at eight o'clock. What caught my eye was a coronet stamped in a corner. A coronet, I say, but in truth it was a crown, the same as surmounts the Arms Royal of England on the signboard of a Court tradesman. I marvelled at the ways of foreign heraldry. Either this family of d'Albani had higher pretensions than I had given it credit for, or it employed an unlearned and imaginative stationer. I scribbled a line of acceptance and went to dress.

The hour of eight found me knocking at the Count's door. The grim serving-man admitted me to the pleasant chamber which should have been mine own. A dozen wax candles burned in sconces, and on the table, among fruits and the remains of supper, stood a handsome candelabra of silver. A small fire of logs had been lit on the hearth, and before it in an arm-chair sat a strange figure of a man. He seemed not so much old as aged. I should have put him at sixty, but the marks he bore were clearly less those of Time than of Life. There sprawled before me the relics of noble looks. The fleshy nose, the pendulous cheek, the drooping mouth, had once been cast in the lines of manly beauty. Heavy eyebrows above and heavy bags beneath spoiled the effect of a choleric blue eye, which age had not dimmed. The man was gross and yet haggard; it was not the padding of good living which clothed his bones, but a heaviness as of some dropsical malady. I could picture him in health a gaunt loose-limbed being, high-featured and swift and eager. He was dressed wholly in black velvet, with fresh ruffles and wristbands, and he wore heeled shoes with antique silver buckles. It was a figure of an older age which rose slowly to greet me, in one hand a snuff-box and a purple handkerchief, and in the other a book with finger marking place. He made me a great bow as Madame uttered my name, and held out a hand with a kindly smile.

'Mr. Hervey-Townshend,' he said, 'we will speak English, if you please. I am fain to hear it again, for 'tis a tongue I love. I make you welcome, sir, for your own sake and for the sake of your kin. How is her honourable ladyship, your aunt? A week ago she sent me a letter.'

I answered that she did famously, and wondered what cause of correspondence my worthy aunt could have with wandering nobles of Italy.

He motioned me to a chair between Madame and himself, while a servant set a candle on a shelf behind him. Then he proceeded to catechize me in excellent English, with now and then a phrase of French, as to the doings in my own land. Admirably informed this Italian gentleman proved himself. I defy you to find in Almack's more intelligent gossip. He inquired as to the chances of my Lord North and the mind of my Lord Rockingham. He had my Lord Shelburne's foibles at his fingers' ends. The habits of the Prince, the aims of their ladyships of Dorset and Buckingham, the extravagance of this noble Duke and that right honourable gentleman were not hid from him. I answered discreetly yet frankly, for there was no ill-breeding in his curiosity. Rather it seemed like the inquiries of some fine lady, now buried deep in the country, as to the doings of a forsaken Mayfair. There was humour in it and something of pathos.

'My aunt must be a voluminous correspondent, sir,' I said.

He laughed. 'I have many friends in England who write to me, but I have seen none of them for long, and I doubt I may never see them again. Also in my youth I have been in England.' And he sighed as at a sorrowful recollection.

Then he showed the book in his hand. 'See,' he said, 'here is one of your English writings, the greatest book I have ever happened on.' It was a volume of Mr. Fielding.

For a little he talked of books and poets. He admired Mr. Fielding profoundly, Dr. Smollett somewhat less, Mr. Richardson not at all. But he was clear that England had a monopoly of good writers, saving only my friend M. Rousseau, whom he valued, yet with reservations. Of the Italians he had no opinion. I instanced against him the plays of Signor Alfieri. He groaned, shook his head, and grew moody.

'Know you Scotland?' he asked suddenly.

I replied that I had visited Scotch cousins, but had no great estimation for the country. 'It is too poor and jagged,' I said, 'for the taste of one who loves colour and sunshine and suave outlines.'

He sighed. 'It is indeed a bleak land, but a kindly. When the sun shines at all he shines on the truest hearts in the world. I love its bleakness too. There is a spirit in the misty hills, and the harsh sea-wind which inspires men to great deeds. Poverty and courage go often together, and my Scots, if they are poor, are as untamable as their mountains.'

'You know the land, sir?' I asked.

'I have seen it, and I have known many Scots. You will find them in Paris and Avignon and Rome, with never a plack in their pockets. I have a feeling for exiles, sir, and I have pitied these poor people. They gave their all for the cause they followed.'

Clearly the Count shared my aunt's views of history—those views which have made such sport for us often at Carteron. Stalwart Whig as I am, there was something in the tone of the old gentleman which made me feel a certain majesty in the lost cause.

'I am Whig in blood and Whig in principle,' I said, 'but I have never denied that those Scots who followed the Chevalier were too good to waste on so trumpery a leader.'

I had no sooner spoken the words than I felt that somehow I had been guilty of a *bêtise*.

'It may be so,' said the Count. 'I did not bid you here, sir, to argue on politics, on which I am assured we should differ. But I will ask you one question. The King of England is a stout upholder of the right of kings. How does he face the defection of his American possessions?'

'The nation takes it well enough, and as for His Majesty's feelings, there is small inclination to inquire into them. I conceive of the whole war as a blunder out of which we have come as we deserved. The day is gone by for the assertion of monarchic rights against the will of a people.'

'Maybe. But take note that the King of England is suffering today as—how do you call him?—the Chevalier suffered
forty years ago. "The wheel has come full circle," as your
Shakespeare says. Time has wrought his revenge.'

He was staring into a fire, which burned small and
smokily.

'You think the day for kings is ended. I read it differently.
The world will ever have need of kings. If a nation cast out
one it will have to find another. And mark you, those later
kings, created by the people, will bear a harsher hand than
the old race who ruled as of right. Some day the world will
regret having destroyed the kindly and legitimate line of
monarchs and put in their place tyrants who govern by the
sword or by flattering an idle mob.'

This belated dogma would at other times have set me
laughing, but the strange figure before me gave no impulse
to merriment. I glanced at Madame, and saw her face grave
and perplexed, and I thought I read a warning gleam in her
eye. There was a mystery about the party which irritated
me, but good breeding forbade me to seek a clue.

'You will permit me to retire, sir,' I said. 'I have but this
morning come down from a long march among the mountains east of this valley. Sleeping in wayside huts and
tramping those sultry paths make a man think pleasantly of
bed.'

The Count seemed to brighten at my words. 'You are
a marcher, sir, and love the mountains? Once I would
gladly have joined you, for in my youth I was a great walker
in hilly places. Tell me, now, how many miles will you
cover in a day?'

I told him thirty at a stretch.

'Ah,' he said, 'I have done fifty, without food, over the
roughest and mossiest mountains. I lived on what I shot,
and for drink I had spring water. Nay, I am forgetting:
There was another beverage, which I wager you have never
tasted. Heard you ever, sir, of that *eau de vie* which the Scots
call *usquebagh*? It will comfort a traveller as no thin Italian

wine will comfort him. By my soul, you shall taste it. Charlotte, my dear, bid Oliphant fetch glasses and hot water and lemons. I will give Mr. Hervey-Townshend a sample of the brew. You English are all *têtes-de-fer*, sir, and are worthy of it.'

The old man's face had lighted up, and for the moment his air had the jollity of youth. I would have accepted the entertainment had I not again caught Madame's eye. It said, unmistakably and with serious pleading, 'Decline'. I therefore made my excuses, urged fatigue, drowsiness, and a delicate stomach, bade my host good-night, and in deep mystification left the room.

Enlightenment came upon me as the door closed. There on the threshold stood the manservant whom they called Oliphant, erect as a sentry on guard. The sight reminded me of what I had once seen at Basle when by chance a Rhenish Grand Duke had shared the inn with me. Of a sudden a dozen clues linked together—the crowned note-paper, Scotland, my aunt Hervey's politics, the tale of old wanderings.

'Tell me,' I said in a whisper, 'who is the Count d'Albani, your master?' and I whistled softly a bar of 'Charlie is my darling'.

'Ay,' said the man, without relaxing a muscle of his grim face. 'It is the King of England—my king and yours.'

II

In the small hours of the next morning I was awoke by a most unearthly sound. It was as if all the cats on all the roofs of Santa Chiara were sharpening their claws and wailing their battle-cries. Presently out of the noise came a kind of music—very slow, solemn, and melancholy. The notes ran up in great flights of ecstasy, and sunk anon to the tragic deeps. In spite of my sleepiness I was held spellbound, and the musician had concluded with certain barbaric grunts before I had the curiosity to rise. It came from somewhere in the gallery of the inn, and as I stuck my head out of my door I had a glimpse of Oliphant, nightcap on head and a great bagpipe below his arm, stalking down the corridor.

The incident, for all the gravity of the music, seemed to give a touch of farce to my interview of the past evening. I had gone to bed with my mind full of sad stories of the deaths of kings. Magnificence in tatters has always affected my pity more deeply than tatters with no such antecedent, and a monarch out at elbows stood for me as the last irony of our mortal life. Here was a king whose misfortunes could find no parallel. He had been in his youth the hero of a high adventure, and his middle age had been spent in fleeting among the courts of Europe, and waiting as pensioner on the whims of his foolish but regnant brethren. I had heard tales of a growing sottishness, a decline in spirit, a squalid taste in pleasures. Small blame, I had always thought, to so ill-fated a princeling. And now I had chanced upon the gentleman in his dotage, travelling with a barren effort at mystery, attended by a sad-faced daughter and two ancient domestics. It was a lesson in the vanity of human wishes which the shallowest moralist would have noted. Nay, I felt more than the moral. Something human and kindly in the old fellow had caught my fancy. The decadence was too tragic to prose about, the decadent too human to moralize on. I had left the chamber of the—shall I say *de jure* King of England? —a sentimental adherent of the cause. But this business of the bagpipes touched the comic. To harry an old valet out of bed and set him droning on pipes in the small hours smacked of a theatrical taste, or at least of an undignified fancy. Kings in exile, if they wish to keep the tragic air, should not indulge in such fantastic serenades.

My mind changed again when after breakfast I fell in with Madame on the stair. She drew aside to let me pass, and then made as if she would speak to me. I gave her good-morning, and, my mind being full of her story, addressed her as 'Excellency'.

'I see, sir,' she said, 'that you know the truth. I have to ask your forbearance for the concealment I practised yesterday. It was a poor requital for your generosity, but it is one of the shifts of our sad fortune. An uncrowned king must go in disguise or risk the laughter of every stable-boy. Besides, we are too poor to travel in state, even if we desired it.'

Honestly, I knew not what to say. I was not asked to sympathize, having already revealed my politics, and yet the case cried out for sympathy. You remember, my dear aunt, the good Lady Culham, who was our Dorsetshire neighbour, and tried hard to mend my ways at Carteron? This poor Duchess—for so she called herself—was just such another. A woman made for comfort, housewifery, and motherhood, and by no means for racing about Europe in charge of a disreputable parent. I could picture her settled equably on a garden seat with a lapdog and needlework, blinking happily over green lawns and mildly rating an errant gardener. I could fancy her sitting in a summer parlour, very orderly and dainty, writing lengthy epistles to a tribe of nieces. I could see her marshalling a household in the family pew, or riding serenely in the family coach behind fat bay horses. But here, on an inn staircase, with a false name and a sad air of mystery, she was woefully out of place. I noted little wrinkles forming in the corners of her eyes, and the ravages of care beginning in the plump rosiness of her face. Be sure there was nothing appealing in her mien. She spoke with the air of a great lady, to whom the world is matter only for an afterthought. It was the facts that appealed and grew poignant from her courage.

'There is another claim upon your good-nature,' she said. 'Doubtless you were awoke last night by Oliphant's playing upon the pipes. I rebuked the landlord for his insolence in protesting, but to you, a gentleman and a friend, an explanation is due. My father sleeps ill, and your conversation seems to have cast him into a train of sad memories. It has been his habit on such occasions to have the pipes played to him, since they remind him of friends and happier days. It is a small privilege for an old man, and he does not claim it often.'

I declared that the music had only pleased, and that I would welcome its repetition. Whereupon she left me with a little bow and an invitation to join them that day at dinner, while I departed into the town on my own errands. I returned before midday, and was seated at an arbour in the garden, busy with letters, when there hove in sight the gaunt figure of Oliphant. He hovered around me, if such a figure can be said to hover, with the obvious intention of addressing me. The fellow had caught my fancy, and I was willing to see more of him. His face might have been hacked out of grey granite, his clothes hung loosely on his spare bones, and his stockinged shanks would have done no discredit to Don Quixote. There was no dignity in his air, only a steady and enduring sadness. Here, thought I, is the one of the establishment who most commonly meets the shock of the world's buffets. I called him by name and asked him his desires.

It appeared that he took me for a Jacobite, for he began a rigmarole about loyalty and hard fortune. I hastened to correct him, and he took the correction with the same patient despair with which he took all things. 'Twas but another of the blows of Fate.

'At any rate,' he said in a broad Scotch accent, 'ye come of kin that has helpit my maister afore this. I've many times heard tell o' Herveys and Townshends in England, and a' folk said they were on the richt side. Ye're maybe no a freend, but ye're a freend's freend, or I wadna be speirin' at ye.'

I was amused at the prologue, and waited on the tale. It soon came. Oliphant, it appeared, was the purse-bearer of the household, and woeful straits that poor purse-bearer must have been often put to. I questioned him as to his master's revenues, but could get no clear answer. There were payments due next month in Florence which would solve the difficulties for the winter, but in the meantime expenditure had beaten income. Travelling had cost much, and the Count must have his small comforts. The result, in plain words, was that Oliphant had not the wherewithal to frank the company to Florence; indeed, I doubted if he could have paid the reckoning in Santa Chiara. A loan was therefore sought from a friend's friend, meaning myself.

I was very really embarrassed. Not that I would not have given willingly, for I had ample resources at the moment and was mightily concerned about the sad household. But I knew that the little Duchess would take Oliphant's ears from his head if she guessed that he had dared to borrow from me, and that, if I lent, her back would for ever be turned against me. And yet, what would follow on my refusal? In a day or two there would be a pitiful scene with mine host, and as like as not some of their baggage detained as security for payment. I did not love the task of conspiring behind the lady's back, but if it could be contrived 'twas indubitably the kindest course. I glared sternly at Oliphant, who met me with his pathetic, dog-like eyes.

'You know that your mistress would never consent to the request you have made of me?'

'I ken,' he said humbly. 'But payin' is *my* job, and I simply havena the siller. It's no' the first time it has happened, and it's a sair trial for them both to be flung out o' doors by a foreign hostler because they canna meet his charges. But, sir, if ye can lend to me, ye may be certain that her leddyship will never hear a word o't. Puir thing, she takes nae thocht o' where the siller comes frae, ony mair than the lilies o' the field.'

I became a conspirator. 'You swear, Oliphant, by all you hold sacred, to breathe nothing of this to your mistress, and if she should suspect, to lie like a Privy Councillor?'

A flicker of a smile crossed his face. 'I'll lee like a Scots packman, and the Father o' lees could do nae mair. You need have no fear for your siller, sir. I've aye repaid when

I borrowed, though you may have to wait a bittock.' And the strange fellow strolled off.

At dinner no Duchess appeared till long after the appointed hour, nor was there any sign of Oliphant. When she came at last with Cristine, her eyes looked as if she had been crying, and she greeted me with remote courtesy. My first thought was that Oliphant had revealed the matter of the loan, but presently I found that the lady's trouble was far different. Her father, it seemed, was ill again with his old complaint. What that was I did not ask, nor did the Duchess reveal it.

We spoke in French, for I had discovered that this was her favourite speech. There was no Oliphant to wait on us, and the inn servants were always about, so it was well to have a tongue they did not comprehend. The lady was distracted and sad. When I inquired feelingly as to the general condition of her father's health she parried the question, and when I offered my services she disregarded my words. It was in truth a doleful meal, while the faded Cristine sat like a sphinx staring into vacancy. I spoke of England and of her friends, of Paris and Versailles, of Avignon where she had spent some years, and of the amenities of Florence, which she considered her home. But it was like talking to a nunnery door. I got nothing but 'It is indeed true, sir,' or 'Do you say so, sir?' till my energy began to sink. Madame perceived my discomfort, and, as she rose, murmured an apology. 'Pray forgive my distraction, but I am poor company when my father is ill. I have a foolish mind, easily frightened. Nay, nay!' she went on when I again offered help, 'the illness is trifling. It will pass off by tomorrow, or at the latest the next day. Only I had looked forward to some ease at Santa Chiara, and the promise is belied.'

As it chanced that evening, returning to the inn, I passed by the north side where the windows of the Count's room looked over a little flower garden abutting on the courtyard. The dusk was falling, and a lamp had been lit which gave a glimpse into the interior. The sick man was standing by the window, his figure flung into relief by the lamplight. If he was sick, his sickness was of a curious type. His face was ruddy, his eye wild, and, his wig being off, his scanty hair stood up oddly round his head. He seemed to be singing, but I could not catch the sound through the shut casement. Another figure in the room, probably Oliphant, laid a hand on the Count's shoulder, drew him from the window, and closed the shutter.

It needed only the recollection of stories which were the property of all Europe to reach a conclusion on the gentleman's illness. The legitimate King of England was very drunk.

As I went to my room that night I passed the Count's door. There stood Oliphant as sentry, more grim and haggard than ever, and I thought that his eye met mine with a certain intelligence. From inside the room came a great racket. There was the sound of glasses falling, then a string of oaths, English, French, and for all I knew, Irish, rapped out in a loud drunken voice. A pause, and then came the sound of maudlin singing. It pursued me along the gallery, an old childish song, delivered as if 'twere a pot-house catch—

> 'Qu'est-c' qui passe ici si tard,
> Compagnons de la Marjolaine——'

One of the late-going company of the Marjolaine hastened to bed. This king in exile, with his melancholy daughter, was becoming too much for him.

III

It was just before noon next day that the travellers arrived. I was sitting in the shady loggia of the inn, reading a volume of De Thou, when there drove up to the door two coaches. Out of the first descended very slowly and stiffly four gentlemen; out of the second four servants and a quantity of baggage. As it chanced there was no one about, the courtyard slept its sunny noontide sleep, and the only movement was a lizard on the wall and a buzz of flies by the fountain. Seeing no sign of the landlord, one of the travellers approached me with a grave inclination.

'This is the inn called the Tre Croci, sir?' he asked.

I said it was, and shouted on my own account for the host. Presently that personage arrived with a red face and a short wind, having ascended rapidly from his own cellar. He was awed by the dignity of the travellers, and made none of his usual protests of incapacity. The servants filed off solemnly with the baggage, and the four gentlemen set themselves down beside me in the loggia and ordered each a modest flask of wine.

At first I took them for our countrymen, but as I watched them the conviction vanished. All four were tall and lean beyond the average of mankind. They wore suits of black, with antique starched frills to their shirts; their hair was their own and unpowdered. Massive buckles of an ancient pattern adorned their square-toed shoes, and the canes they carried were like the yards of a small vessel. They were four merchants, I had guessed, of Scotland, maybe, or of Newcastle, but their voices were not Scotch, and their air had no touch of commerce. Take the heavy-browed pre-occupation of a Secretary of State, add the dignity of a bishop, the sunburn of a fox-hunter, and something of the disciplined erectness of a soldier, and you may perceive the manner of these four gentlemen. By the side of them my assurance vanished. Compared with their Olympian serenity my person seemed fussy and servile. Even so, I mused, must Mr. Franklin have looked when baited in Parliament by the Tory pack. The reflection gave me the cue. Presently I caught from their conversation the word 'Washington', and the truth flashed upon me. I was in the presence of four of Mr. Franklin's countrymen. Having never seen an American in the flesh, I rejoiced at the chance of enlarging my acquaintance.

They brought me into the circle by a polite question as to the length of road to Verona. Soon introductions followed. My name intrigued them, and they were eager to learn of my kinship to Uncle Charles. The eldest of the four, it appeared, was Mr. Galloway out of Maryland. Then came two brothers, Sylvester by name, of Pennsylvania, and last Mr. Fish, a lawyer of New York. All four had campaigned in the late war, and all four were members of the Convention, or whatever they call their rough-and-ready Parliament. They were modest in their behaviour, much disinclined to speak of their past, as great men might be whose reputation was world-wide. Somehow the names stuck in my memory. I was certain that I had heard them linked with some stalwart fight or some moving civil deed or some defiant manifesto. The making of history was in their steadfast eye and the grave lines of the mouth. Our friendship flourished mightily in a brief hour, and brought me the invitation, willingly accepted, to sit with them at dinner.

There was no sign of the Duchess or Cristine or Oliphant. Whatever had happened, that household today required all hands on deck, and I was left alone with the Americans. In my day I have supped with the Macaronies, I have held up my head at the Cocoa Tree, I have avoided the floor at hunt dinners, I have drunk glass to glass with Tom Carteron. But never before have I seen such noble consumers of good liquor as those four gentlemen from beyond the Atlantic. They drank the strong red Cyprus as if it had been spring water. 'The dust of your Italian roads takes some cleansing, Mr. Townshend,' was their only excuse, but in truth none was needed. The wine seemed only to thaw their iron decorum. Without any surcease of dignity they grew communicative, and passed from lands to peoples and from peoples to constitutions. Before we knew it we were embarked upon high politics.

Naturally we did not differ on the war. Like me, they held it to have been a grievous necessity. They had no bitterness against England, only regret for her blunders. Of His

Majesty they spoke with respect, of His Majesty's advisers
with dignified condemnation. They thought highly of our
troops in America; less highly of our generals.

'Look you, sir,' said Mr. Galloway, 'in a war such as we
have witnessed the Almighty is the only strategist. You fight
against the forces of Nature, and a newcomer little knows
that the success or failure of every operation he can conceive
depends not upon generalship, but upon the conformation
of a vast country. Our generals, with this in mind and with
fewer men, could make all your schemes miscarry. Had the
English soldiery not been of such stubborn stuff, we should
have been victors from the first. Our leader was not General
Washington, but General America, and his brigadiers were
forests, swamps, lakes, rivers, and high mountains.'

'And now,' I said, 'having won, you have the greatest of
human experiments before you. Your business is to show
that the Saxon stock is adaptable to a republic.'

It seemed to me that they exchanged glances.

'We are not pedants,' said Mr. Fish, 'and have no desire
to dispute about the form of a constitution. A people may
be as free under a king as under a senate. Liberty is not the
lackey of any type of government.'

These were strange words from a member of a race whom
I had thought wedded to the republicanism of Helvidius
Priscus.

'As a loyal subject of a monarchy,' I said, 'I must agree
with you. But your hands are tied, for I cannot picture the
establishment of a House of Washington, and—if not, where
are you to turn for your sovereign?'

Again a smile seemed to pass among the four.

'We are experimenters, as you say, sir, and must go slowly.
In the meantime, we have an authority which keeps peace
and property safe. We are at leisure to cast our eyes round
and meditate on the future.'

'Then, gentlemen,' said I, 'you take an excellent way of
meditation in visiting this museum of old sovereignties.
Here you have the relics of any government you please—a

dozen republics, tyrannies, theocracies, merchant confederations, kingdoms, and more than one empire. You have your choice. I am tolerably familiar with the land, and if I can assist you I am at your service.'

They thanked me gravely. 'We have letters,' said Mr. Galloway; 'one in especial is to a gentleman whom we hope to meet in this place. Have you heard in your travels of the Count of Albany?'

'He has arrived,' said I, 'two days ago. Even now he is in the chamber above us at dinner.'

The news interested them hugely.

'You have seen him?' they cried. 'What is he like?'

'An elderly gentleman in poor health, a man who has travelled much, and, I judge, has suffered something from fortune. He has a fondness for the English, so you will be welcome, sirs; but he was indisposed yesterday, and may still be unable to receive you. His daughter travels with him and tends his old age.'

'And you—you have spoken with him?'

'The night before last I was in his company. We talked of many things, including the late war. He is somewhat of your opinion on matters of government.'

The four looked at each other, and then Mr. Galloway rose.

'I ask your permission, Mr. Townshend, to consult for a moment with my friends. The matter is of some importance, and I would beg you to await us.' So saying, he led the others out of doors, and I heard them withdraw to a corner of the loggia. Now, thought I, there is something afoot, and my long-sought romance approaches fruition. The company of the Marjolaine, whom the Count had sung of, have arrived at last.

Presently they returned and seated themselves at the table.

'You can be of great assistance to us, Mr. Townshend, and we would fain take you into our confidence. Are you aware who is this Count of Albany?'

I nodded. 'It is a thin disguise to one familiar with history.'

'Have you reached any estimate of his character or capabilities? You speak to friends, and, let me tell you, it is a matter which deeply concerns the Count's interests.'

'I think him a kindly and pathetic old gentleman. He naturally bears the mark of forty years' sojourn in the wilderness.'

Mr. Galloway took snuff.

'We have business with him, but it is business which stands in need of an agent. There is no one in the Count's suite with whom we could discuss affairs?'

'There is his daughter.'

'Ah, but she would scarcely suit the case. Is there no man—a friend, and yet not a member of the family, who can treat with us?'

I replied that I thought that I was the only being in Santa Chiara who answered the description.

'If you will accept the task, Mr. Townshend, you are amply qualified. We will be frank with you and reveal our business. We are on no less an errand than to offer the Count of Albany a crown.'

I suppose I must have had some suspicion of their purpose, and yet the revelation of it fell on me like a thunderclap. I could only stare owlishly at my four grave gentlemen.

Mr. Galloway went on unperturbed. 'I have told you that in America we are not yet republicans. There are those among us who favour a republic, but they are by no means a majority. We have got rid of a king who misgoverned us, but we have no wish to get rid of kingship. We want a king of our own choosing, and we would get with him all the ancient sanctions of monarchy. The Count of Albany is of the most illustrious royal stock in Europe—he is, if legitimacy goes for anything, the rightful King of Britain. Now, if the republican party among us is to be worsted, we must come before the nation with a powerful candidate for its favour. You perceive my drift? What more potent appeal to

American pride than to say: "We have got rid of King George; we choose of our own free will the older line and King Charles"?'

I said foolishly that I thought monarchy had had its day, and that 'twas idle to revive it.

'That is a sentiment well enough under a monarchical government; but we, with a clean page to write upon, do not share it. You know your ancient historians. Has not the repository of the chief power always been the rock on which republicanism has shipwrecked? If that power is given to the chief citizen, the way is prepared for the tyrant. If it abides peacefully in a royal house, it abides with cyphers who dignify, without obstructing, a popular constitution. Do not mistake me, Mr. Townshend. This is no whim of a sentimental girl, but the reasoned conclusion of the men who achieved our liberty. There is every reason to believe that General Washington shares our views, and Mr. Hamilton, whose name you may know, is the inspirer of our mission.'

'But the Count is an old man,' I urged; for I knew not where to begin in my exposition of the hopelessness of their errand.

'By so much the better. We do not wish a young king who may be fractious. An old man tempered by misfortune is what our purpose demands.'

'He has also his failings. A man cannot lead his life for forty years and retain all the virtues.'

At that one of the Sylvesters spoke sharply. 'I have heard such gossip, but I do not credit it. I have not forgotten Preston and Derby.'

I made my last objection. 'He has no posterity—legitimate posterity—to carry on his line.'

The four gentlemen smiled. 'That happens to be his chiefest recommendation,' said Mr. Galloway. 'It enables us to take the House of Stuart on trial. We need a breathing-space and leisure to look around; but unless we establish the principle of monarchy at once the republicans will forestall us. Let us get our king at all costs, and during the remaining years of his life we shall have time to settle the succession problem. We have no wish to saddle ourselves for good with a race who might prove burdensome. If King Charles fails he has no son, and we can look elsewhere for a better monarch. You perceive the reason of my view?'

I did, and I also perceived the colossal absurdity of the whole business. But I could not convince them of it, for they met my objections with excellent arguments. Nothing save a sight of the Count would, I feared, disillusion them.

'You wish me to make this proposal on your behalf?' I asked.

'We shall make the proposal ourselves, but we desire you to prepare the way for us. He is an elderly man, and should first be informed of our purpose.'

'There is one person whom I beg leave to consult—the Duchess, his daughter. It may be that the present is an ill moment for approaching the Count, and the affair requires her sanction.'

They agreed, and with a very perplexed mind I went forth to seek the lady. The irony of the thing was too cruel, and my heart ached for her. In the gallery I found Oliphant packing some very shabby trunks, and when I questioned him he told me that the family were to leave Santa Chiara on the morrow. Perchance the Duchess had awakened to the true state of their exchequer, or perchance she thought it well to get her father on the road again as a cure for his ailment.

I discovered Cristine, and begged for an interview with her mistress on an urgent matter. She led me to the Duchess's room, and there the evidence of poverty greeted me openly. All the little luxuries of the menage had gone to the Count. The poor lady's room was no better than a servant's garret, and the lady herself sat stitching a rent in a travelling cloak. She rose to greet me with alarm in her eyes.

As briefly as I could I set out the facts of my amazing mission. At first she seemed scarcely to hear me. 'What do they want with him?' she asked. 'He can give them nothing. He is no friend to the Americans or to any people who have deposed their sovereign.' Then, as she grasped my meaning, her face flushed.

'It is a heartless trick, Mr. Townshend. I would fain think you no party to it.'

'Believe me, dear madame, it is no trick. The men below are in sober earnest. You have but to see their faces to know that theirs is no wild adventure. I believe sincerely that they have the power to implement their promise.'

'But it is madness. He is old and worn and sick. His day is long past for winning a crown.'

'All this I have said, but it does not move them.' And I told her rapidly Mr. Galloway's argument.

She fell into a muse. 'At the eleventh hour! Nay, too late, too late. Had he been twenty years younger, what a stroke of fortune! Fate bears too hard on us, too hard!'

Then she turned to me fiercely. 'You have no doubt heard, sir, the gossip about my father, which is on the lips of every fool in Europe. Let us have done with this pitiful make-believe. My father is a sot. Nay, I do not blame him. I blame his enemies and his miserable destiny. But there is the fact. Were he not old, he would still be unfit to grasp a crown and rule over a turbulent people. He flees from one city to another, but he cannot flee from himself. That is his illness on which you condoled with me yesterday.'

The lady's control was at breaking-point. Another moment and I expected a torrent of tears. But they did not come. With a great effort she regained her composure.

'Well, the gentlemen must have an answer. You will tell them that the Count, my father—nay, give him his true title if you care—is vastly obliged to them for the honour they have done him, but would decline on account of his age and infirmities. You know how to phrase a decent refusal.'

'Pardon me,' said I, 'but I might give them that answer till doomsday and never content them. They have not travelled many thousand miles to be put off by hearsay evidence. Nothing will satisfy them but an interview with your father himself.'

'It is impossible,' she said sharply.

'Then we must expect the renewed attentions of our American friends. They will wait till they see him.'

She rose and paced the room.

'They must go,' she repeated many times. 'If they see him sober he will accept with joy, and we shall be the laughing-stock of the world. I tell you it cannot be. I alone know how immense is the impossibility. He cannot afford to lose the last rags of his dignity, the last dregs of his ease. They must not see him. I will speak with them myself.'

'They will be honoured, madame, but I do not think they will be convinced. They are what we call in my land "men of business". They will not be content till they get the Count's reply from his own lips.'

A new Duchess seemed to have arisen, a woman of quick action and sharp words.

'So be it. They shall see him. Oh, I am sick to death of fine sentiments and high loyalty and all the vapouring stuff I have lived among for years. All I ask for myself and my father is a little peace, and, by Heaven! I shall secure it. If nothing will kill your gentlemen's folly but truth, why, truth they shall have. They shall see my father, and this very minute. Bring them up, Mr. Townshend, and usher them into the presence of the rightful King of England. You will find him alone.' She stopped her walk and looked out of the window.

I went back in a hurry to the Americans. 'I am bidden to bring you to the Count's chamber. He is alone and will see you. These are the commands of madame his daughter.'

'Good!' said Mr. Galloway, and all four, grave gentlemen as they were, seemed to brace themselves to a special dignity as befitted ambassadors to a king. I led them upstairs, tapped at the Count's door, and, getting no answer, opened it and admitted them.

And this was what we saw. The furniture was in disorder,

and on a couch lay an old man sleeping a heavy drunken sleep. His mouth was open and his breath came stertorously. The face was purple, and large purple veins stood out on the mottled forehead. His scanty white hair was draggled over his cheek. On the floor was a broken glass, wet stains still lay on the boards, and the place reeked of spirits.

The four looked for a second—I do not think longer—at him whom they would have made their king. They did not look at each other. With one accord they moved out, and Mr. Fish, who was last, closed the door very gently behind him.

In the hall below Mr. Galloway turned to me. 'Our mission is ended, Mr. Townshend. I have to thank you for your courtesy.' Then to the others, 'If we order the coaches now, we may get well on the way to Verona ere sundown.'

.   .   .   .

An hour later two coaches rolled out of the courtyard of the Tre Croci. As they passed, a window was half-opened on the upper floor, and a head looked out. A line of a song came down, a song sung in a strange quavering voice. It was the catch I had heard the night before:

> 'Qu'est-c' qui passe ici si tard,
> Compagnons de la Marjolaine—e?'

It was true. The company came late indeed—too late by forty years. . . .

Art's Wedding Present

NEIL M. GUNN

(1891–1973)

'THERE will be great excitement at home,' said Old Hector as he sat on the little knoll, with one eye on the red cow.

'There is,' said Art. 'Morag is dancing about like a hen on a hot griddle, and if she is, Janet and Neonain are not much better, and Mother is ironing. It's no place for a man yonder.'

Old Hector took his pipe out of his mouth the better to enjoy a soft note or two of laughter.

'And Neonain,' continued Art, 'said she was going to get married, and she is only ten past, and when I asked her who she was going to get married to, she said it was none of my business. I told her she hadn't anyone to get married to. Boy, didn't she grow wild then!' declared Art, his eyes dancing.

'She would.'

'She did. You would think,' added Art, 'that a wedding was a great thing.'

'Well,' replied Old Hector, 'it's not a small thing, as a rule. They contrive, one way or another, to make a lot of it.'

The cunning-shy smile came to Art's features and he half looked away. 'Do you think,' he asked, 'that—that women use it to make fools of men?'

'What's that?' asked Old Hector sharply. Then he observed the confused innocence breaking into merriment as Art pivoted on his bare heel, and he inquired: 'Where did you hear that?'

'I heard Father saying it.'

'Did you indeed? He must have been exercised beyond his usual, surely?'

'He was. The Dark Woman was in and she and Mother were talking round the fire.'

'In that case,' said Old Hector, 'I have some sympathy for your father. He would have had a hard time of it.'

'That's what he said. He said he didn't know his own house.'

'He wouldn't,' agreed Old Hector. 'They would be joking and taking fun out of him.'

'They were,' said Art. 'And then the Dark One said something to Father, and Mother and herself laughed out loud, and Morag gave a small laugh, too, but I didn't catch what it was.'

'It was maybe as well,' nodded Old Hector.

'I would like to have catched it, though,' said Art. 'You don't know what it might have been?'

'How could I,' said Old Hector, 'seeing I wasn't there?'

'Why are you smiling like that, then?' asked Art.

'A man can smile if he likes, surely?'

Art smiled too. 'And do you know what Father said about Duncan?'

'No.'

'He said, "You would think he had a sore head."'

'Ho! ho! ho!' laughed Old Hector.

Art laughed too. 'Is that a good one?'

'Fair to middling,' replied Old Hector with bright eyes.

'Do you actually think,' asked Art, 'that Duncan has a sore head?'

'Oh, I shouldn't think so.'

'But perhaps a man has a sore head when he's going to be married. You never know. He might have.'

'He might, of course.'

'There's something wrong with him whatever. Donul asked me to ask him last night if his head was any better, and when I asked him he turned on me and gave me a blow that flattened me.'

'Did he indeed? There would be trouble then.'

'There was,' said Art. 'And Mother took his side, and

Morag, too, and Janet and Neonain, but Father took my side.'

'And what about Donul?'

'He ran away,' said Art, 'laughing.'

'The rascal!' Old Hector bushed up his whiskers to scratch underneath, but Art saw he was smiling in them. 'It's a difficult time altogether.' Old Hector shook his head. 'It's not often I get lumps in my porridge, but lumps there were this morning.'

'Is Agnes great about the wedding, too, then?'

'Who isn't? Three of our young hens have been named for thrawing. It's nothing but presents, presents, and clothes, clothes.'

'Are you making a present yourself?' asked Art.

'Oh, I'll have to give something, I suppose, but it's not much they have left me after many years. All my feathers are gone.'

Art looked at Old Hector's whiskers. Old Hector looked back at Art. Art flushed very slightly and, to change the thought, said: 'They won't be expecting a present from me, will they?'

Old Hector chuckled. 'I doubt if anyone in the two townships will be let off, but the best present you can make is to stay about your home during this difficult time, so that you may do any little thing that's required of you and run a message when you're asked.'

'Why is it always me? It's queer it should always be me who's got to do that,' remarked Art with some petulance. 'There's Donul: he was off the whole day yesterday, and early this morning he was off again, and he said to me—for I woke up as he was going—he said, "I'll murder you if you try to follow me." It's queer it should always be me.'

'Never you mind,' said Old Hector soothingly. 'You'll one day be fifteen like Donul, and then you can be off, too.'

'You were off yourself,' said Art moodily, giving his friend at the same time a suspicious glance.

'I was only off on a visit or two. At a time like this, many strange things have to be done. Indeed I've got to be busy this very minute,' and he looked far around the country-side as if his knoll were a watch-tower. 'Now you be a good boy, and run off home, and . . .'

But it was all very well. Art no sooner put his nose inside his home than it was shoved out. 'Can't you run away and play yourself?'

With whom was he going to play? The whole world had gone queer and hidden things were on foot. A fellow could see by the look of the earth itself that things were moving in silence.

Art went down to his own secret place behind the little barn, and sure as he came there the idea struck him. Donul and Hamish had gone off to the River to catch salmon! Not to poach in the ordinary way—he could think of that readily enough at any time—but to get salmon for the wedding feast *as a present*!

It was a thought, and two thoughts. Ducks, hens, butter, cheese, bakings, cakes with currants, a side of pork, a leg of mutton, eggs and more hens, from this one and from that, from here and from there, puddings and shivering jellies, little pastries and big pies, things Art now heard of but had never seen, much less tasted. And Donul and Hamish were adding to this communal feast the distinction of salmon!

Art looked about him and saw the cat. He had nothing in the world that he could give even to the cat itself, barring a kick. And he never kicked the cat. It wasn't safe.

The distant River slowly drew him by the nose. The farther he went on, the more clearly he saw Donul and Hamish actively engaged at the Hazel Pool.

Skirting Old Hector's cottage at a discreet distance, he paused to spy out the land. There was no sign of Old Hector now. Only women and cows and children here and there. The country was deserted.

He slid down into the hollow beyond, and so entered the Little Glen.

In the Little Glen he was all alone, going away off to find the fabled River and the Hazel Pool, and because this fatal mood was upon him and there was no help for it, he wanted to cry. It was hard on him, having to do all this alone. When the cry mounted he took a little run to himself and the tears that came out bounced off.

Presently he noticed that the glen was quieter and more watchful than when he had gone down it before, perhaps because Mary Ann had been with him then.

But the glen itself seemed to have changed, too. There were curious little places which he had not noticed before, and one or two bends which he could have sworn were not in it the last time. And then he observed, on the other side, the small ravine of a burn which issued in a noisy trickle of water. He certainly had never seen *that* before, so he stood and stared at it until it began to stare back. Whereupon he went on, but with the corner of his left eye on the ravine to prevent a surprise, and while he was thus politely not really looking at the ravine, the earth itself bobbed clean from under his foot and he went face first into a ditch. It was the one he had told Mary Ann how to jump.

So he was on the right road, and even if things could be enchanted, as he had heard Donul say before now, they clearly had not been enchanted entirely.

All the same, they had gone a bit strange, and even if Mary Ann——. The thought of her brought up a vision of the foxgloves which she had called the thimbles of the fairy woman—the foxgloves that grew in front of the wild beast's den, which could not be so very far ahead of him now. Art suddenly stopped.

Mary Ann had said it mightn't be a wild beast's den at all, but the house of the little folk who had planted the fox-gloves in front of it for a garden. To Art at this moment there didn't seem much to choose between a wild beast's den and a house of the little folk.

Back he couldn't go, and forward his feet wouldn't budge, so he went sideways down to the stream in the glen, crossed it without misadventure, and climbed the opposite slope until at last he drew himself up through a tongue of heather and lay on his belly peering all round.

And it was lucky for him that he did so, for now striding across the moor towards the side which he had just left came three strange men. Even at a distance Art could see that they were dressed like the Ground Officer when he went to meet the Factor on the day of the collection of rents. And if it came to a choice of passing close to these Great Ones of the earth or to the wild beast's den, Art would rather take a chance on the den.

So it was fear mostly that held him where he was, while the strange men strode down into the glen. By the stream they paused, glanced about them, and debated together, one pointing this way and one another. The oldest took off his cap, scratched his head thoughtfully like an ordinary man, then looked towards where Art lay. But if he was expecting Art to move he was disappointed, for Art was beyond movement now. He had a heavy dark-grey moustache. The youngest man took a thin book from an inside pocket, opened it, and kept on opening it until it grew into a large bright sheet which he laid on the grass. They grouped round this, and the young man moved his finger along it, glancing up and down as he did so. They all nodded, and the oldest said loudly: 'I told you so.' When the young man had folded the map and put it back in his pocket, they crossed the stream and moved down until they came to the mouth of the ravine which had not so long before stared back at Art. They now stared at it. They nodded. Then, the youngest leading, they proceeded in single file, silently, stealthily, to enter that place.

No sooner were they out of sight, than Art got to his feet and ran on as fast as he could, indeed a little faster, but when he fell he let no yelp out of him now. The next time he fell was from fright at a big black bird that flapped up from below him. As he gazed down the short steep slope, he saw the body of a dead sheep. Where the wool was off its side, the skin was black, and white maggots were crawling over it. A rotten smell attacked his nostrils, and, pushing back his head, he saw, fair across from him on the other side of the small glen, the ravine of the foxgloves and the wild beast's den. He would have run then, but for one infernal circumstance—the roots of the heather above the den breathed out a faint but unmistakable blue smoke.

Art's mind became a whirling place of wild beasts' dens and little houses of fairy folk and legend and dread that set the world itself going up and down and round like the machinery in the meal mill. Then out of the little door, which Art had discovered on the day Mary Ann and himself had set off to find the fabled River, out of the little door that gave entry to the dark den, came the shaggy head of a great beast, and all at once, O torrents of the mountain, it was not a beast's head, but the hairy *oorishk* itself, the fabulous beast-human. There were legends of this human monster that could chill the heart's blood of grown folk. On all fours it came forth, and slowly it reared itself, and looked around, and Art saw, as in a strange and powerful dream, that the *oorishk* was Old Hector.

And Old Hector surely in the living flesh, for who else could scratch his whiskers in that wise and friendly manner while contemplating the heather breathing smoke? But now, like the *oorishk*, Old Hector got down on all fours and crawled in again.

'It's not much,' said Old Hector, as he stood upright in the cave, 'and ten yards up, the smoke disappears entirely.'

'Good for it,' answered Red Dougal, who was switching the froth off a tub of wash. 'You'll believe me now when I said my peat clods were the blackest and best.'

'I believe you,' said Old Hector, smiling. 'You're stoking well, Donul—but go canny. Hold your hand. She'll be coming near it now.' Old Hector lifted a piece of stick and tapped the head of a large enclosed copper pot with a funnel top to it like a chemist's retort.

'Humour her,' chuckled Red Dougal, switching the froth flat. 'The great thing is to humour her first.' His face was blown red and sweating, and charged with hearty mirth and a heavy brown moustache.

Presently Old Hector said to Donul: 'Come here and smell this.'

Donul bent down and smelt the end of a small copper pipe that issued from the foot of a tub. After sniffing once or twice, as though he couldn't believe his own nostrils, he glanced up at Old Hector, saying: 'It's like the scent of roses.'

'The same, but keener,' nodded Old Hector.

'More searching,' said Red Dougal, getting down to have a sniff himself. 'That's the scent of her coming, Donul, boy. Isn't she the lovely one? And when she's kissed you once or twice in the mouth and put her long white arms round you, it's dead to the world you'll be then, my boy.'

Old Hector set a glass jug whose handle was broken under the end of the pipe. And presently there was a crystal drop, another drop, a quick succession of drops, a pause, a trickle in a small gush.

Old Hector smiled as Donul asked him if that indeed was the true spirit.

'Not quite yet,' he answered. 'See!' From the jug he poured a little of the crystal liquid into a coarse tumbler and added some water, whereupon the whole turned a milky blue. 'She's not clean yet.'

'Is this weak, then?' asked Donul.

'No. This is the strongest of all,' answered Old Hector, 'but impure. This is the famous "foreshot".'

'Is it?' said Donul wonderingly.

'It is,' said Old Hector. 'There's nothing like this in the whole world for taking the heat out of an inflamed part, and it's capital for the rheumatics.'

'Do you hear him?' Red Dougal asked the chastened wash. 'Damn me, do you hear him?'

Donul smiled, his face red from the heat of the fire. He

had never cared greatly for Red Dougal, whom he had
hitherto considered to be mostly 'all mouth', but now, somehow or other, the mouth was richer, mellower, and even
those references to white arms which would normally leave
Donul awkward were here less aggressive. Red Dougal was
in his element.

'See how she's clearing,' remarked Old Hector, adding
water to a fresh drop. And Donul saw that the milky-blue
tinge had all but gone. In another minute or two, Old
Hector slipped a small cask under the mouth of the pipe, a
copper filler in its bunghole, and fixed it securely in position.
'You can put on your fire now,' he said to Donul.

When Donul had placed the peat clods in a way that gave
the greatest flame with the least smoke, Old Hector nodded
approval: 'You're coming at it!'

Donul, flushing with pleasure, straightened himself. The
crystal liquid was running in a small but even trickle into
the cask. The rumble of boiling was in the fat-bellied pot.
Donul's eye ran up the pot to the head that narrowed like
the head of a retort, bent over, and was continued in a thin
pipe that would have stretched a long way had it not zigzagged upon itself in so parallel and compact a pattern
that it was contained in little more than half of a gross barrel
or tub. Into this tub, near the foot, water flowed through
a piece of lead piping from the burn outside, the overflow
being drawn away by another piece of piping. The constant
supply of cold water about the zigzagged copper pipe, or
'worm', was sufficient to condense the vapour inside the
worm as it was forced through from the boiling pot. Donul
followed the whole operation and considered it very neat.
Suddenly his eye landed on tiny bubbles breaking on the
surface of the water in the tub. 'What's that?' he asked.

'Ah, dear me,' said Old Hector, stripping off his jacket,
'she's started leaking again. She's done.'

It was a very old worm, lead-soldered in many places, and
when Old Hector had stopped the pin-point leak, he spoke
of ancient days. Red Dougal made a seat for himself of five

uneven peats; Donul sat on a ledge of flat rock, and Old Hector on an up-ended wort-tub.

'I'll hear you better,' said Red Dougal, 'if we try the new run.'

So Old Hector raised the filler, ran some four inches into the tumbler, and replaced the filler without having spilt a drop.

'No, no, try it yourself first,' said Red Dougal, politely shoving back the proferred tumbler.

Old Hector sniffed, and sniffed carefully, and nodded to himself thoughtfully. 'There's no guff in this,' he said. He smoothed back the left wing, the right wing, above his mouth, and then drew down an open hand with natural dignity over his beard.

'Take off your bonnet,' said Red Dougal solemnly to Donul, as he removed his own.

If only a few drops went into Old Hector's mouth, he pondered them with some care before ejecting them with precision into the heart of the fire, where they disappeared like an outraged devil in a wild flash. 'Ha-a-a,' breathed Old Hector, both out and in. Then he nodded finally. 'She'll do,' he said, and handed the tumbler to Red Dougal.

Red Dougal took two heavy sniffs. 'Here's my best respects to you,' and he took a mouthful. He held it for a little as if he didn't know what to do with it, and then let it down in a gulp.

He tried not to show any choking, took in air noisily, and smiled through a flow of tears. 'Boys, it's a good drop,' he remarked huskily. 'I'll say that for you, Hector. It's— kha-a-a—special.' He handed the tumbler to Donul.

'No, no,' said Donul, embarrassed.

'Taste it whatever,' suggested Old Hector.

So Donul, pleased at that, warily lifted the edge of the tumbler to his mouth.

'She won't bite you!' cried Red Dougal, glowing now and laughing at Donul trying to take a few drops without taking many.

This was a more difficult operation than Donul expected, for he was used only to drinking water, and indeed it seemed there was a lot in his mouth once he got it in. Round his teeth it went, stinging his gums not unpleasantly.

'Let it down like a man,' said Red Dougal.

'Spit it out,' advised Old Hector.

Donul didn't know which to do, and at last did both. When he recovered, he breathed out and in quickly, smiling and wiping his eyes. 'It's burning,' he said, 'but it's fragrant still.'

Old Hector looked upon him and smiled with a benign humour. 'It's young,' he explained. 'It has still about it the innocence of creation.' From the tumbler he swallowed a small drop and nodded. 'Yes. Youth itself, as yet unspoiled. The fragrance is the fragrance of the yellow barley under the sun and of the wild flowers in sheltered hollows. It has not yet begun to get old, Donul. With the days it grows rank a little, going through all the green humours as man himself does. Only in advanced age does it get back the original innocence, with something added besides.' Old Hector took another small sip.

'In all languages,' said Red Dougal, 'it's called "the water of life". Isn't that wonderful?' He winked openly at Donul, with a sideways nod towards Old Hector. 'He thinks himself innocent at this moment. Isn't that wonderful, too?'

'It can be abused,' said Old Hector, 'but then so can life itself. So can everything.'

'It can be dear,' responded Red Dougal, 'and so damn dear that the folk who first made it in history—our folk—can now neither make nor get.' Thoughtlessly he stretched for the tumbler, and added: 'That's why I made up my mind we'd have a drop for Duncan's wedding, supposing the whole heaven of the gaugers came down upon us in small bits. So I persuaded Hector. And was I not right? For he is the last of the great makers. Good health to you, Hector, and long may your worm leak in the right place.'

'Thank you,' acknowledged Old Hector with pleasant grace.

'Kha-a-a,' said Red Dougal, pleasantly. 'He's a fine fellow, your brother Duncan, Donul; an upright, decent lad. And his wedding is a time when a fellow is shy and needs—when he needs——'

'We're all the better of a little gaiety at such a time,' interposed Old Hector. 'Indeed we suffer from the lack of it, and sometimes I see a sadness on the land.'

'Sadness bedam'd, and if so who is to blame for it but ourselves? Isn't that what I have always been telling you? But would you listen to me? Not you! You would always say that everything should be measured by right conduct, by what is fair and just. To hell with that, say I! It should be measured by action. And this is the kind of action I mean. We're *doing* things now: not sitting and talking and grieving over the past.' Red Dougal cocked his eye at Old Hector. 'Would you say our conduct is fair and just, now?'

Old Hector's eyes glimmered thoughtfully.

'Here,' said Red Dougal, 'have a pull at this before you answer.'

'Put it round with the sun,' said Old Hector.

Red Dougal laughed and handed the tumbler to Donul. 'You're not frightened of leading the lad astray?'

'Open trust never led a lad astray,' murmured Old Hector, 'in all my experience. And I am sure of Donul.'

With a warm smile of pleasant embarrassment Donul investigated the liquor curiously and handed the tumbler to Old Hector.

'Now you can speak,' said Red Dougal, 'and I'll try not to interrupt you.'

Old Hector shook his head. 'What I have to say, you already know.'

'Are we deceiving the Revenue?' demanded Red Dougal.

'We are,' responded Old Hector.

'Are we breaking the law?'

'We are.'

'What would happen to us if the three gaugers were to descend upon us at this moment?' pursued Red Dougal.

'Because the largeness of the fine would be far beyond us, you and I would be put in prison for a very long time, but Donul would not be put in prison, for he had not anything to do with this, but only happened to light on us by chance. And you will both remember that story carefully,' said Old Hector.

Red Dougal laughed. 'Have I not cornered you now, hip and beard?'

'Not that I have noticed,' replied Old Hector mildly.

'Haven't I proved you the very fount and origin of law-breaking and all that's wrong?' demanded Red Dougal.

'Law-breaking, yes,' said Old Hector. 'But wrong is a difficult word. Many a day I have pondered over it, but I am not sure that I have found the answer. I only have a feeling about the answer and sometimes I go by that feeling. For, you see, laws are necessary, and to break them is wrong. Yet a law can be wrong.'

'And is a law wrong just because *you* find it wrong?' scoffed Red Dougal.

'Yes,' answered Old Hector.

'But the law that's wrong to you is sure to be right to the other fellow, or it wouldn't be in it. How then?' demanded Red Dougal.

'I still must judge for myself, just like the other fellow. That he may have the power to make me suffer does not, of itself, mean that he is right. It just means that he has the power to make me suffer. But it remains with me to judge for myself the outcome of all the elements and to come to a decision on the matter.'

'What are the elements here? Eh?'

'Many and varied they are,' replied Old Hector. 'This is our old native drink, made in this land from time immemorial. We were the first makers, as you have just said. For untold centuries we had it as our cordial in life, distilled from the barley grown round our doors. In these times, because it was free, it was never abused. That is known. Deceit and abuse and drunkenness came in with the tax, for the folk had to evade the tax because they were poor. The best smuggler in my young days was an Elder of the Church. Before he started making a drop, he used to pray to God, asking Him not to let the gaugers come upon him unawares.'

'I have heard of that,' said Red Dougal. 'Tell me,' he added with a curious look, 'did you put up a few words yourself before we started here?'

'I did,' replied Old Hector, looking back at Red Dougal with his gentle smile.

The laugh that had been ready to come out died inward in Red Dougal, and he looked downward.

'For we do not make this drink to profit by it at the expense of the tax,' proceeded Old Hector. 'We do not sell it.

Just as Donul does not sell a salmon he takes out of the River. Nor would we even make it thus for our own use if we could afford to buy it. But we cannot buy it. We are too poor. The men who have made the law have taken our own drink from us, and have not left us wherewith to buy it. Yet they can buy it, because they are rich. I have the feeling that that is not just. I do not grudge them their riches and all it can buy for them.'

'And do you think,' said Dougal, lifting his head, 'that the Sheriff in his court will listen to your fine reasons?'

'I have no foolish notions about that,' replied Old Hector. 'But I am a man whose eightieth birthday is not so far distant, and I had to decide for myself whether my reasons might meet with understanding in a Court higher than the Sheriff's.' There was a pause, and Old Hector looked at the fire. 'There is only one thing,' he added quietly.

'What's that?' asked Red Dougal, eyeing the old man.

'I should not,' said Old Hector, 'like to die in prison.'

There was a little silence, and upon it fell a small sound. The sound came from outside. It was no more than the rattle of a tumbling pebble, but it might have been the sounding of the Trumpet of Judgement upon bodies grown rigid and faces that stared. There was no more sound. Then sound came again, and came nearer. The low doorway was slowly darkened, and before their awed eyes a small human figure uprose in the dim chamber and gazed at them, and the figure was Art.

'God be here!' exclaimed Red Dougal harshly, and though the unstable peats upon which he sat now threw him on his back, projecting his heels into the air, yet he contrived to stare from the ground.

Because of the brightness outside, Art at first could see nothing but terrifying faces in an infernal gloom, and he began to whimper where he stood.

'Art,' whispered Old Hector at last. 'Who brought you here?'

'Is there anyone outside?' whispered Red Dougal harshly.

Terror mounted to a wild cry in Art, but Old Hector soon had him by his knee, soothing him. And presently to the question, 'Is there anyone outside?' Art managed to answer: 'No.'

'Who brought you here?'

'M-myself.'

'Did anyone see you coming?'

'No.'

'Glory be to God,' said Old Hector.

'Holy smoke, you gave us the fright there! Phew!' breathed Red Dougal.

'How did you know we were here?' asked Donul.

Art at first could not answer, but at last he told how he had set out for the River and how he had seen Old Hector from across the glen.

Relief was such that they were all smiling now as at a miracle.

'All the same,' said Old Hector, 'we ought to have had Hamish posted where I said.'

'If I put him where I did,' replied Red Dougal, 'it's because he can command a better approach from the south, and that's the way the gaugers must come. Surely that's sense.'

Old Hector turned to Art. 'And you never saw anyone?'

'Yes,' replied Art, 'I saw three strange men.'

Red Dougal, who had been twisting round for the tumbler, stopped in his twist like a man struck by lumbago.

When they had got Art's story, Old Hector nodded with finality. 'They'll be here in one hour. They're combing the glen.'

'Some rat has informed on us!' cried Red Dougal. 'Some bloody rat must have given us away!'

'Let us think,' said Old Hector.

'Think, bedam'd! We've got to get the stuff away, and double quick. Come on!'

'It's too late now,' said Old Hector, sitting quietly where he was.

Red Dougal raged, ready to tear asunder and save what he could, but Old Hector arose, saying: 'It's all or nothing. We'll take the chance.'

Red Dougal gaped at him. But Old Hector was very calm now. 'Come outside,' he commanded, and went before them with an empty malt sack. They followed, and he turned to Art. When he had given Art instructions how to climb up and crawl along the ridge a little way until he could command the glen, and how to watch and report back, he concluded, 'Will you do that?' with a smile that in its great trust moved Art profoundly.

Art nodded, his chest thick with excitement and fear, for well he knew now who the strange men were.

'You two,' commanded Old Hector, 'take this sack and bring back on it the rotten sheep yonder.'

'What's the sense——' stormed Red Dougal, but Old Hector turned from him and, gathering a nest of decomposing undergrowth, placed in it a pile of sheep droppings. Whereupon he crawled back into the cave.

For a moment he stood looking about him thoughtfully. It was a natural cave, open parts to the front having been built in with solid turfs on which the heather outside grew naturally. The long narrow vent above he would close with a couple of divots, once he had flapped the smoke away.

After covering Red Dougal's wash, he withdrew the cask, placed a wooden bucket under the pipe, draped a sack over both pipe and bucket, and bunged the cask with its small drop of whisky. Into the fire he fed some of the nest until an acrid stench got him in the throat. Raking out the fire from under the pot, he threw the remainder of the nest upon it, and, in due course, stamped out the red embers until the dry putrid stink choked him. Rolling the small cask before him, he reached the outside air, where he lay for a little, gasping and wiping his eyes.

By the time Red Dougal and Donul came back carrying the sheep on the sack, Old Hector was sitting by the mouth of the leaden inlet pipe which ran underground, wiping his forehead. The mouth of the pipe he had choked with a sod and concealed with accidental boulders. The wild contortions Dougal and Donul were making to turn their noses away from the sheep sent a smile into his whiskers as he got up and guided them to where the entrance of the cave had been. As the carcass landed with a sickly squelch, the two bearers grunted in concert.

There was little fight left in Dougal now, for the aroma from the sheep had set up an internal argument with the fumes from the liquor, but still he gaped combatantly for the entrance which had disappeared under Old Hector's hands. 'I'll have—*hic!*—the cask though, though the heavens—*hoc!*'

'Don't *hoc* here,' commanded Old Hector sternly. 'There's the cask. You and Donul clear up the burn. Collar Hamish. Get home. Quick!'

Donul, who had crossed the burn and was sitting amid the tall withered stalks of the foxgloves, his head between his knees, arose and followed Dougal.

Old Hector looked around, smothered an abrasion here,

smoothed a heel-mark there, then took out his knife and cut a hole in the black tough skin of the sheep. Whereupon he retreated hurriedly across the burn, stabbed his knife in the ground to clean it, and climbed until he saw Art, to whom he beckoned.

'Come with me,' said Old Hector, 'and we'll cross over to the other side of the glen.'

This they did, and soon they were lying in the place from which Art had recently seen his friend emerge like an *oorishk*.

Art had a thousand questions in him now, but Old Hector whispered that even whispering would keep them from hearing. Presently he dug Art in the ribs. 'Do you see my heroes?'

Art could see nothing but an old raven sitting on the cave above the sheep, croaking at another old raven, both looking all round. But in Old Hector's eyes Art saw a primordial mirth so warm that he nestled into it.

Time passed.

'They're a long time,' whispered Art.

'Time is longer sometimes,' whispered Old Hector.

It got so long that it must have stopped, and Art was about to formulate his own view of time when Old Hector's hand came gently on his back and pressed him into the heather.

Art was frightened to look at first. Then through the heather roots he saw the three strange men coming down the off side of the glen. They stopped, they talked together, looking this way and that. The young man took out his map, but the man with the moustache waved an impatient arm and strode on. The young man returned the map unopened to his pocket. They drew near, they paused, and, rounding the last bluff, surprised two ravens that rose heavily, croaking, from a dead sheep.

They looked at the ravens, they stared at the sheep, they went slowly through the withered foxgloves and peered into the water. Then the young one lifted his head sharply and stared at the cave. As if struck in the face, he backed away among the foxgloves, a hand to his nose. By the way he made up the burn, an unmentionable disease might have been after the fibres in his throat. The others followed, but more slowly.

They had not proceeded many yards, however, when the man with the moustache, going last, paused, turned slowly round, and sniffed the air like a stag. Old Hector lay very still now, for this was the only one he feared. Art felt the large hand grip in his back.

The man swung round as if to recall the two who were fast disappearing in front. With a hoarse croak of laughter, one of the ravens circled down and alighted above the sheep. The man gave it one look, then followed the others out of sight.

Old Hector's head drooped among the heather. Art asked him if they would come back the same way.

'No,' answered Old Hector, lifting his head slowly and regarding Art with a profound and tender smile. 'You saved your old friend from prison that time.'

'Did I?' Art was deeply moved.

'You did. And you saved Duncan's wedding present into the bargain. Indeed, I doubt if such a great wedding present as this of yours was ever made before. All that remains now is for you to hold it *as secret as the grave.*'

'*As secret as the grave,*' murmured Art, his heart like to burst with the amount of life and loyalty in it.

The Tune Kilmarnock

JOHN MACNAIR REID

(1897–1954)

Is not style an admission that you have found yourself and that, therefore, you are lost? When I said to my heart 'I will take your treasure up into the daylight and explain it to men,' my heart immediately doubted if it had a treasure at all. But I grew reckless as I thought of the chance this was of impressing men by my methods—my choice of words, my deft allusions, my outer rim of nonsense that marks the bull's-eye of sense.

'Yes,' I say to myself, 'you smiled when you thought of people saying, "Now, isn't it strange, but I've often felt such a thing and never could express it!" feeling as you did so powerful, so completely able to express it.

'Then a shadow came on your thought and you frowned. Why did men not add, ". . . but HE surely managed it"? Men read your work and discuss themselves into it, whereas they should see you only in it as it is your property. This treasure in your heart, for instance.'

Style is the body that wears you down and destroys you. It is conduct, three-fourths of life. The other fourth is the material which never goes down and which cannot be destroyed. Great men have had great style. They have stamped the record of existence upon the material Being as a lead embosses paper. I feel on Ayrshire soil that Burns's ribs are sticking out of it. Those great men may not see anything without wishing to impress their personalities upon it. Thus they alter and falsify it. It passes on to the next person—as it must pass on—man-soiled.

I will tell of this thing without style, for I know not how to tell it. I will not ponder on it: I will not be showy.

When I was young my mother said I was always showing off. But that was because she saw me doing things she had never seen little girls do when she was a girl. She knew nothing of little boys.

This thought will restrain me if some night when passing their bedroom door, with the candle shaded by my hand, I hear her saying to my father as they lie in the darkness, 'It's just like him to say he hears something in a tune that no one else has ever heard.' I shall pass on to my own room. They will not know that a part of them both has passed by outside and now lies in another square of the same darkness thinking of them. Such a picture makes me see myself as a tombstone glimmering in the moonlight with their names upon my brow.

But my mother's love would last through all that which she calls showiness, and would through other vices more incriminating. I do not fear her eyes upon my story. With others it is different.

There is Mark Ireland in my mind. We became friends at the time when friends are easily made, and have become enemies now when friends are sorely needed. (I suppose we are enemies now that friendship is over? It must be so when you think of the way things ended.) All my aims and aspirations, my tastes and prejudices were as open country to him. The more he explored the more I wanted to show him. Then, when ultimately my heart was entirely his, and he one of the permanencies of my heart, there came a pause. He seemed to draw back a convenient space to strike. He struck hard and cruelly: my heart shut tight, but it was too late. Now it hides the bruise, and lack of sun and light prevents its healing.

There, then, was someone separate from me, though he used my symbols and had my habits of living; someone from the beginning cast in the mould of enmity against me. If he should read my story he would sneer his sneer which is a duty to himself. And something of my heart would be wounded again.

Mark Ireland has been to Collashaig with me several times. We have slept together in the room above the parlour with its window facing the loch. All the days were spent fishing and mooning around. But on Sundays we went over the moor to the tiny church. He's bound to remember that sometimes. I wonder what his thoughts are when the memory comes and how he puts it from him again. Probably it bores him.

Certain it is that when I go to Collashaig nowadays I am not troubled by memories of him. He has not impressed himself upon the place. I never see his 'slow smile' break where the sun lights up the woods, and Cruachan amid the scurrying clouds stands aloof, as I like to picture him, free from all questionings of vanity. Yet such ears as Mark's have listened to prayer and Psalm in that little church, and such a voice as he possessed once aided in· the praise. He was a voice in the days of my Belief.

My mother had a singing voice. When she first went to that little church on the hill-side at Collashaig one bright Sunday morning, the congregation stopped its breath, far less its voice, to listen to that one throat singing:

> 'I'm not ashamed to own my Lord
> or to defend His cause.'

There was something in her voice that got me. It was a soft contralto, and it was like the crushing of deep purple velvet in my hands. She loved her voice. And when she got a Psalm to sing it was like blending two colours, so suited to the Scottish Psalms was her lovely voice.

My childhood, however she remembers it (and when she talks she recalls window breakings, police chases, school complaints and running after lorries in busy Glasgow streets), is to me a composite picture of still moments in large Glasgow churches, where the sunshine sobered or blinded the vulgar coloured windows, a bowed figure in an exalted pulpit, and a voice swimming in the singing of the choir; that voice which sounded like the yield of rich purple

velvet, or had I known of it then, was like the look of the
faint purplish flush of the bloom of a peach. Yes, and of
Sunday mornings and evenings in the little church at Collashaig, when the leader of the altos of a great Glasgow
church became one of the congregation and mingled her
voice in the quivering and hesitant singing of the rustic
people around her.

Well, then, that is my memory. And it seemed to me that
I was my mother's voice stealing unrecognized into the little
hill-side church last Sunday morning. I am now thirty years
old, and the last time I was in that church I was twenty-five.
The last time my mother sang there I was fifteen. It was
about that time she ruined her voice. One foggy night in
Glasgow she attended choir practice and strained her throat.
Add to that that she caught a chill on the road home. The
purplish flush of the bloom was gone. Now she sings no
more.

The last time, when I was twenty-five, Mark Ireland was
with me. I had told him many times about my mother's
singing, but it was not a topic upon which he could impose
a triumphing example from his own little sphere, and so I
felt that though I had spoken of it my memory remained
undisturbed. When I went to the church last Sunday I knew
I was something older than Mark Ireland, something that
had been beautiful in the world before he was born: I was
my mother's voice. Jubilantly I said to myself, 'Now I'll
hear the magic words, "to the tune, Kilmarnock".'

And sure enough after the first prayer there it was, the
decent minister chap announcing to a passive handful of
people the Paraphrase, number fifty-four . . . to the tune,
Kilmarnock.

The sun was shining mildly on the clear glass windows.
I could see the field below the farm, and beyond its tufted
edge the dark slate-grey line of the loch. A few sheep were
grazing in the field, a wind was bothering some low-laid
clouds, a patch of burnt heather looked like a perpetual
cloud shadow on the far hill-side. The lady with the red hat

was over at the wheezy harmonium, playing the first few bars; a shuffle of feet and we all arose.

The recent craving of my Unbelief, which was to destroy religion, has passed from my mind like a mist that leaves no trace. I say to myself there was once such a craving but it is now unconvincing as remembered pain.

Rejected his father's faith. When did I reject my father's faith? Was there a decisive hour? He took me as a child to a sunlit beach, he got me stripped in a small boat and plunged me into the waters. He was by my side and his gleaming arms were iron rods. Blue and a circle of diamonds were round me and a taste of salt that was the bite of the sunshine, the green, sleek body of the sea slipping past underneath me. 'Jesus, my Lord! I know His name, His name is all my boast.'

Someone who was dead was listening through me to the tune Kilmarnock.

A few shrill soprano voices were leading us all, and the men offered a shy and uncertain harmony. The absence of that other voice which flowed through my consciousness like the blood through my veins made the tune, and in this place, the property of other people. Was it like Mark Ireland's face, which on a meeting now, would pass with a distant stare, the light that animated it for me and shone out recognition of me being withdrawn? The love of this thing was not my mother's love of it, however hard I tried to make it so. It was different from my father's love of it as he had his memories rooted still farther back. It was a love new to man. I touched at the invisible, unformed pain awaiting me in the years of my full heritage and my mind reeled in its immaturity in rank sorrow. Someone who was dead was listening through me to the tune Kilmarnock.

And I do not mean my dead self. That would make the phrase mere chicanery. I was there certainly, my dead self was there: but someone else, or a whole people, was listening to a tune once revered as sacred with a gravity beyond my comprehension.

For if these old people could not understand my Unbelief, I could not comprehend their faith. Kilmarnock sings through me to them, of them to me. They had a formula I apprehend, and never was hate so feared as I feared theirs when in a sickness of love for this glory that is Kilmarnock I claimed their tune to chant my Unbelief. And when they listened to the words, 'Nor will He put my soul to shame, nor let my hope be lost,' the whole thing paused.

The sun was mellow on the clear glass window and the field was green without. That patch of burnt heather darkened the hill-side beyond like a cloud shadow and clouds moved slowly in the sky shadowless. That was the unaltered scene of fifteen years ago. The world of thought had moved on and left this little place a derelict scene in the wastes of long ago.

We were lost, those dead and faithful people and I their son with this handful of worshippers; and with us was an imperishable tune. In illimitable Arctic snows the explorer travels until he drops. All the little, hard, material things he gathered together for his use and safety lie around his melting body in the shifting ice. Some day, years and years onward, his tiny compass may lie in the white palm of a man, highly curious, wise and tolerant. The history of its survival will be recorded. . . . 'What I've committed to His trust, till the decisive hour.'

At the edge of my consciousness where those faces were crowding, Mark Ireland's among them, there was a rim of darkness. Each face had something about it that made it familiar, a something borrowed from my father's face to give it credibility and power. But I knew that while they listened and rejoiced they were blind, and could not explore the calm reserves of sense wherein my existence was secure without even scepticism: an indifference terrible as frozen snowdrifts on winter moors.

Youth stands with beseeching hands yearning toward the past, believing that the very ground he treads has become arid at the touch of his foot. But the ground I tread now is of holy ground for me, for the present must some day complete a past for which I shall yearn and remain uncomforted. The sanction of my Unbelief will then be final and my heart as calm and bleak as moonlight haze on snow. I shall turn my face to the outer darkness and go out. . . . 'Then shall He own His servant's name before His Father's face, and in the new Jerusalem appoint my soul a place.'

O mother, sitting at your hearth, with your black dress gathered round your legs like a silken rug and your white woollen shawl lying idle on the chair's arm near the fire, you have sung as I shall never sing, and as I shall never hear sung again a song that, being intensely grave and holy, is to a mind today only the more intensely pagan. I am standing here, my darling, in the sunlight of the little church, and the green fields are round me and the sheep are grazing in the fields as of old and the loch is still in the distance. Your father and your father's father are listening, and as the voices sing your voice breaks through and grows and grows and grows: it overflows my consciousness: I am dissolving in it; I am become your voice that has visited its old triumphant haunt. Even so I have wandered into the past and am among the lost.

On an Island

NAOMI MITCHISON

(b. 1897)

By morning it was worse Kenny was. She herself had dozed off, for maybe an hour, between black night and the time when the lamp by the window began to look queer. The fire was down, but when she blew on it the peats flared again. The kettle would be boiling in a wee while. He would like a cup tea surely. Nothing to eat, the doctor had said. But how then would he keep his strength up? Maybe an egg——. From where she was by the fire she kept on looking back over her shoulder at him on the bed, not himself at all, a stranger in their own bed, in Kenny's body, pulling at the red blankets.

She made the tea, strong, with plenty of sugar, the way Kenny liked it. But the stranger pushed it away. She hardly knew whether to speak to him in the English or the Gaelic. But he answered to neither.

She looked out; it was low tide. The doctor would cross the ford easy. She had better see to the cow and the hens before he would be coming. Her mother came up past the back of the dyke. She looked at the stranger in the bed, and shook her head.

'Go you to the cow, Beitidh,' she said. 'I will sit with him. Will he not take his tea? Well, well. But it is a pity to waste a good cup.'

After she had fed the hens, Beitidh came back with the milk pail and set the half of it for cream.

'I will churn Saturday,' she said. 'He will be better then.'

For indeed it was a bonny fresh morning and she felt better herself, and that way she had a certainty that he too would be better. But her mother, sitting ben by the bed, gave her a look that spoilt that, and oh, now it came to her that Kenny would never dig his knife into the golden butter, never again, and she sat down on the wee stool by the window and put her head down in her hands, and she had cried the edge of her skirt wet through by the time she heard the doctor's car.

He did not speak much to her, only made her hold the lamp near, for it was kind of dark over by the bed. He was listening and feeling about, and Kenny began to moan, to make noises not like himself, not like Kenny, who was so strong and clever, and her hand shook, holding the lamp, and her mother's eyes on her were sorrowful and certain.

The doctor was speaking and at first she had trouble understanding him.

'But we havena been in an aeroplane, neither of the two of us,' she said. 'He would know——'

'He will not need to know,' said the doctor. 'And all you need to do yourself is to wrap him up warm. I will be with him to the hospital.'

'But—but then—how will I know?'

'You will just go over with Donny's van to Stronbost and you will get Mrs. Morrison at the Post Office to ring up the hospital,' he looked at his watch, 'round about four o'clock, and you will know then.'

'Och, I'm no' just sure—if I want him to go at all, Doctor—not so far—I will need to think it over!'

'Beitidh,' said the doctor, 'there is no time for thinking it over. The 'plane is on its way from Renfrew. Give me some safety pins now and we will wrap him up.'

She felt in the drawer for them blindly. He was taking Kenny away, she had no power to stop him. And what would they do with him at the hospital—och, she would never see him again!

The 'plane came down on the sand, and then, before she was used to it at all, the doctor and a strange kind of nurse had bundled Kenny in, with the red blankets round him, and he not saying good-bye, not knowing even they had taken him away. The door shut on her, and the thing left in a terrible wind and noise, and it was as though part of herself had been pulled away with it.

Her mother had everything straightened up within, and the bed made again, with her other blankets, the old plain ones that she used to sleep under before ever she was married on Kenny.

'If it is the Lord's will,' said her mother, 'we must not be the ones to complain. And maybe it is as well now that you have no bairns. For you will marry again, surely.'

Soon her sister came in and two more of the neighbours, and they put on the kettle again. 'Och, well, well, poor Kenny,' they were saying. 'He was a good lad. It was a terrible pity for him to be going this way.'

And she sat, half listening while they spoke of one or another who had died, either at home or after being taken away to the hospital. And the thing beat on her and now all the months of her life with Kenny had gone small and far. And she began looking ahead, past the things that were to be done. For they would bring back the corpse from the hospital as it had been done before with others. It would come by the boat, and they would go down to meet it. She would need to go to the store for a black dress; she had the coat. There was money saved enough for everything. And of a sudden she saw Kenny's hand putting the silver money into the jug at the back of the press, Kenny's own strong hand, and she burst out weeping and ran from the house. The rest looked on her with compassion and fell again to speaking of the ways of death.

Donny's van was on the far side of the flood, and the boat would be crossing, for it was high tide now. She took her place in the bows; she must carry out the things the doctor had told her; she must receive the news. Old Hamish had a web of tweed to ferry across, but he put it and himself in the stern of the boat and was joined by two of the crofters. They spoke in low voices, aware of her alone in the bows.

She climbed into the van and the road went by and the dark banks of peat and the dark shining water over the peat, and they came into the long scatter of houses that was Stronbost, a few black houses still, like their own, but mostly the new concrete ones. There had been a time when she and Kenny had spoken together of how they would build themselves a white house with a good chimney and maybe a bathroom later on, and he would get the grant from the Board. And that seemed all terrible long ago now.

She went into the store, and whispered to Mrs. Morrison how she needed to telephone to the hospital, and could it be done. Mrs. Morrison said it was the easiest thing in the world and brought her to the telephone and spoke into the thing, and there was clicking and slamming and then it was the hospital, and oh, it was beyond her altogether to speak into it herself, to ask the question and to get the answer! But Mrs. Morrison was brisk, she spoke, she asked. 'Here is the doctor now,' she said. 'Speak you, Beitidh.' And then, calling into the black mouth of the telephone, 'This is Beitidh here, Doctor.'

'He has been through the operation,' the doctor said, 'and he is getting on fine.'

'Oh, Doctor, Doctor!' said Beitidh into the thing, 'is it living he is? Is it living, my Kenny?'

'Aye,' said the doctor. 'Just that. We were in time.'

'Och,' said Beitidh. 'I thought—I thought——'

And then she began to laugh like a daft thing, and the black mouth of the telephone grinned at her, the way it could have been laughing too.

The Goose Girl

ERIC LINKLATER

(1899-1974)

WHEN I woke among the currant-bushes I saw her coming out of the cottage door with her fist round the gander's neck. I heard them too, for she was yelling and the gander was beating the doorposts and beating her thighs with his great creaking wings. Like a windmill in the distance, like the slap of a rising swan's black feet on the water, like clothes on the line thrashing in a breeze: the gander was making nearly as much noise as she was, and she was shouting her head off. There was no leaping tune in her voice that morning. It was just the air in her lungs being driven through the funnel of her throat like steam from a well-fired boiler; and some of the words she was using were no prettier than what goes on in any stoker's mind. I wasn't listening so much as looking. I had heard those words before, but I had never seen a woman's body like hers, so firm and long of limb, like a young reed in firmness and round as an apple where it should be, and white as a pearl. Against the gander's wings, which were a cold white like snow, her pallor was warm and glowing. Not reflecting light, but glowing with it. She was naked as the sky, and the sky, at four o'clock in the morning, was bare of cloud except for a little twist of wool low down in the west.

Now she gripped the gander's neck with both her hands, and even her hands weren't red like any other country girl's, but small and white. They were strong though, and I could see the hardness of her forearms. She was throttling the bird, and its beak was wide open, a gaping stretch of yellow skin, the upper mandible at right angles to the lower. Its eyes were hidden in the ruffling of its little head-feathers. She dragged it through the door, gave a great heave, and threw it with a noise of breaking stalks into some overgrown rhubarb. A splash of dewdrops rose from the leaves and caught the light. For a moment she stood looking at the bird, her arms a little bent and her hair dishevelled, her mouth open, and her breast rising and falling. Then abruptly, she turned and went back into the cottage, slamming the door behind her. I listened, I remember, for the sound of a key turning or a bolt going home; but in this part of the country they never lock their doors. It was lack of custom, not lack of feeling, that prevented her from giving this final emphasis to her act of expulsion.

The gander shook himself, hissing loudly, and broke more stalks of rhubarb as he made his way to a narrow path of little sea-shore pebbles. I had seen him before, half a dozen times with the girl, and always marvelled at the size of him, but now, from where I lay among the currant-bushes, he looked bigger than ever and his ruffled head-feathers stood out like a crown. His neck was as stiff as a broom-handle but twice as thick, and he turned his head this way and that with a twitch of the bill, an angry snap. His little black eyes were swollen and bright, and the broad webs of his feet fell on the path with the heavy tread of

German infantry. He stopped when he saw me and stood for a little while, hissing like a burst tyre; but not in the way of an ordinary gander, with its neck low to the ground and its beak reaching forward. He stood upright, his head swaying back as if to look at me from a greater height, and when he had done with hissing he turned his back on me and went tramping through some rows of cabbage-plants to a gap in the low garden wall where the old turf-dyke on which it was built had collapsed and brought down the stone. It was a plain little garden with no colour in it except some yellow daisies under the cottage windows and a thin growth of honeysuckle beside the door. There was a fuchsia hedge on one side, not in flower yet, and gooseberries and black-currant bushes along the other walls, with a clump of grey-barked elder-trees in the corner. On one side of the dividing pebble-path rhubarb and spring onions, early potatoes and cabbage on the other: that was all. And the gander, marching like a Prussian, flattened the cabbages under his broad splayed feet as if there had been the weight of a man in him. Perhaps there was. He was no ordinary bird, that was certain.

I got up and followed him, cautiously, as he disappeared, and watched him swimming down the little stream that runs behind the cottage to the big loch a quarter of a mile away. I saw his head, still ruffled, still indignantly twitching, behind a bank of meadowsweet; and then he vanished.

I leant against the wall of a cartshed, thinking. The air was still, and the country looked as though no one had ever touched it. The day before had been wet and ugly, and I remembered with a kind of shame how unhappy I had been; and how clumsily I had behaved, getting drunk so that I could tell the truth. But now I felt uncommonly well— and I had done my duty. There's nothing like sleeping in the open air to prevent a hangover, and I had, after long delay, disburdened my mind. The evening before I had gone to see John Norquoy to tell him how his young brother had been killed on the shore of Lake Commachio.

We had been together for a long time, Jim Norquoy and I, in the Seaforths to begin with and then in the Commando, and between Primo Sole in Sicily and that great cold lagoon of Commachio, mud and water and a dancing mirage, we had had our fill of fighting. Jim was hit in shallow water, wading ashore after our boats had grounded on a mudbank just as the sun came up, and I carried him in. But he died on the edge of the land, and his last words were, 'You'll find it difficult to go back too, after all this.'

That was an understatement. I found it impossible to go back to the life I had known before, and when I came north to the islands, to tell his people about Jim and give him what immortality I could, by feeding their pride in him, I was looking for something for myself as well. No more school-teaching for me. I was never meant to be a teacher anyway, either by Providence or my parents. I had only wanted to live—I mean to live in such a way that life came in through my eyes and I could feel it on my skin—but never had I known how to go about it till the war came. And now, when the war was over, I was more at a loss than ever. I couldn't go back to an elementary school in Falkirk, and teach little boys the parts of speech and the more blatant pieces of history, for fear that one of them, some day, might ask me, 'What's it all for? What are we going to say when we've learnt the parts of speech; and if we learn all the history in the world, what would it mean?'

I was no coward, not in the physical sense, and I had been a good soldier—not as good as Jim, though I earned my pay—but when I looked at those questions in the solitude of my mind I knew that I couldn't face them in public. Nor did I want to. I wanted to live, but not to set myself up as a preceptor of living. As a small boy I had gone about in a state of perpetual astonishment; a book or a feather, a mouse or a fish or the dining-room table had all seemed equally miraculous, and I lacked the ordinary confidence in my own reality. I never went to bed without wondering what new shape I might inhabit by the morning. Almost from the beginning I was a disappointment to my parents. They had a position to keep up, and were ambitious too. They took it very badly when I was expelled from the school where my elder brother had been Head of his House and Captain of Cricket.

Now, after six years in the Army, I felt that I had served my apprenticeship to war, but I was still a novice in peace. So I couldn't, in honesty, set up as a teacher, and I had been looking for something else to do. I hadn't much to guide me except negatives. I didn't want to live in a town, for one thing, because I felt, at that time, the need to think; and peace to think, in my view of it, required the open sky.

I started badly, for after I had seen John Norquoy at a cattle market one day, I couldn't bring myself to go and tell him about Jim. I had wanted to make him, and all his friends, so proud of Jim that he would live for ever in their minds like a lighted lamp, to which their love would be as moths, gathering to his memory and beating its wings in the glow of him. Jim was my friend, and even the Seaforth Highlanders had never known a better man.

But when I first saw John Norquoy I realized that it wasn't going to be easy to talk about pride to him, for he knew enough already. That was evident, though it was quite an ordinary occasion. He was looking at a thin-faced cattle-dealer pulling the loose black skin on the rump of a two-year-old heifer. There was nothing of the braggart in him, nothing loud or boastful, but he had the same build as Jim, the same sort of head ten years older, the look of a man who knew what he was after and what it was worth. He was smiling, and there was the same irony in his smile, though he was only selling a beast, as I had seen in Jim's face, grey with the strain of battle, when we had to withdraw from the Primo Sole bridge because our ammunition was spent, and the infantry who should have relieved us hadn't been able to get forward in time. There was nothing I could tell John Norquoy about pride, and when I realized that I put off going to see him. I put it off for about three weeks.

I stayed with the village schoolmaster, a good man who had fought in the last war. I told him about my other difficulty, and he thought I could teach with safety in a country school. 'The children here,' he said, 'wouldn't worry you with awkward questions. They don't grow up with doubt in their minds. Life for them means birth and marriage and death, and they're all natural things. It means hard work and hard weather, and what amusement they and their neighbours can make for themselves. It means dancing and making love when they're young, and breeding a good beast and gossiping when they're older. And if, from time to time, they're troubled about the deeper significance of life, they keep their trouble to themselves. They know that it's an old trouble, and it wouldn't occur to them that you could cure it.'

But I didn't want to teach, either in country or town, so I spent my three weeks in idleness, but kept my eyes open. I had an open mind too, and no accomplishments. I was ready for suggestions; but not for going to see John Norquoy. I met Lydia one day, and talked to her for a quarter of an hour till her mother came out and called her in. The next time I saw her she had the gander with her, and she wasn't so friendly. I felt hurt and disappointed and a little angry, though I didn't realize then what she was really like. We pay too much attention to clothes, and hers were the sort you don't see in a town unless a strayed gipsy has come in. She had a small, beautifully shaped head, but her hair was tangled by the wind and greasy, and her features were so regular that I didn't notice, to begin with, how good they were. Her throat was lovely, long and as white as milk, but her neck was dirty, and when I saw her for the second time it was the same dirt, I'm fairly sure, that still darkened her skin. And yet I felt hurt when she wouldn't stay and talk to me.

I asked the schoolmaster about her, and he told me she was illegitimate, a state of being that's not extraordinary in country districts. Her mother was a grim old woman named

Thomasina Manson, a crofter's only child, unpopular as a girl, who had lived a lonely and blameless life till she was about thirty-five, when she had gone to Edinburgh, and what she did there, except get herself into trouble, no one ever knew. It was generally supposed that she had been in domestic service, and when her baby was born, about three months after she came home, she told the doctor that its father came of the gentry. But that's all she told, and her father and mother, who had married late in life, never recovered from the shock. They were Plymouth Brethren, said the schoolmaster, sternly pious and pitiably dependent on their respectability. They died, one after the other, within a couple of years of Lydia's birth, and Thomasina was left alone to work the croft and bring up the child.

How, I asked, did she come to give it a name like Lydia?

The schoolmaster showed me a register of the village children. About half of them had been christened simply enough: Thomas and James and Mary, Ellen and Jean and William and David, and a few of the girls had clumsy feminine transformations of masculine names such as Williamina and Davidina and—like Lydia's mother—Thomasina. But the rest were a fancy array of Corals and Dereks, Stellas and Audreys, and so forth. 'Their mothers take a fancy to names they've seen on the films or in a magazine,' he said. 'They don't suit our island surnames, but they produce, I suppose, the same effect in the house as a piece of new wallpaper or a set of new curtains. They seem bright and cheerful.'

A moment later he said, 'When are you going to see the Norquoys? They know who you are, and they're expecting you. But they won't ask you to come, they'll just wait.'

'It's not easy,' I said.

'It won't be as difficult as you think. They won't show any emotion, you needn't be afraid of that.'

'I'm thinking of myself,' I answered.

I waited another ten days, and then, one Saturday morning, I went to town—four thousand inhabitants and a little red cathedral—and managed to get a bottle of whisky. I arrived at the Norquoys' about six o'clock, and though I hadn't told them I was coming, they seemed to be expecting me. News travels quickly here, and even a man's intentions become public property as soon as he has realized them himself, and sometimes before. So I sat down to a mighty farmhouse tea in the kitchen, and no one said a word about Jim. They asked me what I thought of the islands, and where I belonged to, and if my parents were still alive, and they all laughed when I mistook a young sister of John Norquoy's wife for one of his daughters. There were ten or a dozen people at table, and I had to be told very carefully who they all were, and they thought it a great joke when I couldn't remember. But no one mentioned Jim.

After tea John Norquoy took me out to see the animals. He had a couple of fine young Clydesdales, a small herd of black-polled cattle, a great surly white boar, and a few score of sheep on hill pasture. We walked in his fields for a couple of hours, and still no word of Jim. But when we came back to the farm he led me into the ben-room; a peat fire had been lighted in it, and going through the passage where I had hung my waterproof I took my bottle out of the pocket. Norquoy paid no attention to it when I set it down, but went to a little table in the window where another bottle, the same brand as my own, stood on a tray with glasses and a jug of water. He poured a couple of deep drams and said, 'It was very good of you to write about Jim in the way you did. We're most grateful to you, and we're glad to see you here. If you're thinking of staying, there's a bed for you whenever you want it.'

I took my drink before I answered, and then, slowly and little by little I told him about Jim, and about the war, and what it means to go through five or six battles with the same friend beside you, and then to lose him in the last one. I realized, in an hour or two, that I was playing the bereaved

brother myself, but I couldn't help it by then. Mrs. Norquoy came in, and their eldest boy, and her sister that I had
taken for Norquoy's daughter, and then two or three
neighbours. I went on talking, and they listened. I got most
of the load off my mind, and if they didn't realize, by the
end of it all, that Jim had been a soldier, well, it wasn't my
fault. And every word I spoke was the simple truth. But when
I got up to go Mrs. Norquoy said, 'We're peaceful folk here,
Mr. Tyndall, and Jim was one of us. How he endured all
that fighting I just can't understand.' It wasn't till a few days
later, when I remembered her words, that I began to realize
how much they had disliked what I had been telling them.
They were peaceful folk, and they didn't approve of war.

But at the time I wasn't in the mood to catch a fine shade
of meaning. Both bottles were empty, and I had had a lot
more than my share. John Norquoy drank moderately and
showed no sign of having drunk at all. He had listened carefully, with little change of expression, and the questions he
asked showed that he was following and remembering all
I said. But he made no comments on my story. One of the
neighbours liked his whisky well enough, but carried it as
solemnly as a cask. I was the only one who seemed to have
taken any benefit from what we had been doing, and Norquoy
insisted on coming with me as far as the main road. I was
walking well enough, but talking too much by then, and I
told him—without difficulty—what I had been waiting for
the strength to tell. I got rid of the guilt on my mind.

For a black minute or two, splashing through the shallows
of Commachio, I had been glad when Jim was killed. Glad
it was he and not I whom death had taken, for we knew,
both of us, that our luck was too good to last, and one or
the other must go before the end. And when I saw it was
Jim I was glad, and the guilt of it had lain on me ever since.
Norquoy said nothing that I can remember, though I think
he tried to comfort me and I know that he wanted to take me
home. But I wouldn't let him.

Soon after we had said good-night it came into my head

that I would like to take a look at the goose girl's house. Lydia's, I mean. The last time I had seen her she had been driving her whole flock, fifteen or sixteen of them with the great gander in front like a drum-major, past a big shallow pool in the stream, where the cattle came to drink, and the whole procession had been reflected in the calm water as if to make a picture. To see her like that, in a picture, had made her more real—or am I talking nonsense? Ideal may be the word, not real. Anyone who's fit to be a teacher could tell you, and tell you the difference between them, but I'm not sure myself. But whatever the word should be, I looked at her on the other bank of the stream, she was wearing an old yellow jersey and a dirty white skirt and her legs were bare among the meadowsweet, and I looked at her reflection in the picture, and that night I dreamt of her, and in my dream she was trying to tell me something, but I couldn't hear her.

So I turned off the main road towards her mother's house, and before I got there I realized how drunk I was. I'm not trying to excuse myself, but the whisky had been mixed with a lot of emotion, and as the result of one coming in and the other going out my knees were beginning to buckle, and when I came to the cottage I had one hunger only, and that was for sleep. There was a south-easterly breeze blowing, chill in the middle of the night, and to get into shelter I clambered over the garden wall, and the softness of the dug soil on the other side seemed very comfortable. I fell asleep under the currant bushes, and what woke me was Lydia's screaming and the clattering of the gander's wings as she threw it out of the house.

Well, after I'd seen the bird go marching off, and disappear downstream, I went round, as I said before, to the lee-side of the cartshed and smoked a cigarette. I had been lying on the packet and they were pretty flat, but I rolled one into shape again, and while I smoked I thought, and came to a conclusion.

I fingered my chin, and it was smooth enough. I had

shaved about five o'clock the afternoon before. I felt fresh
and well. Sleeping on the ground had done me no harm,
for I had grown used to that, and the night had been mild.
My clothes were damp with dew and soiled with earth, but
I took off my coat and shook it, and cleaned myself fairly
well with some cut grass. Then I went down to the stream,
and kneeling on the bank I washed my face and rinsed my
mouth, and drank a few handfuls of water.

The door, the unlocked door, opened easily enough and
I made no noise going in. I stood in a little passage with
some old coats hanging on the opposite wall, and an un-
carpeted wooden stair before me that led to a loft. To the
right there was a door into the kitchen, where the old woman
slept in a box-bed, and to the left was the ben-room with
a closet on the inner side where Lydia slept. The ben-room
door was closed with a latch, or a sneck, as they call it here,
and my hand was steady. I opened the door without a
sound, but only two or three inches, and looked in.

Lydia had put on a long white nightgown, an old-
fashioned garment with coarse lace at the neck, and she was
sitting at the north window, the one that opens into the
yard. She held a looking-glass in both hands, and was
staring at her reflection. Her right cheek—the one I could
see—was pink.

She jumped up with a gasp of fear, a hoarse little noise,
when I went in, and faced me with the looking-glass held
to her breast like a shield. 'What do you want?' she asked,
but her voice was quiet.

I closed the door behind me and said, 'If you had asked
me that a week ago, I couldn't have answered you. I might
have said Everything or Nothing. I didn't know. But that
was a week ago.'

'What does that matter to me?' she asked. 'Why have you
come here?'

'Because now,' I said, 'I do know.'

'You have no right to come into my room,' she whispered.

'I want you to marry me,' I said. 'I want a wife.'

She flushed and asked me, 'Why do you think you can find one here?'

Then I told her, or tried to tell her, why nothing had any force or weight in my mind, after seeing her as I had seen her that morning, but to live with her in the love of a man for his wife, in the love of possession without term or hindrance. She turned pale, then red again, when I said that I had seen her wrestling with the gander, and tried to push me out. But I caught her by the wrists, and spoke as a man will when he is wooing, in fumbling and broken words, of her beauty and the worship I would give her. Fiercely, but in a voice as low as a whisper still, she cried, 'I want no one's worship!'

'Last night,' I said, as urgently but as softly as she spoke herself—for the old woman was sleeping only a few yards away—'Last night my mind was full of bitterness and grief. There had been little else in it for a year or more. But I emptied it, last night, and this morning you came into its emptiness and took possession. And I'm not going to live again like a man who's haunted. I'm not going to live with a ghost in my mind, with a ghost walking on my nerves as if they were a tight-rope, a ghost outside the window of my eyes and just beyond my fingers! I want reality. I want you, in my arms as well as in my mind, and I want the Church and the Law to seal you there.'

She answered nothing to that, and I went on talking, but I don't think she listened very closely, for presently she interrupted and asked me, 'Where did the gander go?'

'Down the burn towards the loch,' I told her.

'That's where he came from. He came here about a month ago, and killed the old one. The gander we had before, I mean.'

'He won't come back,' I said. 'He's had enough of you, after the way you handled him.'

She turned to the window, the one that opens into the yard, and looked out, saying nothing. I went behind her and put my arms round her. She tried to push me away, but with no determination in her movement, and I talked some more. She listened to me now, and presently turned and faced me, and said yes.

The next morning I began my new life of work and responsibility. I bought a boat, a heavily built, round-bellied dinghy, ten-and-a-half-foot keel and in need of paint, for £18. 10s. Two days later I took a summer visitor out fishing, and made fifteen shillings for six hours' easy work. It was a good fishing loch, and there were visitors in the islands again for the first time since 1939. I could look forward to three or four days' work a week, and as trout were selling for 2s. 9d. a pound I sent home for my own rod and tackle, and did quite well on my unemployed days in addition to enjoying them. I could have done still better with night-lines and an otter at dusk and a little caution, but I like fishing too much to cheat at it.

I was still living with the schoolmaster, for £2. 10s. a week, but our relations became a little cooler when his wife discovered that I was sleeping out. That didn't worry me, however, for my happiness that summer was like the moon and the stars, shining and beyond the reach of malice.

It puzzled me a little that I couldn't persuade Lydia to settle a date for the wedding, as I thought there might be a proper reason for it before long, but when I once spoke of it more seriously than usual, she said, 'We're perfectly happy as we are. I don't see why we should bother. Not yet, at any rate. And I'll have to explain to mother, and she's difficult sometimes.'

'I'll do any explaining that's necessary.'

'No, no! You must leave that to me. You won't say anything to her, will you?'

I said I wouldn't. She asked very little of me—she never has asked much—and neither then nor now could I refuse her anything. She had made a good pretence of surrendering, but my surrender went deeper. I had become the roof and the walls within which she lived, but she was the soul of the house. I thought of Jim whenever I looked up at the Kirk hill and saw Norquoy's farm on the slope of it, but to think of him didn't make me feel guilty now. I was no longer obsessed by him, and if a new obsession had taken his place, I had no cause to grumble against it. So June and July went quickly by in that happiness and in good weather, though not settled weather, for the island skies are always change-able, till one day in mid-August, when I came ashore in a rising wind, colder than it had been for weeks, the old woman met me and without a word of greeting said, 'You'd better come home to your tea.'

'That's very kind of you,' I said, and pulled the boat up and took out the two trout which were all I had caught.

'Would you like these?' I asked.

'It's a poor return for a day's work,' she said, though they were good fish, the better one a little over the pound, and slipped them into the pockets of the old raincoat she was wearing without a word of thanks. She had a man's cap on her head, and boots like a ploughman's. We walked along the road together, not saying much, and tea was a silent meal but a good one. She or Lydia had newly baked bere ban-nocks and white bannocks, there was sweet butter and salt butter, and I ate a duck's egg and the half of a stewed cock-chicken. Then when we had finished, she said, 'Lydia tells me that you're wanting to be married.'

'It's what I've been wanting for the last two months and more,' I told her.

'She couldn't agree, and you wouldn't expect her to, until she'd spoken to her mother about it,' said the old woman grimly. 'She's a good girl, and it's a treasure that you're getting.'

I told her, humbly, that I was well aware of that.

'You've been a soldier, she says?'

'For six years I was.'

'I'm glad of that,' she cried, nodding her head. 'It's an ill world we live in, and there's times when the soldiers are all we can depend on, though it's a fool's trade if you look at it squarely.'

I had nothing to say to that, and she went on briskly: 'Well, if you're going to be married you'll be married in a decent manner, with the neighbours there to see it, and something good enough for them to remember too.'

'A wedding,' I said, 'is a woman's affair. I'm willing to be married in any way that suits Lydia. If she wants a big wedding, we'll have it. I've got about a hundred and sixty pounds in the bank. . . .'

'We're not asking you for money,' said the old woman. 'It's not a pauper you're marrying, no, faith! nor anything like poverty neither.'

She went to an old black wooden desk that stood in a corner of the kitchen, with a calendar pinned above it, and took a bank pass-book from a pigeon-hole stuffed with papers. 'Look at that,' she said, and held it open in front of me.

I was flabbergasted. It had never occurred to me that they could have any money at all, but the pass-book showed a credit of £1,207.

'Eight hundred and fifteen pounds of that is Lydia's own money,' said the old woman. 'Five hundred pounds came to her when she was born, and the rest is the interest which I've never touched and never shall. Her money will be hers to spend as she wants when she's of age—you've got three years to wait, so you needn't go to market yet—and the wedding I'll pay for out of my own.'

She gave me a dram then, and took one herself. Just the one each: it was the first time I had tasted whisky since that night at the Norquoys'—and then she put the bottle away in a cupboard with some fancy tumblers and glass dishes. She went out to the byre after that, to milk their two cows, and left Lydia and me together. Lydia had hardly spoken a word since I came in.

The following Sunday the banns were read in the Parish Church, and a few days later the old woman showed me the invitation cards she had had printed for the wedding. She hadn't done it cheaply, that was clear. They were a good thick board with gilt edges, and they read:

Miss Thomasina Manson

requests the pleasure of your company
at the wedding of her daughter

Lydia

to Mr. Robert Lacey Tyndall
in the Ladyfirth Parish Hall
at 6 p.m. on Wednesday, September 6th

R.S.V.P.   Dancing

I said they had a very dignified appearance, and so they had if you weren't so hidebound by convention as to be startled by the prefix to the mother's name. The old woman was very proud of them, and propped one up on the chimney-piece. Then Lydia and I sat down at the kitchen table and began to write in names and address envelopes. The old woman had prepared a list, and there were two hundred and eighteen names on it. But by then I was beyond surprise.

I had no difficulty in dissuading my own parents from coming. I had always been the unwanted member of my family, and I had disillusioned them so often that they could guess the disappointment they would find in my wedding. They had grown accustomed to my disappointing them. I had never enjoyed teaching in an elementary school in Falkirk—that was due to my falling in love, at the age of nineteen, with a female Socialist with red hair and the sort of figure that, in a jersey, is like an incitement to riot—but they were shocked by my choice of a profession. They were less perturbed when, later, I went to sea as a deck-hand on a tramp steamer. They didn't like that, but they regarded it as an escapade. In comparison with the rest of the family I was, of course, an utter failure, for both my brothers had gone to Oxford and done well there, and my sister had married the junior partner in a highly regarded firm of stockbrokers. When Archie, my elder brother, was given an O.B.E. my father was much better pleased than when I got my D.C.M. Neither he nor my mother made any serious offer to come to the wedding. I used to get drunk, when I was younger, and once or twice I had caused them serious embarrassment, so I suppose they thought I should get high, loud, and truculent, and make a spectacle of myself. My father sent Lydia a dressing-case, for which she could discover no purpose at all, and me a cheque for £25. But he missed something by not coming himself.

The old woman wore a black dress that had belonged to her mother, and a man's cap. Not the old ragged tweed one she usually wore, but a new black one such as countrymen sometimes wear at a funeral. She sat in a high-backed chair beside the band, and it was easy enough to guess her thoughts. 'I bore my child without benefit of clergy or the neighbours' goodwill,' she was thinking, 'but my child, by God! will have all the favour and fair wishes that money can buy. My child will be wedded as well as bedded, and no one will forget it.'

And no one who saw her will forget Lydia that night. I realized that I still had things to learn, for though I had doted on her beauty, now I was humbled by it. By her beauty and her dignity. I stood beside her, while the Minister was reading the service, and felt like a Crusader keeping his vigil. The schoolmaster was my best man, though his wife hadn't wanted him to be, and I could hear him breathing, hoarsely, as if in perplexity. He ate little more than I did at supper, and I could eat nothing. I danced twice with Lydia, and the rest of the time stood like a moon-calf while people talked to me. But Lydia was never off the floor, and all night her mother, in the high-backed chair beside the band, sat with a look that was simultaneously grim and gloating.

There was a great crowd there, the fiddlers were kept hard at it, and the wedding was well spoken of. Nearly everyone who had been invited had come, and thirty or forty more as well. All the Norquoys were there, but John and his wife left about two o'clock. Before he went he said to me, 'I'm very glad that you've become one of us, and I hope you'll settle down happily here. You were a good friend to Jim, and if I can help you in any way, be sure and tell me.'

'There's no one can help me more,' I told him, 'than by wishing that as I am tonight, so I may continue.'

Lydia came to say good-bye to them while we were speaking, and after they had gone she said, 'Jim Norquoy was always my mother's favourite among the boys in the parish. She used to tell him that he mustn't be in a hurry to get married, but wait till I grew up and see what he thought of me before going farther afield.'

The schoolmaster came and asked her to dance, and I went outside. The hall was hot and men's faces shone as if they had been oiled, but the night air was cool. There was no wind and the sky was a veiled purple with a little haze round the moon. I could hear the slow boom and dulled thunder of the Atlantic on the west cliffs, four miles away. West of the cliffs there was no land nearer than Labrador, and for a few minutes I felt dizzy, as if I hung in space over a gulf as great as that. The old woman had meant to marry her to Jim, but Jim had died, and I had fallen heir to his portion. 'You won't find it easy to go back,' he had said, as if he knew that another fate would claim me. Nor had I gone back to my own country, but come instead to his, to do what I had to.

I remember sailing once, near Oban, in a little yacht I had hired, and getting into a strong tide and being carried swiftly past a rocky shore though the wind had fallen and the sail hung loose. The moon was pulling the tide to sea, and I was going with it. I was helpless in the grip of the moon, and I felt the excitement of its power.—The sensation came back to me as I stood outside the hall where the band was playing, and listened to the Atlantic waves, driven by the wind of invisible distant clouds to march against our cliffs.

I was moon-drawn again, though I could not see my star. But I knew then that I had come north to the islands, though innocent of any purpose, to take Jim's place, who should have married her but had been killed instead. That was my doom; and I wanted no other. In a little while I went in again and saw the old woman. She was satisfied.

It was nearly seven in the morning when the wedding finished, with the drink done, the band exhausted, and the guests hearing in their imagination the lowing of their cows waiting to be milked. Lydia and her mother and I walked home together, and as soon as we arrived the two of them changed into old clothes and went out to the byre.

Her wedding, however, wasn't the only time when I saw Lydia well-dressed. She had gone to the town day after day, and bought clothes in plenty. Her more ancient garments were thrown away, and her everyday appearance was now smart enough by country standards. She told me one night that it was her mother who had insisted on her dressing like a scarecrow, and often enough wouldn't even let her wash her face for fear of bringing men about the house.

The weeks passed with nothing to spoil our happiness, and I got a job under the County Council, driving a lorry. The mornings and the evenings grew darker, and after a great gale had blown for three days from the north-west the winter came. It was cold and stormy, but after the wildest days the sky might suddenly clear for an evening of enormous calm with a lemon-coloured sky in the west and little tranquil clouds high in the zenith. After the harvest had been gathered and the cattle brought in, the country became strangely empty and its colours were dim. But I liked it. Wherever you stood you had a long view of land and water, and though the sky might be violent, the lines of the hills were gentle.

When I came home one evening about the middle of November, the old woman told me that Lydia wasn't well. There was nothing seriously wrong, but she would have to stay in bed for a few weeks, and she wanted her—the old woman—to make up a bed for herself in the ben-room. I would have to sleep in the loft.

'The doctor has seen her?' I asked.

'No,' said the old woman. 'I don't believe in doctors.'

I had a general knowledge that accidents might occur in pregnancy, but no precise information, and I couldn't make a physiological picture in my mind. I thought of blood and mortality, and the old woman saw that I was frightened.

'Don't fret yourself,' she said. 'She's not going to die yet, nor for many a long year to come. She'll be a brisk stirring woman long after you're in the kirkyard.'

'Is it only rest that she needs?' I asked then, thinking vaguely of some anatomical bolt or washer that might have shaken loose, and needed immobility to re-establish itself.

'Rest,' said the old woman, 'a long rest and a lot of patience. Now go in and see her, but don't worry her with questions'.

Lydia was pale and she had been crying, but when I knelt beside the bed she put her arms round my neck and told me, as her mother had done, that I mustn't worry. And I didn't worry long. Two or three days, I suppose, and then it began to seem natural that she should have to stay in bed. I took to reading to her when I came home from work. My mother had sent a lot of things that belonged to me, including a box of books. I never had many books, I can't remember having had much time for reading when I was younger, but there were some good stories of adventure that I had enjoyed: *Typhoon* and *The Nigger of the Narcissus*, *Kim*, and *The White Company*, and Trelawny's *Adventures of a Younger Son*, *Kidnapped*, and *The Forest Lovers*, and *Revolt in the Desert*, and so on. I've read them all to Lydia at one time or another, and she seemed to enjoy them. I liked reading them again. It was Conrad who was responsible for my going to sea after I had had a year of teaching in Falkirk, and couldn't stand it any longer. I made three or four trips to the Baltic and the Mediterranean in tramp steamers, and a voyage to Australia as a steward in a Blue Funnel boat. But when the war began I had had enough of the sea, so I joined the Army. Lawrence of Arabia may have had something to do with that, or it may have been Kipling.

Only one thing happened to annoy me in the next two or three months, and that occurred one morning when I was taking a load of road-metal to a secondary road we were patching, and drove past the old woman's cottage. It was a dark day, as dark as gun-metal, and the rain was blowing across country in blustering squalls. As I came near the cottage I saw Lydia crossing the road, leaning against the wind with a half-buttoned waterproof flapping round her, and a zinc pail on her arm. I pulled up hard and jumped out.

'Are you trying to kill yourself?' I shouted. 'You're supposed to be in bed, aren't you?'

For the first time since the morning when I'd seen her throwing the gander out of doors, she was angry. Her face seemed to grow narrower than usual, and her lips as hard as marble. She stared straight at me—her eyes are grey, with sometimes a flash of blue in them—and said fiercely, 'I can look after myself. You go about your business, and I'll take care of mine.'

'You're supposed to be in bed,' I said again, stupidly and sullenly. There were some eggs in her pail. They had a hen-house across the road, and she had been feeding the hens and gathering what eggs the draggled birds had the strength to lay in that weather. 'It's madness for you to be stooping and bending and carrying buckets of meal,' I said.

'I wanted some fresh air,' she said. 'I can't stay in bed for ever.'

'Your mother ought to know better, even if you don't. I'm going in to see her,' I said.

'You'll do no such thing!' she cried. 'You leave mother and me to manage our own affairs. Don't you interfere, or you'll be sorry for it. And now go! Go, I tell you. You've got work to do, haven't you? Well, go and do it!'

She was ten years younger than I and a good head shorter, but her words came like the smack of an open hand on my face, palm and knuckles, this way and that, and I stepped back, muttering some limp excuse, and got into my lorry again.

I brought her some oranges at night, that I'd bought from a sailor, and we said no more about it. But two or three days passed before she asked me to read to her again, and then for another six or seven weeks we were calm and happy, though the loft was a cold place to sleep in, and sometimes when the moon shone through the sky-light I woke up to see the rafters and their black shadows, and thought for a moment or two that I was still in the Army, making the best of it in a deserted farmhouse, and once I stretched out my arm to feel if Jim was beside me.

About the middle of February I began to worry about arrangements for her lying-in. Or, to put it more accurately, to worry because no arrangements had been made. I talked with the old woman, who wouldn't listen to me, or wouldn't listen seriously, but I didn't say anything to Lydia in case I should upset her again. And then, before we had come to any decision, I got a telegram from Edinburgh to say that my father had had a stroke, and would I come at once. Archie, my elder brother, was with some Government commission in Washington, and Alastair, the younger, was still in the Army in Rangoon. I didn't want to go, I had never got on well with my father, but the old woman said that if he died without seeing me I would be saddled with regret, like a heavy curse on me, for all the days of my life, and Lydia was plainly shocked, as if by the sight of some fearful wickedness, when I said that he could die as happily by himself as with me holding his hand. So, after a day of argument, I went to Edinburgh, and for a week my mother and I were uncomfortable in each other's presence, and my father slowly recovered. I had been wrong when I said that he wouldn't want to hold my hand. He did. I sat by his bedside for two or three hours every day, and sometimes, with a lot of difficulty, he managed to speak a few words. I was glad, then, that I had done what Lydia wanted. One day my mother told me that he meant to give me a present, and when I went upstairs he smiled and pointed to a leather case that lay on a chair beside him. It was his favourite gun, a fine piece by Holland, far too good for a man who lived in a cottage and drove a lorry for the County Council.

I said good-bye to them in a hurry when a letter came from Lydia to say that she had given birth to a daughter the day after I left her. 'I am very well and so is she,' she wrote, 'and I didn't want to disturb you with my news when you had so much to harass you already. But now, if your father is no longer in danger, I hope you will be able to come home again.'

I said good-bye, but I didn't leave them for another fortnight. My father had a second stroke, and while I was sitting in the train and waiting for it to start, my sister came running along the platform, looking for me, to tell me I mustn't go. He lived for more than a week, but never regained proper consciousness, and then I waited for the funeral. I read Lydia's letter again and again, and two others that she wrote, both of which were full of news about the child. 'I think she may be the most beautiful baby in the world,' she said.

In my mind, when I saw her, there was no doubt at all. She had the perfection of a doll that some dead sculptor— a sculptor too great to be alive in this world—had carved in love from a rosy-veined alabaster. She was very small, and perfect. She was sleeping, and I had a monstrous fear that she might never wake. I put out my hand to touch her, but Lydia caught my wrist and shook her head. 'Let her sleep.'

I made no mention of something I found, a day or so after my return, for I couldn't be certain, then, that there was any meaning in it, and if there was I didn't want to think about it. The sight of it, in the grass, struck deep into my mind like a forester's wedge that splits the fibres of a tree, and for a minute or two I stood trembling. But there was no sense in it, and I didn't want to curse myself with a madman's doubt. I wanted to be at peace, and dote upon the child, so I denied the meaning of it and let it drown in the daily ebb and flow, the tidal waters of common life. It sank into the darker parts of my mind like a body into the deep sea with a sack of coal lashed to its ankles, as I had seen a sailor buried once. Committed to the deep, as they said.

The child grew quickly, and at six months she was like an Italian picture of a cherub, her head covered with small tight curls, paler than gold, and eyes the colour of a hare-bell. The old woman said she could understand already every word we said, and neither Lydia nor I was very serious about contradicting her. For we all thought of her in a way that I suppose is unusual even in the fondest of parents. It wasn't only with pride of possession and a flood of affection whenever we looked at her, but with a kind of glee that never grew stale or sour in the remembrance of its excess.

In May I gave up my job but told the Road Surveyor that I should be glad to have it again in October. He wasn't too favourably disposed to my plans at first, but I had served him well, he was a fisherman himself and knew the compulsion of it, so after a little argument he agreed to let me go and take me back again when autumn came. I painted my boat, put my rod together, and had a week's fine sport before the first of the summer visitors arrived. Then, for three or four days a week till September, I watched my patrons fish, and calculated by the end of September that my own average, on the intervening days, was about as good as the best of theirs. But I fished longer hours than they did, and the price of trout was still high.

Sometimes I used to wake up at night, with Lydia beside me, and see the darkness about us like the mouth of a huge engulfing fear. I had no right to be so happy. No one had such a right. It was like oil on the top step, it was like a German white flag with a sniper lying beside it, it was like a spider telegraphing Walk-into-my parlour over his lethal gossamer. I would lie in the darkness, open-eyed, for perhaps an hour, drenched in fear, but in the morning, waking and turning to Lydia, and then playing with the child for half an hour, my happiness would come back like the returning tide. I couldn't help it. They were both so beautiful.

Once when the child was about fifteen months old, I woke in the first phase of one of my frightened moods, and saw her standing up at the end of her crib. She had taken off her nightgown and she was poised with her head tilted up, her arms out and her hands resting on the side-rails of the crib as if she were addressing a public meeting; or facing her judges, unafraid. There was a late moon that night, and though the window was small there was light in the room. But that wasn't the light that irradiated the child. Her light, unless I'm the simple victim of some cuckoo-born delusion, came from within. Now Lydia's body, on that first morning when I saw her throwing the gander out of doors, was gleaming like mother-of-pearl, or a pearl on velvet, with a light of its own; but never since then had I seen her better than a milky white.—As white as milk and as smooth as curds but not with that radiance.—Yet now the child, naked in the darkness was gleaming with such a light. It was no brighter than the moonlight dimmed by white curtains, but it wasn't in the overflow of moonlight she was shining. It was in a light of her own.

I slipped out of bed, quietly so as not to waken Lydia, and said to the child, 'You'll catch cold, standing up like that. You ought to be asleep.' She looked at me for a moment, as if surprised to see me there, and then twined her arms round my neck and kissed me. I put on her nightgown and obediently she slid down between the blankets.

A year went by and part of another. I came, I suppose, to take my good fortune for granted, and my happiness perhaps lost something of its fine edge and became a rounder contentment. Time, when I look back, seems to have gone very quickly and as smoothly as the water curving over a weir in a polished flow without break or interruption. We were on friendly terms with our neighbours, I saw the Norquoys and the schoolmaster every week or two, and gradually I came to think of the islands as my own place, my proper environment in which I had become an accepted part. But my real life was lived on the old woman's croft, at home. My senses were livelier there, my feelings more profound, my consciousness of life more widely awake.

The old woman could work as well as a man. She could plough and harrow, and between us, when harvest came, we cut and bound and stacked four acres of oats. Lydia looked after the poultry, and singled turnips, took her fork to hayfield and harvest, as well as doing housework and tending the child. We were rarely idle and often our work was hard, though I don't remember that we found it unduly hard because we did it all in our own time, and we had no master to drive us or reprove us or thank us. I couldn't spend so much time fishing as I had done when I first lived there, but I enjoyed working on the land so long as it wasn't continual work.

In the winter months, when I drove a lorry again, I used to read in the evenings. Both Lydia and her mother liked the tales of adventure best. I had some other books, by Jane Austen and Dickens and Galsworthy, that I had never read myself, but we didn't care for them. It was a tale of far-off lands, with the noise of a dangerously running sea, or the thud of a sword going stiffly home, the crack of a rifle, that the women liked. There was something fierce in them, an appetite for deeds, that couldn't show itself in their ordinary life, but there all the time and came out of hiding a little when I read to them. But domestic scenes, and comedy and conversation, bored them.

Well, this good easy life continued—it wasn't physical ease that characterized it, not in those northern winters, but we were all contented—till the child was in her third year, and then one summer day when there fell a flat calm and the loch lay like a mirror, pocked with rising trout, but not one that would look at a fly, I came ashore at midday and on the road a little way past the house I saw five carts standing, three of them loaded with peat and two empty. The loaded ones, coming home from the hill, were John Norquoy's, and the horses between their shafts stood motionless, with drooping heads, their shoulders dark with sweat. The empty carts belonged to a neighbour of his who had started earlier and was on his way back to the hill for a second load. His horses were restless, tossing their heads and pecking at the road with steel-shod hooves. But their drivers paid no attention to them. John Norquoy and two others were squatting on their heels, on the road, and two were leaning against the nearest cart, and in the midst of them, her hands behind her back like a girl reciting poetry at a village prize-giving, was the child. She was talking, and they were listening.

I waited for a little while, some forty yards away, but none of them turned a head in my direction, and when I went up and spoke to them some looked sheepish and embarrassed, but John Norquoy, still on his heels, said to me, 'I could wish you had stayed away and not interrupted us. It's a real diversion, listening to her.'

I picked the child up and asked her, 'What were you talking about?'

'I was telling them a story,' she said, and when I set her on my shoulder she turned and cried to them, 'Good-bye now!'

I don't fully know why, but this small incident annoyed me at the time of it and worried me later. I told Lydia and her mother what I had seen, and said they would have to take better care of the child, for I wasn't going to have her grow up to believe she must always be the centre of attention. I didn't like to see a child showing-off, I said. 'Perhaps,' I went on, 'we ourselves are to blame, for we've always made much of her—too much, I dare say—and let her see that we're proud of her. But we'll have to change our ways if they're going to have a bad effect.'

'We could change our ways a dozen times without changing her,' said Lydia.

'That's nonsense,' I said. 'A child is the product, very

largely, of what she's taught. I used to be a teacher myself. . . .'

The old woman interrupted me with a cackle of laughter. 'It would take more than you,' she said, 'to make an ordinary bairn out of that one.'

Then I lost my tempeɪ, and for the first time we had a proper quarrel. We had had differences of opinion before, and sometimes grown hot about them, but this was different. Now we grew bitter and said things to each other that were meant to hurt, and did. The argument didn't last long, but at night, when Lydia and I were alone, it flared up again. It was she who began it, this time, and when I saw that she was bent on making trouble, her face to put on its fierce and narrow look, her lips were hard—I smacked her soundly on the side of her head, and before she could recover I laid her across my knee and gave her an old-fashioned beating with a slipper.

A week or two passed before she forgave me. Or, perhaps, before she openly forgave me. I knew her fairly well by that time, and I don't think she bore a grudge against me for the beating, but because she didn't want to admit defeat she maintained an appearance of hostility till the affair could be regarded as a drawn battle. Then for a week or two we were in love again with a new fervour.

It was towards the end of February, a few days before the child's third birthday, that the gander came back, and I realized that fear of his return, an unregarded but persistent fear, like the white wound-scar on my leg that I never thought of unless I was tired or there came a hard frost, had always been with me.

There had been heavy snow, piled into great drifts by a strong wind, and for a few days work on the roads came to a stop and I had a winter holiday. The sun came out, the sky cleared to a thin bright blue, and the land lay still as death under a flawless white surface that gave to every little hill and hollow the suavity of ancient sculpture. The loch within a fringe of crackling ice, a darker blue than the sky, was framed in white, and a few swans like small ice-floes swam in a narrow bay. On land there was nothing stirring, and the smoke rose straight from the chimneys of diminished houses.

I had gone out with my gun—the fine piece by Holland—to try and shoot a late hare, and after following tracks in the snow for an hour or two I had got a couple. I was on my way home again when I saw, by the burnside a few hundred yards from the house, the child in her blue cap and her little blue coat. The burn, bank-high, was running strongly, and I hurried towards her with a sudden feeling, as of a man caught among thorns, of nervousness and annoyance that she should be there with no one to look after her.

She stood with her back to me, in her favourite position, her hands clasped behind her, and not until I had come within a few yards of her did I see the gander. He was afloat in a little smooth backwater of the burn, but as soon as he caught sight of me he came ashore, his broad feet ungainly on the snow but moving fast, and I thought he was going to attack me. The child turned and I called to her: 'Come here, Nell! Come here at once!'

But she stayed where she was and the gander came up behind her and opened his wings so that she stood by his breast within a screen of feathers as hard as iron and as white as the snow beyond them. It must have been the whiteness of the fields, with the bright haze of the sun upon them, that dazzled me and deluded me into thinking that the gander had grown to three times or four times his proper size. His neck seemed a column of marble against the sky, his beak was bronze, and his black eyes reflected the sun like shafts from a burning-glass. A low rumbling noise, like the far-off surge of the sea on a pebble-beach, came from his swollen throat.

I'm not a coward and I couldn't have been frightened of a bird. It was snow-sickness, I suppose, that set my brain swimming and undid the strength of my knees, so that I thought I was going to faint. I remember seeing the same sort of thing happen to a soldier in Italy, in the mountains in winter-time. He was a friend of my own, a big fellow as tall as myself. He stumbled and fell, and the strength went out of him. We thought he had gone blind, but after we got him into a house and had given him some brandy, he was all right.

When I came to myself and knew what I was doing, I was on my hands and knees, crawling, and my hands were on fire with the friction of the snow. I had to crawl another twenty or thirty yards before I felt fit to stand up, and then I staggered and stumbled as if I were drunk. I wasn't far from home by then, and I rested for a while in the barn.

When I felt better I went into the kitchen. The child was there already, and as soon as I came in she ran towards me, and pushing me into a chair climbed on to my knee. She began to pat my face and play with my hair, as if trying to comfort me.

Presently I went out again, and found my gun and the two hares where I had dropped them. There was no sign of the gander. They were big hares, both of them, and I took them into the back-kitchen and got a basin, and cleaned and skinned them. But all the time I was thinking: Well, this is the end of pretence. There's no point or purpose in denial now. But what am I going to do?

The women were on the other side, so I couldn't talk to them. Lydia was in love with me, as I with her—there was no doubt about that—and the old woman liked me well enough; but now I knew the dividing-line between us, and I couldn't cross it. But I had to talk to someone.

John Norquoy wouldn't do. I had made a confession to him before, and it was too soon to make another. Nor would he believe me if I did. I had no great faith in the school-master either, but I had to do something, say something to someone, and after tea I set out for his house, walking heavily through the snow, and if he was surprised to see me he didn't show it, but made me welcome. He had spent three or four idle days, with only a dozen children able to come to school, and in his own way he too may have been glad of a chance to talk for a while. His wife left us to ourselves.

I didn't know how to begin, but he helped me. He had been reading a book whose author was trying to prove that modern war was the result of conflicting demands for oil; and he, full of brand-new information, was ready to argue that war had always had economic causes, and no other causes. I didn't believe him, and said so. It was ideas that made war, I said. If an economist went to war, with material gains in view, it was because he was a bad economist, a quack and a charlatan; for any practical economist knows that war is likely to waste far more than it can win. 'But if men believe in ideas, of power and glory, or religious ideas, or even social ideas,' I went on, 'they may go to war for the simple reason that idealists don't count the cost of what they want. They go to war, that is, in despite of the economic arguments against it. And they're always against it.'

We talked away on those lines, getting warmer all the time, and the schoolmaster, really enjoying himself now, went back into history, back and back, till he had proved to his own satisfaction that the Peloponnesian War was due entirely to the imperialism of Athens, and the determination of the Athenians to brook no interference with their mercantile marine.

'And did Agamemnon and Menelaus,' I asked him, 'go to war to win the right of exploiting mineral resources in the windy plains of Troy?'

'If we really knew anything about the Trojan War,' he said, 'we should probably have to admit that that indeed was the cause of it; or something very like that.'

'It's not the generally accepted cause,' I said.

'According to the fable,' he answered, 'the purpose of the war was to recover, from the person who had carried her off, the erring wife of Menelaus. And who was she? Zeus, who never existed, is said to have visited a fictitious character called Leda in the guise of a swan, and the result of their

impossible union was a legendary egg out of which a fabulous being named Helen was incredibly hatched. Helen, says
the story, grew to miraculous beauty, married Menelaus,
and ran away with Paris. You can't seriously regard a
woman who wasn't even a woman, but only a myth, as the
cause of a war.'

'It lasted for ten years,' I said.

'I've been talking history,' he said. 'You really shouldn't
try to answer me with mythology.'

'How does a myth begin?' I asked.

'How does a novelist go to work?' he demanded.

'By drawing on his experience, I suppose.'

He got up impatiently and fetched a bottle of whisky and
two glasses from the sideboard. Then he went out for a jug
of water, and when he came back I said, 'What's worrying
me is this. If a man discovers something within the scope of
his own life that will eventually be a cause of war between
nations, what can he do about it?'

'What could such a thing be?' he asked.

'I can't explain.'

'But it's impossible,' he said. 'War hasn't a simple origin
or a single cause that you can take in your hand like a trophy
to be fought for in a tournament. You have to consider the
whole economy of the rival countries, their geographical
situation, the growth of their population——'

'And their ideas,' I said. 'Their leaders' desire for power,
or a new religion, or a woman.'

'You're going back to your myth,' he said.

'You fought in one war, I fought in another. My experience of war is that you fight for five years, and at the
end of it you see your best friend killed beside you, and
you're glad—you're glad, by God!—that it's he who's
dead, and not you. I don't want another war.'

'Well,' he said, 'whatever starts the next war, it won't be
a woman. You can put that fear out of your head.'

'I'm not so sure,' I said.

The argument went on for a long time, and gave me no

satisfaction. But talking did me good, and we drank a lot of whisky. When I got home I felt calmer, but very old, as if I were a character in a Greek play who saw the enormous tragedy that was coming, and could do nothing but wait for it, and then abide it.

Lydia and her mother were in bed, and I got a lantern from the back-kitchen. I lighted it and went to the stable. Meg, the old black mare, was twenty-seven or twenty-eight, and we dared not let her lie down in her stall for fear she could never get up again, so every night I put a broad canvas sling under her belly, to take the weight off her legs, and she slept standing. She woke as I went in, whinnying softly, and turned her head to watch me.

I stood on a wheelbarrow in the empty stall beside her, and reaching to the top of the wall, where the rafters go in, took down what I had hidden there, and never looked at since, nearly three years before. I had made a parcel of it, with string and brown paper, and now it was covered with thick cobweb. I brushed off the web and cut the string. For a moment or two I held in my hands the cigarette-box—covered with a fine Florentine leather stamped in gold, that I had taken from one of those little shops on the Ponte Vecchio—and then I opened it.

Inside lay the broken shell of a big white egg. I fitted the larger fragments together, and judged it to have been about seven inches long and rather more than four inches in diameter at the widest part.

That was what I had picked up, after coming home from my father's funeral, in the long grass under the ben-room window. It may seem funny to you, but you're not in my position.

Smeddum

LEWIS GRASSIC GIBBON

(1901–35)

SHE'D had nine of a family in her time, Mistress Menzies,
and brought the nine of them up, forbye—some near by the
scruff of the neck, you would say. They were sniftering and
weakly, two-three of the bairns, sniftering in their cradles
to get into their coffins; but she'd shake them to life, and
dose them with salts and feed them up till they couldn't but
live. And she'd plonk one down—finishing the wiping of
the creature's neb or the unco dosing of an ill bit stomach
or the binding of a broken head—with a look on her face as
much as to say *Die on me now and see what you'll get!*

Big-boned she was by her fortieth year, like a big roan
mare, and *If ever she was bonny 'twas in Noah's time*, Jock
Menzies, her eldest son would say. She'd reddish hair and
a high, skeugh nose, and a hand that skelped her way through
life; and if ever a soul had seen her at rest when the dark was
done and the day was come he'd died of the shock and never
let on.

For from morn till night she was at it, work, work, on that
ill bit croft that sloped to the sea. When there wasn't a mist
on the cold, stone parks there was more than likely the
wheep of the rain, wheeling and dripping in from the sea
that soughed and plashed by the land's stiff edge. Kinneff
lay north, and at night in the south, if the sky was clear on
the gloaming's edge, you'd see in that sky the Bervie lights
come suddenly lit, far and away, with the quiet about you
as you stood and looked, nothing to hear but a sea-bird's
cry.

But feint the much time to look or to listen had Margaret
Menzies of Tocherty toun. Day blinked and Meg did the
same, and was out, up out of her bed, and about the house,

making the porridge and rousting the bairns, and out to the
byre to milk the three kye, the morning growing out in the
east and a wind like a hail of knives from the hills. Syne back
to the kitchen again she would be, and catch Jock, her eldest,
a clour in the lug that he hadn't roused up his sisters and
brothers; and rouse them herself, and feed them and scold,
pull up their breeks and straighten their frocks, and polish
their shoes and set their caps straight. *Off you get and see
you're not late*, she would cry, *and see you behave yourselves
at the school. And tell the Dominie I'll be down the night to
ask him what the mischief he meant by leathering Jeannie and
her not well.*

They'd cry *Ay, Mother*, and go trotting away, a fair flock
of the creatures, their faces red-scoured. Her own as red,
like a meikle roan mare's, Meg'd turn at the door and go
prancing in; and then at last, by the closet-bed, lean over and
shake her man half-awake. *Come on, then, Willie, it's time
you were up.*

And he'd groan and say *Is't?* and crawl out at last, a little
bit thing like a weasel, Will Menzies, though some said that
weasels were decent beside him. He was drinking himself
into the grave, folk said, as coarse a little brute as you'd meet,
bone-lazy forbye, and as sly as sin. Rampageous and ill with
her tongue though she was, you couldn't but pity a woman
like Meg tied up for life to a thing like *that*. But she'd more
than a soft side still to the creature, she'd half-skelp the
backside from any of the bairns she found in the telling of
a small bit lie; but when Menzies would come paiching in
of a noon and groan that he fair was tashed with his work,
he'd mended all the ley fence that day and he doubted he'd
need to be off to his bed—when he'd told her that and had
ta'en to the blankets, and maybe in less than the space of an
hour she'd hold out for the kye and see that he'd lied, the
fence neither mended nor letten a-be, she'd just purse up
her meikle wide mouth and say nothing, her eyes with a glint
as though she half-laughed. And when he came drunken
home from a mart she'd shoo the children out of the room,

and take off his clothes and put him to bed, with an extra nip to keep off a chill.

She did half his work in the Tocherty parks, she'd yoke up the horse and the sholtie together, and kilt up her skirts till you'd see her great legs, and cry *Wissh!* like a man and turn a fair drill, the sea-gulls cawing in a cloud behind, the wind in her hair and the sea beyond. And Menzies with his sly-like eyes would be off on some drunken ploy to Kineff or Stonehive. Man, you couldn't but think as you saw that steer it was well that there was a thing like marriage, folk held together and couldn't get apart; else a black look-out it well would be for the fusionless creature of Tocherty toun.

Well, he drank himself to his grave at last, less smell on the earth if maybe more in it. But she broke down and wept, it was awful to see, Meg Menzies weeping like a stricken horse, her eyes on the dead, quiet face of her man. And she ran from the house, she was gone all that night, though the bairns cried and cried her name up and down the parks in the sound of the sea. But next morning they found her back in their midst, brisk as ever, like a great-boned mare, ordering here and directing there, and a fine feed set the next day for the folk that came to the funeral of her orra man.

She'd four of the bairns at home when he died, the rest were in kitchen-service or fee'd, she'd seen to the settling of the queans herself; and twice when two of them had come home, complaining-like of their mistresses' ways, she'd thrashen the queans and taken them back—near scared the life from the doctor's wife, her that was mistress to young Jean Menzies. *I've skelped the lassie and brought you her back. But don't you ill-use her, or I'll skelp you as well.*

There was a fair speak about that at the time, Meg Menzies and the vulgar words she had used, folk told that she'd even said what was the place where she'd skelp the bit doctor's wife. And faith! that fair must have been a sore shock to the doctor's wife that was that genteel she'd never believed she'd a place like that.

Be that as it might, her man new dead, Meg wouldn't hear

of leaving the toun. It was harvest then and she drove the reaper up and down the long, clanging clay rigs by the sea, she'd jump down smart at the head of a bout and go gathering and binding swift as the wind, syne wheel in the horse to the cutting again. She led the stooks with her bairns to help, you'd see them at night a drowsing cluster under the moon on the harvesting cart.

And through that year and into the next and so till the speak died down in the Howe Meg Menzies worked the Tocherty toun; and faith, her crops came none so ill. She rode to the mart at Stonehive when she must, on the old box-cart, the old horse in the shafts, the cart behind with a sheep for sale or a birn of old hens that had finished with laying. And a butcher once tried to make a bit joke. *That's a sheep like yourself, fell long in the tooth.* And Meg answered up, neighing like a horse, and all heard: *Faith, then, if you've got a spite against teeth I've a clucking hen in the cart outbye. It's as toothless and senseless as you are, near.*

Then word got about of her eldest son, Jock Menzies that was fee'd up Allardyce way. The creature of a loon had had fair a conceit since he'd won a prize at a ploughing match—not for his ploughing, but for good looks; and the queans about were as daft as himself, he'd only to nod and they came to his heel; and the stories told they came further than that. Well, Meg'd heard the stories and paid no heed, till the last one came, she was fell quick then.

Soon's she heard it she hove out the old bit bike that her daughter Kathie had bought for herself, and got on the thing and went cycling away down through the Bervie braes in that Spring, the sun was out and the land lay green with a blink of mist that was blue on the hills, as she came to the toun where Jock was fee'd she saw him out in a park by the road, ploughing, the black loam smooth like a ribbon turning and wheeling at the tail of the plough. Another billy came ploughing behind, Meg Menzies watched till they reached the rig-end, her great chest heaving like a meikle roan's, her eyes on the shape of the furrows they made. And they drew to the end and drew the horse out, and Jock cried *Ay*, and she answered back *Ay*, and looked at the drill, and gave a bit snort, *If your looks win prizes, your ploughing never will.*

Jock laughed, *Fegs, then, I'll not greet for that*, and chirked to his horses and turned them about. But she cried him *Just bide a minute, my lad. What's this I hear about you and Ag Grant?*

He drew up short then, and turned right red, the other childe as well, and they both gave a laugh, as ploughchildes do when you mention a quean they've known overwell in more ways than one. And Meg snapped *It's an answer I want, not a cockerel's cackle: I can hear that at home on my own dunghill. What are you to do about Ag and her pleiter?*

And Jock said *Nothing*, impudent as you like, and next minute Meg was in over the dyke and had hold of his lug and shook him and it till the other childe ran and caught at her nieve. *Faith, mistress, you'll have his lug off!* he cried. But Meg Menzies turned like a mare on new grass, *Keep off or I'll have yours off as well!*

So he kept off and watched, fair a story he'd to tell when he rode out that night to go courting his quean. For Meg held to the lug till it near came off and Jock swore that he'd put things right with Ag Grant. She let go the lug then and looked at him grim: *See that you do and get married right quick, you're the like that needs loaded with a birn of bairns— to keep you out of the jail, I jaloose. It needs smeddum to be either right coarse or right kind.*

They were wed before the month was well out, Meg found them a cottar house to settle and gave them a bed and a press she had, and two-three more sticks from Tocherty toun. And she herself led the wedding dance, the minister in her arms, a small bit childe; and 'twas then as she whirled him about the room, he looked like a rat in the teeth of a tyke, that he thanked her for seeing Ag out of her soss, *There's nothing like a marriage for redding things up.* And Meg Menzies said *EH?* and then she said *Ay*, but queer-like, he supposed she'd no thought of the thing. Syne she slipped off to sprinkle thorns in the bed and to hang below it the great hand-bell that the bothy-billies took them to every bit marriage.

Well, that was Jock married and at last off her hands. But she'd plenty left still, Dod, Kathleen and Jim that were still at school, Kathie a limmer that alone tongued her mother, Jeannie that next led trouble to her door. She'd been found at her place, the doctor's it was, stealing some money and they sent her home. Syne news of the thing got into Stonehive, the police came out and tormented her sore, she swore she never had stolen a meck, and Meg swore with her, she was black with rage. And folk laughed right hearty, fegs! that was a clour for meikle Meg Menzies, her daughter a thief!

But it didn't last long, it was only three days when folk saw the doctor drive up in his car. And out he jumped and went striding through the close and met face to face with Meg at the door. And he cried *Well, mistress, I've come over for Jeannie*. And she glared at him over her high, skeugh nose, *Ay, have you so then? And why, may I speir?*

So he told her why, the money they'd missed had been found at last in a press by the door; somebody or other had left it there, when paying a grocer or such at the door. And Jeannie—he'd come over to take Jean back.

But Meg glared *Ay, well, you've made another mistake. Out of this, you and your thieving suspicions together!* The doctor turned red, *You're making a miserable error*—and Meg said *I'll make you mince-meat in a minute.*

So he didn't wait that, she didn't watch him go, but went ben to the kitchen where Jeannie was sitting, her face chalk-white as she'd heard them speak. And what happened then a story went round, Jim carried it to school, and it soon spread out, Meg sank in a chair, they thought she was greeting; syne she raised up her head and they saw she was laughing, near as fearsome the one as the other, they thought. *Have you any cigarettes?* she snapped sudden at Jean, and

Jean quavered *No*, and Meg glowered at her cold. *Don't sit there and lie. Gang bring them to me.* And Jean brought them, her mother took the pack in her hand. *Give's hold of a match till I light up the thing. Maybe smoke'll do good for the crow that I got in the throat last night by the doctor's house.*

Well, in less than a month she'd got rid of Jean—packed off to Brechin the quean was, and soon got married to a creature there—some clerk that would have left her sore in the lurch but that Meg went down to the place on her bike, and there, so the story went, kicked the childe so that he couldn't sit down for a fortnight, near. No doubt that was just a bit lie that they told, but faith! Meg Menzies had herself to blame, the reputation she'd gotten in the Howe, folk said, *She'll meet with a sore heart yet*. But devil a sore was there to be seen, Jeannie was married and was fair genteel.

Kathleen was next to leave home at the term. She was tall, like Meg, and with red hair as well, but a thin fine face, long eyes blue-grey like the hills on a hot day, and a mouth with lips you thought over thick. And she cried *Ah well, I'm off then, mother*. And Meg cried *See you behave yourself*. And Kathleen cried *Maybe; I'm not at school now*.

Meg stood and stared after the slip of a quean, you'd have thought her half-angry, half near to laughing, as she watched that figure, so slender and trig, with its shoulders square-set, slide down the hill on the wheeling bike, swallows were dipping and flying by Kinneff, she looked light and free as a swallow herself, the quean, as she biked away from her home, she turned at the bend and waved and whistled, she whistled like a loon and as loud, did Kath.

Jim was the next to leave from the school, he bided at home and he took no fee, a quiet-like loon, and he worked the toun, and, wonder of wonders, Meg took a rest. Folk said that age was telling a bit on even Meg Menzies at last. The grocer made hints at that one night, and Meg answered up smart as ever of old: *Damn the age! But I've finished the trauchle of the bairns at last, the most of them married or still over young. I'm as swack as ever I was, my lad. But I've just got the notion to be a bit sweir.*

Well, she'd hardly begun on that notion when faith! ill the news that came up to the place from Segget. Kathleen her quean that was fee'd down there, she'd ta'en up with some coarse old childe in a bank, he'd left his wife, they were off together, and she but a bare sixteen years old.

And that proved the truth of what folk were saying, Meg Menzies she hardly paid heed to the news, just gave a bit laugh like a neighing horse and went on with the work of park and byre, cool as you please—ay, getting fell old.

No more was heard of the quean or the man till a two years or more had passed and then word came up to the Tocherty someone had seen her—and where do you think? Out on a boat that was coming from Australia. She was working as stewardess on that bit boat, and the childe that saw her was young John Robb, an emigrant back from his uncle's farm, near starved to death he had been down there. She hadn't met in with him near till the end, the boat close to Southampton the evening they met. And she'd known him at once, though he not her, she'd cried *John Robb?* and he'd answered back *Ay?* and looked at her canny in case it might be the creature was looking for a tip from him. Syne she'd laughed *Don't you know me, then, you gowk? I'm Kathie Menzies you knew long syne—it was me ran off with the banker from Segget!*

He was clean dumbfounded, young Robb, and he gaped, and then they shook hands and she spoke some more, though she hadn't much time, they were serving up dinner for the first-class folk, aye dirt that are ready to eat and to drink. *If ever you get near to Tocherty toun tell Meg I'll get home and see her some time. Ta-ta!* And then she was off with a smile, young Robb he stood and he stared where she'd been, he thought her the bonniest thing that he'd seen all the weary weeks that he'd been from home.

And this was the tale that he brought to Tocherty, Meg sat and listened and smoked like a tink, forbye herself there was young Jim there, and Jock and his wife and their three bit bairns, he'd fair changed with marriage, had young Jock Menzies. For no sooner had he taken Ag Grant to his bed than he'd started to save, grown mean as dirt, in a three-four years he's finished with feeing, now he rented a fell big farm himself, well stocked it was, and he fee'd two men. Jock himself had grown thin in a way, like his father but worse his bothy childes said, old Menzies at least could take a bit dram and get lost to the world but the son was that mean he might drink rat-poison and take no harm, 'twould feel at home in a stomach like his.

Well, that was Jock, and he sat and heard the story of Kath and her say on the boat. *Ay, still a coarse bitch, I have not a doubt. Well if she never comes back to the Mearns, in Segget you cannot but redden with shame when a body will ask 'Was Kath Menzies your sister?'*

And Ag, she'd grown a great sumph of a woman, she nodded to that, it was only too true, a sore thing it was on decent bit folks that they should have any relations like Kath.

But Meg just sat there and smoked and said never a word, as though she thought nothing worth a yea or a nay. Young Robb had fair ta'en a fancy to Kath and he near boiled up when he heard Jock speak, him and the wife that he'd married from her shame. So he left them short and went raging home, and wished for one that Kath would come back, a Summer noon as he cycled home, snipe were calling in the Auchindreich moor where the cattle stood with their tails a-switch, the Grampians rising far and behind, Kinraddie spread like a map for show, its ledges veiled in a mist from the sun. You felt on that day a wild, daft unease, man, beast and bird: as though something were missing and lost from the world, and Kath was the thing that John Robb missed, she'd something in her that minded a man of a house that was builded upon a hill.

Folk thought that maybe the last they would hear of young Kath Menzies and her ill-gettèd ways. So fair stammy-

gastered they were with the news she'd come back to the
Mearns, she was down in Stonehive, in a grocer's shop, as
calm as could be, selling out tea and cheese and such-like
with no blush of shame on her face at all, to decent women
that were properly wed and had never looked on men but
their own, and only on them with their braces buttoned.

It just showed you the way that the world was going to
allow an ill quean like that in a shop, some folk protested
to the creature that owned it, but he just shook his head,
*Ah well, she works fine; and what else she does is no business
of mine.* So you well might guess there was more than
business between the man and Kath Menzies, like.

And Meg heard the news and went into Stonehive, driving
her sholtie, and stopped at the shop. And some in the shop
knew who she was and minded the things she had done long
syne to other bit bairns of hers that went wrong; and they
waited with their breaths held up with delight. But all that
Meg did was to nod to Kath *Ay, well, then, it's you—Ay,
mother, just that—Two pounds of syrup and see that it's good.*

And not another word passed between them, Meg
Menzies that once would have ta'en such a quean and
skelped her to rights before you could wink. Going home
from Stonehive she stopped by the farm where young Robb
was fee'd, he was out in the hayfield coling the hay, and she
nodded to him grim, with her high horse face. *What's this
that I hear about you and Kath Menzies?*

He turned right red, but he wasn't ashamed. *I've no
idea—though I hope it's the worse——It fell near is——Then
I wish it was true, she might marry me, then, as I've prigged
her to do.*

Oh, have you so, then? said Meg, and drove home, as
though the whole matter was a nothing to her.

But next Tuesday the postman brought a bit note, from
Kathie it was to her mother at Tocherty. *Dear mother,
John Robb's going out to Canada and wants me to marry him
and go with him. I've told him instead I'll go with him and
see what he's like as a man—and then marry him at leisure,*

if I feel in the mood. But he's hardly any money, and we want to borrow some, so he and I are coming over on Sunday. I hope that you'll have dumpling for tea. Your own daughter, Kath.

Well, Meg passed that letter over to Jim, he glowered at it dour, *I know—near all the Howe's heard. What are you going to do, now, mother?*

But Meg just lighted a cigarette and said nothing, she'd smoked like a tink since that steer with Jean. There was promise of strange on-goings at Tocherty by the time that the Sabbath day was come. For Jock came there on a visit as well, him and his wife, and besides him was Jeannie, her that had married the clerk down in Brechin, and she brought the bit creature, he fair was a toff; and he stepped like a cat through the sharn in the close; and when he had heard the story of Kath, her and her plan and John Robb and all, he was shocked near to death, and so was his wife. And Jock Menzies gaped and gave a mean laugh. *Ay, coarse to the bone, ill-getted I'd say if it wasn't that we came of the same bit stock. Ah well, she'll fair have to tramp to Canada, eh mother?—if she's looking for money from you.*

And Meg answered quiet *No, I wouldn't say that. I've the money all ready for them when they come.*

You could hear the sea plashing down soft on the rocks, there was such a dead silence in Tocherty house. And then Jock habbered like a cock with fits *What, give silver to one who does as she likes, and won't marry as you made the rest of us marry? Give silver to one who's no more than a——*

And he called his sister an ill name enough, and Meg sat and smoked looking over the parks. *Ay, just that. You see, she takes after myself.*

And Jeannie squeaked *How?* and Meg answered her quiet: *She's fit to be free and to make her own choice the same as myself and the same kind of choice. There was none of the rest of you fit to do that, you'd to marry or burn, so I married you quick. But Kath and me could afford to find out. It all depends if you've smeddum or not.*

She stood up then and put her cigarette out, and looked at the gaping gowks she had mothered. *I never married your father, you see. I could never make up my mind about Will. But maybe our Kath will find something surer.* . . . *Here's her and her man coming up the road.*

Alive-oh !

IAN MACPHERSON

(1905–43)

HE was proud of his name. When he was a child and his namesake's story was read to him he used to send himself to sleep saying 'David Livingstone, David Livingstone' over and over until the sweet pleasure of the sound blurred into the sweeter confusion of sleep and dreams.

As he grew from childhood his father's small business dwindled, and when the old man died it died too. The boy found himself in the world, and all he preserved of his childhood was a very clear picture of his mother ironing, and himself watching her, his small hands level with his face on the edge of the table where she ironed, while she told the often-told story of his namesake.

It made him happy, even now he was grown to manhood, to remember the happiness which filled him then. He had renounced many things. He had closed the doors of his mind against romantic imaginings, he would not go into unknown countries even in fancy, but he could never forget that recollection of his childhood.

His mother did not outlive his father many years, and he found himself alone when she was dead. The pride he took in being wage-earner for them both, eking out the few pounds his father left, evaporated before his mother's death. But he was far from discontented with his clerk's wages, and his unexciting occupation. He was nineteen when she died.

At the back of his mind he was still proud of his name. He was unaware of his pride, for he was humble by nature, and if he had dreamt that he still took honour because he was named after a famous man, he would have been at pains to exorcize his pride. But he was still hero-worshipper in his heart. He gave up the Church after his mother's death. He became infected with a zeal for change. He was gifted with a sardonic wit: he developed an intense zeal for the removal of institutions which had weathered so many years that their utility was not glaringly apparent, and their picturesque air gave them the appearance of ornament, not of use. The Church was chief of such institutions, he despised it, and all its functions, and all its officers. He had a passion for new things, whose purpose shone through them. Sometimes when he met acquaintances, or gathered with his companions in the office by a window overlooking the busy street, he grew eloquent, and sweeping the churches with their spires, the conglomerate mass of ill-planned city, and all the scene with its hidden misery and squalor, into the dust-bin of time, he built new cities for men.

And he was fond of writing his name. In spite of his societies, his earnest young men who listened as if he was a prophet, in spite of the baser sort who enjoyed his wit and drew him on to hear what he would say next, what ancient foundation he would demolish—in spite of his occupations he was lonely. He read with avidity. He lived very simply, in a poor quarter of the town, for as he preached, so he must act, but he spent the money he saved on comfort, buying books.

There was no sweeter moment in his day than the time when, his tea over, his cigarette smoked, his office clothes put off and older clothes put on, he washed his hands and undid the string and brown paper which held his treasures. It was a ritual whose every action was significant. The fair white fly-leaves were like an enchantment. His pen, his ink, were ennobled at this moment, while he wrote his name in tiny perfect letters. And then he slipped from the country of enchantment back to his threadbare restless talkative present as easily as a child ceases to be king when it is called to dinner.

It was childish, and he was a child. The dapper little clerk was more than a little clerk: he had simplicity of heart which made him as great, and as full of promise for the future, as a child. He was small and dark and neat like a thing not meant for use. His complexion was fairer than a woman's and drew many a woman's pitying regard for what it betokened. He knew that he had the seeds of death in him. Had the hectic beauty of his cheeks not warned him, it was plain in his parents' death certificates. But though he knew his disease he did not know how death shone in his face, he did not know why all women were gentle when he was near, and even his harridan of a landlady kept her ill-nature in leash when she spoke to him. Perhaps the simplicity which looked from his clerk's eyes with most unclerkly greatness was not the simplicity of the child which remained alive in him, but of that older inhabitant, who sat with him daily on an office stool, and when he ate his meals, made each meal a communion, and turned the bread and the water into the body of death.

No one was very angry with him when he preached revolution. His boss's large face beamed affectionately at him, like sun through the morning fog of his city, even when he heard his clerk calling down fire to destroy all bosses. One could not be angry with the fragile mite whose eyes' brown gentleness spoke louder than his tongue. The slums of his city and evils of the world had defeated him before he was born.

To himself his disease was not a grief. It belonged somehow to the world's distress, not to himself. Like dirt, and poverty, and all that afflicted men, it was a trouble to the flesh, not grievous to the spirit, for those things had an end. It brought home to him the imperfection of a world where some were rich and some poor, some healthy, some born with death in their bosoms, feeding there. What was wrong could be remedied, his trouble was a part of mankind's, it never came home to himself until one bright April morning he found his pillow bloody, and his mouth salt.

Perhaps because he was so lonely, he cried a long time, but tears, which once could end sorrow, get him kindness and help, would not wipe out this stain. He was not without courage, although life had until now denied him opportunity to show it. When he had cried, he washed himself and suffered the pains as well as the fear of death. By the time he was ready to go to his office, he was prepared. He had died in his heart, the pain was past, he could wait now for the end of his life. If he had not grown up in loneliness he might not have suffered so much at once; he would not have suffered so finally, but now with no intercessor and no friend he met the angel of death, and was defeated, and rose, captive, submissive to his victor's will.

By the time he composed himself it was nine o'clock, and he should have been already in his office. The tremendous thing that had happened came home to him when he looked at his watch, for until now, without fail, he had been in the office by this time. He gathered his coat and hat and put them on. When he saw himself distorted in his shaving mirror he murmured 'Poor David Livingstone' to his image.

A knock sounded on his door and a breathless voice called 'Are you in?'

'Come in, Beldy,' he said. A girl opened the door and slipped into the room. Words tumbled from her.

'You're late. Did you not know you were late? Did you sleep in?'

He nodded his head.

'I slept in,' he agreed.

'Hurry!' she said. 'Ma left your breakfast—it's cold. She's out.'

They looked with understanding at each other, knowing his landlady, and the girl smiled.

He thought it strange that she should smile so happily. He had never noticed until now that her body, set though she was not yet fifteen, and her shrewd old face, had youth in them. He glanced from her face to his hands, and from his hands to his own face in the mirror. The new thing he saw in her was in himself also. His eyes hurried round the room, and everything he saw was new. He seemed to see things as if a glass screen had been taken from before his eyes.

The girl shook his arm impatiently.

'You'd better hurry,' she said, and then 'You ill?'

He shook his head.

'Oh!' she exclaimed, looking at his pillow.

'A tooth,' he explained, 'tooth come out, Beldy.' He had never realized how alive she was. She held the door open for him.

'I'll fix it all right,' she said casually. 'Best not let Ma see. Best not say a lot, eh?'

His go-to-work habit sent him over the street to a tram-standard. The streets were empty of the children he usually saw going to school. He looked a little for them before he realized what was missing. The conductor on his tram was one of his acquaintances. Forbes heard all the gossip of the town and retailed it above the noise of the tram to friends. His news was often useful to such small revolutionaries as Livingstone; in an argument the clerk often made use of the stories of rent-racking and sharp practice which Forbes had told him in the morning. David Livingstone was not proud of the source of his knowledge, he did not like Forbes's leer when he spoke of business men and their love affairs, but he consoled himself and rebuked himself with the thought that it was all for the good Cause. In spite of that he did not like the man, and he did not like to be singled out, to have scandal hurled at him across a line of stout old ladies, and to be made into a red revolutionary to the horror of passengers, to the tune of a clacking ticket-punch.

But this morning he did not shrink when Forbes hailed him. He had the lower deck to himself, and sat white and

small and forlorn in a corner while the conductor rushed
upstairs. The curious nakedness with which his room, and
Beldy, appeared to him, was general. He felt elated. He felt
as if he was deeply alive inside, and he saw the livingness of
the scene with a feeling almost of ecstasy, as if he was alive
outside himself as well as in, and the crowds, the morning
air as yet uncontaminated by smoke, and he himself, had
a communion which was unknown until now. The street was
almost terrifying to his sharpened senses. He was for the
first time in his life deeply aware of the life around him. He
saw an old woman walk slowly down the gutter, between
the throng of people and a stream of cars. She was tall,
and the baskets she carried in either hand did not make her
stoop. She sauntered down the gutter crying in a loud clear
voice 'Caller Dulse! Caller Dulse!' Her cry, the dignity of
the old woman, moved him.

Forbes tumbled down the stair in his hurry to meet his
friend. 'A bit late old boy, what?' he cried, ringing the bell
twice to restart the tram. 'Easy now, madam,' he urged an
old lady who clambered aboard. He rushed her into the seat
beside Livingstone and sat down opposite them.

'You're looking white about the gills, boy,' he said. 'Out
on the binge, now?' His head shook reproving his own levity.

'No, I know,' he went on in less sprightly tones. 'Needing
a rest, needing a holiday. "What a hope," sez you! Fat
chance of holidays for the likes of us working blokes. If we
was rich men's sons now—d'you hear 'bout young Frazer?'

He rambled on. To Livingstone his talk was vague, and
yet important. Names, names, and every name a living soul;
what living things there were in the world, how queer the
gift of life, a little proud thing wrapped in clay; everything
that was a name a living thing. It looked through their eyes,
it was in their flesh, their voices, how strange and terrible
it was to be alive.

Forbes checked his oratory.

'Your stop, old man, your stop. See you later, cheero.'

When David recalled this morning, and it came often

into his mind during the month that followed, he thought wistfully of his own strange adventure. He did not go to the office, but led by random impulses, now by the sight of men working, now in pursuit of that goal to which a stream of people seemed to have their faces set, he walked along busy quays, down muddy lanes between shipyards, and from the point of masonry where the harbour ended and rock began, he weaved his way inland, by suburban streets, to a little hill on the country's outskirts. The country stretched before him.

Everything he saw excited him. Like a thread of scarlet silk his path wound through the city, and everything he saw was lovely, even when it frightened him; long weeks afterwards he traced his path through the city, and wondered why the morning ended.

In the afternoon he went to the office. He was tired out. Bobby roared and back-slapped his way through a story of the streets, an encounter, and the bawdy conclusion. The office laughed, dutifully, for Bobby was the boss's nephew.

The day was over and it left him nothing but a tired body and an almost insufferable feeling of futility. He was so tired that he could not stand by a tram station, in the home-going rush; he began to walk towards his lodgings, and reached them, almost collapsing.

His landlady was still out. Beldy set his tea, brought hot water for his face and hands, and helped him off with his coat. She brought his kipper in, and sat over from his table, with sewing in her lap. He ate by force of will, and drank four cups of tea. The girl bit a thread through, and with one end still in her mouth she mumbled: 'You gotta get out of here, Dave. You gotta go to the country.'

He shook his head.

Suddenly her head dropped in her hands and she began to sob, crying, 'Dave, you're gonna die and leave me. For God's sake don't leave me.'

He leaned over her, patting her shoulder. 'Don't, Beldy,' he said in a shaking voice. 'Please don't.'

'Don't!' she flared. 'How can I? You've gotta get out of here.'

'I can't,' he said. 'You know I can't.'

'Oh me, oh me,' she went on, not heeding him, 'what'll I do, whatever'll I do?'

She looked at him and tried to smile.

'Sorry, Dave,' she said. 'I'm no damn good.'

'Yes you are,' he murmured. 'You're very good to me.'

'Am I, Dave?' she demanded. 'Am I really?' She shook her head. 'You're just saying that,' she said.

'No, Beldy, it's true. You know I wouldn't tell you lies.'

'Why'd you say it was your tooth then?' she cried. 'Why'd you say that, Dave?'

'Oh, Beldy, I'm so tired,' he said.

'Poor Dave,' she murmured, laying her hands on his shoulders and drawing him down until he was kneeling beside her. She drew his face close to her heart. 'Poor Dave,' she said; 'rest now, boy.'

In the month that followed he thought more and more of the morning he spent walking through the streets of his city, and the old occupations of his mind gradually slipped away. He was always on the alert, eager to recapture that morning's vision, and although it eluded him, there were instants when he waited on the brink of a revelation, and once or twice he saw common drudgery in that morning's light.

He searched for what he had found and lost; he rose in the bright May mornings and followed that morning's way through the empty streets, ending always on the hill which had the city before it, and the country reaching out on the other side.

Although he saw the light which illumined that morning only in glimpses, he began to find solace, instead of ecstasy. He found two easeful things. One was Beldy. The other was the country, from whose edge he no longer looked back upon the city. Instead he watched rooks in the woods which lay like smoke in the valley.

He went at last secretly to a doctor and had the term of

his life told him. From the doctor's he went to draw his small savings from the post-office. And one morning in the merry month of May he walked with Beldy along the familiar way until they came to the hill he had found. They looked for the last time at the city, where he had put his name on books. It was grey in the morning sunshine; its dust had killed him, but he saw a vision in it. Then, poor city fools, they turned their backs on it, and walked down to the valley, sitting often to rest because a little exertion tired him; they never turned their heads to look at what was everything. The Dark Continent waited for his coming.

Number Two Burke Street

GEORGE SCOTT-MONCRIEFF

(1910-74)

NUMBER two Burke Street was smaller and thinner than its neighbours. I remember being told that a murderer had once lived in it. Thereafter I looked at it with particular interest, trying to detect a sinister quality in its tranquil face, ghostly bloodstains on the wall. I learnt the true story eventually. No murder had taken place in the little house and, by the standards of the day, the culprit hardly qualified as a murderer. He was a Captain Grant and he shot his man in a duel in the neighbouring Meadows in the year 1785. The tragedy started with an argument over a sedan chair outside the Theatre Royal where Sarah Siddons was acting to packed, excited houses. The chairs were chiefly carried by Highlanders who wore tartan jackets and were a source of entertainment with their antics and loud shouts and limited English. Captain Grant considered that he had secured a sedan for the lady he was escorting, when a gentleman deftly handed in another lady. 'Words ensued' and in the morning a challenge. Grant seems to have been the more provocative and to have fired to kill. His opponent was the son and heir of Lord Mailes, and Grant had to get out of the country immediately, escaping aboard a French cargo-boat sailing from Leith. He seems to have spent the rest of his time and energy trying to obtain a pardon, but his victim's relatives remained as implacable as they were influential. Grant died an exile in Boulogne nearly thirty years after his duel: a long time in which to nurse regrets and empty hopes.

His house was bought by another captain, but this time a half-pay Naval officer, Captain Gillespie of the frigate *Penelope*. On the night of June 5th, 1792, the tall drawing-room window of number two was amongst those smashed by the George Square rioters, for Captain Gillespie joined his colleague and neighbour, Admiral Duncan, when the Admiral came out with his walking stick and assailed the mob until a hail of stones drove the gentry back into their houses. It was the King's birthday and the occasion was being celebrated by the expression of forceful dissatisfaction with the Government for its rejection of the Bill for the reform of the Royal Burghs. The evening ended bloodily, with troops firing on the mob, and next day corpses were picked up in the Meadows. Captain Gillespie was also the friend and supporter of another Naval captain, James Haldane, a nephew of Admiral Duncan who retired from the sea to become, what was considered remarkable in an officer and a gentleman, an evangelical preacher whose quarter-deck tones sometimes addressed a congregation of ten thousand on the Calton Hill before he was appointed preacher to the Leith Walk Tabernacle.

Captain Gillespie must have been an old man, pious and salty, when he died in 1820, just at the end of what has been called the Golden Age of Edinburgh. Thereafter his house became the home of various persons apparently of no singular distinction but no doubt registering in themselves, their activities and interests, the changes that followed one another between the Regency days, through the long age of

Queen Victoria to the new century. By that time the Church of Scotland had purchased number two Burke Street as a manse for the Mungo Smith Memorial Church whose harsh Gothic-style protuberances broke into a newer, but socially declining, street on the far side of George Square.

It was as minister of this church that the Rev. John Bruce came to Edinburgh. He came at the beginning of the century, already middle-aged, bringing with him his sister and his brother, Acky. Acky was a 'natural': his 'pottiness' had certainly nothing to do with complexes but simply with some physical flaw in his brain. Everybody referred to him as Acky, tacitly implying that, even when his hair was white with age, he was as a child.

Some years passed since the evening on which I saw the two brothers from the window next door before I was to see them regularly, as neighbours, generally going along the street together, both dressed in black except that Acky usually wore a grey gravat—or scarf. By this time I was at the University and, my mother having gone to live in the south, had moved into lodgings in number seven. The minister and his brother were, after the houses themselves, the most familiar sight in the street. They knew everyone, but nobody well. They passed the time of day with unfailing, bright-eyed enthusiasm: the minister in clear, resonant pulpit tones, his brother in a mumble. They never went into any house but their own, and none of the people who lived in the street went to Mr. Bruce's church.

If people saw them pass the window and were short of a topic of conversation they might remark, 'There they go. Look at them,' perhaps adding, 'He's very good to his brother,' or, alternatively, 'I don't think it can be good for him, spending all his time with that brother of his.' Sometimes one heard more: 'He came here from the north-east years ago. Poor Acky came with him. Their father was a ploughman. They say the minister was a brilliant student at Aberdeen. Everyone expected him to have a great career, but it doesn't seem to have come to anything.'

Or, again, 'When they first came their sister kept house for them, but since she died they've only had a charwoman. They're always quite neat themselves, but I'm told the house is a perfect pigsty.'

I used to hear more emphatic comment upon the menage at number two from Mrs. Murphy, who took boarders at number three. Two fellow-students of mine, Adam Kennedy and Colin MacPhee, stayed there, and at one time I was often in the house. Mrs. Murphy was a huge, fat Irishwoman, an atrocious cook but cleanly and, despite a richly critical tongue, extremely good-natured. She would work herself into a cheerful fury over Mrs. Gibson, the thin, grey-faced charwoman who came to number two. 'Look at her—that old scabby cat! What's the use of taking a carpet out into the garden when you don't leather it more than you would a new-born babe! It bleeds my heart to think of those poor old men with no more of a woman than that to mind them. Och, but she's sullen, or I'd go into the house myself and give it a proper dust-up, wouldn't I indeed!'

It was true enough, the windows of number two looked dim as though a world of dust lay behind them. It was quite surprising to see the two old men come out of it looking so bright and lively: the minister with a full white moustache, Acky clean-shaven with white down left along his cheekbones. They both had clear blue eyes. They wore shepherds' boots with bulging turned-up toes, and one could easily imagine them in their native Aberdeenshire walking the rigs beneath a windy sky. Perhaps in spirit they had never really left it, for their lives seemed hardly fused into that of the City about them for all that they were so familiar a sight.

I knew the minister no better than anyone else until one day I was drawn, if only a little way, into his life, both literally and metaphorically into the hall of his house. It was early evening and I was walking back to my digs. As I was about to cross the street, opposite their house, the two old men came abreast of me and I paused to wish them good evening.

'Good evening,' replied the minister. My eyes turned to Acky, but he showed no sign of recognition. His eyes were shut, and the fantastic thought came to me that he was about to die. He stumbled. I was near enough to catch him before he fell. I heard his brother call out, 'Acky!'

Between us we helped him up the steps, his legs dragging. The minister got the door open and we helped Acky into the hall. Inside was a chair piled with papers. The minister pushed the papers on to the floor and we sat Acky in it.

'Acky,' the minister was saying, 'Acky!'

I remembered Dr. Watson next door, 'I'll get him,' I said, 'I'll get the doctor.' I looked again at Acky's face, and I was sure he was dead now.

I turned and went quickly out of the dark, dusty hall into the bright evening, down the steps, up the steps of the doctor's house, and rang the brass bell. I told myself Acky was not dead: how should I know? I had never seen a dead man.

Yes, said the maid, the doctor was at home. She insisted on my coming in, through the hall into the waiting room. I was left there while she fetched Dr. Watson.

'It's Acky—Mr. Bruce,' I told him. 'I think he's dead.'

The doctor stared at me.

'Next door,' I explained. 'Mr. Bruce, the minister's brother. He's ill, he can't speak.'

'All right, I'll come.' Dr. Watson led me out into the street again and back to the hall where Acky still sat in the chair, his brother bending over him, chafing his hand. I stood in the doorway, my numbness beginning to give place to awkwardness, while Dr. Watson made his brief examination. 'He is dead, Mr. Bruce,' he said, straightening.

'Dead!' replied the minister, then, after a pause: 'Will you give me a hand to carry him ben?'

Every house in the street was represented at Acky's

funeral. It was as though words of friendship that could never have been spoken could at last be expressed by merely standing in a cold wind on the edge of the little pit that is the last worldly service that the living render the dead. In a cemetery there are no houses to change possession, to become happy homes or sad homes, with open doors for visitors: only silent graves that maintain a great sameness whatever monstrous memorials may be raised above them. 'Ashes to ashes, dust to dust . . .' the Reverend John Bruce's words came and went finely on the wind.

It was moving and impressive, this last dignity done to the 'natural', Acky. I was so impressed that the following Sunday I went to the eleven o'clock service at the Mungo Smith Memorial Church, although at the time I had conscientiously given up going to church in order to justify my declared agnosticism. There was the merest handful of a congregation as I slipped in, rather late, and sat in one of the empty pitchpine pews: fourteen, I counted. The church had an appearance of eternal emptiness.

Probably when it was built, in the Scottish way to canonize a deceased tobacconist, the Mungo Smith Memorial Church was already redundant. Even for massively church-going Victorian days the streets around were amply provided. This late Gothic extravagance seemed particularly ill-accommodated to the Presbyterian worship for which it had been designed. Its apse was a kind of shrine for organ pipes; the acoustics were strange, uncanny. In abrupt contrast with the pinnacled elaboration of the exterior was the ironbound starkness of the interior, still observing the Gothic plan but stripped of all conceits except for a stencilled frieze of curlicues around the walls. Small squares of pink glass alternated with green in the windows, casting a sickly light over the dun-coloured woodwork. Only the pulpit was draped with solemn, ecclesiastical red.

The singing was necessarily thin, and rather tuneless. I waited patiently for the sermon: I had come partly to hear it, being so impressed by Mr. Bruce's few words at the

graveside, partly as a gesture to him and his brother. But
when at last Mr. Bruce ascended the pulpit and a spate of
words gushed from him, I was aghast. True I was an
agnostic, without respect for theology, but as a third-year
student of Moral Philosophy I felt I knew what theology
was, or ought to be. There seemed to be none at all in Mr.
Bruce's sermon, simply a surge of words with only the flot-
sam and jetsam of scholarship tumbling about, broken up
and meaningless, out of context, without direction or
discipline, serving only to hinder any natural expression of
ideas. Although his voice and accent were pleasant, his
words themselves lacked all lucidity, bedevilled by pulpit
clichés and fragments of lore.

Embarrassed, I encouraged my attention to wander.
I counted the congregation again: ten females including the
organist, four males including myself. I looked at the heavy
brass lamps, oil lamps clumsily converted for electric light.
I tried to read the words on a distant bronze tablet let into
the wall. Then I found my attention caught by the preacher
again. Not exactly listening to his words but, as it were,
watching him with my ears as well as my eyes. After all,
there was something there, even although his words did not
express it: there was a potent suggestion of goodness, of
a triumphant unwearied innocence in the man. It was as
though he really knew something that his tongue could not
express. There was manifestly neither bitterness in him
that his career should have been a failure, his church almost
empty, his natural gifts dissipated, nor any consoling
pretence that things were other than they were. He was a
failure, and he did not mind, not because he was afraid of
facing failure but simply because it did not matter to him.
Therefore it seemed necessary to suppose that he was perfectly convinced in some value outside those of this world.
It seemed I was watching a man who really had faith,
although his words told me nothing about it.

I saw him lean forward, look down at his listeners and
cry pressingly, as though answering muddled questions—

perhaps his own: 'He loves us!' With that the sermon was over and Mr. Bruce climbed down from his pulpit.

This recollection remains with me, although of course I did not then pursue the train of thought that it started. I had far too many ideas yet to seize and worry before I could see beyond my academic and contemporary education and know that there was more to man than ideas, other motives than our appetites and the theories we spin from them.

I met Mr. Bruce in the street the next day. He said, a little surprised, 'I saw ye in the kirk.'

'Yes,' I said awkwardly for I had no intention of going again but yet I held him in new respect. Feeling I must say more, I added, rather uncertainly, 'I liked your sermon.'

He looked positively puzzled, 'But I'm no preacher!' he exclaimed: a perfect confession of failure for a Presbyterian minister. He smiled and moved on, 'It's a bonny day.'

After Acky's death he seemed to dwindle a little: but perhaps this was only because where we had been used to seeing two black-clad figures we now saw only the one, passing up and down the street several times a day. He was still there when I left. When he died the Mungo Smith Memorial Church was sold and became a furniture warehouse, and the manse was bought by the University authorities and used as an annexe to the offices next door.

The Last G.I. Bride wore Tartan

FRED URQUHART

(b. 1912)

I

'I'M goin' to grab the last Yank in London,' I said.

We were standing at the top of the escalator in Piccadilly Circus tube. My girl-friend, Violet, said: 'What's that? What're you muttering about, Jessie?'

But I didn't take time to answer. I grabbed her arm and cried: 'C'mon!' And I ran down the escalator ahead of her. I'd just seen an American soldier disappear down it, only his head and shoulders, like he was in a boat being carried over the Niagara Falls. It was only a glimpse, mind you, but it was enough. He was the first Yank I'd seen for weeks. Almost the first Yank I'd seen since I came to London. And I'd come to London to get a Yank. Honest to goodness I had. For months before I left Scotland, you could almost say for years, I'd thought about nothing else but getting a Yank. But there was no hope in a wee village like Birnieburn. All I could do was read about them in the papers. Every time I read about G.I. Brides I got real mad, wishing I was one of them. And when I got like that I read *Gentlemen Prefer Blondes* again and made up my mind that what Lorelei Lee did when she came to England I'd do when I got to the U.S.A. Only worse. Lorelei was going to have nothing on me. And so when finally I got round my mother to let me go to London to a job as a waitress in her second cousin's café I had really only one thing in mind: and that was to get a Yank.

But it wasn't as simple as all that. The war was over, and almost all the Yanks had gone home or had been sent to Occupied Germany. And those that were in London all had girl-friends already who clung on to them like grim death and who'd have fought tooth and claw for them. I wasn't half mad, I can tell you, that the war hadn't lasted a bit longer. All the last year of it I kept hoping it would keep on long enough for me to be eighteen so that I could sort of say to my mother: 'Well, I guess it's time I went places and did things.' But it didn't; it stopped when I was seventeen years and seven months. And could I have wept!

But I didn't weep long. I put *Gentlemen Prefer Blondes* in a case along with my Stewart tartan skirt and my few other duds, and I went to London. The job in my second cousin's café wasn't so hot, but I chummed up with Violet, another waitress, and we went places.

This night we'd been to see Lauren Bacall's new film, and when I saw this American disappear down the escalator in Piccadilly Circus tube I just rushed after him. Because he was really the first American I'd seen by himself.

I was so excited I didn't wait to see if Violet was following. I rushed down two steps at a time.

It was all right for a minute. I could see him straight ahead of me. He wasn't walking; he was standing, leaning on the rail of the escalator. He had nice broad shoulders. And then for a few terrible seconds I couldn't see anything else. You see I'd forgotten that I'd been in London only a month and that I hadn't gotten used yet to the moving-staircases in the tubes. At first I'd always stood on them, partly because I was terrified to walk down them and partly because I liked to get a good eyeful of the people who were travelling up the staircases on the other side. But after the first week I plucked up courage and now I could walk up or down them all right and still watch the people.

That night, however, I was in such a panic when I saw this Yank I forgot I wasn't fully acclimatized and also that I was wearing pretty high heels. And so, before I knew properly where I was, I went head over heels and went rolling down the escalator.

They were a few terrible moments, I can tell you.

And then before I knew where I was, there I was lying at the foot of the escalator and the Yank and two or three other people were bending over me. Away up above Violet was flying down, shouting: 'Oh, Jessie, are you hurt?'

Honest to goodness, I didn't know whether I was hurt or not. I was so surprised. But what I was most surprised at, I think, was the sight of the Yank's face.

He was no oil-painting.

II

'He wasn't worth taking a tumble for,' I said to Violet as soon as we were safely in our tube. 'I wouldn't have had him with a pound of tea!'

'What did you want to follow him for anyway, love?' Violet said. 'You're crackers! Whatdja want a Yank for? All the best of them have been grabbed. Anyway, you wouldn't want to go away to America and leave all your friends, would you?'

'Chance me!' I said.

'Of course, I'd go like a shot,' I said. 'I want to go to Hollywood and get into pictures, and how'm I goin' to get there if I don't get a Yank? How'm I goin' to pay the fare?'

Violet giggled. 'Ooooo, Jessie, wot things you say!'

'What's wrong with what I say?' I said. 'I'm hard. Hard. That's me!'

'Coo, but you ain't as hard as all that,' she said. 'You'd never marry a bloke, would you, then ditch him?'

'Whatdja think I'd do? Sit and twiddle my thumbs and watch him?' I laughed like I'd heard Hedy Lamarr laugh in a film when she was giving a bloke the run around. 'No, sister, not me! I'm gonna grab a Yank and get to America and then divorce him as sure as my name's Jessie McIntyre.'

'Coo, but you *are* hard,' Violet said, and she looked at me as though I was the Statue of Liberty or something.

'You have to be hard in this world if you want to get on,' I said.

But I wasn't feeling as hard as I'd like to make out. I felt like crying. I'd hurt my knee when I fell and it was beginning to bother me. I was crippling a bit when we got out the tube, and Violet got real worried.

'Let's take a taxi, love,' she said.

I said: 'Ach away, don't be daft, I can easy walk.' But before I could stop her, she'd shot up her arm and yelled, and a taxi that was crawling past stopped.

'Number seven Mavisbloom Avenue,' Violet said, opening the door.

We'd just got in when the door opened again, and an American soldier jumped in. 'Sorry, girls,' he said, sitting down opposite us. 'But I sure had to get a cab and this was the only one in this God-forsaken bit of London. Which way you goin'?'

'Well, of all the cheek!' Violet said.

I couldn't say anything. For a moment I thought it was the Yank on the escalator who'd followed us, but then I realized it wasn't; this guy had the same kind of broad shoulders, but that was all they had in common. This guy was a perfect picture.

'Listen you,' Violet said. 'We don't want to share this taxi with anybody, so you'd better skedaddle—and skedaddle quick!'

'Aw, have a heart, sister,' the Yank said. 'I want to get to a place pretty damn quick, and if I drop you girls first it'll be quicker than waiting for another cab. See my point?'

'I see nothing,' Violet said. 'Except the shine on your brass neck. It's blindin' me.'

'Aw, nuts!' he said.

'Look, I'll pay for the cab,' he said. 'After I drop you dames. . . .'

'Listen, brother,' Violet said. 'Whatdja think we are? You get out of here pretty quick or I'll tell the driver to stop and call a policeman. Don't you know it's illegal to share a taxi. . . .'

'Aw look, baby!' he said.

The taxi had stopped at some traffic-lights and they were shining right in full on him. He was leaning forward, grinning. Honest to goodness, I must say he looked good. But I was determined to be on my high-horse the same as Violet.

'My girl-friend has asked you to go,' I said as icy as I could. 'So please do so. No gentleman would stay where he wasn't wanted.'

'But I ain't no gentleman, baby,' he said, laughing. 'I'm just a simple guy from the Middle West. Name's Lew Winnegar. What's yours?'

'Come, Violet,' I said. 'We'll just ask the driver to drop us here. We can easy walk the rest. Since this gentleman's in such a hurry that he's forgotten his manners we might as well show him that at least *we've* been well brought up.'

'But your leg, ducks!' Violet cried. 'You can't walk with it.'

'I'll do my best,' I said on my dignity. 'I think I'll be able to bear the pain. Anyway, tomorrow's my day off, so I can rest then.'

'Look, sister,' the Yank said. 'I don't want to bother you, honest I don't. But I simply gotta be at this place by a certain time, and cabs are mighty difficult to get. Have a heart. Please!'

'Have a heart yourself,' Violet said. 'Think of my girl-friend's leg.'

'Which she hurt through the fault of another American soldier,' she said with a snap.

'Well, we haven't far to go now,' I said, musing like. 'I daresay we can let you share it. . . .'

'Say, that's swell,' he cried. 'You're a coupla peaches and I'm mighty. . . .'

'But kindly don't talk to us,' I said, leaning as far back as I could in my corner. 'We aren't interested.'

I could see we were getting near Mavisbloom Avenue. Violet was getting all ready to say something, but I gave her a dig and she shut up. The Yankee started to say something too, but he gave it up. We drove the last few minutes in silence.

The taxi stopped and me and Violet got out. Violet leaned in to pay the driver, but before she could say anything the Yank said: 'Okay, driver, make it the one fare. Drive me now to Grosvenor Square. Goodnight girls, thanks a lot!'

And before we could say anything the taxi drove off. Violet and me just stood and looked at each other. 'Well, of all the cool cheek,' Violet said as soon as she'd got her breath. 'He might at least have stopped long enough to thank us properly. I thought we'd got off with him.'

'So did I,' I said.

III

The next morning when I was reading *Gentlemen Prefer Blondes* for the sixteenth time and wondering what new wrinkles I could get, Mrs. Percy, the landlady, knocked on the door. 'This just came by taxi,' she said, handing in a large cardboard box.

It was addressed to 'The Young Lady in the Tartan Skirt'.

It was full of carnations that must have cost a fortune, and on top of them was a card: 'Will you meet me at three o'clock in the Café Lenore in Shaftesbury Avenue and I'll apologize for last night? Lew Winnegar.'

'What a cheek!' I said.

At ten past three when I went into the Café Lenore he was sitting at a table near the door. He jumped up and pulled out a chair. 'Park yourself, sis,' he said.

'Good afternoon,' I said on my dignity.

But he wasn't the kind that could be frozen. He was even nicer in the daylight than I'd thought. He had pale grey eyes that looked even paler because of the thick fringe of

black eyelashes. Like lots of Americans I'd seen he looked
as if he'd been poured into his uniform. It was kind of
tight across the seat. But for all that he was all right.

In less than a week he was my steady fella. I was a G.I.'s
moll like I'd always wanted to be. And in less than a fortnight I was a G.I. Bride. And so I quit work and settled
down to live on my allowance, and when Lew was sent
back to Germany I had a rare old time, gadding around
London.

I got a right kick out of writing home and telling my
mother I was a married woman now and that I was all set to
sail for the U.S.A. as soon as the authorities could arrange
my passage. And I got a bigger kick when I was able to go
home to Birnieburn for a couple of weeks and show off all
the new clothes Lew had bought me. My mother was a bit
flabbergasted when she saw them and she said: 'But where
did ye get all the coupons, Jessie?'

'The black market,' I said. 'Lew paid two bob a coupon.
He bought about eighty.'

'Lord preserve us, Jessie McIntyre,' my mother said.
'Ye were daft to let him spend all that money on ye. My
word, if I'd been in London beside ye I'd have put my foot
down good and hard. The clothes ye had already were fine;
ye werenie needin' new ones.'

'Aw nuts,' I said.

'I'll aw nuts ye!' she said. 'Maybe ye're a married woman
now, but that'll no' prevent me frae gi'en ye a scud on the
jaw if I have any more o' yer impiddence.'

So I said 'Aw nuts!' to myself this time. I was hard put
to it to keep my temper that fortnight I was at home, for my
mother found fault with everything. She was right rattled
that I was going away to the States where she wouldn't be
able to come into my house when I got one and tell me how
to run it. 'I just hope yer man's mother is a sensible body,'
she said. 'I hope she'll keep her weather eye on ye and see
that ye feed him right and that ye don't get led away wi' too
many o' yer daft notions.' She kept weeping every now and

then, saying: 'It's such a long way to Americy. Yer puir faither and me'll never be able to afford the fare to come and visit ye, so it's hardly likely we'll ever see ye again in this world.'

'And not in the next if I can help it,' I said to myself. My mother gives me a pain.

So I was right glad when I got a telegram from Lew to say he'd left Germany and was coming to London on his way back to the U.S.A. And so I got on the first train and said good-bye to Birnieburn and all the folks without much regret. At least I thought I did, and you can imagine how annoyed I was just after my mother and father had seen me off in the train at Dundee when I had to go to the toilet in case I burst into tears in the compartment before a lot of strangers.

Lew was in London only two days before he sailed for New York, so we made hay. The last night he was like a kid: almost blubbering. 'I hate to go and leave you, Jessie,' he said. 'I'll be countin' the days until you come and join me in Struthers Bridge, Minnesota.'

'Ach away!' I said.

'I sure got a case on you, babe,' he said.

'Ach away!' I said.

'Honest,' he said.

'Ach away!' I said. 'I don't believe you.'

All the same I wept buckets when we said good-bye, and as soon as he'd gone I made a bee-line for the American Embassy to see how soon it'd be before I got a passage. They were awful nice, and so were the people at the shipping company. They all said they'd give me a passage as soon as they could, and they gave me a booklet called *A Bride's Guide to the U.S.A.* and they told me to go home and study it and to content myself.

But I practically parked myself on their doorsteps for the next few weeks, and while I waited for visas and all the other things I read *Gentlemen Prefer Blondes* and this booklet time about. And the tips in this booklet were right funny,

I can tell you. By the time I'd read it two three times I felt
I knew America from top to bottom. And so I was real glad
when there was a phone-call to say another G.I. Bride had
fallen ill and would I like to take her passage on a boat. I
didn't stop to wonder what had happened to this dame;
I collected my duds and got on the first train for Southampton. I was on my way to America at last, and 'California,
Here I Come' was my theme-song.

IV

There were a lot of G.I. Brides on the boat. I shared
a cabin with three others. They were all older than me and
because they'd been married longer and had gone with lots
of Yanks they ribbed me no end. They were a bit snooty
about my clothes, so I sure had a nice time with them.

'Why d'you always wear that old tartan skirt, Scotty?'
Isobel said. 'Haven't you got any other clothes?'

'Sure,' I said. 'I've got a lot of clothes, but they're all in
the hold in my trunks marked "Not Wanted On The
Voyage".'

'That's not gonna do you much good,' Letty said, fixing
her face in front of the mirror for about the nineteenth time
that day.

'Well, they won't wear out there,' I said.

'Proper Scotty aren't you!' Isobel laughed. 'Whatya mean
keepin' them for, kid? Your grandchildren, etc. etc.?'

'No,' I said. 'But it says in the G.I. Bride's Guide that
you should dress smartly for first interviews, so I'm keepin'
them for that.'

'D'ya expect your mother-in-law to give you the once over
before she lets you share a room with her blue-eyed boy?'
Cora said.

'Nuts for my mother-in-law,' I said. 'I'm keepin' them
till I get to Hollywood.'

'But you ain't goin' as far as Hollywood,' Isobel said.
'Where's your knowledge of geography? If you'd read your

G.I. Bride's Guide carefully you'd see that a knowledge of
American geography is necessary before you can become an
American citizen. You aren't likely to make the grade if you
don't know that Struthers Bridge, Minnesota, is sixteen
hundred miles north-east of Hollywood, etc. etc.'

'I do so know that,' I said. 'But all the same I'm goin' to
Hollywood sometime—and not before too long either!'

'Hubby gonna take you there?' Cora asked.

'Not on your life!' I said. 'I'm goin' myself. I'm gonna go
into films.'

'Greta MacGarbo the second!' Letty giggled.

'Ach, you can laugh if you like,' I said. 'But I'm goin'.
What do ye think I'm goin' to America for? Do ye think
I grabbed a G.I. just so's I could settle down in a wee house
in the Middle West? Not on your lives! I'm a lot harder
than you dames seem to think.'

'Well, I must say, Scotty, it shows a very nasty spirit,'
Isobel said. 'I don't know what's comin' over the girls
nowadays.'

'G.I.s,' Cora said.

'I'd never dream of leading a guy up the garden like that,'
Isobel said. 'Mind you, I'm no angel myself, but I always
believe in putting my cards on the table, etc. etc. I'd never
of dreamt of marryin' my Mervyn if I hadn't been in love
with him hook, line, and sinker.'

'Nor me,' Cora said. 'My Alvin would strangle me if he
thought I was goin' to America just to go on the movies.'

'Well, Lew'll just have to make the best of it,' I said.
'I told him before I married him that I was hard. If he won't
let me go to Hollywood to see what I can do, then he can
just divorce me. I won't mind.'

'That's not the proper spirit, Scotty,' Isobel said. 'And
speaking of spirit—what about a little snifter, girls?'

When she came aboard Isobel had six bottles of whisky
and gin that she'd brought with her from Germany where
she'd had a job with the Allied Control Commission. Her
loot, she called it. She said she was keeping it until she got

to North Dakota so that she and Mervyn could celebrate their reunion. But before we'd been long on the voyage she opened the first bottle, saying: 'One bottle less won't mean a thing to Mervyn, and us girls certainly need it to keep up our morale, etc. etc.'

She said the same about the second bottle, and about the third. By the time she'd opened the fourth bottle she'd forgotten about it, though.

'Well, here's to us all!' she said now.

And so then Cora took out her loot. She had boxes and boxes of hundreds and hundreds of cigarettes. She was right mean about them, and whenever she left an open box lying around she dusted the fags with black powder so that she'd see if anybody had been tampering with them.

But that night she was all hail-fellow-well-met and come hither and take a fag. And so the rest of us weren't slow in coming forward.

'I'm just crazy to get to Rhode Island,' Cora said after a while. 'I'm just crazy to see my Alvin again.'

'You're crazy enough already,' Letty said.

'That's an obvious wisecrack,' Isobel said. 'You shouldn't be obvious in this world. Now Scotty here is far far too obvious. If she acts like she's doing, her hubby and his people will chuck her out neck and crop before she's been with them a week.'

'And serve her right too,' Cora said. 'It's not nice of Scotty to act so gold-diggerish like the dame in that book she's always reading. I'd be ashamed to act like her.'

'Not that I need to,' she said, taking another drink. 'Because I adore my Alvin. I'm just crazy about my Alvin.'

'I'm crazy about my fella too,' Letty said, going to the mirror and taking another decka at herself. 'I'll always remember the first night I met Bill. I heard the Wolf Call and I answered it.'

'Well, I didn't hear any Wolf Call,' I said. 'Lew barged into the taxi I was in, and I was right annoyed, I can tell you.'

'I know another girl who met her G.I. in a taxi,' Isobel said, pouring out more drinks. 'She went to his people in Arkansas last year, and was it a flop! Do you know, they lived in a shack beside the railway where they sold snacks to the railwaymen. This friend of mine was proper peeved, etc. etc. After him telling her he owned a chain of restaurants!'

'My Alvin would never do anything so mean as that to me,' Cora said, taking another swig. 'He's on the level, my Alvin is. He's a partner in a firm of solicitors in Providence, R.I., and he's got a swell apartment waiting for me.'

Cora was all prepared to launch out into another description of this apartment, so I said: 'Did I show you the cartoon my mother sent me from a paper?' And I rummaged in my bag and found it and passed it round. It certainly was a right take-off on all the G.I. Bride stories. It showed a G.I. and his Bride and their kid arriving at his old homestead, a terrible shack in the backwoods, with all his family lying around in rags. They were all smoking pipes, from the old granny in her rocking-chair to the wee baby playing in the dust without any clothes on. I had thought it right funny when my mother sent it, though I hadn't been so pleased at what she'd written on the back. 'Be Warned!'

The girls passed it from one to another, and they all laughed, but nobody said anything. Then Cora said: 'What about gettin' another station on the radio? Somethin' lively. I'm tired of this Drink to me only with thine eyes stuff. Let's have Beat Me, Daddy, with a Bottle of Gin. That's what I call Life!'

But we couldn't find anything lively, so we had some more drinks and then Isobel began to tell us about one 72 hours'. leave she'd had in Berlin and about the juicy experiences she'd had. And she got fairly going about some fella she'd met on a train who'd taken her around the night clubs, and how they'd sat up almost all night drinking in a hotel. But I didn't listen much to her, I kept looking at this G.I. Bride

cartoon and thinking about Lew, who after all was more or
less a stranger.

V

The night before the boat docked there was a dance
aboard. There was a right kick-up in our cabin while we got
ready for it. Letty would have hogged the mirror all the
time 'lashing herself up', as she called it, but we weren't
having any.

'Get away from that mirror you,' Isobel said. 'Give us
a chance to get lashed up, too.'

'It would take a lot of lashing,' Letty said, without moving.
'Especially Scotty there! She looks out of this world in that
get-up.'

'What's wrong with my get-up?' I said.

'Nothing, dear, nothing,' Isobel said quickly. 'I'm sure
it was a very nice frock and in the height of fashion in 1939.'

'Ach, go and fry your face,' I said because I couldn't
think of anything else to say. But I was real mad and I
wished I'd never been such a fool as to listen to Violet when
she told me not to wear my best duds on the voyage. But
I was determined I'd show them as soon as I got to New
York. And when I got to Hollywood—well, they'd laugh on
the other side of their faces when they saw me on the
movies, looking like a couple of million dollars. They'd just
be plain American housewives by that time, going to the
movies once a week regular as clockwork, and it was nice to
think of them sitting back in their seats, saying: 'Gee, I
came across in the same boat as that dame. She's gone
places since then.'

Anyway, I didn't see anything wrong with my pale blue
organdie. It had been good enough for the Hammersmith
Palais de Danse, where I'd had my moments even after
I married Lew. So I reckoned it was good enough for an
old dance on a tub like this.

I was right. We weren't five minutes in the ballroom

before a fella came up and asked me to dance. I wasn't surprised at this, but the other dames were. Because this was an awful high-hat sort of fella called Paul Whittaker that all the dames had been trying to make ever since the boat sailed. He was a journalist or something, going to the States on a lecture-tour. He was a real smasher, so I gave the girls the wink as I fox-trotted away with him.

I knew a lot of gen about Paul already because news travels fast aboard ship, but while we danced and then after, while we sat the next one out, he told me a lot more. He was a pretty high-up guy in the newspaper world it seemed, and he knew everybody it was worth knowing. So I told him a few things about myself and about how I aimed to go to Hollywood, because I figured maybe he might have contacts there which would come in handy when the time came.

By the time the dance was half-way through Paul was all over me, but I was keeping a grip of myself. I was kind of attracted, mind you, for he was tall and he had a nice pink and white face that I wouldn't have minded smoothing over with my hands. And his close-cropped golden hair just shouted out to be touched. But I kept telling myself I was a married woman and that the next day Lew would be waiting on the dock for me. Though it was awful difficult because I hadn't had such a good time with a fella for quite a long time.

And so when he said to come up on deck for a breather I went like a shot, but telling myself to watch my step. And I watched it all right, too, though he drew me into a dark corner beside one of the life-boats and put his arm round my waist.

'You're far too young to be married, Jessie,' he said. 'A girl like you should have a good time before you settle down to married life.'

'I can still have a good time and be married,' I said. 'I don't see why gettin' married should make any difference.'

'That's what you think,' he said. 'But what would your husband's views be?'

'Ach, if he doesn't like it, he can lump it,' I said. 'I told him before I married him that I was out to have a good time and that I wasn't prepared to settle down into a housewife for a long time yet.'

'You talk hard, Jessie,' he said, and he gave a bit laugh. 'But really you're a nice girl underneath, aren't you? Come on, own up!'

'I'm not a nice girl at all,' I said.

'Ah, but you are,' he said. 'If you weren't you'd have proved it to me already.'

I didn't say anything to this, because I was trying to figure how Lorelei Lee would have acted in the same situation.

'I knew you were a nice girl as soon as I set eyes on you,' Paul said. 'The funny thing is that as a rule I don't like nice girls. They bore me to tears. But you're different.'

'Ach away!' I said.

'Yes, you are,' he said. 'I don't think I've ever met anybody quite like you—and I've known lots of girls in my time. But the odd thing is that I've never met one I'd rather be with than you.'

'Ach away!' I said, and I was so busy trying to think of something else to come-back with that I didn't make any move when he put his arm a bit tighter round me. It was real pleasant to stand there in the darkness close to him, with the moon shining on the ripples of the sea far away below us.

I don't know how long we'd have stood like this and I don't think we'd have gone any farther, but just then somebody giggled beside us, and Isobel said: 'Don't make yourself cheap, ducky!'

And so for spite I reached up and kissed Paul right before the eyes of Isobel and Cora and Letty. I was right mad at them. They had no call to come and butt in like this just because they were jealous.

But Paul took away his arm. 'What about you and your friends coming for a drink?' he said.

'That would be swell,' Isobel said, and she put her arm through his.

We were moving towards the Cocktail Bar when a steward went past shouting: 'Everybody in Ball Room, please! Everybody in Ball Room. The Captain has an important announcement to make. . . .'

VI

When we got into the ballroom the Captain was standing on his hind legs on the platform beside the band, but he was waiting for everybody to come in before he said his little piece. We all stood around, wondering what it could be about, and there were lots of speculations. Some of the dames had the wind up, saying they were sure we'd struck an iceberg or something disastrous. But I knew we hadn't felt any jolt, and so I was right amused at them saying: 'Maybe this is going to be another *Lusitania*.'

At least, I would have been amused if I hadn't been so annoyed at Isobel and Co. butting in the way they'd done. It wasn't that I was so desperately keen on Paul, but I hadn't had a man put his arms round me and kiss me for at least a fortnight, and so I was real burnt-up. I tried to edge him through the crowd, away from Isobel and the others, and when I'd manœuvred this, I said: 'I'm afraid my girl-friends were a bit rude just now.'

'One picks one's own friends,' he said kind of distant like.

'Well, I didn't pick these,' I said. 'The shipping company picked them for me.'

'Anyway,' I said, 'one isn't to blame for what one's friends say.'

'Possibly not,' he said, but he kept that frozen look on his face and he never made any more moves to be friendly.

I was just figuring out what I'd do when the Captain held up his hand for silence and said:

'Ladies and Gentlemen—and G.I. Brides!'

He paused for a laugh, and of course he got one.

'I have a very important announcement to make,' he said. 'As you are all aware—indeed how could we possibly be unaware of the presence of so many charming young ladies— there are a number of G.I. Brides on this ship. To be exact there are ninety-seven of them. Ninety-seven charming young women who are on the threshold of attaining American citizenship. Let's all give them a big hand!'

And so while everybody cheered and clapped us G.I. Brides stood and tried to look as if butter wouldn't melt in our mouths—and I must say it must have been a difficult job for some of those dames. But I knew I didn't need to pretend to look starry-eyed and simple.

'Now as you know,' the Captain continued, 'the United States Government has sponsored the voyages of these charming young ladies to their new homes in this great country. But unfortunately the United States Government do not feel that they can go on doing this indefinitely, and so they have decided that the last official G.I. Bride is sailing on this ship. Of course, there will still be a great many more G.I. Brides coming across the Atlantic, we hope, but these young ladies will have to come without official sponsoring. That does not mean that they won't be welcomed with open arms by Uncle Sam and his boys—especially his boys!'

He stopped for another laugh and took a drink of water or something.

'But this ship is carrying the last official G.I. Bride,' he said. 'And now my problem is to say which of you ninety-seven lovely young ladies is that privileged person. It is a hard task. A far harder task than a poor weak male like myself cares to tackle! But the United States Government has given me an order, and so as a loyal simple-minded seaman I am going to do my best to carry out this order.'

He paused while everybody whispered and looked at each other. And we were all on tiptoe when a couple of stewards propelled a huge barrel on to the platform and set it end up beside the Captain.

'I've racked my brains as to which is the best way to solve this problem,' the Captain said. 'At first I thought I would make the youngest bride on board the last official bride, but I came to the conclusion that this wouldn't do. I didn't fancy asking all these ninety-seven young ladies to produce their birth certificates. I felt it would be un-chivalrous! And so I've thought of another way out. In this barrel there are ninety-seven envelopes. Each envelope is sealed. Inside each is a slip of paper with a number. I must now ask all the G.I. Brides to line up and come forward and take an envelope from the barrel, and I must also ask them to wait until I give the word before she breaks open her envelope.'

There was a lot of giggling and pushing as we all lined up, and everybody was doing her best to look coy. Isobel and Cora and Letty and me were well at the head of the queue, I can tell you, and we all blushed like nobody's business as we got up on the platform and took an envelope from the barrel.

I was just itching to rip my envelope open, but of course none of us dared do it until the Captain gave the word. We were all wondering what number we'd got—not that it mattered much as he hadn't said which number was the right one—and we all kept holding them up to the light to see if we could see. But the envelopes were pretty thick and we could see nothing.

'Now,' the Captain said when the last dame had taken her envelope, 'now that you have all got your envelopes, I wish you to open them, and then I want the young lady who has. the number ninety-seven to step up here. She is the last official G.I. Bride!'

VII

There was such a ripping open of envelopes as you never saw. Not that I saw much of it; I just heard the rustle. I was too busy ripping open my own envelope.

I had the number ninety-seven!

Of course, I could have told that before the envelope was open, long before the last dame had dipped into the barrel, because every girl knows that she has got the lucky number. All the same you could have knocked me down with a feather, and my knees were shaking so much I could hardly get up on the platform.

I was still in a daze when the Captain took my hand and shouted: 'Ladies and Gentlemen, may I present—the last official G.I. Bride!'

'What's your name, dear?' he whispered.

I tried to whisper it back, but I could hardly make my lips move and I had to say it twice before he got it.

'Ladies and Gentlemen,' he cried. 'Allow me to present MRS. JESSIE WINNEGAR!'

After a lot of clapping and cheering lots of people cried: 'Speech! Speech!' But I hung back, and the Captain said: 'The little lady's shy, so we mustn't embarrass her more than we can help. Let me just greet her in my official capacity, and welcome the last G.I. Bride.'

Then he kissed me on the cheek in quite a fatherly way.

'I think,' he said, 'that if I'd carried out my original plan of asking all these young ladies to show their birth certificates in order to find the youngest, Mrs. Winnegar would still have been chosen, so you other young ladies mustn't be disappointed that you didn't pick the lucky number.'

'I'm right, my dear, amn't I?' he said to me. 'How old are you?'

'Eighteen,' I whispered.

'There you are!' he cried. 'I was right. Mrs. Winnegar is

only eighteen. Am I right in thinking that none of you other young ladies are *quite* so young as that?'

There was a lot more laughing and clapping, but I saw some of the other brides looking real mad at me. However, I didn't mind. The Captain was holding my hand in a right nice and fatherly way, and I felt safe standing beside him.

I was still feeling so good after the dance finished that when I went back to our cabin I was singing: 'I'm the last of the Red Hot Mommas.'

'Positively the last, ducky,' Isobel said in a catty way. 'But you'll cool down quick enough, too, when you get to that little hick town in the Middle West. It won't be long before you're singing "Don't Fence Me In", etc. etc.'

VIII

The next morning passed in a daze. There was all the excitement of seeing the Statue of Liberty and the New York skyline, and then getting ready to disembark. And then an official party came on board, the Mayor of New York and a lot more officials, and before I knew where I was they were greeting me like a long-lost sister, telling me the whole city was mine. I was fair away with myself and I didn't mind the photographers and the radio guys with microphones at all. I wasn't in the least little bit shy. The funny thing was that I didn't mind a bit not having got my new clothes out of the hold, because everybody admired my tartan skirt. I fair enjoyed myself, and so did Isobel and Cora and Letty, for they hadn't been long in announcing they were my buddies and horning in on the photographers and the radio. I'll never forget Isobel saying in an awful posh tone into a microphone: 'I am ever so pleased to come to America and I am sure that my life here will be ever so happy. I am looking forward ever so much to becoming an American citizen, and I am sure my little friend, Jessie Winnegar, is too. Jessie is a very nice girl and I am ever so glad that she has been chosen to be the last official G.I. Bride. But I'm even more glad that we are to be near neighbours in this great country. On the steamer coming over she was a familiar sight in her tartan skirt, and I am sure that you will all love her as much as we do. Once you can understand her Scotch accent Jessie is a very very nice girl and ever so sweet, and I am looking forward to going to visit her in her new home at Struthers Bridge, Minnesota, after we've both settled down to becoming American housewives, etc. etc.'

I couldn't help giggling at Isobel saying 'etc. etc.' even when she was at the mike, though I was annoyed at her hogging it so much when all the radio guys had done had been to ask her to introduce me. But I didn't get time to think of all this because one of the guys waved me forward and there I was!

I don't know what I said, but I guess I managed all right. I only said a few words, and I stammered most of them. I clean forgot about what the G.I. Bride's Guide said about trying to retain your own accent because Americans like it. I wish I'd remembered and put in a few 'Ochs' and rolled my Rs for good measure, but you can't think of these things at the time. I did remember what I'd seen Carole Lombard do in a film, but I was too scared to do it. I wonder what would have happened if I'd said: 'Are ye listenin', Ma? This is yer wee lassie speaking all the way from America. I hope ye're well, Ma. I'm all right. Ta ta, Ma!'

But even if I'd said it I guess my mother wouldn't have heard it because she would be in the wash-tub at the time, and anyway she wasn't likely to be listening to an American radio station. Still, it's a pity I didn't do it, because they might have put headlines like TARTAN-CLAD G.I. BRIDE SAYS HELLO TO HER MOTHER IN SCOTLAND instead of putting things like TARTAN-CLAD G.I. BRIDE HAS MIKE FRIGHT.

And the next thing was Lew was there, kissing me right in front of everybody with the cameras going nineteen to the dozen. And Cora's Alvin was there, too, and so was Letty's Bill. But Isobel's Mervyn couldn't come all that distance from North Dakota—though Lew had come just as far for me. Still, she tagged along, and the seven of us went places and did things in New York that evening and for several days after that. And I must say Isobel being with us was a right nuisance because she kept making up to Lew. In a way I don't blame her, for he was the swellest looking guy of them all, but I got real mad sometimes when she clung on to his arm and kept treating him like he was her property. Personally I wouldn't have given two dimes for Cora's Alvin, and why she'd made all the song and dance about him is beyond me. He was as thin as a pole and about six feet four. Cora herself was about five feet ten, which made Isobel say to me: 'Goodness knows what their kids'll be like! Six feet six at least! It'll be kinda hard on the girls, if they have any!' There was one good thing about it all, though. Letty discovered the Du Barry Beauty Salon and she was never out of it, so that left her Bill free, and Isobel was able to hitch on to him sometimes. Though if I'd been as soft as I look she'd have had me tag along with him while she monopolized my Lew.

Isobel is all right, and I quite like her, but I must say I was glad when Lew and I said good-bye to her at St. Paul. We'd had her company all the way on the train and I was a bit sick of it. We clung to each other and kissed, and Isobel said: 'You'll keep in touch, won't you, Scotty? We'll always be friends, won't we?' And I said: 'Sure, sure, I'll always remember you, Isobel.' Though I didn't mean this in the way she meant. I was thankful that Rivers End, North Dakota, was a tidy step from Struthers Bridge, so I thought I was safe in saying: 'We'll see each other soon,' as we waved good-bye.

And so you'll know how I felt when she appeared on my front porch a week ago, saying: 'Honey, I've left my husband. Can you put me up until I make my plans?'

IX

Of course, a lot of water had flowed under the bridge in the month before this happened, so I'd better put it all down first.

Lew had told me Struthers Bridge was quite a small place and that his father owned the main store. Lew worked in this store and until we got a home of our own we were to live with his parents. 'You'll like my Mom,' he said. 'She's swell. You'll like my Pop, too. He's looking forward to meeting his new daughter-in-law.'

I was kind of nervous, hoping it wouldn't turn out to be a wee place like Birnieburn—though I told myself even if it did I wouldn't be there such a long time after all, because pretty soon I'd be lighting out for Hollywood.

But it turned out to be a fairly decent-sized place, and it even has a cinema. We're only twenty-five miles from St. Paul and we go there whenever we want to hit the high spots. Lew likes to go places as much as I do. He says Struthers Bridge is kind of cramping after being in the army.

Pop Winnegar's store is quite large, almost as big as a Woolworths in Perth or Dundee. I'd been picturing Lew in a white apron serving behind the counter, but it turns out that he sits in a small office dealing with accounts and running the business for his Pop, who has more or less retired now that Lew has quit soldiering. This makes Lew a pretty important guy in Struthers Bridge; the Winnegars are pretty important people, and Pop has been Mayor of the place for years and years.

But in a way Pop being retired is right wearing for me. Because he spends a lot of time at home, sitting on the front porch or fiddling around with the radio. I reckon I've enough to deal with when I've got Mom Winnegar at my tail all day without having the old man always butting in, too.

Mom Winnegar is tall and thin, with a florid complexion. She is very dignified and what she calls better class. According to her there are three grades: no class, better class, and class. She is too much of a lady to say which grade she belongs to, but I know she reckons she is class in Struthers Bridge, but only better class in big places like St. Paul and New York. She is a great one for the Social Register. She wears toques like Queen Mary, only they are usually black or dark brown. She says her admiration for the Queen Mother has gone down in recent years because she keeps on wearing pastel shades. 'I reckon it ain't dignified for a lady of her age to wear such light colours,' she told me. She asked if I'd seen the King and Queen close, and when I said I'd never seen them at all, she said: 'My land, if I lived in London I'd just hang around Buckingham Palace and hang around until I saw them.'

'I reckon you should study the pictures of Princess Elizabeth, Jessie,' she said. 'You'd be well advised to take a leaf out of her book when it comes to dress. She's got class.'

But I turn a deaf ear when she says this, because when it comes to dress I don't need anybody to tell me what's what. And anyway, if I felt the need to study anybody I'd rather study Ginger Rogers or Betty Grable. I know what suits me. I guess it's a pity Mom Winnegar doesn't. She should take a decko at herself sometimes in those dark-coloured toques.

So it isn't so hot living with Lew's people, but I guess I could bear that all right. What gets my goat most is the various old friends of the family who are always dropping in or asking us to visit them. It's not my idea of pleasure to go and sit on somebody's porch in the evening and listen to two three old people about seventy talking about the weather and each other's ailments. And it's not Lew's idea either, thank goodness. Like me he likes nothing better than to get into the automobile and head for St. Paul. There have been quite a few rumpusses about this, especially nights when Mom Winnegar has invited people over for coffee and cakes and me and Lew have lit out. She never says a great deal about it at the time, but sooner or later she drops something out about: 'Of course, Lew ain't his Mom's baby any more.

Poor Mom'll have to remember that her baby's got a wife who takes first place.'

The first week I was here Mom Winnegar spent a lot of time quizzing me about my ancestors and about Birnieburn. I had to tell her where exactly it was, how many miles from Perth and how many miles from Dundee. She got out an atlas and looked up the map of Scotland, following all the details. And she got fair excited and said: 'My land, you must come from right near the place where old Mr. Neill's grandfather came from.' And nothing would stop her until she'd asked this old Mr. Neill along one evening for coffee and cakes, to meet me. It appeared that Mr. Neill's father and Mom's mother had been brought up in places right near each other in Pennsylvania, but otherwise they had nothing in common because he had been what she called 'a no account cattle-thief'.

Still, she asked him along one evening, and it was right boring for me and Lew. Because Mom made me wear my tartan skirt, and we all sat there on the porch while old Mr. Neill spoke about some book called *The Bonnie Briar Bush* and about his clan and his clan's tartan. 'I'm seventy-seven,' he said. 'But there's life in the old hoss yet, young lady. And one of these days I aim to make the trip and see the land of my fathers.'

All I can say is the quicker he makes this trip and gets away from Struthers Bridge the better I'll like it. I sure am tired of him skirling 'Scotland for ever!' every time I meet him on the street. And I'm running out of excuses to keep from going to listen to him playing his bagpipes.

But I guess the biggest menace of all is Mrs. George Boddler. She is Mom's greatest friend. Mom can't do anything unless she consults Louise Boddler. They are always out and in each other's houses, though Mrs. Boddler is oftener in ours than in her own. She is a large shapeless dame, and she is always panting and out of breath. She and her little fat poodle, Bunny-Wunny, are a pair. If I'm not tripping over the one, I'm running full tilt into the other.

It seems that Mrs. Boddler and Mom Winnegar have been great friends ever since they discovered they were both born on the 7th July. 'That was forty years ago,' Mom told me. 'Forty years since Louise came to stay in Struthers Bridge, and when she told me she'd been born on the seventh of July, too, right there and then we became buddies and we've been buddies ever since.'

Mom Winnegar is a great one for coincidences, but all I can say is it would take more than a coincidence like this to make me buddies with any of the other girls in Struthers Bridge. I reckon none of them like me much on account of Lew. They all thought they'd make him, so it was one in the eye for them when he brought back a bride from overseas. I can't say I blame them, because he's the nicest looking fella in town.

Still, it's real wearing on me when one of them'll say sweet as you like: 'I always reckoned Lew was to be *my* Mr. Right. He had quite a case on me, honey, before he went away to the war. Of course, I've got over him, *but* . . .'

When I hear things like that it makes me more determined to hang on to him. It's funny about me and Lew. When I grabbed him I was all set to be hard and calculating. I reckoned I was only marrying him so's I could get to Hollywood easy. But since I came to Struthers Bridge I'm not so sure about that. I've got kind of used to having Lew around. He's easy on the eye and he sure makes love in no uncertain fashion. I guess I'm getting kind of crazy about him.

This is what made me so mad when Isobel turned up unexpected a week ago.

X

I was on the porch mending a run in my stockings, listening to Pop Winnegar tell me all about the Struthers Bridge election campaign of 1911 when we saw the afternoon bus from St. Paul go past. 'Bus is on time today,' Pop said.

'Where's Mom? Reckon it's about time we had a cup of tea, ain't it, young woman? Gee, I must say I've sure got quick into your Scottish habits.'

Mom was in the lounge with Mrs. Boddler, so I shouted: 'Four thirty, Mom! Pop's getting anxious about his tea!'

I bent over my stocking, trying not to hear Pop and hoping Mom wouldn't shout back she was too busy to make tea and would I make it. I was so busy pretending to be busy that I didn't notice anybody approaching the house until Bunny-Wunny began to yap and then I heard Pop say: 'Here's a strange young woman luggin' some baggage!'

I looked up, and there was Isobel, smiling as bold as brass and shoving Bunny-Wunny away with the edge of one of her suitcases.

'Darling!' she cried.

'Well, what do you know!' I said.

'How are you, dear?' she said, kissing me and looking at Pop as though she were all set to kiss him, too.

I introduced them quick, wondering what Isobel was doing here. I didn't like the look of those cases at all.

But in no time she'd told me it all. 'I couldn't stand Mervyn another minute, honey,' she said as soon as we were upstairs in my bedroom. 'Honest to goodness, ducky, what a poor fish he turned out to be. And what a joint that Rivers End is! My God, it's more like Worlds End. You never saw such a one-horse place, etc. etc.'

'So I've left him,' she said.

'Well, what do you know!' I said.

'I couldn't think where to go,' Isobel said. 'And as you were the nearest. . . . You don't mind putting me up, do you, honey, until I make up my mind what to do?'

'Well,' I said, but before I could explain about this not being my own house and about Mom and Pop, she said: 'You're a pal, Scotty! I knew you wouldn't let me down. So if it's all right by you I'll just park myself here until I make up my mind whether I'm going straight back to Britain or whether I'll stay here until I get my divorce, etc. etc.'

'Now I must lash myself up to meet your folks,' she said, going to the mirror. 'Like Letty! Good old Letty, I wonder how she's gettin' on?'

'Fancy!' she cried, heaving on the lipstick. 'Mervyn had the nerve to keep saying to me why didn't I try to look a bit more like Rita Hayworth. D'ya ever hear the like! I reckon he was pretty lucky to have somebody like me in a dump like Rivers End. Honest, ducky, you never saw such a dead-end hole. Rita Hayworth. . . . Huh, what's she got that I haven't got, etc. etc.? D'you know, kid, I've half a mind to stay here and try my luck on the movies. What say you and me hit the trail for Hollywood together?'

'Well,' I said.

'It would be nice to have a chum in a place like Hollywood,' Isobel said. 'At first, anyway, until we got properly going. We could live on our alimony.'

I was real thankful when Mom Winnegar shouted upstairs at that moment that tea was ready. I just didn't know what to make of Isobel, and I hustled her downstairs as quick as I could. 'Just a tick,' I said at the door of the lounge. 'I must collect my silk stockings from the porch before Bunny-Wunny gets a hold of them.'

'I never thought I'd find you mending the ladders in your stockings, Scotty,' Isobel said, following me on to the porch. 'I must say I thought Lew would of been able to keep you supplied with so many nylongs from his store that you wouldn't of bothered about runs.'

'Nylongs aren't so easy to get as all that,' I said.

'Well, for crying out loud,' Isobel said. 'Don't tell me Lew's a tight-wad! I must say I thought once or twice in New York . . .'

'Lew's all right,' I said. 'There's nothing wrong with Lew.'

'C'mon in and meet the folks,' I said, opening the lounge door.

Isobel was hardly introduced to Mom and Mrs. Boddler before she'd launched into an account of how she'd quarrelled with Mervyn and what she said to him and what he said to her. 'Of course, I should never have married him in the first place,' she said in her poshest tone. 'I should have made certain that he was able to keep me in the style to which I've been accustomed, etc. etc. It really is terribly hard on a girl like me when she discovers that the man she's given her all to is such an out and out blackguard. Why, there wasn't one thing that he'd told me true! He told me he was an executive in the oil business—and when I got there I found he worked a gasoline pump!'

'But I'm glad to see my little friend, Scotty, so happy and well settled,' she said, dabbing her eyes. 'I'm glad to see she's struck it lucky. She deserves it, because she had a hard time before she came over here, being a waitress, etc. etc.'

'Another cup of tea, Isobel?' I said.

'No, ducky, no thanks,' she said. 'But I'll have a cigarette, if I may.'

'But perhaps I shouldn't smoke,' she said, keeping her case half-in and half-out her bag. 'Perhaps your mother-in-law may object?'

'You don't mind, do you, Mrs. Winnegar?' she said with a gushing smile. 'But of course, you must be used to it by this time with Jessie smoking like a furnace!'

'Jessie doesn't smoke much,' Mom Winnegar said. 'Just two three a day is all Jessie smokes.'

'My, Scotty, you must have turned over a new leaf!' Isobel cried. 'A cigarette never seemed to be out of your mouth in the old days.'

'You and Jessie are old friends?' Mom said.

'Oh yes, we've known each other for ages and ages,' Isobel said, leaning back and crossing her legs so that Pop Winnegar could get a good view.

'I must go now,' Mrs. Boddler said. 'George'll be home at any minute.'

She rose most unwillingly, keeping her eye on Isobel, hoping, I guess, she'd say some more before she finally went. But Isobel was smiling at Pop.

'I always like to be in when George comes home,' Louise Boddler said. 'I think a wife should always be there to greet her husband coming back from work.'

'Scotty's lucky in that respect, isn't she?' Isobel said. 'I'm sure she never needs to bother about being home to receive her husband when his mother's on the spot.'

'You *are* a lucky bag, Scotty!' she said. 'I bet you go gadding to the movies most afternoons, knowing that Mrs. Winnegar here will see to Lew's tea, etc. etc.'

'Jessie never goes to the movies without Lew,' Mom said.

'I really must go,' Mrs. Boddler said. 'Come along then, Bunny-Wunny. Home! Say good-bye to the ladies!'

'What a sweet little dog,' Isobel said. 'Isn't it, Scotty?'

'But of course, I forgot,' she said. 'I've just remembered that you loathe dogs.'

'I never——' I began, but just then Lew came in and Isobel rushed to him, crying: 'Lew! Lew love, how nice to see you!' And she kissed him before he knew where he was.

'I really must go now,' Mrs. Boddler said. 'I daren't put off another minute.'

And so she went, and I knew that before bed-time it would be all over Struthers Bridge about Isobel's arrival and what she'd said.

XI

'How long does that girl aim to stay here?' Mom Winnegar said on Isobel's third afternoon with us.

'Search me,' I said. 'I wish I knew.'

'She ain't doing herself any good staying here,' Mom said, sifting sugar into a basin with flour.

'Nor you,' she said, reaching for a packet of shredded suet.

'If I was her man I'd come and tan the pants offen her,' Mom went on, beginning to stir her cake mixture. 'She's no class. She's just no class at all. I can't think how you ever took up with her, Jessie.'

'I didn't take up with her at all,' I said. 'The shipping company put us both in the same cabin.'

'Well, all I can say is it ain't right of the shipping company to do such things,' Mom said. 'She's no account, and the quicker she gets on her way out of Struthers Bridge the better.'

But Isobel wasn't showing any signs of moving. She kept saying she was making her arrangements, but I couldn't see when she was doing them.

'Where is she now?' Mom Winnegar said.

'She said she was going to the Post Office,' I said.

'Well, girl, if I was you,' Mom Winnegar said, stirring quickly and not looking at me. 'If I was you,' she said, 'I'd go out and meet her. I reckon you should keep an eye on that young lady.'

'Okay,' I said, and as I walked slowly down the street towards the Post Office I thought maybe I'd misjudged Mom Winnegar a bit when I first came to Struthers Bridge. She wasn't a bad old stick. She had the size of that Isobel all right.

There was no sign of Isobel at the Post Office. Mamie Jones behind the counter said she'd been and gone an hour ago. I bought some stamps and began to walk back home. I was passing Pop's store and I thought maybe I'd go in and see Lew, but as I was turning in the door who should come out but Isobel.

'Hello, ducks!' she cried, hitching her arm into mine. 'Out for a little constitutional? I must say I've enjoyed mine! I'm absolutely starving. Let's hurry back and get something to eat. I hope that mother-in-law of yours has the tea ready.'

'I was goin' in to see Lew,' I said.

'He's terrible busy, etc. etc.' Isobel said. 'He just about flung me out on my neck. Don't bother him just now, ducks. Come on!'

She began to draw me up the street, so I went, not wanting to make any fuss. I'd seen old Mr. Neill heading for the store anyway.

'Hello, how's my little Scottish friend today?' he shouted, waving his stick.

'Fine, thank you,' I called, and I waved, but I didn't make any move to stop.

'Who's that old geezer, honey?' Isobel said. 'God, I must say there are a lot of queer guys in this dump. You've certainly landed amongst them, etc. etc. The quicker you get out of it and away from them the better.'

'Och, it's not a bad place,' I said. 'And old Mr. Neill isn't a bad old soul.'

'Don't make me laugh,' Isobel said. 'What about packing up and lighting out with me tomorrow for Hollywood?'

'So you're going tomorrow?' I said.

'Well, I haven't made up my mind definitely yet,' she said. 'I've been trying to figure out how much money I've got. Can you raise any?'

'No, I guess not,' I said.

'What about the Winnegars?' she said. 'Would they loan me some?'

'Well, really, Isobel,' I said, feeling I'd just about had enough.

'All right, if you don't want to help me,' she said. 'I guess I'll get along all right with what I've got. But I just thought because we were pals, etc. etc.'

'If you're as dependent on the Winnegars as all that,' she said.

'But I'm sorry for you, Scotty,' she said. 'With that old battle-axe of a mother-in-law. I bet you'll be glad when you get your divorce.'

'Who said anything about a divorce,' I said. 'You needn't think because you and Mervyn can't hit it off that everybody's like you.'

'And there's nothing wrong with my mother-in-law,' I said. 'She's been very nice to me.'

So Isobel shut up then, and after we'd had tea she went away and wrote letters.

XII

I'd thought Lew had been kind of funny ever since Isobel came, but I'd put it down to him not liking her very much and to her landing on his folks in this way. Still, that evening he hardly spoke, and he went away to bed early. Normally when he went to bed early he'd say no matter who was there: 'C'mon, honey, beddy-byes!' and he'd practically push me away in front of him. But that night he just picked up a magazine and said: 'Well, I'm hittin' the hay.'

He was lying with his back to me when I went into our room, and he never spoke or turned round while I undressed. 'Are you asleep already?' I said, but he never answered.

I got in beside him and I put my arm round him, but he shoved my hand away with his elbow and said: 'Aw, lay off me, can't you! I've had a heavy day and I'm tired.'

I lay and looked at his broad shoulders for a few minutes, then I put my arm round him again.

'Darling,' I said.

'Aw for Chrissake!' he said. 'I was near asleep.'

'What's the matter, honey?' I said.

He shoved my arm away again.

'Can't you leave a fella in peace?' he said. 'Move over to your own side of the bed.'

'But darling,' I said.

'Aw, go to sleep,' he said.

I lay for two three minutes, then I started to cry.

'Aw shuttup,' Lew said. 'If you don't quit it I'll go to the spare room.'

I cried all the louder at this.

'What's the matter?' I said. 'What've I done?'

'What've you not done!' Lew said.

'That Isobel,' he said.

'Yeah, that Isobel,' he said again. 'Pal of yours. Just the

right kinda pal for a dame like you. She came into the store today and did she open her mouth and spill it!'

'Yeah, did she spill it,' he said, heaving round on to his back.

'So you thought you'd play me for a sucker, did you?' he said.

'And how soon do you plan to file suit for divorce, Mrs. Winnegar?' he said.

I was weeping buckets by this time. If that Isobel had been within reach I don't know what I'd have done to her.

'I'm not,' I said. 'I'm not aiming to file for divorce.'

'Since when?' Lew said. 'Isobel told me you had your mind made up to file for divorce before you left England.'

'I had not,' I said.

'You had so,' he said. 'Isobel told me.'

'Isobel's a liar,' I said.

'Isn't that just like a dame,' he said. 'She can't even stick to her pals.'

'You just married me so's you could get to the States,' he said. 'Everybody on the boat knew it.'

'I did not,' I said.

'I love you,' I said.

'Tell that to all the other guys,' he said. 'You're just practising so's you'll have it word perfect when you get to Hollywood.'

'I'm never going to Hollywood,' I said.

'Don't let me stop you,' he said. 'I wouldn't want to ruin your career.'

'I don't want a career,' I said. 'Not any more I don't.'

'I just want you,' I said.

'Well, think again,' Lew said.

And he got up and went to the spare room and locked the door. I was going to beat on the door until he opened it, but it was right next to Isobel's room, so I didn't. I went back to bed and wept and wept until I fell asleep.

XIII

The next morning when I got up Lew had left for the store. Mom Winnegar was in the kitchen and she just gave me one look and then she said: 'If I was you, girl, I'd do somethin' about those eyes of yours before that Isobel gets up. I reckon your pillows must be sopping.'

'And I wouldn't worry if I were you,' she shouted after me. 'That Isobel's gonna get a spoke in her wheel or my name ain't Gert Winnegar.'

I didn't think much about this at the time, I was too busy figuring how I was going to put a spoke in Isobel's wheel on my own. But I remembered it later when Mervyn arrived.

Isobel was having her breakfast and I was giving her a good piece of my mind when Mom Winnegar came in and said: 'Guy here to see you, Isobel.'

And there right behind Mom was a tall fella that I recognized at once from his pictures.

'Mervyn!' Isobel yelled.

'What're you doin' here?' she said.

'I've come to take you home,' he said. 'There ain't never been a divorce in our family.'

'There ain't never been a divorce in our family either,' Mom Winnegar chipped in. 'And there ain't gonna be one if I can help it. You'd better find out here and now that America ain't just what they make it out to be in the movies. Folks like us don't go in for divorce as much as they make out.'

'Howd'ya know I was here?' Isobel said.

'A little bird whispered,' Mervyn said.

'A pretty big bird I should think,' Isobel said, looking at Mom Winnegar.

'Yeah, I phoned him yesterday when you were down at the store making mischief,' Mom said. 'But I guess it's the last mischief you're gonna make here.'

'You bet,' Mervyn said. 'Better get your stuff together, honey. We're leavin' on the next bus.'

'We are not,' Isobel said.

She got into a right paddy then and yelled and yelled. But it was no good. Mervyn and Mom were as firm as a couple of Rocks of Gibraltar. 'You get her on that bus, young man,' Mom said to Mervyn. 'Then you can thrash things out for yourselves.'

'Though it's her I'd thrash,' she said. 'Soundly.'

'I'm right sorry for that boy marryin' a tramp like that,' she said when they'd gone. 'I reckon she won't go a step farther than St. Paul.'

'Still, it'll be the best thing for him if she don't,' she said.

'Now you go and get your face fixed,' she said to me. 'Then go down to the store and tell that husband of yours he's a sap to listen to anythin' a tramp like that 'd tell him.'

XIV

Lew wasn't at the store. One of the girls said he'd got in the flivver and left soon after they opened. 'Looked kinda funny, Lew did,' she said. 'Kinda peaky.'

'He didn't sleep well last night,' I said. 'His stomach was bothering him.'

Louise Boddler was in when I got home, and she and Mom were having a right good session in the kitchen, so I went up to my room.

I was in a real panic. I thought about all the things that had happened last night and I sat down in front of the dressing-table and wept and wept. I could have strangled that Isobel. I was so mad at her. What right had she to come here and make trouble between me and Lew? I just hoped Mervyn would give her a good hiding. Though I reckoned Mom was right and Isobel wouldn't go a step farther than St. Paul. I bet she'd take the first boat back to England like so many other G.I. Brides. And that was the right place for her, I reckoned. Good riddance to bad rubbish and all that. The lousy tramp. It was real bad luck that I'd been put in the same cabin as no class dames like her and Cora and Letty.

I bet they'd lit out by this time, too, and were on the middle of the Atlantic. Pity the boat wouldn't sink and drown them all.

I got so het up thinking about them that I stopped crying. I sat and looked at myself in the glass. You'd have thought with all the crying I'd done in the past twenty-four hours that I'd have looked a sight. But I didn't look any too bad. In fact I looked all right. I looked pretty good. As good as Ginger Rogers or Bette Davis when they were having a big weepy scene.

Better than them, I thought, giving myself the once-over. The way the tears were hanging on my lashes was real artistic. I bet if a director saw me like this he'd sign me up and put me on the first train for Hollywood.

Of course, Hollywood was out of the question now. I'd been daft ever to think of such a thing. I wasn't thinking about anything else now but Lew. I was for Lew in a big way. I just didn't want anything but him and for him to put his arms tight around me.

I went down and helped Mom prepare the lunch. Mrs. Boddler hurried away after her session with Mom, so excited she could hardly take time to say hello to me.

We laid the lunch, but though Pop came in Lew never appeared. We waited a while, then we had ours. Mom put aside Lew's to keep hot for him, saying: 'I'll make his ears hot for him when he comes.'

But three o'clock came and he never turned up. Then four o'clock. I began to get in a real stew, wondering what had happened to him, and I had all sorts of visions of the flivver having gone over a cliff with Lew lying at the bottom among the wreckage. . . .

XV

It was six o'clock before he turned up. Mom and Pop had gone out visiting, and I was walking up and down, up and down. Because by this time I was near demented.

'Where've you been?' I cried.

'What does it matter to you where I've been?' he said.

'It matters a lot,' I said. 'Keepin' folk worryin' about you.'

'Fat lot of worryin' you'll do,' he said.

'Bring on the eats,' he said. 'I'm starvin'.'

'Bring on the eats,' I cried. 'Here am I near demented and all you think about is your stomach.'

'Well, I couldn't sleep last night on account of my stomach,' he said. 'So Kitty in the store told me.'

'It was news to me, I must say,' he said, parking himself at the table.

'Well, it'll be news to you, too, that Isobel has gone,' I said, putting his hotted-up lunch in front of him. 'Mervyn came and took her away.'

'Whyn't he take you, too?' Lew said, beginning to wolf. 'Or are you waitin' for this Paul Whatsisname to come and cart you off?'

'What Paul Whatsisname?' I said.

'You know,' he said. 'Fella you fell for on the boat.'

'I didn't fall for any fella on the boat,' I said. 'I only fell for you.'

'Don't try to come the bag,' Lew said. 'Isobel told me about this Paul guy.'

'Isobel's a liar,' I said.

'So you told me last night,' he said. 'I still don't believe it.'

I started to weep then. It was about time. 'You'd believe Isobel before you'd believe me,' I said.

'Why shouldn't I?' he said.

'But I'm your wife,' I said.

'Thought you were gonna sue for divorce,' he said.

'Oh, Lew!' I cried.

'You know I wouldn't,' I said.

'Paul meant nothin' to me,' I said. 'He was just a guy I danced with on the boat.'

'Isobel said she saw you kissin' him,' Lew said.

'What if I did,' I said. 'It was just once. I couldn't help it. I was thinkin' about you at the time, and he reminded me of you. Honest he did.'

'So I'm to spend my life watchin' out for fellas that remind you of me,' Lew said, getting up and switching on the radio.

'You know you aren't,' I shouted to make myself heard above a dame crooning *Give Me Five Minutes More*.

'Looks like it,' he said, sitting down and opening a magazine.

'Listen, honey,' I said.

'You know I'm for you in a big way,' I said, wiping my eyes. 'Ever since that night in the taxi.'

'That taxi,' he said.

'Why won't you believe me?' I said, weeping harder than ever.

'Aw, cut it out,' he said. 'Let's call it a day.'

I don't know what I said next, but in between crying I tried to tell him all about Birnieburn and wanting to go to Hollywood and how I didn't want to go there any longer and how I'd never been and never would be in love with anybody but him. And then quite suddenly he put his arms round me and said: 'Aw, honey, let's forget it.'

'Stop cryin', sweetheart,' he said after a while. 'You're gonna make your eyes all red, and I wouldn't like that.'

'I can't,' I said, 'I can't.'

And I couldn't, because the harder I tried to stop the harder I cried. I laid my head against Lew's shoulder and he took my hankie and wiped the tears as fast as they fell. We stood like that for a long time, and then I said: 'Let me go, love. I must go and fix my face before Mom and Pop come back.'

But Lew held on to me tight, humming: 'Give me five minutes more, only five minutes more, let me stay, let me stay in your arms. . . .'

'Ach, you'll get plenty of time for that yet,' I said. 'Lemme go.'

'Aw, what's the hurry,' he said.

'Do you remember that last night in London?' he said.

'Will I ever forget it?' I said.

'That's the way I feel now,' he said.

'That's the way I'll always feel about you, baby,' he said.

'Me too,' I said.

'Now I really must go and fix my face,' I said, and I kissed him and ran upstairs.

And while I was lashing myself up so that I'd be all right for Mom and Pop coming home I noticed the G.I. Bride's Guide lying on my dressing-table, and I thought of all the things it didn't tell you. And I thought, as I ran downstairs to Lew, that maybe one day I'd try and write a better one myself—if I could get time to get round to doing it between films.

Madame X

MORLEY JAMIESON

(b. 1917)

ANOTHER day had begun. Madame X now wholly dressed went to the window and drew up the blind so that the sunlight filled the bedroom to the utmost corner. It revealed too the pallor of Madame X's delicately shaped features and the metallic dullness of her blonde hair as she gazed for a moment on the surrounding countryside. Madame X was not feeling very well and had spent a restless night. She left Jim-Jim yawning in bed and went downstairs to get the milk. As she opened the door the sunshine met her again and welcoming it she impulsively took a deep breath but it hurt so much that she felt dizzy. She bent down and lifted the bottle of milk from the step, but almost in the same moment

it slipped from her grasp and smashed with a spray of whiteness on the concrete. Her neighbour Mrs. Braun was coming
up the garden where she had been hanging out a washing
and when she saw the smashed bottle she uttered a loud
clicking noise of commiseration. 'Oh,' she said, 'you've done
it now, but wait a minute and I'll see if I can spare you a pint
to go on with.' And she went into her house reappearing in
a moment or two with a pint of milk which she put into the
arms of Madame X who had been unable to move from the
door.

'That's kind of you Mrs. Braun.'

'That's all right—now don't you drop it.' And Mrs.
Braun stooping hastily gathered the broken fragments of the
bottle and put them in the dust-bin.

'You can have your porridge after all, you look as if you
wanted something to strengthen you.' Then she vanished
once more through her own doorway as if embarrassed and
wishing to cut short her gratitude.

As Madame X turned to go upstairs Jim-Jim came
lumbering down and she knew how that noise must irritate
those in the house below. He stopped when he saw her.

'What's wrong?'

'I dropped the milk,' she said, 'and Mrs. Braun gave me
a pint of hers.'

He took the milk bottle and put his arm round her helping
her up the stair to the sitting-room. As she sat down she
clutched at his hand and began to cry, partly with weakness
and self-pity, and partly with a renewed tenderness for
Jim-Jim. He patted her hand, wiped his black moustache
first on one side and then on the other with the back of his
hand, and went through to the scullery to get the breakfast.

Then it was time for him to go to work and when he was
ready she looked him over carefully as was her daily practice
to make sure that there was no ouder on his collar, no hairs
on his shoulder, and that his tie was straight. It was a kind of
ritual with her and she prolonged it as long as she could.

When the clock chimed the half-hour his going was like an eternal parting to her and she fought off the moments gaily as if she hoped to stave off the depression which threatened to assail her once he was gone. Something in the resigned manner in which he pulled on his coat and said 'Well dear, I must be off' was infinitely pathetic. She had never grown used to this attachment to a man twice her age and to the agitation which his going or coming wrought in her. Poor old Jim-Jim: if he had transgressed it was chiefly on her account, but that was in the past; and she remembered that he had been the first man who was really nice to her.

'You're all right with me,' he said, and she was and had been ever since she married him.

When the door finally closed on him and she went upstairs again to watch him walk along the street she seemed to slide back into the horror of that other life when she had first met him. This generally happened when she was tired or ill, and Jim-Jim who was so intimately bound up with the past was also the barrier against its insistent memory. The sight of his lanky figure and familiar features returning in the evening would once more resolve that fateful period and their happiness push it into the background. He seemed like a homely symbol of all that was at variance with the old life: but now when he went the old came back.

Even though she was not feeling well and easily tired, the housework did not keep her long, and by mid-morning with the sun shining out of a clear blue sky she went out and sat in a deck-chair in the lee of the house. In the sunshine drab memory began to melt and she cheerfully passed the time of day with Mrs. Braun as she hung out more washing. There Madame X sat most of the day enjoying the warmth, and sometimes looking up at the blue hills with an expression of query on her face like a child asking awkward questions: then she resumed the book or tract she was reading, for Madame X had taken to religion; and she was inclined with the old life behind her to give up so many things that had made life pleasant as if everything that related to pleasure was sinful and abhorrent. Yet like a naughty child she persisted in some things, unable to part with them, so that she sat in a semi-coma of devotion, praising the Lord in her heart with the lipstick in a great scarlet daub on her mouth bespeaking to all who saw her something other than purity and praise.

Mrs. Braun when she met a friend out shopping said to her in a voice of unusual feeling, 'Have you seen Madame X today, God she looks awful.'

She may have only referred to the pallor of Madame X, but there were times when Madame X looked not what she was now, rather what she had been. The hollow eyes and cheeks told the tale of innumerable bottle-parties, dance halls, and midnight gaieties on the foreshore, while the thin figure had paid its debt to sensation. These were the obvious things: yet Madame X still looked like a tart in the way in which she wore her black and white tailored clothes, or even in her demureness which was accentuated by her favourite furs; and she had a way of smiling which did more than conversation to win her attention, especially from the men. Nevertheless there was a peculiar dignity and independence about her, the remains of an old habit which she early learned to be elegant and avoid the customs and habits of ordinary trollops and to keep off their beat, the pubs and coffee-stalls. She was the illegitimate child of a butler and a housemaid, and in her youth had been convinced that the master, or perhaps the butler and the mistress were responsible: in consequence she built up an edifice of fantasy in which surrounded by admirers she enjoyed the opulence and luxury she imagined should have been hers.

Later in the afternoon when she set out to walk to the head of the road to meet Jim-Jim off the tram, she teetered on impossibly high heels and wore her special silver-fox fur on her shoulders. She went slowly up the road where as it chanced the building contractors had not yet been let loose, and on one side was a cornfield with a good braird of green on it while on the other side loomed the barracks grey and oriental echoing with the sound of immense virility, and by the roadside were chestnut-trees whose branches swept the air above her head, bowing in a ceaseless obeisance. Every few yards she went up the road the hills behind her raised their crests still higher so that by the time she reached the tramways and turned for a moment they were enormous and filled the whole horizon. Their grandeur awed her and impressed her shallow religious ideas bringing to mind the familiar phrases and texts like trumpet calls: she could almost see the Beatitudes emblazoned on the gigantic billboard of the sky:

> Blessed are the poor in spirit:
> For theirs is the kingdom of heaven.
> Blessed are the meek:
> For they shall possess the earth.

She was repeating them to herself when she met Letty Morice.

Letty was a respectable housewife, comfortable and with few cares; and though a near neighbour of Madame X had always taken good care to avoid her, all the more since they had been classmates at school. There was a time not long distant for Madame X when to meet with people who knew her in former days was an acute embarrassment, but now she was strangely interested in the fortunes of all those miscellaneous and apparently meaningless lives which had crossed her own at one time or another.

'Hello Letty,' she said, 'how are you?'

Her one-time companion was surprised by her greeting and for a moment the conflict of respectability versus curiosity showed plainly in her face; and curiosity in the name of pity won: she stopped a yard or two off, glancing furtively at the passers-by and then at Madame X:

'Hullo Daisy, how are you?'

'Oh I'm not so bad,' and Madame X warming to her old companion asked after those girls who had been in the same class and of whose fate she had formerly been so indifferent.

They reminisced for a few minutes on those gawky, long-legged, big-mouthed days and watched each other, taking each other in, greedily absorbing the present and the past. Finally they parted amicably with uplifted hands of farewell.

When Letty reached home she flung her message bag on the kitchen table and plunged next door to tell of her encounter:

'And what do you think she had the neck to say to me when I came away . . . "Oh," says Madame,' and she imitated Madame X's husky voice, ' "Oh it doesn't matter what you've been or how you've lived so long as you love God in the end," . . . and after all that she's been—the bitch, preaching to me.'

Madame X sunned herself at the tram-stop and watched the trams sweep off to the left down a long vista of trees which seemed to her like a felicity that somehow, some day, she would realize. The sunlight caught by the stretch of wall behind her was pleasant and comforting, giving her a sense of security and a quiet happiness. Then Jim-Jim dropped off the next car, and when he saw her his eyes brightened and he crossed the road to where she stood; his whole bearing, his expression, and even his gesture was of solicitude for her. The sun never did her so much good as Jim-Jim and they walked down the road arm-in-arm like young lovers oblivious of the passers-by, engaged at once in the inconsequential recital of the day's doings even though such a superficial variety must serve them as a subject for the rest of the evening.

As the summer advanced the walk to and from the tram-stop came to have a growing sweetness for Madame X and she began to associate happiness with its familiar objects. Her walk was slow and she became aware of the changes in the landscape, the corn ripening, the cones of white blossom on the chestnut-trees, even the birds in the hedges fascinated her with their bright careless movements. She had acquired that last earthly resort of the chronic sufferer, communion

with nature. Formerly, too, she had known that her liveli-
hood depended to a large extent on her being accepted by
the community at least nominally, though she herself had
not accepted the community: by being a type, an agreeable
and obliging type, she preserved herself in the midst of a
hostile and sometimes disagreeable people. Now, however,
when she looked so obviously what she had been, she was
more aware of being at one with common humanity and
was conscious of the meeting ground of virtue and vice in all.
She was eager now to talk to people and by that mysterious
agency which welds society, especially in cities, she was
absorbed into the community; and though she might be
pointed out, it was as a curiosity and not as an object of
derision and contempt.

For one with her reputation she had a startling innocence
and naïveté which made the shopkeepers smile and not
grin. Even the doctor when he called did not hurry in and
out with a frown on his face, but sat for a few moments
looking at her and talking about the best treatment for
rheumatics.

'Take care of yourself,' he said, 'eat as much as you can,
butter, eggs, pork chops, and drink plenty of milk, don't go
out in the rain . . . you'll be all right.'

Though she knew that his cheerfulness was only a bedside
manner she accepted it simply, grateful and comforted by it.
And just as she thought the doctor engaging with his stories
about his cases, the corns, the flat feet, and measles, all
seemed wonderful to her: even the gloomy people attracted
her and she longed that they might be happy like herself.
She wanted to do some great work of mercy and to make
some sacrifice, but even to distribute leaflets was too much
for her.

On inclement days when she couldn't go out she missed
her walk and sat by the window watching the road and
fidgeting till Jim-Jim came home. She read her Bible but
somehow the red-lettered texts did not sting and burn into
her consciousness as they generally did. She realized then

how avid she was of life and that the outer world drew her,
the new world of sensation which had been unknown to her:
she rebuked herself for her vanity and tried to turn away
from the rain purling down the window and the sight of the
hills cloaked with rain-clouds. She felt a concern for the
lovely world under the liquid lash, the corn, the twittering
sparrows and especially the trees on the road heaving their
branches about in the wind so that the white blossom
fluttered and was lost in the hedge or stuck to the wet
macadam.

She remembered reading in the potted psychology
columns of the Sunday paper how the tree was a symbol of
life; and in a muddled way she liked to think that the Cross
might have been cut from such a tree as those on the road.
Her road and her tree.

Then one afternoon in the late autumn it rained, driving
off the hill with a fury from the south-west. Madame X
laid the tea-table and made a few jam-tarts which Jim-Jim
liked so much and at the back of five o'clock when all was
ready, with a comfortable glance at the clock she sat down
to wait. By himself Jim-Jim only took six or seven minutes
to reach the house from the tram-stop and it surprised her
when he was not in at quarter to six. She told herself that he
had missed his tram or been delayed at business, but at half-
past six her uneasiness had grown to a dread of the unknown
and unusual. Something out of the ordinary must have happened because Jim-Jim didn't indulge in casual drinks
with old friends for he didn't seem to have any old friends
at all.

She tried to allay a premonition of disaster by praying
but the words were dry and unreal: peas rattling in a bladder
like any other hocus-pocus; and she went about the house
touching the familiar objects to reassure herself. The rain
stopped about half-past seven though it still lowered over
the hills. A blink or two from a watery sun deceived her
and she decided that she would go up the road to meet him.
In her haste she forgot both umbrella and her raincoat and

went out meeting people hurrying home who glanced at her curiously as they passed. Each man in the distance wearing a mackintosh was Jim-Jim, only to disappoint her as he drew near.

Before she got very far a shower of rain blattered down, and with the wind in an airt that made the trees useless as shelter she was soon wet. She was suddenly so exhausted that she had to stop and rest in the middle of it, turning away from the wind for it caught her breath. She clung to the fence post, quivering a little, feeling the wind and anxiety between them stretching her to breaking point. Before her was the corn partly cut and the stooks standing awry or blown over by the wind, while the rest of the crop lay flattened and lank; immediately the parable of the sower and the seeds came back to her:

. . . some fell by the wayside and was trodden down and the fowls of the air devoured it. And other some fell upon a rock : and as soon as it sprung up it withered away because it had no moisture. And other some fell among thorns : and the thorns growing up with it choked it. And other some fell upon good ground : and being sprung up yielded fruit a hundred-fold. . . .

Her strength returned to her as she thought of this, and with renewed hope she went on up the road. When she reached the tramways she rested against the wall and animal-like pressed to it for a protection it couldn't give. Darkness closed the final gap in the lowered sky and the lighted trams coming up the hill from the town seemed to drag themselves up from some hateful avernus, raising in Madame X a variety of hopes, fears, and memories: but the vehicles passed on with noisy traction without bringing Jim-Jim.

She grew cold and felt her body like a clod, even fancied herself at times as distinct from it. She began to chatter involuntarily and three youths on their way to the beershop looked at her knowingly. One of them said something and turned away abashed by his own impertinence, ashamed of his remark even while he made it. At that they went on out of earshot but presently they were all three guffawing on the sidewalk at some private joke. The incident stabilized Madame X because she was furious with the young men for their insult, feeling it with something like her old arrogance: she indeed, who had never needed to solicit, to be thought canvassing: and even the renewed shame of her position was mixed with this alien element of rage at being taken for a common trull.

She hugged the wall praying for Jim-Jim to come and rescue her from this nightmare of dread and felt helpless against the monster city which claimed him. Then she became aware that a man was standing before her: he was like Jim-Jim but something about him choked her greeting in her throat: his face was strangely drawn and white. At last he spoke in a harsh angry voice:

'What are you doing here on such a night as this?'

'Oh Jim-Jim I missed you . . . where have you been . . . what kept you?'

He turned his head hesitating, and as she saw his profile in the lamp-light she was aghast at his expression.

'You're soaking wet, you shouldn't have come out.'

He slipped off his mackintosh and put it round her shoulders.

'What kept you so late Jim?'

'I met in with some one.'

They walked slowly because she was stiff with standing but happy in having him again she talked on though still puzzled and anxious about his strange appearance. He was distraught but had not been drinking and she asked him a mild curiosity:

'Who was it you met with?'

'I met my wife.'

At first she thought she had misheard him and she laughed as if he had made a joke but he gave her a quick look which stifled her: and when he turned away as if in revulsion at the

whole situation she knew that it was true: that he had met
his wife. Her legs trembled and she fell against him and as
he caught her Jim-Jim was sobbing in restrained gasps of
grief so that he could hardly hold her.

'Hullo,' said a voice out of the darkness, 'what's the
matter?'

'It's my wife,' said Jim-Jim, 'she's not well, she's taken
a fainting turn.'

'Hold on.'

The policeman's bulk as he bent over Madame X almost
hid her completely and Jim-Jim did not see the man's
cold face change as he recognized Madame X. When he
looked up again his wide face had an official poker-expres-
sion.

'You'd better get her off home now she's come round.'

But Madame X couldn't walk and with a quick movement
Jim-Jim lifted her bodily.

'Manage?' said the policeman.

'Yes I'll manage—it's not far,' and the policeman stood
in the middle of the road till Jim-Jim had gone down the hill
out of sight.

When he got her home she lay on the sofa and cried, not
loudly or hysterically but with a low grief that cut him in
two. Tears always disturbed him and now her agony added
to his own almost demented him; but from habit he went
about the house putting things to rights. He got her a hot
drink and put a hot-water bottle in the bed and at last persuaded her to take off her wet clothes and go to bed. She
stopped crying and watched him coming and going, not
with the old fondness but with a new expression in her
bright feverish eyes; and conscious all the time of her gaze
he desired passionately to return to the old happiness. He
dreaded an explanation and reproaches, and each time he
tried to right his ideas the effort was too much for him. After
she was in bed he sat a long time by the fire in despair,
seeing his mistakes too late.

When he had tidied up he went through to the bedroom

and began to undress. Madame X had fallen asleep and under the soft light her flushed cheeks gave her a momentary appearance of radiant health. As he lifted the bed-clothes to get in she started awake and looked at him in horror.

'You can't get into this bed,' she said, and then gaped as if in surprise at herself denying another woman's husband the right to share her bed.

Jim-Jim stopped half in and half out of the bed:

'I want to be near you,' he said.

'I don't care, you can't share this bed any more.'

Jim-Jim was unwilling to precipitate a scene and went into the next room where he stripped the blankets off the bed and returning he made up a makeshift with some chairs. He turned off the light in silence and lay down, but was awake most of the night listening to her moaning and tossing and turning.

Next day Madame X was in a high fever. The doctor called, wrote out a hasty prescription and when he spoke to Jim-Jim in the hallway the frown had come back to his face. He seemed in a hurry to get away.

'She's had some kind of shock,' he said, 'was she out in the rain yesterday?—ah I thought so, she's got a bad chill, I don't like that at all.'

And after giving Jim-Jim some instructions he hurried away to the comparative ease of mumps, measles, or worms. It was not that the doctor was unaccustomed to people dying but the complexity of human feelings disturbed him: the body was simply a mechanism that ran down, but before the last gasp something gazed out of the eyes and sometimes mouthed itself in delirium, whether it was terror, insanity, horror, love, or indifference: it was all here in Madame X.

Jim-Jim who had so long nursed her anyway tended to her in his quiet systematic manner, expecting her to demand an explanation or to reproach him with his deception. After a time he saw that the explanation and the deception did not matter any longer, not because Madame X was a woman of the world but because she had grown remote from the world where such things did matter. She accepted the situation simply because she could not remedy it. Jim-Jim thought that away from the dissipation which clouded moral conduct she was now a prey to extravagant sensibility in yet another direction. Her religion he regarded as a shallow growth though he encouraged her in it because the texts and large promises seemed to comfort her. But now it was a strange growth indeed. Her refusal to let him sleep with her struck him at first as absurd; an unnecessary prudence: but he could see that her earnestness was established deep in her and was not simply the obstinacy of an invalid.

Mrs. Braun readily came in to attend to her during the day: her tremendous activity, what between endless washings and cookings, seemed only to give her an added zest for more to do. She was large and coarse and made jokes in her loud voice in an effort to rally Madame X who appeared to enjoy having her. When Jim-Jim came home in the evening he felt her presence dominate the house: she trampled like a great unwitting animal on the shattered fragments of the intimacy that had been between Madame X and himself. Their extravagant love-making and the rosy, deliberately fostered, illusion of their life together had been momentary while this new situation was eternal.

He sat beside her bed reassuring her with talk of the day's doings and the inconsequential gossip and anecdote which had amused her in the past. But now they did not hold her. Her frail strength was divided by concern for him and what seemed wholly irrelevant abstraction. She was even reluctant to let Mrs. Braun go in case something should betray her into that old passionate relationship with Jim-Jim, while he tried gently to regain the old atmosphere with memories and the familiarities of their past enjoyments. Now and then the soap bubble of illusion, mysteriously coloured and intransient, would engage them for a brief moment. She divined his purpose, however, and became difficult, struggling with her affection for him, praying aloud for mercy and refused to be comforted, crying, why had she not been allowed to die in peace. She accused him of cruelty, not for having a wife already but for letting her know. That always agitated Jim-Jim and his moustache twitched so that he looked like a baby who is reproved and about to cry. When Madame X saw that, she was repentant in a moment, kissing his hand and crying over him.

Gradually, however, even these painful episodes were less frequent and Jim-Jim was suddenly aware of her purpose: instead of him resigning her and bidding an unspoken farewell to the cherished body and the well-loved person, she was resigning him. Whenever he came into the room her unearthly blue eyes followed him about with their gaze, silently denying him, giving up all claim on him, and drawing from her exhausted frame all the power she had in one supreme act of abnegation.

The time was gone by for protestation: and in the end he was robbed of his feelings and unable to feel clearly and distinctly the responsibility for their situation, nor the desire for forgiveness and all the regrets and decent grief, but he was left instead with a confused and congealed remorse. All these things Madame X claimed and absorbed, monopolizing and heaping them on herself with a kind of fervour. And when she closed her eyes she took them all with her.

Peacocks and Pagodas

DOROTHY K. HAYNES

(b. 1918)

SHE awoke, knowing it was light, but not knowing the time. The alarm-clock was still on its face, the only position in which it would ring, and for the moment she could not think to put out her hand and lift it. Then the bell came sounding across the quiet morning, a soft, falling tone to stroke the faithful awake. The notes dropped from the grey belfry, sinking through mist and green leaf, and belling across the pink purity of the sky, and Mrs. McCallum lay in a trance of pure peace. It was only half past five, too early to get up; but somewhere, in the green lawns and walks surrounding the chapel, there would be a fluttering of doves and nuns; and elsewhere there would be nothing but grey and dusty loneliness, over the silent market, and the slumbering railway station, and the hundreds of houses with not a drift of smoke from their chimneys.

There were cocks crowing as Mrs. McCallum savoured her last half-hour of rest. She liked waking early. It 'gave her the benefit,' she said, of being in bed. Beyond the recess curtains she could see the fireplace, with a sooty square of light trembling on the black kettle, and above it, the swan neck of the gas laid by against the wall. The window was covered by an old red tablecloth, hooked on to two nails, and the light came through, dim and warm, with a few beams lancing silver through the slits.

Here, in the bed recess, it was doubly dim. Her husband lay with his mouth open, and his shirt open to below the red V on his neck. Above his head was a greasy mark on the wallpaper, and Mrs. McCallum eyed it fiercely. Tonight, if all went well, that mark would be gone; and so would the faded paper, the curly peacocks and bunches of grapes and green and purple pagodas. She had liked the pattern well enough, when it was new, but now it was dirty, and Sandy complained that he traced every curlicue in the feathers and climbed every pagoda before he got to sleep. For herself, she was always too tired to bother.

But she wakened early; and today, not waiting for the alarm, she slid out of bed and began to put on her clothes. Quietly, she gathered her kindling, and went down the stairs without waking her husband. The bell was quiet now, but the air was sweet with the murmur of pigeons and a rushing river of birdsong.

In the yard, the stones were warm already, and the weeds green in the bright day. Inside the washhouse was a smell of water and dankness. A flood of glass lipped the tub under the tap, and the tap went drip, drip, a little song like the plink of a banjo. Mrs. McCallum ruffled the water with a dipper and poured a cascade into the brown boiler. A few splashes starred the stone floor and sparked at her stockings.

Throwing away her match, she watched smoke curl and lose itself, heard the breath of flame and the quick crackle of sticks. On her knees, she built up the coal, bit by bit, with a good shovelful thrown in when it had caught. It was six o'clock now, and all the clocks striking, and she slammed the fire door and went up to see to the breakfast.

Sandy was up, bald and heavy, moving slowly about the kitchen. He was not a man to speak much in the morning. With the family married, and the two of them left alone, things were as they had been forty years ago, the early rise for Sandy to go to the quarry, and the tacit agreement of silence. Only now they were slower, and the early rise a little more burdensome, and the evening reunion one of peace rather than passion.

'Isn't six o'clock early enough for you now?' he asked.

'I was down lighting the boiler,' she told him. 'I'm doing the bed today.'

'Oh?' He turned from the mirror, a froth beard giving him grandeur. He hated odd nights on the bed settee, with the window in the wrong place, and a draught at his back. 'How long will *that* take?'

'We'll be back in it by bedtime, if all goes well.' She looked at the sky, invisible with sun, and the grape blue of slates in the shade. This was the time to get on. By seven o'clock she had the bed stripped, and the curtains and valance on top of the pile, grey streaked and smelling of dust. They would need a good soak before she could wash them.

The fire was roaring red, and the water hissing. Strong, she straddled the drain in the floor, print-fresh, her dust-cap down to her brows. The long blankets came from the wringer like ropes, looped and caught in her red hands, and the sheets boiled in a rainbow sapple. She was through with her washing before the bairns had done scuttering to school.

She crossed the street with her basket, went through a whitewashed close, and into a walled garden. The green was neglected, great silver tufts pluming the posts, and the brick path weedy and broken; but a rose tree bloomed on a ruined wall, and there was a tangle of honeysuckle, and nasturtiums making a green honeycomb of the border. To Mrs. McCallum, who used this green by the courtesy of a neighbour, this was the highlight of her day. She dreamed, sometimes, that the garden was hers, to walk in and tend, and rest.

The washing hung straight down, not a breath of air to move it. Back in the house, she pummelled the mattress out of bed, dragged it to the landing, and flopped it half out of the window on a couple of chairs. The bed boards were strewn with magazines, going back about forty years, and every year she dusted them, stacked them upon the dresser, and put them back again. She kept them all, *Home Notes*, *Home Chat*, and hundreds of *Weldons*; she could no more throw away magazines than burn her wedding lines.

One by one, she cleared them away, and then she lifted the heavy boards from their supports, and sluiced and scrubbed them with disinfectant. When they were clean and fresh, she propped them opposite the landing window to dry and bleach in the sun. Impatiently, she cleared the recess of its clutter, the boots and the bath, the big portmanteau where she kept her sheets, and the spare pieces of linoleum. Now, at last, she could get on. With an old scarf over her dust-cap, she slapped whitewash over the ceiling, and watched it critically as it dried. There, that was better. Now maybe she could have a cup of tea and carry on when she was refreshed a bit.

She had a pie with her tea; Mrs. McCallum was a great lover of pies. As she ate, she could hear the railway horse stamping in the road below, as the lorry was unloaded. Every morning it brought tools and coils of wire and big straw-stuffed crates to the ironmonger's store, and there was a great ceremony of feeding the horse and the pigeons that fluttered in the lane. On warm days, Mrs. McCallum worked with the window open, and sometimes the pigeons became so bold that she had to flap at them with her dish-towel.

She quartered her pie, dipped it in tomato sauce, and turned over an old *Weldons*. Gallant, picture-book boys stared at her, and little girls with Dorothy bags and sashes. Children's fancy dress . . . no good keeping *them*, she thought. Besides, fashions changed. Some of the coats looked just silly.

But you never knew. Most of them came round again, in time. And the other magazines—some were so far back she had forgotten the stories, and the stories she remembered seemed far more vivid than anything she read nowadays. The modern writers didn't seem to write *about* anything.

Well, she thought, this won't pay the rent, or buy the bairns a new pinny. She clattered away her tea things, and then, triumphantly, went into the room and reached down the rolls of wallpaper from the wardrobe. Plainer this time; plain greyish fawn, with a grain in it, and a tendril of rose-buds here and there, so faint you had to look for it. She tried it up against the wall, pushed the kettle nearer the fire, and

mixed up the flour for the paste. And let Sandy start marking *this* paper with his head——!

It went on smoothly, covering up the curly birds and the
pagodas, till the recess was no longer an Oriental nightmare.
With great satisfaction she washed out her basin at the sink,
and looked out at the mixter-maxter of roofs she called the
view. She had never thought it dull. The tiles changed
colour with the sky, and the skyline was stabbed with
steeples, the old clock tower, the wee church with its flyaway
weather cock, and the beautiful spire of the chapel sending
its bell notes over the trees. She could not imagine what it
would be like to worship in such a church. She was a
Presbyterian, a douce, sober-minded kirk member, but
nothing in her religion touched her like the sound of the
chapel bell and its faint falling sadness. 'The peace of God,
which passeth all understanding. . . .' She always thought
of the bell when she heard that phrase.

But this wasn't a time to be thinking of bells. There was
much more to be done. She went down the dark stairs again,
through the white close, and there was her washing, bone
dry, and a drone of bees drowsy with brown bumbling.
There never seemed time, somehow, to linger at the green.
She mounded the clothes all warm and fresh in her basket,
and in her kitchen she wiped the sweat from her face and
put the irons on to heat. Once she got the ironing done,
and everything back in its place, she could tidy round and
get the dinner ready for Sandy coming home.

The scrubbed floor of the bed recess was dry and sweet,
and Mrs. McCallum sighed as she cluttered it up again with
the heavy portmanteau, the bulky bath, the wringer and
washboard, and the boots, all dusted in a neat row. If only
she had more room to put things! The boards rang and
echoed as she dropped them into place, and then she spread
the magazines, lovingly, their bright covers and old advertise-
ments hidden for another year. Panting, she humphed the
mattress in, kneading the flock in its blue ticking, then she
made the bed with the fresh sheets and the fluffy blankets

and the covers warm from the iron. When she had shaken
the rugs and polished the floor and put a gleam on the
dresser, then it would be time enough to put up the curtains.

She delayed the pleasure, setting the table first, peeling
the potatoes, and seeing to the stew on the hob. Now it
would have to be done, or Sandy would be in on top of her.
She threaded the curtains with clean tape, and looped the
middle of the tape over a nail to keep it from drooping, then
she poised the pelmet dainty and delicately above. The
valance was tricky. It had to be pleated into place with
drawing pins, and then the bed cover brought down so that
the fringe just covered the join. A man could never make
a recess bed properly. When Sandy did it, he left it all
humped and hollowed, and the cover still folded on a chair.
Ten to one he'd never notice the work she'd put out on it
today.

She would not point it out to him. Time for that later.
First thing, he needed a wash, to lave the red dust from his
pores, and then he needed his dinner. She was ready for
something herself, when she thought about it. She watched
him bowed over the sink, his shirt botched with sweat and
his hair fuzzed round his ears, and above the sound of the
tap the chapel bell called over the chimneys. Six o'clock.
A blessed hour of the day, with her man home, and a meal
on the table. . . .

Later, as he sat with his pipe, she took her chair into the
room and set it at the window. There was a pinkish light in
the streets, and below her, on the opposite wall, a child
bounced her ball and caught it.

> 'Mademoiselle,
> She went to the well,
> She never forgot
> Her *soap* nor towel . . .'

The picture-house was open, and she could see in as far
as the pay-box, the couples drifting in and disappearing.
Maybe it was cooler in there. It was certainly not cool in

the chip shop. Steam welled out at the door, and there was a savoury smell of frying, and two men leaned against the wall with papers in their hands, their fingers poised, their mouths round in the delicious agony of hot potatoes.

As she watched, Mrs. McCallum saw other windows open, and, shadowy in dim rooms, the figures of other women enjoying the evening. And suddenly, she realized that all day she had not spoken to a soul. Some days you couldn't work for gossiping. You met one, and then another, and somehow you couldn't break free; but today had been blessed by silence and she had not felt lonely. She sat there for a long time, till the pink light faded a little, and the air turned colder. The clock struck, the white pigeons wheeled, a silver flash, a gold gleam, a silver flash as they turned, and when she looked back into the room she could hardly see for a moment.

The chant was still coming from below:

> 'She washed her hands,
> She dried them well,
> She said her night prayers,
> And *jumped* into bed.'

Yes, that was the idea. It was early, but they were both tired. She shut the window and went through to the kitchen, hooking the red cloth over the window and folding the counterpane as carefully as she had spread it. Sandy would come when he had finished his pipe. A man was always a little later, on principle.

She was almost asleep when she felt him climb over her, and the heave as he settled himself next to the wall. The match scraped as he lit his last pipe. In forty years he had never set fire to the sheets, but she still dreaded it. 'Mind now,' she said sharply, 'mind your head on that wallpaper!' He grunted, struck another match, and grunted again. Maybe it was approval; she did not know; but as she strained her eyes to see the faint thread of roses on the walls, she half regretted the grotesque and garish curlicues she had covered. Would she ever see them again? Last time she had papered, she had stripped the walls, and each layer, half forgotten, had brought back its own memories. Perhaps, years later, if she was spared, she might go right back again to this quiet, plain paper, and remember the day she had hung it, such a perfect day, so hot and still, and everything going like clockwork; and farther back, farther yet, she would recognize the queer peacocks and pagodas, and remember the last time she had looked at them, a morning of sun and birdsong, and the falling tones of a bell.

The Money

IAN HAMILTON FINLAY

(b. 1925)

AT one period in my life, as a result of the poverty I was suffering, it became impossible for me to tell a lie. Consequently, I became the recipient of National Assistance money. But it all began when I applied for Unemployment Benefit money at the little Labour Exchange in the nearest town.

As I entered the building, the typist turned to the clerk and I heard her whisper, 'The artist is here again.' No, she gave me a capital—'Artist'. The clerk rose, and, making no attempt to attend to me, crossed to the door marked 'Welfare Officer' and gave it a knock.

The clerk was seated. Presently the Welfare Officer appeared. He is, or I should say, was then, a rather stout, unhappy looking person in his early forties. This afternoon, as if he had known I was coming to see him, he wore a fashionable sports jacket and a large, arty and gaudy tie. My heart went out to him as he advanced towards the counter saying: 'I've told you before. We have no jobs for you. You are simply wasting our time.'

Somehow I had got myself into a ridiculous *lolling* position, with my elbows on the counter and my hands supporting my chin. I gazed up at the Welfare Officer and replied timidly, 'I haven't come about a job. I have *been* in a job. Now I have come to ask you for Unemployment Benefit money.'

As I spoke, I could not help glancing at the large, locked safe that stood in the far corner of the room. Out of it, distinctly, a curious silence trickled, rather as smoke trickles out of the stove in my cottage. I had no doubt it was the silence of The Money I had just referred to.

'What!' exclaimed the Welfare Officer, raising his black, bushy eyebrows. 'You have been in a job!'

I nodded. 'I was editing a magazine.'

'And may I ask what salary you received?' he said, his tone disguising the question as an official one.

'One pound, three and sixpence,' I answered, for, as I explained, I could not tell a lie.

'Per month?' he suggested.

'Per week,' I replied with dignity. 'And it was only a part-time job.'

'Hum! In that case, *assuming* that you have been in part-time employment and did not leave it of your own accord you will be entitled to claim part-time Unemployment Benefit money from this Labour Exchange,' he informed me, all in one breath.

'What? But that isn't fair!' I retorted. My cheeks crimsoned; I took my elbows off the counter and waved my hands. 'That isn't Just! I paid *full-time* National Insurance money. So I should draw *full-time* Unemployment Benefit money from this Labour Exchange!'

My impassioned outburst brought a nervous titter from the typist and an astonished rustle from the young clerk. The Welfare Officer, however, only glanced at me for an instant, turned his back on me, strode into his office and shut the door.

I waited a few moments. Then, 'Do you think I have

offended him?' I asked the clerk. 'Am I supposed to go away now? Do you know?'

But, before I had received an answer to my unhappy question, the Welfare Officer appeared once more, bearing two large volumes—no, *tomes*, in his arms. CRASH! He dropped the tomes on the counter, right under my nose.

Then he opened one of the tomes; and slowly, silently, with brows sternly knitted, he began to thumb his way through the thick and closely printed sheets. Page 100 . . . Page 250 . . . And he still had the second of the tomes in reserve.

I moistened my lips, and said weakly, 'Very well, I give in. I am only entitled to draw part-time Unemployment money from this Labour Exchange.'

'That is correct,' observed the Welfare Officer. Closing the tome, and flexing his muscles, he bent to push it aside. Then he took a step or two towards the safe. That, at least, was my impression. Looking back on the incident, I see that he was really going to the cupboard to fetch forms.

But the sight of his too-broad figure retreating to fetch me The Money touched my heart. True, he had won a hollow victory, but I did not mind, and I wanted him to know I did not mind.

'Thank you,' I said, in low, sincere tones.

The Welfare Officer stopped at once. He turned to face me again. 'Thank you? Why are you saying thank you? You haven't got the money yet, you know,' he warned me.

'I know that,' I said, and I apologized to him. He appeared to accept my apology, and, turning, took another step or two towards the cupboard—or, as *I* thought, the safe.

Again I was touched. It was the combination of my poverty, his pathetic appearance in his rich clothes, and the thought of The Money he was about to give me. It was as if he was generously giving it to me out of his own pocket, I felt.

'But honestly,' I sighed, 'I'm awfully grateful to you. You

see, if you give me The Money, I'll be able to work . . . I'll be free to work—at last!'

'Work? What work?' exclaimed the Welfare Officer. He halted, flew into a rage, and once more turned to face me. 'If you are going to be working you cannot claim Unemployment Benefit money! Don't you understand that!' he shouted.

At this moment, the typist intervened, saying, 'He doesn't mean *work*. What he means is, taking pictures. Like that one—I forget his name—who cut off his ear.'

I, too, flew into a rage, and not only at this mention of *ears*.

'*Taking* pictures? TAKING pictures? PAINTING pictures if you don't mind!' I fixed the typist with my eye, and as a sort of reflex action, she bent forward and typed several letters on her machine. Then, looking at the Welfare Officer, I asked: 'Just tell me, yes, do tell me, how is a person to work when he is in a job? I can only work when I am NOT in a job! When I am in a job I CANNOT work, do you understand?'

'Are you working or are you not working?' shouted the exasperated Welfare Officer at the very top of his voice. 'Think it over will you, and let me know!'

So I thought it over, and that very night, by the light of my oil lamp, I wrote a polite, regretful letter to the authorities in the Labour Exchange. In effect, what I said was: 'I resign.' And the following morning, I handed the letter to the postman when he delivered the bills at my mountaincottage.

But in the afternoon, when I was painting in my kitchen, I happened to look through the window, and I saw a neat little man. Clothed in a pin-striped office-suit and clasping a brief-case, he was clinging rather breathlessly to the fence. Several sheep had ceased to crop the hill-side and were gazing at him with surprise.

As he did not look like a shepherd, I at once concluded that he must be—could only be—an art-dealer. Overjoyed,

I thrust my hairless brushes back in their jam-pot, threw the door open, and ran out into the warm summer sunshine to make him welcome.

My collie-dog preceded me. 'Don't be afraid!' I shouted to the art-dealer. However, he had already scrambled back over the fence, and was standing, at bay, in the shade of the wood.

Calling the dog off, I opened the gate, and, smiling, advanced to meet him with outstretched hand. 'Good afternoon. I'm very glad to see you,' I said. The art-dealer took my hand, shook it warmly, and replied, 'I am from the National Assistance Board. Good afternoon.'

It was then I noticed he had been holding *forms*. The collie still bounded about us, leaping up on the stranger so as to sniff his interesting, office-y smells. 'Fin McCuil,' I ordered, 'you mustn't touch *those*. Bad. Go away, now. Chew your bone instead!'

Then I turned to the National Assistance man, and I explained to him, with many apologies, that I had resigned.

He listened sympathetically, but when I had finished speaking, he came a step nearer to me, placed his arm around my shoulder, and said softly, 'Son, there is no need to feel like that, you are perfectly entitled to take this money.'

He tapped his brief-case. He meant, of course, the National Assistance money.

'But I don't feel *like that*,' I assured him. 'Believe me, I feel grateful . . . I mean, ungrateful . . . bringing you all this way . . . But I have resigned . . . I don't think I fit in very well, you see . . .'

'Son,' said the National Assistance man, speaking as no art-dealer ever did, 'I understand your position. No, don't look surprised. I do understand it. You see, my own brother is a violinist . . .' And breaking off for a moment, he stared down the steep and rickety, old path up to my house. 'He lives in a garret,' he continued. 'He is in the same . . . er . . . position . . . you see, as you are. He sits up there all day playing his violin.'

So it was just as I thought, and almost as bad as if I had told a lie. 'But I don't play the violin,' I pointed out. 'I don't play anything. You see, there's been a mistake.'

'No, no, I understand. You don't play the violin. You paint pictures,' said the National Assistance man soothingly. Suddenly he looked me straight in the eye, and he asked me, point-blank, 'Son, do you want this money?'

I could not tell a lie. 'I do,' I said.

So he thrust his hand into his brief-case. He offered me The Money, and, without looking at It, I put It in my pocket as fast as I could. Money is a great embarrassment when you are poor.

'Just fill those in,' he explained.

So, I thought to myself, they are not pound notes; they are postal-orders. But when we had shaken hands and said good-bye to each other, I found they were not postal-orders, either; they were forms. . . .

And I filled them in. And thereafter, till my truthfulness got me into fresh trouble (for, of course, I had been brought up to look on charity as trouble) they sent me a regular weekly cheque. For my part, I was requested to fill in a form stating what Employment I had undertaken during the week and how much money I had earned by it. As painting was not Employment, though it was Work, I very carefully wrote the words 'None' and 'Nil' in the appropriate columns. After five or six weeks they gave me a seven-shilling rise.

Then I sold a picture. And I was inspected at the same time by an unfamiliar National Assistance man.

It was a breezy, blue and golden day in early autumn when he arrived at the door of my cottage. No sooner had I answered his knock than he cheerfully apologized, 'Sorry, old chap. Can't wait long today. Two ladies down in the car. . . .'

'I expect you are going for a picnic,' I observed, wondering if I ought or ought not to return his wink.

'Ha, ha, old boy, you are quite right there!' he answered.

'Well, do come in for just a moment,' I said. 'I shan't keep you, I promise.'

Lifting my easel out of the way, and hastily removing my wet palette from a chair, I invited him into my kitchen, and he sat down. On my palette, as it happened. He had sat on the chair on to which I had removed it; I at once ran for the turpentine and the cloth.

When we had cleaned him up, I put in tentatively: 'There is something I wanted to ask you. It's er . . . it's about those . . . er . . . forms. . . .'

'Forms?' His bright face clouded over. I was spoiling his picnic with my Prussian Blue paint and my silly questions.

'Those . . . er . . . weekly forms that you send me. . . .'

'Oh, those. You mean that you complete those, do you?' He seemed astonished that I did.

But I could not tell a lie. 'I'm afraid I do,' I confessed. 'Do you think it matters very much?'

'Ah, well, no harm done, I suppose.'

'Then there is a difficulty,' I announced. And quickly, so as not to keep the ladies waiting, I mentioned the awful problem I was now faced with. Painting, I explained, was not Employment, though it was *Work*. And even if I stretched a point and called it Employment, still it was not Employment undertaken *this week*. The picture I had sold had been painted a whole year ago. . . . How was I to inform them of the money I had received for it?

'I want to be quite truthful, you see,' I added. 'The form applies only to the present week. . . . So, you see, it is difficult to be truthful.'

'If you want my advice, old boy, *be* truthful,' he answered. 'Yes, be truthful, that is always best. Or nearly always best, eh? HA HA! Ah, hmm. . . .' He rose, and moved to the door. 'I say,' he whispered to me, 'do I smell of turpentine?'

I sniffed at him, and assured him that he did not. 'The very best of luck then, old chap.' We shook hands. Halting to wave to me at frequent intervals, he hurried down the path, and I returned to the house.

There and then, determined to be truthful at all costs, I set about filling in my weekly form. 'Employment Undertaken—None.' And under 'Money Earned', I carefully wrote—'£5. 5. 0.' It had, I reflected, that slight suggestion of paradox one expects with the truth.

I posted the form, and, by return of post, I was sternly summoned to the central office of the National Assistance Board.

When I entered the building, and gave my name at the desk, I was at once led, like a very special sort of person, down several long passages and into a room. There, I was awaited. Several men, all of whom, it was plain, were awaiting me, were seated rather grimly around a table. On the table lay my form. Strange to say, it looked completely different there; *absurd*.

On my arriving in the room, one of the men—their spokesman or perhaps the head one—pointed to my form, and said, 'What is *that*?'

'That? Why, it's my weekly form,' I replied.

'Can you explain it to us?' another asked me.

'Yes, easily,' I answered. And I proceeded to explain it to them. Time. Money. Work. Truth. When I had completed my explanation, one of them got up from his chair and fetched a tome. It was a signal, for, at this, they all left their chairs and fetched back tomes. They threw them open on the table.

I grew nervous. After a while, I looked at the one who had first addressed me, and, pointing to *his* tome, I said, 'You are wasting your time. *I am not in it.*' He looked at me, but he did not smile or reply.

'Gentlemen—,' I began, interrupting them. 'Gentlemen, I think it would be best if I gave up The Money. I don't fit in, I quite see that. I sympathize with you. So I resign.'

At this, there was a sudden and very noticeable change in the atmosphere. They were obviously relieved at my decision. They smiled at me. But one of them said: 'There is no need to be hasty.' And another added: 'We wish you well.'

'Then I am to go on taking The Money, am I?' I asked.

But once more there was a change in the atmosphere. The men became grim again, and put on frowns.

'I see,' I said. 'Then I have no alternative but to resign.'

Smiles. Relief. Opening of silver cigarette-cases. 'There is no need to be hasty.' 'We wish you well.'

'I believe you,' I assured them. 'Will you send on the forms or shall I just fill them in now?'

'Now!' said the men, speaking all at once.

So I completed the forms of resignation, and I left the building a free man.

GLOSSARY

A', *aa*, all.
Ablow, below.
A'body, everyone.
Ae, *ane*, one, a.
Aff, off.
Aff·o', from.
Ahint, *ahent*, behind.
Aik, oak.
Ain, *awn*, own.
Aince, once.
Airt, direction.
Albainn, Scotland.
Aneugh, *eneuch*, enough.
Arle(s), earnest money.
Asclent, aside.
Atower, up above.
Auld, old.
Auld Lichts, members of a body of Presbyterian dissenters.
Auld Reekie, Edinburgh.
Ava', at all.
Aye, always.

Back-ganging, in arrears.
Bairn, child.
Baith, both.
Bass, mat.
Bawbee, a halfpenny.
Bear, *bere*, barley.
Begude, began.
Behove, to be incumbent or to feel bound to.
Beltane, May Day.
Ben, (towards) the inner room of a house.
Besom, slut.

Bestial, cattle.
Bide a wee, stay for a little while.
Bield, shelter.
Bien, comfortable, prosperous.
Birl, to move round rapidly.
Blaud, a piece, passage (of verse).
Blude, *Bluid*, blood.
Bogle, ghost, goblin.
Borrel, simple.
Bothy, hut, lodging for farm-workers.
Boyne, tub.
Brae, hill.
Braid, broad.
Braird, sprouting of grain.
Brak, break.
Brash, a brief storm or shower.
Brunstane, brimstone.
Buik, *buke*, book.
Buik-lear, book learning.
Burn, stream.
But, the outer room of a two-roomed house: without.
By-ordinar', more than usual, extraordinary.

Callant, young man.
Caller, fresh, crisp.
Canty, cheerful, lively.
Carlin(e), old woman.
Chaft, jaw, cheek.
Chalmer, room.
Change-house, inn.
Chap, strike, knock.
Cheil(d), fellow.
Clachan, hamlet.

Claes, clothes.
Clought, clutch.
Clour, blow.
Coats, petticoats.
Cogie, two-handled cup or bowl.
Collieshangie, noisy dispute.
Corbie, raven.
Corp, corpse.
Coup, cowp, to tumble, upset.
Coupit his creels, turned head over heels.
Cranreuch, hoar frost.
Crouse, self-confident.
Cromag, shepherd's staff.
Cruisie, a primitive lamp.
Crunluadh, a movement of the pibroch, *Crunluath*.
   breadach, a quick movement.
   c-mach, the fastest part of the pibroch.
Cummer, gossip.

Daffin', pastime.
Dander, dauner, saunter.
Daur, dare.
Dear years, time of famine ending A.D. 1700.
Deave, deafen.
Deid, death, dead.
Deidly, deadly.
Deil, devil.
Delate, accuse.
Deray, disorderly mirth.
Diarmaid, a Campbell.
Dirl, rattle.
Ding, dang, thrust down.
Divot, turf.
Dominie, schoolmaster.
Douce, sedate, gentle.

Dour, grimly determined.
Dreich, tedious.
Dub, puddle.
Duds, duddies, clothes.
Dunch, push.
Dwine, dwindle, decline.
Dyke, wall.
Dyvour, bankrupt.

Eas, waterfall.
Een, eyes, evening.
Eicht, eight.
Ettle, attempt, intend.

Fair, quite, completely.
Fash, fasherie, trouble, nuisance.
Feadan, chanter, the melody pipe of the bagpipes.
Fee'd, engaged as a servant.
Feint a, devil a (emphatic negative).
Fell, remarkably.
Flauchtered, feal, sliced turf.
Fley, frighten, drive off.
Flyte, scold, rail.
Forbye, too, in addition.
Forefolks, ancestors.
Forjaskit, exhausted.
Fou, fu', full.
Fuff, puff.
Fusionless, weak, characterless.

Gab, talk, oratory.
Gabbart, lighter.
Gae, go.
Gang, go.
Gate, gait, road, way.
Gey, gei, very.
Gie, give.
Gilleasbuig Grumach, Archibald the Grim, 7th Earl of Argyll.

Gin, if.

Ging in til't, go into it.

Girn, make a wry face, complain.

Goblet, iron pot with handle.

Gowk, cuckoo, fool.

Grane, groan.

Grat, wept.

Grue, shiver (with horror, disgust).

Gude, *guid*, good.

Gudesire, grandfather.

Guff, smell.

Guidwife, housewife.

Habber, stutter, growl.

Hae, Bell, take this, Bell.

Haill, hale, whole.

Haver, to talk nonsense.

Heid, head.

Hirdie-girdie, topsy-turvy.

Hirsle, creep.

Hodden-grey, cloth of undyed wool.

Hoddle, waddle.

Hoo, hou, how.

Hoo's a' wi' ye? How are things with you?

Howe, (of the Mearns), the inland valley of Kincardineshire.

Howff, favourite haunt, shelter.

Howlet, owl.

Ilk, the same.

Ilka, every.

Ill-getted, illegitimate.

Iolair, eagle.

I'se warrant, I feel sure.

Jackanape(s), ape, monkey.

Jaloose, Jalouse, suspect.

Jiled, imprisoned.

Juist aff an' on, having ups and downs.

Keel, red ochre.

Ken, know.

Kirk-officer, beadle.

Kisted, coffined.

Kye, cows.

Laigh, low.

Laird, landowner, squire.

Laith, loath.

Laroch, ruin.

Lammas, the first of August, often a time of floods in Scotland.

Laochain, hero, comrade.

Leal, loyal, trustworthy.

Leasing-making, sedition, slander.

Limmer, ill-behaved woman, thief.

Linn, lynn, waterfall.

Littlins, children.

Loan, loaning, lane.

Londubh, blackbird.

Loon, youth.

Loup, leap.

Low, flame.

Lown, calm.

Luckie, elderly woman.

Lug, ear.

Mail, rent.

Mair, more.

March, boundary.

Mart, cattle market.

Maun, must, man.
Mear, mare.
Meck, *maik*, halfpenny.
Meikle, *muckle*, large.
Merk, 13s. 4d. Scots money
 (15½d. sterling).
Mind, remember.
Mirk, dark.
Mistrysted, disappointed.
Mony, many.
Moss, marsh.
Muckle, much, great.
Muckle Friday, day of the feeing
 fair when farmers engaged
 their workers.
Muils, slippers.

Nae, *na*, no.
Namely, well-known, famous.
Neb, nose.
Neuk, corner.
Nicht, night.
 The nicht, tonight.
Nieve, fist.
Night-hag, nightmare.

Old-word, proverb.
Or, before.
Orra, occasional; *Orra-man*,
 odd-job man.
Ouder, fluff.
Ower, over, too much.
Oxter, armpit.

Pace, Easter.
Paich, *pech*, gasp.
Park, field.
Parochine, parish.
Pawky, sly.

Pibroch, *piobaireachd*, sym-
 phonic bagpipe music.
Pickle, *puckle*, a little.
Pirn, bobbin, yarn wound on
 reed.
Pleiter, mess.
Pletted toys, pleated mutch-like
 caps.
Plouter, floundering in water,
 mud.
Pock, *poke*, bag.
Port (piping), dance tune.
Professor, one who claims to be
 orthodox.
Puir, poor.

Quaich, two-handled cup.
Quean, girl.

Raid, rode.
Reddin', setting in order, clean-
 ing.
Reishle, rustle noisily.
Rig, ridge, strip of arable land.
Ripe, search out.
Routh, plenty.
Rug, to pull sharply, a good
 share.

Sair, sore, very.
Sal (exclamation), upon my
 soul.
Sark, shirt.
Saugh, willow.
Saul, soul.
Scowp, drink.
Screigh, shriek.
Sculduddry, indecency.
Scunner, loathing, disgust.

Session, Kirk session, the parochial court of the church, which before 1845 controlled poor relief.

Sheep-fank, sheepfold.

Sheiling, hut on a high pasture.

Sholtie, pony.

Shoother, *shouther*, shoulder.

Shoon, shoes.

Sib, of kin.

Sic, such.

Siller, money.

Single Questions, the questions and answers of the Shorter Catechism without the 'proof texts' of Scripture which support them.

Sinsyne, since.

Siubhal, allegro.

Skeich, easily startled, skittish.

Skelloch, shrill cry.

Skelp, beat.

Skeugh, crooked.

Sleekit, smooth.

Slocken, quench.

Smeddum, spirited good sense.

Smoor, smother, be smothered.

Snod, neat, well trimmed.

So, here.

Soddy, soda (water).

Soss, wet, dark.

Sough, whisper, soupçon.

Spaul, *spule*, shoulder.

Speer, *spier*, inquire.

Speerings, news.

Speirin' her, proposing to her.

Spunk, active spirit.

Spunkie, small fire.

Steek, shut.

Steer, stir, din.

Stend, leap.

Stocking, cattle and equipment of a farm.

Stot, bullock.

Stotter, stumble.

Straucht, straight.

Stravaig(u)in', wandering.

Suld, should: *they suld hae ca'd her*, I think she was named.

Swack, nimble.

Swat, sweat, sweated.

Sweir, lazy, unwilling.

Syne, ago, since, after that.

Taigle, delay, confuse.

Tash, stain.

Tass, cup.

Thae, those.

Thegether, together.

Thir, those.

Thirled, bound (by law).

Thrapple, throat.

Thrawn, twisted (of a fowl's neck in killing it).

Threap, *threep*, repeat incessantly.

Tink, tinker, gipsy.

Tippenny, ale.

Tod, fox.

Toon, *toun*, town, farmstead.

Toom, *tume*, empty.

Trauchle, fatiguing or confusing effort.

Tyke, dog.

Unco, extraordinary, uncanny.

Unstreakit, not laid out for burial.

Urlar, groundwork or adagio of the pibroch.

Usquebaugh, whisky.

Wanchancie, unlucky.

Want, lack, be without.

Ware, spend.

Wark, work.

Warlock, wizard.

Waur, worse.

Wean, child.

Wha, who.

Wheen, a not inconsiderable number.

Whiles, (at) times.

Whurlie, mill.

Wreaths, snowdrifts.

Wuss, wish.

Wynd, alley.

Yett, gate.

Yowl, howl.

OXFORD

MORE OXFORD PAPERBACKS

This book is just one of nearly 1000 Oxford Paperbacks currently in print. If you would like details of other Oxford Paperbacks, including titles in the World's Classics, Oxford Reference, Oxford Books, OPUS, Past Masters, Oxford Authors, and Oxford Shakespeare series, please write to:

UK and Europe: Oxford Paperbacks Publicity Manager, Arts and Reference Publicity Department, Oxford University Press, Walton Street, Oxford OX2 6DP.

Customers in UK and Europe will find Oxford Paperbacks available in all good bookshops. But in case of difficulty please send orders to the Cash-with-Order Department, Oxford University Press Distribution Services, Saxon Way West, Corby, Northants NN18 9ES. Tel: 01536 741519; Fax: 01536 746337. Please send a cheque for the total cost of the books, plus £1.75 postage and packing for orders under £20; £2.75 for orders over £20. Customers outside the UK should add 10% of the cost of the books for postage and packing.

USA: Oxford Paperbacks Marketing Manager, Oxford University Press, Inc., 200 Madison Avenue, New York, N.Y. 10016.

Canada: Trade Department, Oxford University Press, 70 Wynford Drive, Don Mills, Ontario M3C 1J9.

Australia: Trade Marketing Manager, Oxford University Press, G.P.O. Box 2784Y, Melbourne 3001, Victoria.

South Africa: Oxford University Press, P.O. Box 1141, Cape Town 8000.

OXFORD BOOKS

THE OXFORD BOOK OF ENGLISH GHOST STORIES

Chosen by Michael Cox and R. A. Gilbert

This anthology includes some of the best and most frightening ghost stories ever written, including M. R. James's 'Oh Whistle, and I'll Come to You, My Lad', 'The Monkey's Paw' by W. W. Jacobs, and H. G. Wells's 'The Red Room'. The important contribution of women writers to the genre is represented by stories such as Amelia Edwards's 'The Phantom Coach', Edith Wharton's 'Mr Jones', and Elizabeth Bowen's 'Hand in Glove'.

As the editors stress in their informative introduction, a good ghost story, though it may raise many profound questions about life and death, entertains as much as it unsettles us, and the best writers are careful to satisfy what Virginia Woolf called 'the strange human craving for the pleasure of feeling afraid'. This anthology, the first to present the full range of classic English ghost fiction, similarly combines a serious literary purpose with the plain intention of arousing pleasing fear at the doings of the dead.

'an excellent cross-section of familiar and unfamiliar stories and guaranteed to delight' *New Statesman*

OXFORD BOOKS

THE NEW OXFORD BOOK OF
IRISH VERSE

Edited, with Translations, by Thomas Kinsella

Verse in Irish, especially from the early and med-
ieval periods, has long been felt to be the preserve of
linguists and specialists, while Anglo-Irish poetry is
usually seen as an adjunct to the English tradition.
This original anthology approaches the Irish poetic
tradition as a unity and presents a relationship
between two major bodies of poetry that reflects a
shared and painful history.

'the first coherent attempt to present the entire
range of Irish poetry in both languages to an Eng-
lish-speaking readership' *Irish Times*

'a very satisfying and moving introduction to Irish
poetry' *Listener*

ILLUSTRATED HISTORIES IN
OXFORD PAPERBACKS

THE OXFORD ILLUSTRATED HISTORY
OF ENGLISH LITERATURE

Edited by Pat Rogers

Britain possesses a literary heritage which is almost
unrivalled in the Western world. In this volume, the
richness, diversity, and continuity of that tradition
are explored by a group of Britain's foremost literary scholars.

Chapter by chapter the authors trace the history
of English literature, from its first stirrings in Anglo-
Saxon poetry to the present day. At its heart towers
the figure of Shakespeare, who is accorded a special
chapter to himself. Other major figures such as
Chaucer, Milton, Donne, Wordsworth, Dickens,
Eliot, and Auden are treated in depth, and the story
is brought up to date with discussion of living
authors such as Seamus Heaney and Edward Bond.

'[a] lovely volume . . . put in your thumb and pull
out plums' Michael Foot

'scholarly and enthusiastic people have written in-
spiring essays that induce an eagerness in their readers to return to the writers they admire' *Economist*

THE OXFORD AUTHORS

General Editor: Frank Kermode

THE OXFORD AUTHORS is a series of authoritative editions of major English writers. Aimed at both students and general readers, each volume contains a generous selection of the best writings—poetry, prose, and letters—to give the essence of a writer's work and thinking. All the texts are complemented by essential notes, an introduction, chronology, and suggestions for further reading.

Matthew Arnold
William Blake
Lord Byron
John Clare
Samuel Taylor Coleridge
John Donne
John Dryden
Ralph Waldo Emerson
Thomas Hardy
George Herbert and Henry Vaughan
Gerard Manley Hopkins
Samuel Johnson
Ben Jonson
John Keats
Andrew Marvell
John Milton
Alexander Pope
Sir Philip Sidney
Oscar Wilde
William Wordsworth

PAST MASTERS

A wide range of unique, short, clear introductions to the lives and work of the world's most influential thinkers. Written by experts, they cover the history of ideas from Aristotle to Wittgenstein. Readers need no previous knowledge of the subject, so they are ideal for students and general readers alike.

Each book takes as its main focus the thought and work of its subject. There is a short section on the life and a final chapter on the legacy and influence of the thinker. A section of further reading helps in further research.

The series continues to grow, and future Past Masters will include **Owen Gingerich** on *Copernicus*, **R G Frey** on *Joseph Butler*, **Bhiku Parekh** on *Gandhi*, **Christopher Taylor** on *Socrates*, **Michael Inwood** on *Heidegger*, and **Peter Ghosh** on *Weber*.

**Oxford
Paperback
Reference**

OXFORD PAPERBACK REFERENCE

From *Art and Artists* to *Zoology*, the Oxford Paperback Reference series offers the very best subject reference books at the most affordable prices.

Authoritative, accessible, and up to date, the series features dictionaries in key student areas, as well as a range of fascinating books for a general readership. Included are such well-established titles as Fowler's *Modern English Usage*, Margaret Drabble's *Concise Companion to English Literature*, and the bestselling science and medical dictionaries.

The series has now been relaunched in handsome new covers. Highlights include new editions of some of the most popular titles, as well as brand new paperback reference books on *Politics*, *Philosophy*, and *Twentieth-Century Poetry*.

With new titles being constantly added, and existing titles regularly updated, Oxford Paperback Reference is unrivalled in its breadth of coverage and expansive publishing programme. New dictionaries of *Film*, *Economics*, *Linguistics*, *Architecture*, *Archaeology*, *Astronomy*, and *The Bible* are just a few of those coming in the future.

Oxford Paperback Reference

THE CONCISE OXFORD COMPANION TO ENGLISH LITERATURE

Edited by Margaret Drabble and Jenny Stringer

Derived from the acclaimed *Oxford Companion to English Literature*, the concise maintains the wide coverage of its parent volume. It is an indispensable, compact guide to all aspects of English literature. For this revised edition, existing entries have been fully updated and revised with 60 new entries added on contemporary writers.

* Over 5,000 entries on the lives and works of authors, poets and playwrights

* The most comprehensive and authoritative paperback guide to English literature

* New entries include Peter Ackroyd, Martin Amis, Toni Morrison, and Jeanette Winterson

* New appendices list major literary prize-winners

From the reviews of its parent volume:

'It earns its place at the head of the best sellers: every home should have one'
Sunday Times

THE CONCISE OXFORD DICTIONARY
OF OPERA

New Edition

Edited by Ewan West and John Warrack

Derived from the full *Oxford Dictionary of Opera*, this is the most authoritative and up-to-date dictionary of opera available in paperback. Fully revised for this new edition, it is designed to be accessible to all those who enjoy opera, whether at the opera-house or at home.

* **Over 3,500 entries on operas, composers, and performers**

* **Plot summaries and separate entries for well-known roles, arias, and choruses**

* **Leading conductors, producers and designers**

From the reviews of its parent volume:

'the most authoritative single-volume work of its kind'
Independent on Sunday

'an invaluable reference work'
Gramophone